TURNOVER

A Novel

by

John P Warren

ISBN: 0615929532
ISBN 13: 9780615929538
Library of Congress Control Number: 2013921991
PineLands, New Wilmington PA

Turnover is dedicated to the American voter, sometimes an unwitting accomplice to political greed and power.

AUTHOR'S NOTE AND DISCLAIMER

*T*urnover is a work of fiction, the product of my imagination knit to real events surrounding the 2012 presidential election. Major party nominees have been largely invented, though similarities to real persons exist. With notable exceptions, their speeches, dialogue, and other commentary are what I believe they might have said or could have said, but there should be no confusion with actual speeches or positions articulated by representatives of the two major parties.

That I have fictionalized other public figures and media journalists underscores the assertion that views expressed in *Turnover* are my own. If, indeed, there are similarities, they are entirely coincidental. Polling and other news events selected, on the other hand, are close facsimiles of the 2012 election cycle, as reported by news organizations, including *The New York Times,* CNN, *The Wall Street Journal*, and *The Washington Post,* to name a few. General information about the IRS scandal as well as the Benghazi matter came from one or more of the above purveyors, and others.

Internet queries on electronic voting and voting systems generated pointers to websites of several actual providers. In *Turnover*, however, the firms portrayed, and everything about them, are wholly invented. The US Election Assistance Commission does, indeed, exist, but to my knowledge, issued no contract such as the one described.

Having served stints in the US Army Security Agency and with the US Office of Personnel Management as an investigator, manager, and executive, I can assure readers that most public employees are dedicated and conscientious servants of all the people. That some staff members of one or more agencies allegedly perform as pawns in a latter-day spoils system is an issue for the American people to remedy.

As to OPM's Federal Investigations Service, it has been well led and deserves its reputation for excellence.

Underlying the plot of *Turnover* is a real threat, all but invisible, to a fundamental right most Americans hold dear: the ability to vote and to have it count in the way we intend. Even casual research reveals that a wholesale theft of a presidential election—or any other election—is possible, and easily so. Because a national election may be determined by one or two states, the likelihood of tampering will become all the more irresistible to some, if it hasn't already.

I present no evidence that the 2012 election was manipulated on behalf of any candidate, but is there any person in authority who can assure the American people—to a reasonable degree of certitude—that it can't happen here?

FEBRUARY 2012

USA Today/Gallup Poll
February 16-19
President Averell Williams 46%
Governor Winston Hardy 50%

T hwack! The backboard shivered with the slap of the Spalding
Never-Flat. It was a sound somehow out of place on the grounds
of the White House.

"Sonofabitch!" The guttural sound flew from the throat of Joseph
P. Morrison, thirty-nine year-old vice president of the United States,
when his bank shot twanged on the rim and fell back into his hands. The
usually surefooted moves of his five-foot-nine-inch frame had become
less so as too many Washington dinners clung to his midsection.

Glancing at his usual opponent, Morrison felt certain Agent Cox
could not know the epithet was really intended for President Averell
Harriman Williams, a man he had once admired but had come to
despise. Morrison's ego elbowed him, not for the first time. *Why are
you so little trusted by the president? Isn't it true, Joe, that the missed
shot is just a metaphor for the last three years of your political career?*

Will he keep me on the ticket? In anger and frustration, the ball
Morrison cupped in the splayed fingers of his right hand became a
launched missile.

Marty Cox ran to retrieve it. "C'mon, Joe," he said. "Things can't be
that bad."

With cold blue eyes, Morrison passed Cox a look to wrinkle the
leather of his Secret Service credentials. In possession of the ball once

again, the VP took two more steps before attempting a layup around his erstwhile opponent. He missed. "Jesus H. Christ!"

A few more minutes of sloppy ball helped the men notice that the wind on the late winter day had stiffened, and despite nature's bid for a bit of sunshine, the air shouldered a chill that had not been there earlier. Morrison let his gaze follow the rays of the morning sun to a window in the upper floor of the White House, and glimpsed a face shadowed there.

"Bad karma today, that's all it is." Morrison's voice was louder than it needed to be.

Just then, Remy Carlson, the vice president's chief of staff, bounded out of the West Wing and hailed the man a heartbeat away from leadership of the free world. "Mr. Vice President," she called. "Sir, you did want me to remind you if Senator Riordan called, didn't you?"

Morrison nodded.

"He's on the phone, sir, and hopes you're available."

"Tell the majority leader I'll be right there." Toweling his neck and the dripping edges of his jet-black hair, he turned to the agent who'd been on his detail since the 2008 election. "You had an easy game today, Marty. That won't be true next time."

"Yes, sir," Cox said, as beads of sweat began to run from his close-cropped, blonde head. "Those missed shots'll getcha every time. Like turnovers. They can be game changers."

"You're right," he responded with sarcasm. "They make all the difference." *But I'll make the key shot when I need to*, he pledged to his ego as he turned and walked quickly toward the door from which Remy Carlson had summoned him. He hoped the call was important.

President Williams studied the slapdash game from the second-floor window of the official residence. There was a time, he mused, when he would have whupped the two on their very best day. In fact, when he'd begun his first term, he'd played a few games with some of the more agile members of the White House staff. It had been good politics that pictures of the president making a clean shot found their way to the news circuit, but that was then.

Now, at sixty-seven, Williams acknowledged the creeping age and health issues that had begun to nag at him. At six foot four, he rivaled Abe Lincoln himself as the tallest man in the office, but the two were of very different skin color. While Lincoln was dark-complexioned compared to the sallow skins of contemporaries who never worked a farm, Williams was definitely a black man, elected, in part, because Lincoln had emancipated his forebearers so many generations before.

In the window's reflection, Williams saw the years piled upon his chronological age by the office he held. It had happened to every president. The accumulated weight of his responsibilities accompanied him wherever he went, and he wondered: *Did every president endure the same cardiac stresses?* Even his skin, stenciled with age spots near the span of wrinkles surrounding very dark eyes, seemed washed out. It was as if someone had dusted a glove-gray powder on the edges of his rich features.

As the question of his longevity—in life or office—crossed his mind, he blocked it out as a self-pitying waste of time. The call he was waiting for—the sole reason for coming back upstairs this morning—might remind him just how precarious his health might be. Glancing at his discrete Baum & Mercier watch, he knew with a certainty that Commander Bolling's call would come promptly at 9:30 a.m. as promised, and not a moment before.

Pulling a side chair closer to the window, he watched his number two fumble around the court. That was unlike Joe Morrison. "Uh-huh," he said softly. "I'll bet we're thinking about exactly the same thing—his future." When he realized he'd spoken aloud, he pulled his thoughts back into the silence of his very keen mind.

It was almost March, and if he let it, the coming campaign would command his every waking hour—even those treasured times alone with Andrea, his still-gorgeous wife of thirty-one years. This campaign was going to be his last, and hardest, and a key question remaining in the grand strategy was a simple one: *Do I want to keep Vice President*

Morrison on the ticket? He vowed that no matter what, the first African American presidency was not going to be a one-act play.

As he watched his VP, he remained unsure. He'd given him few tasks in the previous three and a half years, mostly because Morrison was shallow and callow, a ticket pick largely because the young senator from Texas was expected to bring in the western vote. To everyone's relief and surprise, Morrison had had no bad baggage. One wife, two children, and an unremarkable record, not to mention his good looks, helped boost him to the second spot.

Every other day, it seemed, Sheldon Ingber, his longtime adviser and campaign manager, nagged him about it. "You need to shake it up, Av. What Joe gave us in the first run won't get us a second term. That I can tell you." Williams remembered Ingber's bushy head catching the morning light that filled the Oval Office. He supposed the man's heavy mustache was there to round out a picture of hirsute masculinity, and Williams rarely teased him about it.

"Why are you so sure, Shelly? He's pleasant enough, gives a good stump speech, and will help us get Texas, New Mexico, and this time maybe Arizona, not to mention Colorado—states that would otherwise go red."

"Maybe," Ingber had cautioned him just that morning. "Maybe," he repeated. "If Winston Hardy turns out to be our opponent, Morrison may come in handy, but Av, you can do better."

Williams eyed the man who had guided him to a win in every campaign over twenty-eight years. As a young Assemblyman from Buffalo, Mario Cuomo's Lieutenant Governor, Stan Lundine, had introduced him to Ingber. They took to one another immediately, and it was Ingber who convinced Williams to run for Congress. After four terms in Washington, it was Ingber again who caught the scent of a better opportunity and pushed him to run for state office back home in New York. Williams took the unheard of step in returning to Albany, but it was one of the smartest moves he ever made. After a two-term stint as attorney general, he became lieutenant governor, and then held the top seat for two terms of his own.

Born in the iffy environs near Buffalo's Broadway Market, he was named for another New York governor, the fabled Averell Harriman, a man many said had dreamed of the presidency for himself. Harriman's illustrious career as a governor, statesman, and diplomat helped make him the idol of Wilson Williams, the president's father and first mentor.

The president never forgot his path to the Oval Office. Wilson Williams, he loved to recall, was a reliable precinct worker in Buffalo's boiling black neighborhoods, and could deliver the votes in good times and in bad. He knew, too, that his father labored all the harder to ensure his only son would not have to perform a lifetime of party favors to earn a living.

"The truth is," he told his son, "we will always be Democrats, but not even FDR and Harriman did much for us." The problem, he explained, was that Republicans stopped giving a damn about blacks before the Coolidge Administration, and working for the Democrats offered a way out of the slums. "For us," the president never forgot his father saying, "it's between bad news and worse. The Republicans want us to pull ourselves up without a rope, but the Democrats give us too much rope. Some of our people get so tangled in it, they never get to climb up. At least with the Democrats, we won't go hungry."

It had never been easy for him. He worked his way through Canisius College driving a Checker around Buffalo. That, plus hard work in everything else he did, especially the campaigns, helped create a future where one would otherwise not exist. He left the work of community glad-handing and megaphone management to the pretty boys long on talk and short on actual accomplishment.

As a Democrat, he thrived politically during the presidency of Jefferson Harper and found a way to get along with George Bush during 9/11 and its aftermath.

Then he watched as people in his own party, including Joe Morrison, blew hot air into the housing bubble. When it burst, Ingber seized the chance of a lifetime as hapless Republicans tried to tread water. By that time, the country was ready for an African American to reach for the top, and Shelly Ingber made it happen.

It was in 2008 that Ingber had come into his own as the shrewd-est man on the political circuit, someone even the fabled Bush guru, Gardner Stewart, admired. The president admitted to himself that Ingber's carefully plotted campaign may have unlocked the front door of the White House for him, and though Joe Morrison, a choice born of convenience and geography, had played his part well, he was of no help whatsoever in the battle with the nation's deep recession. It had become an intractable mess.

Only because of his own doubts about Morrison did Williams begin to hear the plaintive words of his storied manager. He knew he had to listen. Morrison's unimpressive footwork on the court below shouldn't have affected his judgment about him, Williams knew, but it did. The VP's inability to score a basket seemed to round out a picture of a man who might not continue to score well with the voters. But time was running out, and soon he'd have to make a decision. In closing their last conversation, he had promised, "I'll think about it, Shelly."

Somewhere behind him, Mary Beth Frederick—"Freddie" to every-one in the circle closest to the president—cleared her throat noisily. "Commander Bolling is chasing you down, Mr. President. Shall I have him come up here?" Her voice seemed to carry urgency.

"Stay calm, Freddie. I've been expecting him, and you can tell him to save his feet. We'll talk on the phone, and when I'm through, I'll come back down." He glanced at his assistant, pert and pushy, and teased her. "And you can quit following me in my own house." Williams smiled at her and then turned his head back to the court just in time to see Morrison disappear into the copse of trees below.

"Mr. President," Commander Bolling began, "would you prefer that I come up, given the sensitivity of the topic?"

"No need to take so much of your time, Jeremy. You have other people to worry about. Let's have it." The president ignored the metal-lic clicks on the line.

Bolling chuckled. "Sir, you're my number one patient, and I never forget that." The clicking continued. "As we discussed earlier, Mr. President, the biopsy confirmed my earlier diagnosis. The results show that the cancer has engulfed one entire side and part of the other.

Unless you're interested in the actual numbers..." Bolling went quiet for a moment. "Sir, what's that clicking on the line?"

"Oh, it's the damn phone system—probably installed in Lyndon Johnson's time. Pay no attention, and you're right, I'm not interested in the details. Keep going."

"Yes, sir. I should tell you that this particular type is moderately aggressive, and you should consider action within the next few months."

"Jeremy, you've been around me for a while now. Think about it. This is a campaign year. If you're telling me it's not immediately life threatening, then we'll tell no one—not the media, not the First Lady. Got that?"

Dr. Bolling said nothing. Only the clicking sound was heard.

"Jeremy?"

"Yes, Mr. President."

"I didn't hear an answer."

"I understand, Mr. President, but usually we tell the public everything."

"Not everything. Besides, the press and the public would go nuts just hearing the C word. It'll become the GOP's biggest issue, when in fact it isn't one. Are we okay on this, Jeremy?"

"Yes, sir. I understand. While it's serious, it is not...well, you know. And indeed, there's much to consider. We'll continue doing blood work."

"Later, my good doctor. We'll talk more later."

When Joe Morrison walked into the West Wing and picked up a private telephone, he expected to hear Senator Harrison Riordan's gravelly voice on the other end. Instead, electronic clicks punctuating snippets of another conversation altogether sputtered in his ear.

"Christ Almighty," he said under his breath. He was about to follow the accepted protocol by hanging up and having Carlson get Riordan on the phone again. As his right arm began to obey his brain's command to replace the receiver, he realized he'd been tapped into no ordinary conversation. First, he heard a syllable or two of President Williams's unmistakable voice, followed by a silence. Then, there was something about a biopsy and a diagnosis. He was enthralled by the fact that, somehow, he was listening to a private conversation of, arguably, the most powerful man in the world.

When the next words in the string filled his ear—something about action necessary, right after the word *aggressive*—Morrison found it frightening. He wanted to hang up the phone and walk quickly away.

Unable to command a single fiber of muscle, Morrison clutched the receiver like a life preserver. After fascination and fright came a cool elation when he heard the commander in chief extract a promise from the White House physician to keep the entire matter under wraps. Morrison understood withholding information from the media—it happened every day—but about the president's medical checkup? And keeping it from the First Lady herself? The last part he heard was the president's reference to the *C* word just before the line went dead.

"Oh, my God," the vice president whispered to himself. "Cancer?" So startled was he by his own voice and the thump of his heart against his chest wall that he turned and looked around to make sure no one had heard him. Replacing the receiver, he sat still while he flipped through the ramifications as he would a political Rolodex. Williams could die in office, and should it happen, his own constitutional role would instantly move from one of relative insignificance to one of immeasurable prestige and power.

Because Williams had chosen not to employ Morrison's skills—a management flaw about which Morrison's wife reminded him at least once each month—the vice president found plenty of time on his hands. To his closest friend and confidant, Morisa Rivera, with whom he had grown up in Texas, Morrison once said he suspected every single man in his position had secretly conducted the same survey. Only eight men had succeeded to the presidency unelected, all but one upon the death of the incumbent. The exception was Gerald Ford, who may not have even suspected his fate.

Morrison mused that, since 1840, four presidents had died in office due to illness: William Henry Harrison, Zachary Taylor, Warren Harding, and Franklin Roosevelt. Save Ford, the remainder of ascensions to the highest office in the land had been upon the assassination of the nation's leader.

Then, it hit him again. There had been speculation of late—a trial balloon by Ingber?—that he should be replaced. At all costs, Morrison knew he had to remain on the ticket. Equally important, the Williams-Morrison ticket had to be victorious on November 6. He felt a rush of both guilt and eager anticipation when he considered the possibility that Williams might actually follow FDR's example.

John Nance Garner, a Texas homeboy himself and two-term veep under Roosevelt, once said to his press buddies that the office "wasn't worth a bucket of warm piss." History books of the day cleansed the comment to make it a bucket of "warm spit." Morrison chuckled to himself. Old man Garner had it right. The VP job had its perks but wasn't worth a damn to anyone with youth and ambition. Then FDR replaced Garner with Henry Wallace in 1940, and Wallace with Truman in '44.

Now, he thought, it was different. As he sat motionless and lost in the realm of his own political lust, one more thought occurred to him. If, indeed, Williams had an aggressive cancer, Joseph P. Morrison would be the only holder of his office in history to have knowledge of the president's death months, maybe a year, in advance. Like the clasp of a handshake, two objectives became tightly intertwined: stay on the ticket, and get reelected. *No matter what.*

"Mr. Vice President," Remy Carlson said softly. When Morrison did not move from the alcove chair, or even acknowledge her presence, she said, "Sir?" in a voice louder than she would otherwise use.

Morrison looked up. "Yes, Remy? His voice was dreamlike. "What is it?" In an instant, he'd become irritated—to be interrupted in thought was one thing. To be surprised out of a most pleasant reverie was another. His heart rate had yet to return to normal.

"Sir, did you ever talk to Senator Riordan? He's on the phone again."

"This line was dead." His voice had become flat, uninterested. "Can you patch it to my office? I'll go right now."

When he'd situated himself behind his desk, he snatched up the instrument. "Harrison. I thought you were back home in Missouri buying more votes."

"Mr. Vice President, your humor eludes me." The near-ancient senate majority leader had held his post each time the Democrats managed fifty-one or more seats, and that had been true on three occasions over the past twenty years. For the half term Morrison had spent in the Senate, it was one of the few periods Riordan had not had the majority to be elected leader, and the old man had taken a liking to him, using his fabled energy to school the Texas freshman in all the ways of political and legislative manipulation he could manage.

"You always think every conversation is overheard, Harrison, and..." As soon the words slipped out of his mouth, he realized the implications of his experience only moments earlier.

"Yes, and that's a good thing to keep in mind, my young friend."

"As always, you're right, but we're both very busy, and so I suspect you called with a reason."

"Are you close with Jackson Armitage, Ingber's deputy?" Riordan's tone was solicitous, but forewarning.

"Not particularly. What's he saying now?"

"In part because he's the same race as the president and often thinks himself his spokesman—nearly always, inappropriately so—there have been times when the good Mr. Ingber has used his second's penchant for garrulousness to float an option."

"Meaning?"

"Meaning there are better choices for the old man than you this time around. You know, Joe, this election will not be a piece of cake. The economy stinks, we've got problems in the Middle East, and the public's love affair with an African American in the White House may be waning. And I'm sure you saw the latest polls."

"Enough, Harry. I've heard all the reasons. Is Armitage whispering to our friends in the media, or just on the Hill to see who salivates?"

"Oh, he's been everywhere with it. He's even mentioned Daryl Perelman as a possibility."

"That's crazy. Perelman's older than Williams, for Christ's sake, and he's from Connecticut to boot." His response was too quick, he realized. "Too many things wrong with that ticket. Armitage will have to do better."

"Well, I thought I'd better let you know. It's too late this year for you to attend a bunch of Martin Luther King dinners, so you'd better find some way to prove your value to our beloved president." Sarcasm laced with rich irony was a Riordan trademark.

"I'll be on it, Harry. Don't you worry."

It's never easy in this town, Pete Clancy told himself as he observed the stream of traffic heading east on Little River Turnpike from the I-495 interchange just over his right shoulder. He never second-guessed his decision to move the National Investigations Service's headquarters just inside the main DC beltway. It made going and coming for field staff based there as convenient as anything could be in the nation's capital.

For him, too, the location allowed him to go opposite the flow of traffic from his residence in Alexandria's Old Town. For the past dozen years, he'd attended Mass at St. Mary's every morning before making the trek to the office. It was a commute for which there was a fairly direct route, and his routine of church and long hours at the office were preferable to mind-numbing traffic and, because he was a widower, to the empty house on South Fairfax Street.

The tall coffee from the McDonald's out front steamed on Clancy's desk while he waded through the flood tide of e-mail sinking his Microsoft Outlook in-box. He scanned the messages quickly, knowing there were at least one or two from his government masters to which he would need to immediately respond. For a moment, he permitted himself a few memories.

As a contractor to the federal government's central personnel agency, the US Office of Personnel Management (OPM), Clancy knew his company would always be under the gun. He knew, too, how the beltway world played its games, and long ago he made up his mind to play them well. At just over five-feet seven, his presence did not command a room, and the thinning, dark hair atop a lined face with bushy eyebrows he overcame with leadership, work, and pluck.

He'd been a founder and principal officer of NIS, the forced privatization of a federal entity under Former Vice President Al Grayson's thumb. With Clancy's program knowledge, the company thrived when most federal customers thought the new firm—staffed by fired feds—wouldn't last six months. That was in 1996, and NIS had performed brilliantly.

Then, when the Defense Department's cadre of in-house investigators bankrupted itself, NIS was tasked with hundreds of thousands of new cases, checking the backgrounds of staffing clerks and generals alike. NIS had creatively and effectively taken on the task, proving beyond question how flexible and responsive a private company could be when confronted with a seemingly impossible workload.

Calamity struck NIS the day after 9/11, however, when the government demanded the company stand on its head to help staff entire new agencies at higher quality and production standards. Clancy chuckled quietly. *The government always demands service that's faster, better, and cheaper, when they themselves never seem to manage any two of the three.*

Eleven years later, and the pressure had not let up. Under the Williams Administration, federal employee rolls had grown dramatically, and the demands on NIS to support two wars, a huge and growing welfare state, and a burgeoning government class were beginning to collect their tolls. Clancy noticed his calendar signaling February's end. *I damn well will not be in this chair a year from now.*

His computer beeped, heralding incoming mail, and he groaned when he saw the email from Kristen Bartley, OPM's Director for Investigations. It was marked, "High Importance." *Weren't they all?* He sighed. Skimming her entire message to see if any grenades were about to go off, he exhaled in relief that it was just another emergency request from the Office of the Vice President.

Since OPM was on the short list of VP responsibilities, the incumbent spent a fair bit of time manipulating—and draining—its resources. This time, a number of Special Scope Background Investigations (SSBIs) on nominees for the vice president's National Commission on the Elderly had to be completed in very short order to satisfy political favors. No problem, Clancy thought. Although his company's 3,400 field investigators were working night and day to clear soldiers going to Iraq, Afghanistan, and God knew where—not to mention the nation's border patrol staff, all its federal prison personnel, EPA inspectors, atomic energy workers, and the like—he would see to it that the day's "emergency" demand would be met.

Picking up the phone, Clancy hit three on his speed dial and waited for the inevitable answer. At the second ring, the voice of Janice Dern claimed the electronic ether.

"Did you see it?" he said.

"Yep. Know how many high-importance-red-exclamation-mark messages I get every day, Pete?"

"No." He chortled. "That means you need to train your subordinates better."

"Funny. I don't know why you bother calling. You know I'll get right on it."

Clancy ignored Dern's mood. "There are some other workload matters we need to cover, and now's a good time. While we're on the phone, I'll bet Bartley will fire two more missiles, and we'll deal with them as well."

For several minutes, the two covered staffing, cost estimates, and the myriad concerns of field investigators performing one of the most invisible, thankless, and unglamorous jobs a man or woman could want in a career. Yet, those who thrived on independent work, travel, and using their wits—because no weapons, subpoenas, or threats were in their back pockets—enjoyed interviewing their fellow citizens in a free country, all in support of the national security.

At the end, Clancy asked Dern to tender his regards to the Columbus staff, and asked her to remind everyone that Ohio would be getting a lot of attention this coming election. "No one wants the spotlight on NIS."

Hanging up, he sipped his chilling coffee and was comforted that once the task was in Dern's hands, it would be done to the nines. This wasn't the first priority request from Vice President Morrison, and it wouldn't be the last.

"Jackson," Sheldon Ingber said. "Tell the president what you heard." The Oval Office walls seemed to shiver with the late winter blast of wind and snow blitzing the capital.

"It was interesting, Mr. President," Armitage began, shivering too. "When I made my rounds floating the idea that Joe Morrison might not be on the ticket this time, there was definitely a mixed reaction."

Williams sat impassively while the tick of the mantle clock behind him filled the pause. He knew his own reputation for letting silence speak louder than words, and appraised the young man before him. Armitage's inexperience as a spokesman in national politics could be catastrophic, yet, his skills in a vote-getting ground game were unmatched.

"As you might expect, sir," Armitage continued, "the vice president has supporters around town. He's done a lot of favors for people, and he's still a hit with a crowd."

"But?" Ingber nudged.

"But there are more than a few snide remarks about his unwillingness to think things through before he acts. The older hands in the Senate put a good face on things, but privately, there's not a lot of respect there. Harry Riordan remains his rabbi, however."

"Jackson, tell the president what Lightner said—and what many have repeated." Graham Lightner, everyone in the room knew, was a five-term senate Democrat from Florida, and though past his prime in more ways than one, his words continued to carry weight.

"Yes, Jackson?" Williams said, speaking for the first time.

Armitage cleared his throat, shifting uncomfortably. "Some have reported that in more than one cloakroom conversation, Senator Lightner said, 'Morrison is as dumb, and as useful, as an ashtray.'"

The president's lips turned upward on one side, but otherwise betrayed no reaction. "Thank you, Jackson," Williams said, shifting his gaze to Ingber.

Taking the hint, Armitage excused himself.

Waiting until the door closed, Ingber pressed. "We talked about this in '08, Av. One: he'd barely served one half of his first term in the senate, and most of that time he spent campaigning for the job you now hold. Two: he's always in campaign mode—the only thing he seems to know how to do well. That, and doing little favors for people. Even now, presiding over the senate, few on the hill know him or what he's all about, except perhaps Harrison Riordan. Three: he knows nothing about world affairs and his social positions remain farther to the left"—here Ingber paused for effect—"than even yours."

"So?" the president said with bemusement.

"What do you mean, 'so'? He's a lightweight, and that was just an appetizer. Surely, you've picked up on the growing noise about Morrison in the media? He's a loose cannon."

"But he's our loose cannon, Shel. Look, my friend, if I paid attention to every media twit on a slow news day, I'd have traded you out ten times by now. And Lightner? An old gasbag. Lucky thing he's on our side. Of course, you're right. Morrison is not the sharpest guy we've ever met, but in politics, he's not alone. What he does have is energy and stump appeal. He can draw in women and the young in ways I no longer can."

Ingber said nothing, but his face revealed his feeling of helplessness, as if he was watching a man trying to drown himself.

Williams caught Ingber's frustration. "Shelly, you're the smartest political strategist drawing breath right now, and you know I respect your opinion, so I'm open to convincing, but I gotta tell you, it'll be a long pull."

A rap at the door preceded the entrance of Freddie Frederick, the aide who started out in Albany with Williams over a decade earlier. Her very dark red hair framed a face still freckled despite its age. "Mr. President, you have two appointments here, and we're a bit behind this morning."

"Thanks for the hint, Freddie." He turned to his campaign director. "This needs to be a longer conversation. Come back in—"

"An hour," Frederick said, finishing the sentence, knowing the president wouldn't mind her keeping him closer to the clock.

Williams smiled and nodded. "An hour, Shelly."

"Mr. Vice President, this is Enrique McCord." So introduced the bundler—a megafundraiser to anyone else—as the three sat down to a lunch in the veep's private office in the White House complex. Silverware on white linen glinted as cold sunlight flooded the table. Morrison appreciated the more formal introduction because it would then be he who could say, "Just call me Joe," to the right kind of donor.

"Mr. McCord, how good of you to join me for lunch. I always appreciate it when..." He looked at the bundler begging for help.

"It's Tom, Mr. Vice President."

Morrison was embarrassed about his memory lapse. *Better get in campaign mode, Joe!* He'd have to make it up to "Tom," one of many self-important flacks he'd have to schmooze until November.

"Of course, Tom. My deepest apologies," he said affably. "I have to tell you, Mr. McCord," he continued, "Tom is one of our strongest supporters, and since it was he who insisted on me meeting you, can I assume you're from the great state of Texas?"

McCord beamed. "Why, yes, sir, Mr. Vice President, I'm from San Angelo. Not exactly Dallas or Houston, but we do love the fact that one of our own sits right here at the seat of power."

Glad to have cleared the hurdle, Morrison moved into his element. Such a first meeting would have been more comfortable at the official residence in Bethesda, or perhaps, at the JW—Marriott, that is—but the vice president never underestimated the power of a West Wing visit. He pressed on. "So tell me about yourself, Mr. McCord."

"As Tom may have mentioned, I'm the founder and CEO of SoftSec, an election software business. We're headquartered in Cincinnati—the Midwest is where a lot of our new customers are."

"At what customer level are we talking about?"

"Why, the various states and major cities primarily, sir. You see, all of the states are now equipped—to one degree or another—for electronic voting. That wasn't true in '08. And there are only a half dozen companies in the field, along with another smattering of outfits picking up places like Idaho."

For the next forty-five minutes, during a lunch of club sandwiches and Saratoga chips, McCord delved into electronic election management. "So there are no more paper ballots?" the VP said at one point.

"That's a yes and a no. You see, Mr. Vice President, in some locales, a paper ballot is produced for the voter, and it is then scanned for tabulation. Of course, there's the older punched card ballot and, more recently, there's DRE."

"DRE?" Morrison could feel his eyelids drooping.

"Direct Recording Electronic voting, sir. In some locations, the voter still uses an electronic interface, casts the ballot, and it produces a card—like the famous ones with the hanging chad in the 2000 election. At the end of the day, those cards are collected and run through a high-speed tabulator, which produces the vote count. That is getting to be very old-fashioned, but is still around in some places.

"So, DRE is the newest and best technology," McCord continued, "because we eliminate paper altogether. Using a similar electronic interface, probably touch screen, the voters cast their ballots, which reside on flash memory devices, like thumb drives, and at the end of the voting cycle, each device connects to a master tabulator and the vote count is produced. It's much faster, and again, there's no paper. Very green. Very efficient."

"SoftSec produces both the hardware and software for both devices?" Morrison asked, more interested.

"Indeed we do, and we're now in twenty-two states."

"Really." The chief listener was impressed, and fully awake. For the first time, he sized up his guest as a Texan should. The self-made entrepreneur spreading mayo on the last triangle of his sandwich had strong features, was fairly tall for someone of Hispanic descent, and had rich, curly hair framing a face with a natural, bright smile. This guy could run for office, Morrison mused.

"I shouldn't mention this," McCord added conspiratorially, "but in 2011, we bought VoteCounts, a firm about half our size. It's in five of the states where we already have a presence, but it gives us a foothold in six more."

"Why is that a problem?"

"Right after we bought VoteCounts, the Justice Department, along with the Federal Election Commission, brought an antitrust suit against us. It's still working its way through the system. It would be a shame if we had to divest ourselves of those assets before November."

"To be sure, Mr. McCord, to be sure." The rough-toothed wheels in the Morrison mental machine whirred at higher speeds. "Well, sir," he said, appearing to regret his next words. "This has been a real delight, and although I'd like to hear more, I'm sure the president has a few chores for me."

The intimation of power washed over McCord like baptismal waters in a cathedral. "Yes, sir. I understand, sir. And by the way, it's Ricky."

"And when we're together like this, Ricky, you can call me Joe."

"Sure thing, Joe," he said with a smile as broad as the Rio Grande is long. "If you ever need anything, you just let me know."

Morrison flashed his famous grin. "You never know, Ricky. You never know."

"Okay, Shelly, let's review the bidding," the president said with zest in every word of a favorite phrase. "I know you're going to remind me we have a hell of a race in front of us, but don't bother." Williams perched on the edge of his preferred seat.

"You're damn right, Av. This will not be a walk, but we have a couple of aces in the hole."

"One is the GOP has no ground game and we do," said Williams. "Acorn did a nice job getting it set up in '08, and it's a good thing we kept it going."

"But that may not do us much good if the economy stinks up every voting booth in the nation. And your problem is that you can't keep blaming Bush and the Republicans."

"I hear ya, and you're right again," Williams said, scratching the side of his nose. "Besides, we both know we had as much or more to do with the crash than Bush. That poor bastard's been our punching bag long enough."

"Jesus, Av, is the recording system on?"

Williams laughed. "You know, Shel, George Bush knew I was gonna pound him. That's the game, and believe it or not, I've tried to make amends to him more than once for the beating he's taken."

"Now you sound like Harry Truman. I understand he made a point of inviting Hoover back to the White House after the Roosevelt crowd made him look like cyanide to the American public for almost sixteen years."

Again, Williams's mood sparked a chortle. "I heard that one. What's the other ace?"

"Maybe it's not the cards we don't have. It's the cards *they* don't have, but even I am embarrassed to mention that the print and electronic media remain in our camp."

"Are you surprised, Shelly? Look, survey after survey has shown that somewhere between eighty-five and ninety percent of all media types are liberal, and not to blow my own horn, but I've given them a hell of a lot of good reasons to be on our side. They damn well better be. Without me and the liberal majorities in the House and Senate for the first two years, we wouldn't have had a stimulus package or an immigration bill or a greater entrenchment of abortion rights."

"I sure didn't mean to wind your crank."

"You didn't, but why wouldn't they be with us?"

"To name just two: You made a big thing out of closing Guantanamo 'the first day,' and it's still open. Worse, the economy still sucks three years later on our watch."

"I may not have closed Guantanamo, but we've begun giving terrorists basic rights—just like any American citizen." The president sat straight up, raised his voice for effect, and pointed his famous index finger in Ingber's direction. "Our liberal base *and* the media love it. And as to the economy, surely you've noticed that the stories about unemployment across most of the media—except News Global of course—are about the corporate responsibilities for hiring people, not about the horrors of hungry job seekers. That's a tone that hasn't hurt us. So let's not worry about the media. They're like the ground game—all ours."

"As long as you continue to make nice with them, and as long as we continue to do the controlled interviews, we'll be okay, I think."

"And we have another edge with them. What's different about today, unlike the JFK versus Nixon race, is that some of our mainstream friends don't even bother with the appearance of neutrality." Permitting himself a small snicker of satisfaction, the president then asked, "So, what's it look like on the other side?"

Ingber shifted his large frame on the couch where Oval Office guests and those being grilled for one reason or another always found themselves. He began to rattle through the points he'd prepared about Governor Winston Hardy and other wannabes. The president took it all in.

After about twenty minutes of back-and-forth, Freddie Frederick once again presented herself. "Mr. President, CIA Director Warner and Secretary Grantham need some of your time—something about Libya."

"Shelly," Williams said with a wry smile, "our campaign would be so much easier to manage if it weren't for this damn job."

All laughed sympathetically.

"Freddie, please make sure Mr. Ingber and I get another hour tomorrow—uninterrupted. Thank you."

Pete Clancy picked up the phone and, for the thousandth time, was grateful for caller ID. "Yes, Kristen, how can I help you?" The air in his office seemed suddenly cool.

He could easily picture her workspace in the old Investigations Program enclave at 1717 H Street NW not fourteen miles from where he sat. She would be ensconced behind a veritable aircraft carrier of an oak desk, beautifully refinished to show the detail and the grain of the wood. Nearby was the fabled brown leather, government-issue couch that had been in the same spot since the early 1950s, when the program received its impetus under the Atomic Energy Act. The details of

Bartley's office were familiar to him because, as he would only occasionally mention to visitors, it used to be his office, his desk, his couch.

"I take it your people are already working on the special cases we sent you this morning?"

No hello, he noticed. Just business. "Kristen, I'm always surprised when you call about just a few of the forty-five thousand cases we have going for OPM at any given time." Clancy was always careful, but not obsequious, in his approach to Bartley, a tall, wiry woman, whose angular facial features caught light and shadow as if carved by her no-nonsense personality. Now unattached, Bartley's priorities in life were coffee, cigarettes, and the investigations program—in reverse order. It was a set of preferences Clancy frequently reminded himself to never forget.

"Pete, you know exactly why I'm calling. Those cases have Vice President Morrison's interest, and I hope you understand that priority."

As an old investigator for the US Civil Service Commission—later OPM and before privatization—Clancy knew all about White House work. He and his colleagues had done cases for high, sensitive positions in the government since the Nixon Administration and for every Republican and Democrat since.

What had proven a challenge for him was that when he'd decided to take the NIS job, OPM in turn decided not to promote his suggested replacement, but instead brought Bartley over from an investigations unit in the Treasury Department. She'd had no hesitation in turning his painstakingly constructed federal entity upside down, yet he never understood why she'd taken a professional liking to him. What was perfectly clear, however, was that she hated the whole notion of privatization. Wondering if the white-collar union mentality so prevalent at Treasury influenced her agenda seemed a silly exercise to him. It was all about protecting federal jobs and bennies. Nothing more.

Since privatization, Bartley and her federal colleagues tasked with managing the program's principal contractor, NIS, did so with a vindictive zeal, as if Clancy and the hundreds of men and women tossed out of the federal government had had any choice in the matter. The new reality had not been altogether pleasant, and he had not always understood why.

"Of course, we understand, Kristen. Better than most, you know that. Do you really think you needed to make this call?"

The line was silent for a moment. "Pete, you and I have established a fine relationship, and for the most part, you've made my job easy. Which makes me want to ask you about noises I hear that you plan to bail in a year or so. Is that right?"

"Should you be asking that question of your contractor, Kristen?"

"I'm just letting you know," she said quietly. "Not long after you go, this will be a federal program again."

This was the first time she had ever been so plainspoken. "I've heard that said." Clancy took a chance and went further. "So I take it you have no qualms about thwarting the wishes of Congress and the last Democratic administration."

"Vice President Grayson and his staff were misguided and you know it. They had no other intention than to fire a warning shot at the FBI."

"I'm surprised to hear you be so blunt about it, my friend."

"Stop there, Pete. We're not friends. I admire you for leaving OPM and taking the risk of getting NIS on its feet. Nobody else could have done that. But that was then, and this Democratic administration likes federal power."

Clancy noticed her words were neither mean nor cold. Her tone, however, might have been one reserved for her ex-husband—a role, he was relieved to say, that had never tempted him. "Kristen, I know this is a conversation we might not be having, but NIS's existence saved the Investigations Program, and you have to admit we made it an efficient machine that has brought you pride before your hundred customer agencies. How can you just take it back?"

"Like I said, that was then. Don't forget that I'm a whiz at numbers and what graphs and charts can do. And I'm the one who testifies before Congress, not you."

"Why is this such a mission for you, if I may ask?"

"I'm well aware that you and your team built this program and its reputation from fifth class to world class, which allowed OPM to actually handle what the Defense Department and 9/11 threw at us. And you know, too, that when the Civil Service Commission was born in 1883, and the country developed the need for background investigations over two world wars and then the Cold War, we were the right ones to do, quietly, what the FBI chose not to."

"And?" said Clancy. That she needed to recite history for him rankled.

"And you have to agree that this is a program that's inherently governmental."

"No argument necessary, because it is in federal hands. You and your folks manage the living hell out of it while NIS does all the field-work far more effectively than we ever did as feds. And I suppose it doesn't matter that it's far more costly to the taxpayer when it is done by federal employees, not to mention that there's been far more case falsification by feds than by contractors like NIS."

"Just don't get in my way, Pete. This conversation—that we never had—is over. And you can mark my words—the current situation will change. NIS served its purpose. And I'm younger than you. I'll get this done, but after you're gone."

"All right, Kristen, I hear you." He paused, changing the tone once more to that of a contractor addressing his customer. "As to today's business, the Commission on the Elderly cases are already in the mill."

"Don't disappoint us, Pete."

"We won't."

"And by the way, with the election season heating up, get ready for a slug of cases from the Election Assistance Commission in a few weeks or so."

"Got it." Clancy heard the line click without the old "Bye, bye" in her western Maryland lilt. He shook his head. Nothing she'd said was new. She'd just added a bit of reality to years of speculation. Besides, she may be the head of the program, but she would need White House authority to accomplish her objective, and as far as he knew, she didn't have it.

Occasions such as this reminded him he was no longer the lone ranger heading his company. He now answered to a board of directors and, in the past year, a new corporate owner. For his people to have kept their jobs, his supervised stewardship was a small price, but it was one he had not been prepared to pay indefinitely.

He flipped his calendar to 2013 and sighed. There was nothing he could do about Kristen Bartley and her plans. And in the meantime, he had work to do.

"Sorry about that long interruption, Shelly, but as Yogi Berra loved to say, 'It's déjà vu all over again,' and now you have my undivided attention." President Williams and his guest settled themselves in their usual places.

"Av, I don't need to tell you this is the last day of February, and we need to give this some time." Ingber knew these were early days in the months-long sprint for the presidency, but after so many meetings in the Oval Office, one tended to blur into the others. He sat himself down on the couch and faced his friend.

Williams jumped right in. "I know you're impatient with me, but you know there's nothing I like better than being elected. Since 2012 is my last one, I'm going to be highly invested in that objective, no matter what. Don't let anyone in the campaign ever get any idea my heart isn't in it. Ha! Let the Republicans think that. Now, what are they up to?"

"I don't need to tell you March Madness is next week, and I don't mean basketball. By the way, I hope you filled out your bracket. The media sports mavens will want to know. As to the GOP, there are still seven who think they have a shot, but only three who can get there."

"So who are you eliminating?"

"It's too early to cross any of them off, but for our purposes, Ron Paul is not going anywhere, despite his appeal to the hard core." Ingber dismissed Johnson, Huntsman, and Perry, and said, "That leaves us Santorum, Gingrich, and Hardy."

"Do you want to pare it down a bit further?"

"Not yet."

"Okay, but I know what you're thinking." The two dissected the remaining three for the better part of forty minutes. Then Williams said, "Let's get Sondra in here for a minute. We'll talk about our side of things, no matter who wins the GOP race."

Ingber rose and walked to the rounded door leading to outer sanctum. "Freddie, find Sondra will you? Thanks." He returned, stroking his mustache.

Williams decided to take a risk. "When are you gonna get a regular haircut and trim that thing over your lip, Shelly? Your wife and I have been looking at it go gray, for heaven's sake."

"I like all the hair I have, thank you—Audra's never seen me any other way."

The two men exchanged grins of friendship and bonding neither would ever trade. Both turned to look as Sondra Thompson, Williams's chief of staff, entered and sat. All three basked in the filtered sunlight invading the windows behind the Resolute desk, from under which JFK Jr. famously poked his towhead some fifty years before.

Having expected the invitation, Thompson's words were playful. "Well, guys, are we finally ready to talk about the next six months?"

"Shel knows why I bring you in when talking about the campaign, so let's make sure everybody knows where they stand. Shel is in charge of the campaign and Sondra is in charge of the White House support of that campaign. It's that simple, and between the two of you, we can't lose. But before we get gushy here, I know you two will respect the lines of authority. The reason I have you two together on stuff like this is there are no better political thinkers in the country right now." Williams cast his glance across the off-white decor of the Oval Office, as if there was a world listening, and added, "And Gardner Stewart, that includes you."

His listeners beamed, and remained poised, like trained beagles.

"I hate to give George Bush's electoral guru such attention, but until you two came along, he was the best."

"If you boys are through having fun," Thompson threw in, with no disrespect, "let's get at it."

"All ears," Ingber said.

"Here's the way I see it, Mr. President. It's going to be about nothing but the economy. All the other stuff will not matter, not even Joe Morrison."

Ingber rolled his eyes, making no effort to conceal his feelings.

Thompson continued. "The other side will throw eight point three percent unemployment at us every chance they get. That's number one. Two, they'll talk about the deficit and untamed government spending." She looked directly at the president. "Three, sir, they'll point out that you haven't done anything about gridlock in Congress."

The trio spent another twenty minutes discussing the counters to the likely GOP attacks.

"That's one side of things." Shifting his gaze to Ingber, the president asked, "Any good news, my friend?"

He shrugged his shoulders. "Well, I think so. You know, many red-state strategists haven't yet absorbed the fact that we took Texas in '08, and it would be damn nice," he said, acknowledging the big con to the mini campaign against Morrison, "if we took it again. That said, all this noise by the cable crowd that we're cooking up some nine-state strategy is something we should let run. Just smile whenever we're asked about it."

"I'm not following," Williams said.

"It's just this, and I'm sure Sondra will agree. Assuming we take Texas again, it all comes down to four states: Ohio and Florida principally, with Virginia and Colorado thrown in for good measure, but we don't even need the last two."

Williams smiled. "Phew. That makes the real campaigning a bit more focused," he said, enjoying the irony. "I get it, and if it's Hardy, I want Colorado." He paused. "And if we could put Virginia in the bag, that would be icing on the cake, wouldn't it? Ha. I love it. Once again, Shelly, you've zeroed in on it. I salute you."

Turning to Thompson, he said, "What else, Sondra?"

"Well, besides our ground game, we have Emerson Grantham, our secretary of state, do we not." It was a statement.

"How so? As a federal employee, he can't be a part of the campaign."

"Precisely, gentlemen. Unlike 2008, there will be no powerful alternative voice on our side running against us. And that means his kissin' cousin will be neutralized as well, but we should factor in that Grantham and Former President Harper are personally, not politically, estranged."

"Kissin' cousin?" said Ingber, inclining his head toward Thompson.

"They both acknowledge some distant relationship, but Emerson Grantham is from the patrician branch of the family in Connecticut, while Jefferson Harper comes from humble and not-so-polished Tennessee beginnings. No love lost there."

"Let's not be shy about this," the president said. "As far as Jeff Harper and I are concerned, no love lost here either, but we'll need him to get off the couch this fall." He looked directly at his listeners, stretching his lips into the famous grin. "Ha! Good thing those two aren't close."

"So it will be a bit tricky," Thompson noted. "Jeff Harper will remain very quiet in this campaign unless his cousin has a clear path for 2016. With those two, family still trumps party."

President Williams nodded. "And whether he campaigns for us may make all the difference, so we'll have to figure out a way to shift him out of neutral."

"Okay, we'll work on it," Ingber said. "In the meantime, Av, I hope you'll think about our earlier conversation."

With a question formed in his arched brows, Averell Williams looked across at his manager.

"About Joe," said Ingber.

"Don't be shy, Shelly. I'm sure that's crossed Sondra's mind as well."

Sondra nodded. "You bet it has."

"Look, you two." Williams's tone was playful, but he knew his listeners would take him seriously. "I don't want to hear any more whining about Morrison unless you give me a valid alternative. Got it?"

"Right," they both responded in unison.

Freddie Frederick, the clock's grim reaper, appeared and pointed out that Secretary Grantham and Defense Secretary Roberts were waiting.

MARCH

NBC/Wall Street Journal Poll
February 29-March 3
Williams 50%
Hardy 44%

F orbes Flannery faced the camera on the News Global set. "You have just entered *The FactZone*, and on deck is Gardner Stewart with his insights into the Republican primary race."

Off camera, Stewart shambled up to the single seat facing the one occupied by his host, the unchallenged and long-running champion of cable news. He noted with amusement that Flannery's seat was cranked at least two inches higher than the one reserved for his guests.

In his most affable mood, Flannery introduced his guest and got right to it. "Okay, Mr. Stewart, in the interest of full disclosure, we should point out you're a News Global contributor, and that you've managed two Republican presidential campaigns. But that aside, tell us what's going on with the current GOP mob scene."

Stewart gave his host and the News Global audience his Mona Lisa smile, as if he would never reveal his deepest secret. "Well, Forbes, the gentlemen to whom you're referring think there's still a chance because the Winston Hardy campaign has yet to catch fire."

Flannery closed his eyes, seemed to throw his head over his left shoulder, and offered a deprecating chortle. "Do you seriously think the governor can change his message sufficiently to make the turn he needs?"

"That remains to be seen, doesn't it?"

"If you were advising Governor Hardy's campaign, Mr. Stewart, what would you tell them?"

"The advice I might offer is that while he needs to appeal to the conservatives, he does not need all of them. He should pick his issues and remember constantly that in the general election, it will be the independents who win it for him."

"At this point, I remain dubious. Thank you, Mr. Stewart."

Joseph P. Morrison didn't mind enjoying the trappings of an office to which the current president attached no power, and he missed few opportunities. As his limousine drew up to the Jefferson Hotel in the 1200 block of busy Sixteenth Street, he warned himself to be careful, as always. Washington's many fine dining establishments existed because the capital was the center of power and, politically, the center of money.

In setting up the dinner with Election Assistance Commission personnel, his staff realized that all four seats on the commission were vacant. They decided that the EAC's Executive Director, Jim Sommers, and a number of electioneering practitioners, including his new Texas acquaintance, Enrique McCord, could work out well. *What's the point of it all if one Texan couldn't lend a hand to another?*

Morrison's Secret Service escort was caught unawares when, after stepping from his limousine, he took six steps and stopped. He turned his head skyward to admire one of the most massive and imposing iron and glass marquees in the entire city, especially since he now commanded every square inch of its cover. That a dumb Texas kid would one day be walking into the Jefferson inside a Secret Service circle never ceased to amaze him. When he thought about others who would be amazed, he allowed himself an arrogant grin. "Eat shit," he said under his breath.

As he strode through the hotel's massive bronze doors, he delighted in the fact no one knew what was behind his toothy smile. Still unbelieving in the truly pleasant coincidence gleaned from a staff report on SoftSec, Morrison savored its potential value much as a Labrador retriever eyed raw meat. What Ricky McCord had not told him in their earlier meeting was fleshed out by Remy Carlson: McCord's company was owned by the largest newspaper chain in the heartland, the *Missouri Courier* in St. Louis—home to his political rabbi, Harrison Riordan. *What luck!*

Even more arresting was the knowledge that the *Missouri Courier* had been bought in 2011 by Appalachian Shires, the investment machine of the second wealthiest man in America—just behind Bill Gates—Milton Jennings himself. And Jennings, the Iowa livestock baron who became an East Coast investment genius and liberal dilettante had long been a staunch Williams supporter. "Only in novels," the man in the beautifully tailored tux said to himself as he crossed into a fairytale of hotel living. "Now to see what power can do."

A sumptuous lobby greeted the vice president, and he enjoyed the sound of his Allen Edmonds shoes across the black-and-white marble floor. Replete with seven-foot potted palms under the arching backlit skylights, the venue created a mood with *Titanic* stirrings.

Guests were cocktailing in the private room when Morrison and his cordon made its way in. Flashing his famous smile, the vice president shook hands all around, giving one CEO a special introductory massage.

"Jim Sommers," Morrison said. "I want you to meet Enrique McCord, a fellow Texan—not that that would have any bearing on any relationship you might have. I want you to understand that, Jim." The smile was captivating, Cheshire in its breadth.

"Naturally, Mr. Vice President. As EAC's executive director, I'm glad you were kind enough to host this gathering so that we on the federal side might better be acquainted with those who actually do the vote counting for us."

The thirty-some guests relished the opportunity, not to mention the food. These included representatives from a number of states key to any election—people like McCord, there to hustle their services in a friendly arena, and Morrison himself, who keynoted.

"My friends," the vice president said, after an impeccable lamb feast, an irony that made him wonder if the guests there knew who were the lambs and who were the lions. "You are among the most important people in the nation this year, yet no one will ever know who you are. Why? It is you, in one fashion or another, who will ensure our destiny as a free nation confident in its vast system of election practices."

Morrison droned on for the scheduled ten minutes, and after brief but hearty farewells, he made a brisk departure. Alone among the gathered, he had accomplished the only real objective of the dinner, courtesy of the US taxpayer. Entering the backseat of the Cadillac Escalade for the ride to Bethesda, he smiled to himself. "Now that was easy money," he murmured to no one. After all, for a quick introduction at a small dinner, that was the fastest quarter million to fall into his campaign chest.

"Governor Hardy," Lisa Hoxworth said as she looked at her candidate's hair, its silvering prominent under the glaze he had learned to use in earlier campaigns. They were in a quiet, paneled room of the candidate's Colorado estate, a place where candid conversation was expected. "This is not going to be a cakewalk, as you must already know."

"Are you talking about the fall campaign or the battle we're in now?"

She chuckled. "Both, I suppose."

"So lay it out for me—as you see it."

"Look, Governor, we're not connecting with the hard core."

"No surprise there. Lisa. I'm not one of the hard-core right and never will be. The positions some of these guys take on foreign affairs and immigration are in my opinion, just plain goofy. They're not in sync with most Americans, for sure, and I think I am."

"Let's break this down, and take first things first. You have to win in the primaries, where the hard right is a major force in many of the states we need to win early on so that the momentum is ours. That means your message now—on gun rights, foreign aid, abortion, welfare, and health care—has to be a bit more conservative than you may inherently feel."

"That's very hard for me to do, Lisa. I am what I am, and for me to suddenly concoct such views just to please the fringe will be phony and everybody will know it."

Hoxworth sighed the sigh of a Donna Quixote. "Let's talk about this a bit. I know you hold strong Second-Amendment views, for example. Why can't you talk that up a bit, and maybe a commercial or two of you on hunting trips when you were governor here would buttress that view."

Winston Hardy peered out the window of his giant estate on the reserved land of the Ken Caryl Ranch southwest of Denver, his gaze toward the foothills of the Rockies. Hoxworth saw the wistful expression on his face, almost as if he could transport himself back just a few years to when he inhabited the Governor's Mansion in downtown Denver. She waited.

"I'll do what I have to, Lisa, but only insofar as my conscience will allow. On gun rights, that's not so hard, but don't let anyone ask me about assault weapons or expanded background checks, because I could never support the first, and we desperately need the other."

"I'll take it."

"On abortion, I'm sticking to the views I held as governor: I'll abide by the law permitting first- or second-trimester abortions—although privately, I abhor them all—and I'll fight to the end to prohibit all abortions in the third trimester.

"Two things on that," Lisa interjected. "When you talk about the first or second trimester, make sure you always add something about incest, rape, or the life of the mother." She saw Hardy's nod. "And two, if you're careful about it—and this is a risk—you might tease Williams out on the whole third-trimester thing. I understand that if pressed, you and Williams share the same view. He just never talks about it."

"He doesn't have to. It's so much easier to let Morrison take the point. He's on the record in Texas, of all places, in support of letting babies die who are born alive in botched abortions." Hardy shook his head, his eyes shut as if in prayer. "I do not know how a civilized human being can harbor such a view."

"Well, Morrison has a lot of views, and they play well with the hard left, of course. And that, Governor, brings me to another sensitive issue."

"That being?"

"Religion. At some point, you might be forced to do a Kennedy-in-Houston encore, and I suggest we actively seek the right venue for the greatest effect."

"I suppose you're telling me that a Mormon can't get elected. In 2012?"

"Look, Governor, we're not talking about Colorado or Utah or Idaho. On the liberal side, you shouldn't even concern yourself with their views. They wouldn't vote for you if the planet switched its poles. And to most independents, it will be a nonissue—they will applaud you, however, if you deal with it."

"So once again," he said, traces of anger in his voice, "we're left with my friends on the right. I have to convince them I'm a genuine Christian and a genuine conservative—the C words. That's what it gets down to, doesn't it?"

"We come full circle. In all the upcoming primary debates, you have to fashion your answers with a bit more care—even if you don't win them over, you have to do two things: don't offend them, and look better than the opposition. Above all, sir, you've got to remind people over and over that you're electable because you have what it takes to get the economy moving again and none of the others—especially Williams—have the right stuff."

"We're a week away from Super Tuesday, so I guess we have a lot of work to do. But don't forget something, Lisa."

"What's that, sir?"

"We're going to win. It may be slow, it may get a bit ugly, but we're going to win. So let's work on my near-term strategy with the C words, and after next week, maybe we can start thinking a bit long-term."

"Sounds like a plan."

The vice president's official residence since the time of Nelson Rockefeller nestled into the acreage of the US Naval Observatory in Bethesda, and millions had been spent over the years to make what had been an aging Victorian pile a suitable place for the one-heartbeat-away occupant of the office. In the second floor residential quarters, Sharon Morrison ruminated about the place—and about her place in the world. Her iPhone chirped, and she knew it was her sister, Margo, calling from Houston.

"What good timing you have. I just put the last one to bed. That little Joshua just will not give his mommy any rest." She laughed into the ether and heard her younger sibling respond in kind.

"You lead some life, and I don't know how you do it," said Margo.

All at once, as if her sister had rung all the right chimes, Sharon Morrison burst into tears.

"My God, Share. What did I say? You were just laughing out loud. What's wrong?"

The second lady—a title never used because no woman would stand for it, or so Barbara Bush was alleged to have said when she occupied the dubious seat—let her tears subside. She didn't hurry and didn't worry about what her sister thought—they loved each other and it would never matter. Finally, she found her voice. "Oh, hon, I love Joe and I love our kids, but I just can't stand this!"

"What are you saying, sis? I thought you loved all that pomp and baloney."

Sharon struggled to find a chuckle. "It is baloney. But we're left out of most of it. For some reason, the president doesn't want to give Joe anything of substance to do, and—oh, my God, Margo, you can't repeat this to a soul—he spends most of his time playing basketball, doing silly photo ops, and piddling around with the second-rank agencies he's allowed to touch. Christ, it's a disgrace."

"Of course, it is. He's the vice president, for cryin' out loud. What's Williams afraid of?"

"I guess he just doesn't think Joe is up to it—God, that's the first time I've ever said that out loud. I can't believe it."

"Oh, that can't be true. Jesus, he helped Williams win the election. Why would he put the screws to Joe like that?"

"I don't know, but maybe it'll end soon."

"What are you talkin' about?"

"Oh, you know—the rumors. I don't suppose they're a part of everyday conversation in Houston, but DC is a political town, and I can hardly show my face. People say things—people who should know better."

"What things?"

"That Williams will dump Joe because the economy is so bad his campaign needs a shake-up."

"That is just bullshit, and it makes no political sense. They need Texas and our electoral votes, and they need Joe's energy on the campaign trail."

"God, you sound just like one of these politicos." They both laughed out loud. "You know, I don't know what to wish for. If Joe left office, we'd have a more normal life, but the adjustment would be horrendous because we're not prepared for it—not to mention humiliating as all hell." She started to cry again.

"So what's Joe going to do?"

"I don't know. He just keeps telling me not to be such a worrywart."

"What do you think he has in mind?"

"Oh, I have no idea, but he just smiles and says great days are ahead."

"Janice, this is Pete," Clancy said while idly flipping the pages of his datebook. Outside, an ice and sleet event shrouded Little River Turnpike and snarled the homeward rush.

"Yes, sir. How's the political weather in DC?"

"Heating up, I think. You know, I've been at this business for nearly forty years—that's ten presidential election cycles—and each time it plays out a little differently for us."

"I've been around for a few of those cycles myself, but what do you mean?"

"It was one thing when we were a federal agency. We were insulated, protected. Now we're the private pawn of a federal agency, one that reports to a sitting vice president. Surely you've noticed, even out in Columbus, this regime has seen fit to politicize nearly everything within the reach of the federal government."

"I'm not sure I agree with that. Look, Pete, you're the best boss I've every worked for, and I respect you fully, but you've already figured out we differ politically. You're a bit conservative, and I'm a bit more liberal, and I don't feel guilty for having voted for Williams. And my being a black woman has nothing to do with it, so get that thought out of your head."

"Whoa, Nelly. You and I are pros, and we keep politics out of everything, but sitting where I sit, this crowd is every bit as bad as it was during the Nixon years. They keep score and remind people of it daily."

"Okay, I won't argue the point, but what's this all in aid of?"

"I've decided to hit the road, visiting you guys and the other regions as well. I want to remind our investigators about our political neutrality as an organization and put them on alert about things not to say. You know the drill. We don't have the same Hatch Act restrictions on our speech, but no federal host agency wants to be embarrassed by their contractor. And I don't want us firing somebody because they wore a Williams button to an interview—same goes for the other side, whoever that will be."

"Good idea. The troops always like to see you. Do you have a schedule yet?"

"I'll have to hit all the hot spots in the next sixty days, so I'll get back with you on some dates for Columbus."

"Got it. I always look forward to seeing you." She chuckled into the phone. "Even if you can't think straight politically."

Laughing too, he added, "You know, Janice, we've done this management thing for a while now, and I wouldn't want anybody else in your seat. Thanks for the good stuff you do out there. Talk to you soon."

❖

"Ricky! Good to see you again."

"And you, too, Joe. Thank you for the invitation." Enrique McCord wore his broadest smile. "Only somebody like you could arrange for us to play at Oakmont in March. It doesn't get cooler than that!"

Joe Morrison beamed and was enjoying the moment on a number of levels. His first choice for a golf venue had been Burning Tree, practically down the street from Bethesda, but BT was out. Its exclusion of women would not sit well with the NOW crowd and more than one segment of the liberal base.

"My pleasure, Ricky." Steamrolling the powers that be in Oakmont's rarefied atmosphere had given him a great deal of satisfaction. *Just who did these Pittsburgh people think they were, anyway?* As much as anything else, it was the reason for the famous grin he flashed at the software mogul now at his side.

"I have to admit I was pleasantly surprised by your call," McCord said.

McCord seemed nervous, as if he expected to make another donation. "Relax, Ricky. We're going to have a fun time this morning," said Morrison as he signaled his Secret Service detail to follow in a separate cart. He and McCord jumped into their own and set off for the first tee.

The holes flew by and Morrison was up by three strokes. Then they came to Hole Four, a six-hundred-yard par five from the black tee. It was famous for the so-called church pews—sand traps—running perpendicular to the left side of the fairway. Morrison was not a long-ball hitter, however, and hit a so-so, fairly straight ball that managed to fly the gauntlet safely. Next, McCord teed up and, with his two-wood, knocked it out 175 yards but into the rough on the right.

"Oh, tough shot." Morrison couldn't hide his mirth. "Now we'll see what you're made of." Though he considered himself a very competitive player and enjoyed his advantage, he didn't want to beat his opponent too badly. McCord had something he wanted, and he had to keep him in a good mood. The unseasonably warm day helped.

"Enjoy it, Joe, because I don't plan to make it easy for you."

The two struggled through the hole, both capturing a bogie. The rest of the first nine sailed by uneventfully, with Morrison ahead by one stroke as they made the turn. "You know, Ricky, I want to hear more about your election software when we get to lunch."

McCord smiled back, as if to suggest Morrison was being merely polite.

"Seriously, I think you and I are made of the same Texas cloth, and you might be able to be of great service to our nation."

McCord eyed him with both respect and surprise. "Whatever I can do to help. I'm sure you know I'm a big fan of the Williams-Morrison team."

As they finished Hole Thirteen, Morrison thought that his comment had had the very nice effect of flattering McCord and distracting him. He grinned his way through the last five holes and enjoyed his four-stroke win. As in most other things, Morrison muttered to himself, too softly for anyone else to hear, "Whatever it takes."

"Did you say something, sir?"

"Not a thing, Ricky, except that it was a great round against a formidable partner. And since I invited you, lunch is my treat. Let's go into the clubhouse, and spend some good talk time together, just the two of us."

McCord glowed.

Morrison returned the smile, knowing that McCord was a second-generation Latino and a fervent Democrat, someone who could be useful in the one way the Williams-Morrison ticket needed it most.

"So what do you think, Joe? Who will the Republicans throw at you guys?"

"In my humble opinion," Morrison said with a grin, "it won't matter. They have no candidate and no game."

"What if it's Hardy, Santorum, or Gingrich? Gingrich is a great speaker—though not as good as you or President Williams," he hastened to add.

"I know both Newt and Rick personally—their campaigns have no legs," Morrison replied.

"And Hardy? He could be tough—successful businessman, former governor, and all that."

"That's what we've been thinking all along, Ricky. And that's partly why I wanted to talk with you privately. When we were last together,"

Morrison said, and he leaned in with a conspiratorial air despite their total seclusion, "you talked quite a bit about your business."

"Sure, Joe, I remember."

"I'd like to know which states use your software and just how foolproof the system really is." The mile-wide, shark-white grin showed itself. "I'm all ears."

Over a cold Diet Coke and a tall glass of ice water just off the sixteenth green, the two men talked for a quarter hour more about the broad capabilities of McCord and his people.

"You seem to be very concerned about this November, Joe. You think there'll be some vote fraud?"

"I'm beginning to feel certain of it," Morrison said. He paused, wanting his next sentence to seem an afterthought. "While I'm thinking about it, there's a quick-path Election Assistance Commission contract up for grabs right now, and your company will be just right for it."

"Look, gentlemen," News Global's Flannery said. "The folks want to know what's going on in the Republican race, and you guys are the best."

Gardner Stewart and Jack Rispoli sat opposite their host like Dickensian characters unwillingly joined for the political duration. They chuckled in friendly unison.

"Here in *The FactZone*, ladies and gentlemen," Forbes continued to the camera and his nine million viewers, "we want you to know that Mr. Stewart was a longtime member of a Republican administration, and Mr. Rispoli is a seasoned Democratic campaigner and strategist, and also a News Global contributor. The two of them will join us from time to time to help us understand the ins and outs of this year's presidential race." Looking to his guests, he said, "So Super Tuesday has come and gone, and what say you, Mr. Stewart?"

His chalkboard materializing like magic, Stewart began speaking with his characteristic half-smile. "Hardy leads the pack," he said, displaying the current tallies. "So, it's beginning to become an easier path for the nomination."

"I don't necessarily agree," Rispoli chimed in. "As you were saying not long ago on this very show, Hardy's message is not catching on, and the Democrats—not to mention the people in Hardy's own party—are having a field day with his wealth and lifestyle."

"As for his lifestyle," Stewart said, "the man was a hugely successful mining engineer, headed the state's prestigious School of Mines, and served two terms as governor. The guy is wealthy. He's earned it. The media needs to get over it."

Rispoli scored what his smile said was the victory point. "Too late. Those stories and commercials have played before millions of people and their initial impressions of Hardy are there."

"And the other so-called news outlets—most of them—ought to be called, collectively, 'State Media.' I don't know, Forbes, shouldn't the networks and your cable competitors be required to register as super PACs aligned with the Democratic Party?"

Laughing out loud, Flannery said, "I see that gets under your skin, Mr. Stewart, but let's answer the question. Has Hardy got it nailed?"

"In my opinion, very likely."

"So, what do you think, Shelly? Is it all over for the other guys?"

"Do you mean, is it Hardy? Yeah, I'd say so." Ingber had parked himself on one of the two facing yellow brocade couches in the Oval Office, his file folder next to him protected as if it were part of his long and enlarged body. He looked over at the president, still seated behind the famous Kennedy desk after finishing his call with Senator Riordan. Williams's head was bowed to his pen, concentrating on a note to himself, and Ingber couldn't help but notice the white streaks creeping through the president's full head of hair, hair that not many years before had been a black halo around the sculpted deep walnut face. It was a noble head, fit for a Roman bust.

Having completed his written thought, the president ambled to his favorite spot. "For my money, we couldn't have a better opponent. By the way, where's Thompson?"

"She'll be here in a minute, Av. And you're right about Winston Hardy. His problem—in his party, and in politics in general—is that he's a true Boy Scout."

"Oh, God, he sure is," Williams said with a chuckle. "He just doesn't know what he's in for. He has no idea that the New York political machine is about to roll over him, that in this game, anything goes. From what I hear, he's been an astoundingly successful businessman, but never ruthless."

"That's his problem. Our job will be to make sure his ideas never get traction."

Sondra Thompson walked in with a frazzled bearing. It wasn't so evident in her face but in the disarray of her ordinarily perfect light brown hair. "Good afternoon, Mr. President. I haven't seen you since this morning."

"And Sondra, our days are going to get crazier. Everything under control out there?"

"Yes, sir. More crap about Solyndra. The gang at News Global just won't let go."

"What about the others? CNS, Newshare, ABS, and the rest?"

"Hardly a word, and just the way we like it."

"Am I supposed to ask how you guys manage that?"

Ingber and Thompson looked at each other. Ingber nodded to the chief of staff.

With a bit of a smirk on her face, Thompson said, "There's somebody on my staff who has a great e-mail thing going with a particular blogger very friendly to us. No names mentioned. The blogger has a private e-mail list of her own, and two or three times a week, she spits out to her media buddies a few points that happen to match what our staffer has written. The blogger has a reputation as a thoughtful progressive, and to the White House Correspondents Association, most of whom are just like us, getting some inside thinking is never a bad thing."

Williams nodded. "So, Sondra," he said, as if the previous exchange hadn't happened, "you were saying the other day it'll be all about the economy."

"Yes, sir, and of course, the Republicans will throw the national debt at the public every chance they get. May I suggest, sir, that we craft a few moves to show how you've attempted to work with House Speaker Whitaker on a four-trillion-dollar deal?"

Williams smiled. "You know what'll be so great about that is that we've been to Ohio twenty-six times already this term, right in John Whitaker's backyard, and I have no problem camping in Cincinnati to tell that story over and over."

"Well," Ingber joined in, "that'll be the tack for the next six months. You've tried to work with Whitaker in the House and Marshall in the Senate, and it's been they who have refused to budge. Switching gears a bit, if I may, the other prong of our campaign is to steal the national security thunder right out from under Hardy and company."

"Right, Shel," Thompson added. "The Republicans have owned that issue for too long."

"I hate to say it, but Joe Morrison has been working on a great line that goes something like, 'General Motors is alive and Osama is dead,'" Ingber said.

"And al-Qaeda is definitely on the run," Thompson pointed out. "We'll have to polish that one up a bit," she said, making a note on her pad. "But let's save it for the summer."

"Back to Hardy," the president said. "How're we going to play him?"

"He might be a Boy Scout, but he's a rich one, so it'll be a natural to portray him as an out-of-touch capitalist who wants to buy the office. We'll have a lot of help with that, I'm sure. Reporters will ask him tough questions about the high life and won't let it go. Just where he stands on issues like gun control, welfare, abortion—all of those will trip him up in his own camp and distance him from everybody else."

"What about the Independents?" Thompson asked Ingber.

"Good question. We just have to make sure our ground game gets out our own vote, and we get as many fence-sitters as we can, certainly women who'll be scared of a Republican regime on abortion rights."

"Exactly," she said. "And it should be no trick to have our PACs do some of that work for us. Let's not take for granted the African American vote. We'll need every one of them."

"Not ninety-two percent or ninety-five percent but ninety-nine percent if that's possible," Ingber said.

"Should I ask how're you going to do that?" Williams wanted to know.

"I don't know yet," said Ingber, "but we'll have to make it happen. The Republicans are making inroads with the white, college-educated voters, and he'll get a bunch of Independents on the fiscal issues."

"We've got to take the Hispanic vote from them, Shelly," the president said. "Remember, George Bush got forty-four percent of those votes in '04, and we took some back in '08, but they're ours, dammit, so let's do what needs to be done."

"I think passage of the 2010 Immigration Act should seal that one for you," said Ingber.

"But the GOP will get some credit since they cosponsored it."

"That's where our ground game in the barrios will trump anything they do."

"Let's hope so." Williams looked at his strategists, unconvinced. "Any other angles to play?"

Ingber asked, "Is there any way to limit their fundraising?"

"How do you mean?" said Thompson.

Ingber stroked his mustache. "Oh, I don't know. I just wondered if we shouldn't put the Tea Party crowd under the glass."

Quickly, Thompson said, "You and I should talk later on this."

"That'll be another thing you two never tell me about," Williams insisted, and he made direct eye contact with Thompson as he spoke. "Want to talk a bit about Morrison, Av?

"Maybe not now, Mr. President," Thompson said. "Freddie warned me to keep you on schedule this morning. You have a meeting with your Jobs Council. You haven't had one this year, and we think you'd better get one on the record."

"Yes, ma'am," Williams said with a salute, and he shifted his glance from one to the other of his companions. "I'm off to Seoul next week, but right after I get back, we're going to settle this Morrison question once and for all."

At the suburban Denver ranch, a bit less glamorous than the Hardy retreat in Aspen, Lisa Hoxworth and her deputy met with their candidate while readying for the Wisconsin and Maryland primaries on April third. Hardy asked for an update.

"There's a fair amount of good news, Governor. You know, of course, that since Super Tuesday, winning most of the marbles in Wyoming, Alaska, Mississippi, Missouri, and Illinois puts you nicely ahead of the pack."

"Don't forget Louisiana," the deputy added. "Winning in the southern states—where they could have voted for the others had they wanted to—boosts your standing with conservatives."

"After Wisconsin and Maryland, Governor, you get a three-week break before the five primaries in the Northeast—all blue states. During that interregnum, Jerry and I have you scheduled for two stops in Ohio, one with Speaker Whitaker in Cincinnati and another with Governor McNickle in Columbus. I'm checking the schedule now, but at some point—sooner rather than later—you've got to get to southeastern Ohio, a part of Appalachia a lot of conservatives and evangelicals call home."

"Just how important will that area be, do you think?"

"Probably more than we know. Without strong margins in places like Scioto County, you have no chance to offset Cuyahoga County, meaning Cleveland, where Williams rules. And without Ohio, Governor—"

"I know, Lisa. I know." Hardy's bright blue eyes lasered on Hoxworth. "I have to admit I'm a bit worried about those folks. I'm having trouble enough convincing some that I'm a conservative like them, but I'm wondering whether the evangelical crowd will ever give me a chance. A lot of them are Harry Riordan fundamentalists."

There was a long pause while his aides absorbed the candor of their usually ebullient leader. Hoxworth's deputy jumped in. "Governor, it's like this. Unlike you and Lisa, I'm not Mormon. I'm just a regular old

Presbyterian from Kentucky, and I can tell you this: when you're with folks for whom religion is a big deal, it wouldn't hurt you to make the right kind of reference to Jesus Christ once in a while. Letting them know he's your savior too will go a long way."

Hardy forced his lips into a thin, straight line. "I hear you, Jerry, but it's just not like me to talk so openly about my religious beliefs."

Supporting the deputy who had taken a bit of a risk with the governor, Hoxworth spoke up. "Win, if you can't do it, you're just convincing those folks you're not one of them, and they won't even go to the polls in November."

Hardy remained pensive.

"It's also important for those voters out there to call you by your first name. 'Win' has its own karmic power, I'm thinking."

"Okay," Hardy conceded. "Jerry, let's do more with that idea, but not over the top."

"Yes, sir. I know it's a small thing, uh, Win, but if you want people to think they can enjoy a beer with you, it'll be huge."

"Jerry, don't you know that with Mormons it's ice cream, not beer?"

"Whatever you say, sir," he said with a bright smile. "And as the campaign moves forward, I'll get you more polling and issues analyses than you'll ever want."

Hardy nodded appreciatively.

With all three smiling, Hoxworth said, "Now for some other news. The national polls are beginning to matter and there's definitely some opportunity for us."

"I'm listening," Hardy said, though he was beginning the mental adjustments he needed for the campaign trail. It wasn't just his message. It was the messenger. That messenger, Hardy knew, had to look and act like the common man in some ways, but be just tall enough to earn their respect.

"According to a CNN/Opinion Research matchup between you and Williams, he has you by seven. What's better for us is that the president's approval rating is barely over fifty percent, and his disapproval level is at a pretty high forty-five percent—and that poll came out just this morning."

She continued, "So to sum up, Governor, what we have to work on is the religion question and your presumed lack of foreign affairs experience. On the plus side, we have to hammer home your business experience creating jobs and the fact that the incumbent has done little to change the economic picture."

The deputy held up his index finger as he glanced at his iPhone. "Governor, you may have an opening on the foreign policy point—the president said something very interesting in Seoul."

"This is Peter Marsden here with *The World Journal*, and in Colorado today, we have our Tony Duke. So tell us, Tony, what's it like out there in Aspen among the rich and famous?"

With the Rocky Mountains as his backdrop, Duke positioned himself so that the camera would capture not only the panorama of the snow-caps but also, glimpses of a few of Aspen's mega mansions. "I haven't met many as yet, Peter, but as you can imagine, it would not be hard to do in this enclave of wealth few Americans are privileged to enter."

"Have you been able to talk with any of the Hardy family, Tony?"

"I have not, Peter, despite our requests for an interview. Reportedly, Governor Hardy is in Colorado this week, but until yesterday, it had been unknown whether he would take refuge from conservative attacks here or in one of his other homes in Maine, Michigan, or Florida."

"How does the campaign respond to charges that Hardy is so rich that he's out of touch with everyday Americans?"

"It's already clear that despite the recent Hardy primary victories, his approval rating is taking early hits because of the questions about his wealth." Duke paused and turned to his left. "And here we have Lisa Hoxworth, a long and trusted Hardy associate. What do you say about all this, Lisa?"

"Thanks for having me, Tony. First, Governor Hardy has had successful careers in business, education, and politics, and we should be focusing on how many jobs were created as a result of the governor's business enterprises, how much he's contributed to mining science when he ran the School of Mines, and his great record as Colorado's Governor. Those stories are not being told."

"But Lisa, what about people who lost their jobs under his leadership?" Duke said, sugar oozing through his words. "Just what responsibility does Governor Hardy take for those people?"

"The governor is always saddened when the economy turns and employees have to look elsewhere for employment, but Win Hardy cannot be responsible for every unfortunate occurrence. By the way, what's wrong with success? Isn't that every American's dream?"

"Thank you, Lisa." He turned to the camera with Hoxworth now out of frame. "It remains unclear whether average Americans can identify with the governor when they see how the Hardys live—their houses and cars aplenty. To put it more specifically, can Joe Six-Pack picture Winston Hardy at a cookout in a blue-collar backyard? Back to you, Peter."

"Thanks for that insight, Tony. Meanwhile, President Williams meets in Seoul with the world's nuclear powers, and carries with him the weight of the issue as North Korea and Iran vie to see which will be the next member of the atomic-weapons club. As we can see from our live feed, the president's energy level does not seem to have suffered from the long flight halfway around the world, and no doubt he hopes to prevail in dealing with the Russians, among others."

Marsden paused to let the viewing audience absorb the majesty and power of the venue with the US president involved in a seemingly important exchange with the Russian leader.

"This is Barnes Ward with *NewsFlash!*" The brassy logo filled the News Global Service screen at its usual 6:00 p.m. time slot, and the boyish face of the host appeared, somber eyes over a toothy smile. "There's breaking news from Seoul, Korea, tonight, as it becomes clear that President Williams was unaware of an open microphone in front of him when he made what sounded like a promise to the Russians some have called troubling. Joshua Powell, who is traveling with the president, has a brief report. Joshua?"

"Good evening, Barnes. The news from here tonight is not what one might have expected from a bilateral nuclear summit with the Russians. CBS News has the open-mic recording in which the president is conveying more flexibility in a missile deal after a November election win. This incident recalls a similar one not four months ago in which Williams was caught saying to French President Sarkozy some unflattering things about Israeli Prime Minister Netanyahu."

"Does the Williams Administration have any comment on this incident?"

"Not as yet, Barnes."

"Thank you, Joshua. We'll have the panel in later this hour to comment on this and another story we're following for you. It seems that Senate Minority Leader Jordan Marshall, Republican from Kentucky, held a press conference today in which he claimed that several of his constituents have been unduly hassled by the IRS in obtaining 501(c)(4) status from that agency. As you may know, it is the IRS that rules whether an organization can qualify for nonprofit and, therefore, non-taxable status in the United States. Senator Marshall joins us now. What do you have to tell us, sir?"

"Thank you for asking, Barnes. It appears none of the other news outlets have any interest in reporting what may well be very disturbing abuses by the IRS in carrying out its regulatory responsibilities."

"What exactly has been reported to you, senator?"

"Several conservative groups, some of which are affiliated with the Tea Party, have sought 501(c)(4) status from the IRS. Their offices, by the way, are located in Covington, Kentucky, just across the river from Cincinnati. And it appears to me the questions asked by the IRS and the demands made by them are way out of line. What is just as troubling is that as of this date, I have not received even the courtesy of a response from Acting Director Hellman."

"This is the first we've heard of this, Senator Marshall, and we will continue to cover this story as it evolves."

Other news about late winter storms and the stubborn level of unemployment over 8 percent, not to mention the fact that "real" unemployment was in the midteens, filled the airwaves for several more minutes before William Herzog, Steven Harrison, and Marta Andresson appeared with their anchor. "William, as to the incident in Seoul, what are your thoughts?"

Clearing his throat, Herzog delivered his view with a practiced certainty. "Once again, this president needs a minder around an open microphone. Careless words are one thing, as occurred with President Sarkozy. While they do damage with the Israelis, a quiet apology usually does the trick. As to Seoul, that is a different matter. President Williams appears to be striking a bargain with the Russians, contingent upon his reelection—of which he seems unduly certain—and it is the flexibility at which he hints that we may find most troubling."

APRIL

Gallup Poll
April 11
Williams 45%
Hardy 47%

As Joe Morrison clambered into the Escalade idling in front of the official residence, what commanded his concentration was the encounter with Navy Commander Jeremy Bolling. Their meeting had been totally unanticipated but serendipitous in a number of ways. For the half-dozenth time since the morning before, when he twisted an ankle going for a simple layup and needed Bolling's services, he replayed their conversation, insignificant though it first appeared.

"Joe, I keep telling you, playing a light game of basketball for media appreciation is one thing, but playing like a college boy with the likes of Marty Cox, who's in far better shape than you, is quite another."

"What difference can it possibly make?"

"All the difference in the world when you don't know what the future holds. In your position, the Boy Scout motto could never be more apt."

"Okay, okay, Dr. Bolling. I'll follow orders." His jocularity was genuine, and other possible meanings behind Bolling's words did not occur to him until much later in the day. When he thought about them—thought about them again and again, putting a more satisfying spin on them each time—he made two conclusions vital to him personally, which brought a contentment interrupted only by the usual departure noises of his small motorcade.

As they left the Naval Observatory grounds and proceeded to the West Wing using the Plan D route Morrison returned to a more important thought process.

Commander Bolling's words seemed to reassure him first that he had a future in the White House, and second, that it was a future for which he needed to be prepared. If true, his first concern about 2012— whether or not he'd remain on the ticket—was, as they say, history. That President Williams had not consulted him on the matter was balanced by the fact that his marching orders for robust speechmaking had not been curtailed. No news was the best news, he assured himself.

Nonetheless, he applied a rigid discipline clarifying his objectives. Being on the ticket was one thing, but before history could anoint him a presidential successor, there was one all-important hurdle in between. He had to work like hell for Williams's reelection, and if hard work didn't make it happen, he smiled, *smart work would have to do the trick.*

Amber Bustamente rose from the queen bed and ambled toward the bathroom. She paused only to peer from the box bay window in their apartment above Graeter's Ice Cream Shop in Cincinnati's Hyde Park Square.

From the far side of the bed, Nathan Conaway raised himself on an elbow as he watched her as she stood near the sheer curtains screening her from viewers below. Finally, he spoke through all the curls on his large head. "What's out there, Amby?"

"Nothin', hon. Just a buncha drinkers on the corner outside the Cock & Bull."

"Wish I hadda picture of you standin' there in the moonlight."

"You take a picture of this body, Nutsy, and I'll be heavin' your fat ass out this window, and you don't wanta spoil Graeter's business, do ya?"

"No, ma'am. How come I can't take a picture?"

"Because pictures of fat girls like me ain't gonna exist, that's why."

"Awwww," he whined.

"You just like big girls, Nutsy, and I'm glad you do. I'll make you even gladder when I get back." With that, she moved toward her destination.

Moments later, Amber lay on her stomach and let herself be the recipient of a long, slow, gentle massage from the nape of her neck to the rounding of her heels with a pause or two along the way. "Hey, Nutsy," she murmured, "I noticed those papers on your desk. What kinda forms are they?"

"I'm not supposed to tell you what that's about, Amby."

"Well, I couldn't help but notice you gave your weight as two ninety-five, and you always told me you weighed only two seventy. What's up with that?"

"You ain't supposed to be readin' my personal stuff, kiddo." It was annoying to be caught in a lie, especially by this girl, whose own weight most certainly eclipsed his own.

"So what's that all about?"

"If you must know, Ms. Nosey-pants, my company just got a hush-hush federal contract, and I have to get a security clearance. Can you believe it?"

"Somebody's gonna investigate you? Right here in Cincinnati?"

"Yep. What I'm fillin' out is a Standard Form 86. The feds use it for all kinds of security clearances. And I have to list who I'm living with, so somebody will probably be talkin' to you."

"What?" Her shriek sounded genuine, but delighted. "Me? What am I supposed to say?"

"Listen, Amby, and listen carefully. You can tell 'em we're living together—that's not a big deal—but for cryin' out loud, be careful what you say about pot. I don't want them to think I got a problem. Get it?"

"Yeah, I got it. I saw where you listed Nutsy as your nickname. How did you get that name, anyway? Do people think you're crazy?"

Nathan's laugh was so deep and full that his naked mass shook the bed and the sheets independently of one another. "No, silly."

Amber rolled to her side, and he looked into her cocoa eyes to make sure hers followed his to a place where a physiological reaction was beginning to occur. "It's because I gotta real pair, and I'll bet you're glad I do."

As if her curiosity was more important than anything else at the moment, she went on. "I saw where you listed a lotta people who know you—more than a few women. Any of them know you have a real pair, you big hunk?"

"Nope. Nada. Never. I barely have time for you."

"Oh, I get it. Barely. You're so funny." Her voice was flat.

"Don't you ever worry about me, Amby. There's plenty of you to keep me busy for a long, long time." He stroked her thigh with the lightest touch his sausage-like fingers would permit.

Amber tittered. "But Nutsy, why would a guy working for an election software company need a security clearance? What kinda secrets are you gonna have, anyway?"

"Have no idea, darlin'. But gotta do it. And besides," he said as he stroked his curly beard, "whether you know it or not, you're talkin' to sharpest software wizard you're ever gonna know." He caressed one of her pendulous breasts, and kissed her heavily on the lips.

"Oooh, Nutsy, you can keep doin' that." She kept her eyes open.

"I will, but first, tell me what *you* weigh!" They laughed, rolled, and fell out of bed together, quaking the floor and everything connected to it.

The venue at the elegantly turreted One Observatory Circle was gala but the food, highly forgettable, Joe Morrison lamented. Everything was set, but the cook staff at the vice-presidential residence was definitely not in the same league as that of the White House, and in his opinion, much better fare could be had in Texas.

He felt Sharon did the best she could as the wife of a second banana, but the odds were good that he would fade into history whether he stayed on the ticket or not. She'd often said their life in Texas was grand, full, and rewarding. In Washington, grand was all it was, and that could be a very empty word.

The vice president continued to fuss with his black bow tie and cummerbund before heading to duty. Glancing out the one window of his dressing room, he noticed the first limousine's headlights curling up the drive.

It was Secretary of Defense Jensen Roberts and his wife. Representing the only African American at a senior cabinet post, Roberts was actually a holdover from the Bush years. Immediately following them were Missouri's fabled majority leader, Senator Harrison Riordan, and his companion for the evening, Former House Speaker Angela Tesoro, from Maryland. The pairing was almost laughable inasmuch as the two couldn't stand each other. How Tesoro would get home after dinner was a detail, he'd let her work out.

With nearly half of his guests walking in the front door, Morrison perceived it a good time to appear in the mansion's foyer. On his way from the master suite, he whispered to Sharon how beautiful she looked, that he would see to their guests, and that she could join them when she was ready. He wanted her to feel her best. When she grimaced, he simply said, "Just go with the flow, hon. Just go with the flow."

Downstairs, Morrison cranked up his broadest smile for the four people already there and kept his grin alight for the three couples yet to appear. Just as he finished greeting them, CIA Director Andrew Warner—the only other senior African-American in the administration—and Attorney General Norton Sweeney, along with their wives, made their entrance.

When Sharon Morrison stepped into their presence and the hellos were properly executed, the last couple appeared. Morrison beamed at the perfect timing. He knew most of his guests would wonder about the presence of an unknown—in Washington, unless you were a somebody that the in crowd considered a somebody, you were definitely a nobody.

He took advantage of the opportunity with his first words. "Ladies and gentlemen, most of you know each other, but I'm guessing none of you have had the pleasure of meeting my fellow Texan and his wife, Enrique and Bridget McCord. The McCords happened to be in town, and I wanted to include them tonight." The smile on McCord's dark-skinned face could not have been in larger or higher contrast to the older, Washington veterans around him.

The unorganized parade proceeded into the grand parlor for cock-tails and conversation, both all too predictable. With some amusement, Morrison noticed the government class being only politely interested in McCord's business. *They must think he's somebody they'll forget after tonight. That might be a good thing.*

At table, Lobster bisque left the white-columned dining room to make way for a nondescript green salad and small filet mignons bright-ened and sweetened with a warm béarnaise. The oven-roasted potatoes were further accompanied by steamed asparagus dressed in melted butter and a grated cheese of some sort.

Morrison glanced at his wife and was glad to see she was relaxed and enjoying herself. He was glad, too, for the deference shown to both of them by their guests. It was a bit of Washington subtlety not to be overlooked. That all of the invited guests accepted their invitations meant that no one was ready to write him off as a historical footnote. *How quickly that could change.*

Imported gelato followed by a sip of Limón cello completed the repast. When Morrison raised the subject of the political opposition in the fall, there were actually hoots of derision for the other side. No one thought Winston Hardy and whomever he chose as a running mate could match an encore of the Williams-Morrison ticket.

The hosts led their guests on a short tour of the Naval Observatory gardens, abloom with sprays of orange and red tulips, hot-pink azaleas, and banks of light-lavender rhododendron. An hour after dinner, with no real news items worth repeating to their friends over Sunday break-fast, the party showed signs of evaporating.

It was then that Joe Morrison actually perked up in making his farewells because of the very private meeting he'd arranged with Harry Riordan and the attorney general. *Thank God the Roberts's will take Angela Tesoro with them.* Politely, Morrison suggested that the McCords, houseguests at the mansion, might make themselves com-fortable while he conducted a little business. With a wink, he looked at McCord and said, "Ricky, you and I should have a nightcap together later. Shall we?" Sharon Morrison and her remaining guests moved to a comfortable sitting room.

In the vice president's walnut-paneled study with shelves full of election trophies and other doodads in place of impressive volumes Morrison had no interest in reading, three men sat with their Bailey's over ice.

"I can't remember, Joe, is this house a smoke-free zone?"

Morrison laughed at the question from Harry Riordan, a man who would tease the honored guest at his own funeral. "Whatever you want, Harry, and I won't report you to the Secret Service."

"But you'll have to ask the attorney general for a waiver of GSA regulations," Norton Sweeney chuckled, a willing conspirator. "So what's on your mind, Joe?"

As innocently as he could manage it, Morrison responded, "Nothing all that special. Sharon and I just wanted to entertain a very few people we trust and enjoy, and we're very glad you're in that group."

"Thanks, Joe, but why would you want to hang around with a guy like Harry Riordan, for cryin' out loud?" They laughed at the jab, as Sweeney folded his frame into a comfortable chair and rested his chin on the bridge formed by his bony hands, each extending to an elbow pinned to a chair arm. His blue eyes focused on his host.

"Because Harry always looks out for me, and being from the middle of the country, he seems to have a three-hundred-sixty-degree view of things. Don't you, Senator?"

The aging Riordan brushed back the wisps of whitening hair from his brow, and worked the muscles in his jaw before responding. "As always, Joe, you give me too much credit, but like Norty here, I'm wondering what you have in mind."

"Putting it simply, how do you guys see our chances this fall? And don't give me any patronizing bullshit, either."

Neither man was surprised by the bluntness of the question, as both knew what had been said at dinner was for polite consumption only.

"Of course, I'm coming from the apolitical part of the house," said Sweeney.

His companions snickered in derision.

"But I give you and Av a good chance, Joe. Though, right now, no better than fifty-fifty." He reached up and adjusted his dark-blue, dotted bow tie. It didn't need adjustment, but he evidently needed something to do.

"What's your reasoning?" Morrison asked.

Sweeney employed his usual technique of blinking his eyes several times while he composed his answer. "Pretty simple. We haven't been able to crack the economy thing. The machine is stuck in the mud, and unemployment seems locked in at over eight percent. Then, we didn't close Guantanamo. Lastly, he needs every black voter to turn out again as whites bleed away toward Hardy, and the immigration bill simply did not have black support. That's it in a nutshell, but there are other reasons for people to bolt to the right."

"You agree with that synopsis, Harry?"

Riordan didn't bother to use energy for a word. He just nodded. When no one spoke, he added, "It ought to be clear to both of you that we need every advantage." He looked at Sweeney directly. "And, Norty, is there any way your guys at Justice can, shall we say, dampen media opposition to our side?"

"What media opposition, Harry? There's only News Global. And what the hell do you mean by 'dampen'?"

Riordan gave his friend a half smile and shrugged his shoulders. "However you want to interpret that, Norty, but that crowd, along with the Tea Party nuts, is having an effect."

"There are other ways to get at the Tea Party, men," Sweeney said, "but my department's options are limited. As to the media, well, we have to be careful there. In this country, anyway, we usually don't go after the fourth estate." He looked around to see that everyone understood his trump.

Morrison took his turn to nod, not uttering even a syllable in the affirmative. It was as if each man remembered the possibility of a recording device somewhere. Then, he said, "My new best friend, Ricky McCord, may be able to help us."

"How can a guy in his position help us?" Sweeney wanted to know.

"All I might suggest," and he extended his gaze to include Riordan, "is that we want to avoid all questions of hanging chad in this election. It has to be clear and convincing that we win, and things have to be such that a recount will make no difference."

Morrison wanted his wide-eyed listeners to understand two things: First, he was not as inept as some would make him out to be. Second, they should ask no further questions. In their business, men knew as an article of faith that deniability was everything. Their conversation wound down from there, and in short order, they thanked their host for, as Riordan put it, "an evening of enlightenment." Morrison savored the uptick in their demeanor from politeness to respect. *Someday, I will need them, and they'll need me.*

Morrison policed the glasses in his study, opened the window to vent Riordan's cigar smoke, and considered how to approach the second objective on the only to-do list that mattered in 2012. When a tactic soon evolved, he went looking for Enrique McCord, the man who could serve as the vital but invisible thumb on the scale of the presidential election.

In a high school football stadium in Madison, Wisconsin, the candidate was pleased to see posters and banners saying "Win with Hardy" occupying every space a person wasn't. Mounting the platform, he and his wife, Susan, waved to the increasingly noisy crowd. It was as if their flailing arms somehow turned up the volume knob on the swarm.

"When I announced my candidacy for the presidency in June 2011, I did so because we are a nation at risk," he said, making the microphone in front of him come alive. "Susan and I could easily have passed on this uphill struggle and spent our lives doing many productive things—not to mention spoiling our grandchildren—but we are here, together, as the Hardy team that will give new meaning to White House leadership.

"What has Averell Williams accomplished since January 2009? Unemployment has gone up to over eight percent and the debt is nearly sixteen trillion dollars.

"You may say, my fellow Americans, that those are just numbers, but tell that to real people like Sandy Jorgensen, a bagger at Copps Food Center, who told me she works two jobs without benefits just to feed and house her small family. Tell Lee Silverman, who was just laid off from his mechanical engineering job, that these are just numbers.

"So what's the big deal? The big deal, ladies and gentlemen, is that this president is just not up to the job if all he knows is how to make the government larger, spend your money on boondoggles for his friends, and spend his days doing photo ops. What Averell Williams has never figured out is that how they do things in New York is not how we do them in the rest of the country."

Applause filled the air.

Lisa Hoxworth scrambled to the major network reporters covering her candidate. To one she said, "Nothing compares to Governor Hardy's record of leadership and stewardship. Throughout his career, people who have put money in his business and voters who have put trust in his leadership have never been disappointed."

Tony Duke of CNS next asked, "Why is it, Lisa, that the governor's message does not seem to be catching on with the public in general?"

Hoxworth could not resist, and knew she would regret it. "He will certainly have trouble with his message if networks like yours don't give it airtime, Tony."

At the Easton Mall's Bon Vie on the eastern edge of Metro Columbus, Pete Clancy and Janice Dern sat at the bar, a Sam Adams for him and a Blue Moon for her to wash down the artichoke dip. "Sorry about the venue, Pete," she said while they waited for their sandwiches. "I didn't realize this place would be so crowded on a Tuesday in April."

"Don't think twice about it, Janice. I love this place. The bar has all the beer we can drink, it's not all that noisy, and besides, you know what a political junkie I can be—it's not much past eight, so the election results should be coming in soon."

Dern laughed out loud, and no embarrassment flushed her flawless brown skin. "Don't expect me to get interested in what the Republicans do, Pete, and remember our deal."

"Yeah, yeah. We won't talk politics. But I can listen, can't I?" They both laughed.

The bar's two televisions permitted sports and political fans to have their way, and the one facing Clancy and Dern showed Peter Marsden giving the evening's rundown on the Republican Primary fight. "It's looking like a clean sweep for Governor Hardy in the District of Columbia, Wisconsin, and Maryland. Tony Duke spent time with the governor's campaign in Madison today. Tony, the Hardy campaign seems to be picking up steam, doesn't it?"

"It does, Peter. Hardy will likely pick up an additional eighty-nine delegates after today, and that gets him that much closer to the magic eleven hundred and forty-four."

"And that also means the other guys are beginning to feel the spring chill without tidy delegate counts to warm them up."

"You've got that right, Peter, but what continues to trouble the Hardy campaign is the lack of zeal, of fire, if you will, and that will be in sharp contrast to the campaign presence of President Williams. Listen to this exchange I had with the Hardy campaign manager, Lisa Hoxworth."

The broadcast cut to the previously recorded clip.

"Why is it, Lisa, that the governor's message does not seem to be catching on with the public in general?"

"He will certainly have trouble with it."

Clancy turned on his barstool. "Okay, I promised not to comment on network bias, so I won't mention how that clip was edited." He took a good swig of the Sam Adams while feeling the cool condensation under his fingers.

"You just did. Now let's talk about your visit with the gang tomorrow."

"Since we last talked, I'm getting a lot of pressure about production and quality."

"That's not fair," said Janice. "We had to hire so many new people after OPM began raiding our top guns, and the newbies' investigative reports are not ready to go without a good review."

"I'm just telling you that unlike any other customer, they can drop any number of cases on us anytime they want to, and their expectations are always the highest. OPM could never meet its own standards, yet we have to. Nice position to be in, ain't it?"

"You're ruining my day, Pete."

"Speaking of bad days, word is there will be a bunch of cases coming from the Election Assistance Commission *before* the election."

"You almost never hear of those people," Dern said. "All everyone talks about is the Federal Election Commission. Are you sure your source has it right?"

"It's from the top," said Pete. "And she doesn't make mistakes. Of course, these cases underscore the point for my visit to the regions. All I know so far is there will be less than a dozen cases, with most of the work in Cincinnati. Nearly all the work will be in your territory, I expect."

"Gee, thanks. By the way, do you have any idea why we'll be doing these cases—now?"

"All I heard—and this was from somebody else in DC—was that they involve a private contractor who'll be in some way monitoring the vote counts in a bunch of states. Company called SoftSec, I think."

Sondra Thompson and Sheldon Ingber passed the few minutes before the rendezvous with tension as their companion. In the cherished office space she occupied in a corner of the West Wing, she felt the location was the best perk of her eighteen-hour-a-day job. Her three west-facing windows allowed her to cast an occasional glance in the general direction of Buffalo, New York, where she was raised and where she first met and admired Assemblyman Averell Williams. For a woman whose long Polish name had been changed at Ellis Island a hundred years earlier, and whose unlettered forebearers sweat blood to raise and educate a brood of new citizens, she felt honored to devote her unceasing labors to a man and to the country that made her accomplished life possible.

As for Sheldon Ingber, she liked him immensely, despite their differences in background, religion, and approaches to problems. Having waged campaigns together for longer than she could remember, Thompson trusted Ingber, and she knew the reverse was true. Neither would ever throw the other under the bus, and neither one's loyalty to the occupant of the Oval Office would ever be breached. "That's why he trusts us, Shel," she said, tilting her head toward the office down the corridor.

"Because?"

She laughed. "Because we know too many secrets about each other."

Ingber smiled then looked at his watch. "What time did you say he was coming?"

"He should have been here a few minutes ago. Let me call."

"Held up at the gate," she said, putting down the receiver. "In a minute, we'll go upstairs. I don't want this meeting to take place here."

"Understood."

They entered the small, comfortable conference room where Gordon Hellman, Acting Director of the IRS, stood waiting. Hellman was a portly specimen, not of great height, and with a few wisps of stringy hair on top, his polished head caught whatever light was in the room. His glasses seemed small for his face, and his off-the-rack suit appeared to have been worn too many times since the last dry cleaning.

"Ah, Mr. Hellman. It's been a few weeks," said Thompson. She introduced Ingber and the three sat. Looking Ingber's way, she said, "You may remember that Mr. Hellman was a holdover appointment from the Bush Administration, and—"

Hellman poked an index finger into the air. "Not exactly, Ms. Thompson."

"First names, shall we?"

"As I believe I pointed out at a previous meeting, Ms....er...Sondra, I was the IRS Center Director in Covington, Kentucky—a career, non-political position—before I was made Acting IRS Director. It's been over three years now."

"The arrangement seems to have worked out for you, Gordon," Thompson said. "You should assume, then, that the administration has been happy with your work, and am I guessing correctly that you'd like to be appointed and confirmed—officially, that is?" Her tone was more gentle than pointed.

Hellman hesitated, then said, "Well, I hadn't expected that question to come up today, uh, Sondra. I thought this was one of my regular meetings."

Ingber glanced at Thompson, a clear question in his eyes.

Thompson placed her hand on the table near Ingber's arm, the only signal for patience she gave him. To Hellman, she said, "Of course, it is." She noticed Hellman was clasping his briefcase for all its worth, his fingertips whitening more every second. "We're making no offer of a permanent appointment as yet, but I assure you, the president continues to be keenly interested in the capabilities of the IRS."

"When will we be sitting down with President Williams to discuss what we've been doing?"

"The president has an unbelievable schedule, so a sit-down with him is unlikely. That's why he has us, but certainly we'll get you a photo op with him one day soon."

"What else would you like of me?"

"We want you to heighten your focus on certain groups, now that the campaign is beginning to heat up," Thompson said.

"More than what we've been doing?"

"Yes. It has been noted with some alarm that certain radical, conservative groups are seeking 501(c)(4) status, and some might wonder if groups such as these should have such status and benefit from the tax deductibility of their contributions."

"Like?"

"CrossingPoints, for example?"

"Is that the group Gardner Stewart is part of?"

"We do not know what role he plays or doesn't play," Thompson said. "But CrossingPoints is raising millions, as are the Tea Party groups that have sprung up."

"And?" Hellman asked.

"And none of these groups support the president Americans elected to lead us," Ingber said, his own tone now more pointed than he'd intended. "These groups are frustrating policies the people want."

"I'm well aware of their aims. The IRS has already been identifying these groups and taking appropriate action, although I should point out, they are likely legitimate under federal law."

"I'm not sure you understand, Gordon," Thompson smiled, as if tutoring a child. "No one would ever ask you to deny these conservative groups their rights, but their legitimacy must be investigated. Your own regulations require it, do they not? And such inquiries take time. Lots of time."

"It is interesting that you bring up that approach," Hellman said. "I already have several letters from Senators—Illinois, Montana, and New York—asking us to investigate the groups to which you refer."

Ingber and Thompson nodded in pleasant surprise. Ingber spoke to Thompson. "So we need not be the spur to the horse here. We could let nature take its course, as it were."

"We could," Thompson said. "But we have always appreciated progress reports on IRS activities. Gordon, as Director of the IRS—Acting, for now—you continue to have many reasons to come over here for discussions of tax policy and the like, specifically in connection with the immigration issues that popped up with the passage of our bill, and it would definitely be better if these matters were not discussed by phone or, God forbid, e-mail."

"Most assuredly," Hellman said. "Coming by once a week or so has been my habit for the past three years, and I'm not sure there's a need for change, even in this campaign season. Am I correct?"

"Correct," Thompson said. "We wanted to see you today to underscore the need for your continued good work, and I wanted Sheldon to meet you finally. As usual, you'll see one of my key staffers, probably Ron Shope."

Hellman became visibly nervous. "Sondra, I'd like to point out what risks we're taking and how difficult this has been. Over a hundred employees have become involved in this long-term project. While I know the two of you are close to the president and wouldn't be asking me to manage these matters unless interest came from on high, I'm nevertheless reluctant to amp up our activities without some further cover of legitimacy."

"I understand your point, Gordon," Thompson said. "We want you to be comfortable in what you're doing, and you have our personal and professional assurances that no recriminations will be forthcoming. Besides," she added, forming her words carefully, "unless you or your people say something, who will ever know? The IRS does what the IRS does."

❖

After Hellman closed the door behind him, Ingber gave his partner in crime a hard look. "How long has it been going on? And when were you going to tell me about this?"

"When the campaign got into gear, as it is now. Remember, Shel, you may be Williams's old buddy, but you've not been an official member of this White House, and there are some things you had no reason to know. Now you do. As to the 'how long' part, we talked to Hellman sometime in '09 and have kept him on the string ever since. The IRS has been doing, shall we say, a close examination of administration 'unfriendlies' for a long time."

"Whew! Why am I not surprised? New York politics at work, and I should have known. Does the president actually know about this stuff?"

"You shouldn't ask and I shouldn't answer, but I can tell you he and I have never had a direct conversation about it. That's all I'll say."

On his exit from the West Wing, Gordon Hellman took several deep breaths. He didn't know how long he could continue to play a double game, but at least he made it through another high-profile meeting. Although the two political operatives with whom he had just met should have known better, a few pretty obvious facts must have escaped their notice.

For the past three years, he'd acted as if using the IRS for political purposes was a most difficult thing to do. The truth was such a proposition would only be true if everyone were still living in the Nixon era. Didn't they understand that Nixon's Enemies List surfaced only because most IRS employees were Democrats and they found a way to make it surface? Didn't they get the fact that the IRS had a strong union that made hefty contributions only to Democrats and that suggesting to certain IRS people they spend their days bedeviling conservatives was like suggesting to a kid that he have another candy bar?

As Hellman walked to his waiting car, he hoped only that he could maintain the ruse long enough to secure the permanent appointment he craved. As to the IRS employees, no one was going to change their political leanings, so why not ride the wave?

"Here they are again," said Forbes Flannery at 8:07 p.m., like a barker at a carnival, "Gardner Stewart and Jack Rispoli, to give us the latest on this Monday evening, April sixteenth. It should be pointed out that four hours from now, Eastern Time, is the deadline to file your taxes, and of course, what we pay and where it goes is, in part, what this campaign is all about. Gardner, I understand you have some interesting news to report."

"I don't need my chalkboard to share with your viewers the news that according to Gallup's recent poll, if the election were held today, Winston Hardy would be ahead of President Williams by two percentage points, forty-seven to forty-five."

"Nice try, Gardner," Rispoli said, his congenial chuckle betraying his possession of a counter. "The CNN/Opinion Research poll, out just today, shows the president with a nine-point lead. And let's not forget the Democratic Party's ground game—awfully hard to beat."

Flannery all but cackled. "And there you have it, ladies and gentlemen, from two men who have yet to agree on the day of the week."

In a private dining room at the Capital Grille, just off the Navy Memorial in downtown Washington, DC, Joe Morrison sat across from his new friend, Enrique McCord. It was just the two of them. No spouses. No other friends. No staffers. The waiter brought McCord a Grey Goose and Schweppes with a slice of lime, and in front of the vice president, he placed an iced glass of gassed Perrier.

"You're not drinking, Joe?"

"You may not have noticed, but I never do. I've been a teetotaler my whole life, and that's no baloney. Since we're Texas boys, we both know that in some families, alcohol can be closer than a blood relative. That was true in mine, and I've never forgotten that. What's more, Ricky, being all about sober helps me keep my head when all about me are losing theirs." Morrison laughed broadly at his own joke.

"I understand, sir, I mean, Joe, and I'm sorry I asked. Do you mind if I do?"

"No offense taken, friend, and no, I don't mind, but before we go further, I have to be sure of one thing."

"What's that, Joe?"

"That alcohol will never loosen your tongue. What the president and I may need your help on can never be divulged. Not to a fucking soul, alive or dead." Morrison's language suggested an intimacy between men with shared experiences, and that was the way he wanted it.

"So how can I help?" McCord said, leaning in.

Morrison's smile claimed all the facial real estate south of his nose. "I'm glad you always ask that question." At that moment, the waiter reappeared. "Let's give this young man our complete order, and then he won't have to make so many trips back here," he said for the benefit of both his listeners.

Morrison ordered a pasta with chicken, broccoli, and a rich cream sauce, while McCord indulged with a small filet mignon, smashed red-skin potatoes, along with peas and pearl onions.

Morrison looked at the waiter and said, "Sonny, don't be surprised at what a guy like me eats. I come to places like this because I'm expected to, but give me a chicken pot pie anytime." The thrilled young man left on his mission.

Morrison waited until McCord had all but finished his vodka and tonic, in part because he knew the Capital Grille never skimped on its drinks. It wasn't that he wanted to take advantage of him. There were other ways to do that, but hoped the Grey Goose would make his guest just a bit more pliable.

"Ricky, did you see the Gallup poll numbers today? Hardy is ahead of President Williams. Unbelievable. Unbelievable."

While Morrison talked, McCord nodded furiously at his companion's commentary. "You're right, Joe, I don't understand it either."

"Do you think we could lose this?"

"You're asking me? I support you and the president, but I'm a lifelong Democrat, so who else is there? Otherwise, I know nothing about politics."

"Then I hope you're willing to trust me," Morrison said, inviting the full attention of his listener, "because I wouldn't want you to run afoul of anything these days."

"Afoul of what?"

"Well, like that contract with the Election Assistance Commission you received not long ago." Morrison leaned forward. "You can be sure the right words were whispered in the right ears, but of course, I couldn't officially have any part in that process." He laughed. "Anything for a fellow Texan."

"Yeah. Anything." McCord echoed.

"Well, I wanted you and your company to have a piece of the federal pie—whether we're reelected or not."

"Oh, Joe, the game is far from over, and—"

"You're damn right it's not over, but those crazy conservatives and their groups—like the Tea Party—they might influence a lot of votes. You never know."

"Well, if it gets to that point, two of us can play at that game."

"What do you mean?" It was asked in the most innocent tone Morrison could muster.

"As I may have mentioned, Joe, our company is in a lot of places, and we supply both software and hardware. SoftSec is in a position to actually see the vote counts before they're official, and if you need a few votes here and there..." He let the sentence hang.

Feigning shock and surprise, Morrison challenged him. "You mean you could actually do that?"

"You bet, and with this EAC contract, it'll actually be easier because we should be able to see the vote totals compiled by other providers. And in those situations where there's no paper in the mix, it would be impossible to prove anything. Totally impossible. But there's a small problem regarding our purchase of VoteCounts—the antitrust suit I mentioned a while back."

"That's one decision I may not be able to change, but if we slowed it down until after November, that should give you plenty of time to reap the benefits of your acquisition, right?"

"That's all it would take, Joe."

The vice president inhaled deeply, as if he'd just been told he and the president were evacuating to Mars. "I would never have asked you to do a thing like this, Ricky, but it's nice to know it's even possible—in the off-chance we would ever need a little help, I mean." In his most humble manner, he added a benediction. "Our nation has had many silent heroes, and now I know that should you be called upon, you would rank high in the eyes of the president and all of our people."

Morrison could see the effect of his words as McCord's eyes glistened at the edges and his lower lip quivered. *Damn! He baited his own hook and took it.*

Sheldon Ingber traversed the familiar steps across the West Wing, making his way through the oval corridor into the space where Freddie Frederick served as gatekeeper and timekeeper. Her pert face looked up from the phone conversation engaging her at the moment, and she nodded to him to go on in.

Ingber took the three big steps to the slightly curved door beckoning visitors into the most famous office in the world. He knocked and pushed the door ajar.

"C'mon in, Shel. I know it's you," called the familiar voice, now more careworn from too many stump speeches, too many fundraisers, too many stops in the campaign that did not end in November 2008. Ingber knew where to sit and to unbind his folder of talking points for the day's meeting. All of this occurred without an additional syllable between them.

When he was ready, the president moved to his chosen station from which he could merely incline his ear to better hear Freddie when she appeared over his left shoulder. From his vantage point, Ingber noticed, he could also enjoy the three great nine-over-nine windows looking out into the copse of strategically placed trees just behind his desk. Even so, the light from their southern exposure was never harsh, and the morning's sunshine filtered by the colonnade washed the room with a comfortable glow. Williams presented his friend a broad, welcoming smile, seemingly carefree.

"Gee, Av, for a guy who's neck and neck with his competitor, who's leading a stagnant economy, who's saddled with an intractable Congress, who's...well, I needn't go on. Just what the hell are you all smiles about?"

Williams's smile turned into outright laughter. "Look, Shel, it was tough as hell to get my black self elected the first time, and despite the bad news, we have all the levers of power at our command. Do you realize that in the last hundred years, only four—four, Shel—incumbents who ran for reelection lost? And three were Republicans: Taft, Hoover, and G. H. W. Bush. No Democrat—except Carter—lost the White House if he ran for a second term, and I do not intend to be partnered in history with Jimmy!" Affability reigned alongside his bravado.

"Glad to hear you say so, Av, because we have a lot of work to do. Let's deal with it." For the next several minutes, Ingber named a topic and the president offered his counters. Together, they tuned his message.

"Keystone? That hits both our union allies and the jobs issue."

"We're going to delay on that one. I don't want to piss off the environmentalists, and neither do I want to destabilize the world's other oil producers when their economies are at risk. That's an issue hard to explain, I know, but I'll leave it to you and Sondra and Jack to figure that one out. We'll have to see how the polls are trending."

"It's funny you mention Jack Sennett. He's been your press secretary for all four years and has done a terrific job for you. How big a role do you want him to play in this campaign?"

"Let's keep Jack right here in the White House facing those media alligators every day. That's where he's best. He sticks to his script and we'll keep him out of certain key discussions—we want him to be able to truthfully deny what we don't want out there."

"Okay, what do you want to say about the national debt? And you can't avoid it, because the Republicans are going to make it a big issue."

"Let 'em. Just let 'em. Most people out there don't understand a trillion dollars, and what's more important for us is that as long as their checks keep coming for their lifetimes, they don't care. Only about half of the people even give a damn about it, and they don't vote in the same reliable numbers as our folks do."

When the president became reflective for a moment, Ingber held his fire.

"And besides, it's simply our philosophy that the federal government is the only—the only—institution large enough to make a difference with the monies we can put in the marketplace. The more we can get in the hands of our voters, the more they'll spend, and the more likely the economy will move in the right direction.

"And the national debt wouldn't be so damn high if the rich would kick in their fair share. It's just that simple, and that's how I'll keep banging away at it in the campaign. We're actually lucky that if it's Hardy, he's one rich son of a bitch. When the real people think about him and his kind not paying a decent amount in taxes, they'll be energized to vote for me, and you can take that to the bank."

"Damn! I'm glad I didn't wind your clock on a bad day." They both laughed at that. "Now, Av, we get to the nutcracker, so I suppose we need Sondra to join us on this one."

"I'm warning you, Shelly," he said playfully, "if this is about Morrison, this is the last time we talk about it. Got that?"

"Yes, sir," he said, and went to Freddie Frederick's door.

Two minutes later, Sondra Thompson deposited herself on the couch and said in mock despair, "I guess I know why I'm here."

"You can't avoid it, Sondra," Williams said. "We're going to put this whole ticket matter to bed, once and for all. We've got to get past this now because I'm hitting the trail—three preemptive stops in Ohio, and I don't want any media confusion on this. So what do you two conspirators have for me?"

At the word *conspirators*, Ingber and Thompson exchanged quick and careful glances as the president checked a copy of the day's schedule lying on the table next to him. "I believe that Sondra and I are of one mind on this, but of course, she can speak for herself. Both of us do not get good feelings from anybody but the unions about Joe Morrison remaining on the ticket."

"That's a big constituency, and we owe them," the president said.

"There's a pretty classy alternative," Ingber said.

"Who is?" Williams was growing impatient with the dance.

"Naturally, Emerson Grantham would be an ideal candidate and one you should seriously consider. He's widely respected by our own party members, is loved by many independents, and would garner some crossover votes from Republicans unsure about Hardy."

"I thought we buried this possibility two months ago."

"I'm sorry, Av, I thought we left it open," said Ingber.

"As did I, Mr. President. I believe he would jump at the chance because it would enhance his chances in 2016."

"Let me be blunt about this. The biggest reason I wouldn't take him in '08 had to do with famous relative. If he'd become vice president, the two of us would have been viewed as in the orbit circling Harper's sun, and the comparisons would have been both constant and annoying. I knew he could handle the State job because he's well qualified, and serving for both terms will make him practically unbeatable next time around."

"I see that," said Ingber. "In the past four years, you and Grantham have had a chance to be your own people. It worked, but that was then and this is now. It could work to your advantage, and this move might solve the other problem: moving Jefferson Harper out of neutral."

"I knew you two were going to try this one again," Williams jabbed them like a father having to put up with the repeated bad behaviors of his children. "And I've thought a lot about it, for all the reasons you give. But expecting Jeff Harper to give his all for a relative with whom he barely speaks doesn't compute with me. Besides, we gain nothing. Jeff now lives in New York and Emerson was a senator from Connecticut, and we'll get all those electoral votes whether he's on the ticket or not. Keeping Texas and a few other western states is a more important question. That depends greatly where Morrison is this fall, and that's a risk I find it unnecessary to take. Case closed."

Thompson raised her index finger, begging leave to continue. "Mr. Ingber won't ask you this question, but we're both curious, Mr.

President. If you don't mind us...me...asking, have you talked with Morrison yet?"

"Glad you asked that, because it's something I shouldn't be taking for granted. The poor bastard is probably wondering as well."

"Word is that he's a pretty unhappy guy," said Ingber. "He feels ill-used, if you know what I mean. He might just think he's pretty valuable to you and want a better cut of meat, so to speak."

"I've wanted to ask you about that, sir," Thompson said. "What's held you back about Joe, if you don't mind another question?"

"You know," Williams said, "I've always thought we New Yorkers had it all over those guys from Chicago. On my home turf, when we get things done, we're not so damned obvious about it."

The president stopped to catch his own thought, and then continued. "If New York politics has a fine touch about it, and Chicago is more ham-handed, then Texas has always been a veritable slash-and-burn operation. There are no secrets there at all. At least, that's my own considered opinion."

"And?" said Ingber.

"And if you think about it, this presidency has been pretty free of scandals. The Solyndra mess wouldn't count for much if it was the only one, but if Joe had his Texas hands in too many things, just how many Solyndras do you think we could handle?" Williams paused.

"I get your point, Av."

"I hope both of you do. I expect to stay in power, and expect you to do whatever is necessary to make that happen—but no scandals. Clear?"

"Clear," Ingber and Thompson said in unison.

Pete Clancy had easily approved Janice Dern's choice of the Hilton Garden Inn south of Columbus, just off of I-71. It was an easy drive for eighty-some investigators, all tasked with conducting background investigations on federal applicants and employees in the tri-state area. Not least in importance for Clancy was the fact that the Hilton was a nice place but not too nice. He never liked the idea of government employees or their contractors frolicking at high-end spas, all on the taxpayer's dime.

He had chosen Columbus as his first stop because of the cluster of cases showing up in that region having vice-presidential interest. Although the Commission on the Elderly may not be politically sensitive, the cases coming from the Election Assistance Commission certainly would be. There was a far more political (small *p*) reason for his choice: the president and vice president had spent more time in Ohio than in any other state, and that simple fact upped the chances for a problem no one wanted.

Promptly at 8:30 a.m. on Wednesday the eighteenth, he opened the conference with a short talk on overall workload expectations from the Department of Defense in particular. Nine Eleven and the wars in Afghanistan and Iraq changed everybody's plans, but now there was talk of the wars winding down, Clancy reminded his listeners. As always, OPM was insisting on faster case production with higher quality, he said, and investigators had to do a better job before submitting their casework.

"Is it true that OPM wants to take over the entire program and that we could be federalized?" asked a woman from Louisville.

Janice Dern spoke up. "You ask me about this every time we talk," she said, not unkindly. "And yes, that may be the future of the OPM Investigations Program, but for starters, the agency will likely want to take over high-level and unusually sensitive stuff, particularly overseas work. Isn't that what we're hearing, Pete?"

"That about says it, but I hope those rumors do not encourage a flood of applications back to the federal government." Clancy managed his patience as best he could. "You know, when President Harper and Vice President Grayson decided to give us the axe back in '96, it was NIS that came to everyone's rescue and provided the same salary and benefits we had as feds. Because we were an employee-owned company, everyone was able to reap the rewards, and we all had a say in it. Why anyone would want to go back to those that tossed us out the door like so much trash is beyond me."

Clancy saw Nelson Evers raise his hand and pointed to him. He didn't know all that many field people on a personal level, but Evers was someone Janice Dern talked about often. She was sensitive about matters of race, and NIS had gone the mile to reflect the nation's face in its ranks, but he and Dern knew how hard it was to recruit African-Americans and Latinos when they could get great jobs doing less for more. He glanced at Dern briefly, knowing she was proud of the man beginning to speak. As Evers rose, everyone looked his way with respect.

"I've been around a lot longer than most of you. In fact, I was one of the first blacks ever to become an investigator. That took a long time after the end of slavery, I can tell you. And yes, like you, I came from OPM, and if I was younger, maybe I'd be thinking another way, but NIS was there for me, so I'm darn well going to hang in with them till the bitter end."

The applause in the room was more than polite, Clancy was glad to see, but he wondered what actions many would take if given the opportunity. He glanced around the room and said, "Thanks, Nelson. It's always good to hear from one of the old pros." He paused, readying his real message. "Okay, gang, let's get back to business for a bit. You all know this is a political year, and it seems that every four years, I have to give this speech. As feds, we were limited by the Hatch Act as to what we could say about our political views, and most of you remember that made our jobs a whole lot easier—no debates with the citizens when we rang their doorbells.

"As private sector employees, however, our role is far trickier, in my opinion, and I do not want any of you caught in an airplane propeller on this. Janice?"

For the next thirty minutes, Dern deftly demonstrated her PowerPoint skills and fielded all of the usual questions. When she was finished, she turned it back to her boss for a wrap-up.

"Thank you. Nicely done. Before we leave the political stuff, however, here's the bottom line for me: whether you're for Williams or for the Republican, it's nobody's business in the office or out there on the street. Legally, you're permitted to use bumper stickers and buttons, but you're a plain idiot if you do so, and management will not defend your poor judgment if there's a complaint." He chuckled. "How's that for clarity?"

Marlyn Burdette, a feisty young woman, short, auburn-haired, and sharp as they come, raised her hand. "Pete, you know, right across the river from where I work in Cincinnati is the big IRS Center in Covington, Kentucky."

"Yes?"

"They have a gazillion employees there, and of course, we do some of their cases, so I'm there maybe once a month or so."

"I know there's a point coming, Marlyn."

"Look, it's no skin off my nose, but when I do interviews with employees in their workspaces, I see tons of Williams-Morrison stickers, and believe me, I wouldn't want to be a Republican at that place. How is it that they're so open about their politics?"

"I suppose that's a management question for the IRS, don't you think?"

"It's more than that, though," she said. "The cracks they make tell me harassing Republicans is part of their program. In fact, they think it's funny."

"How do they get away with that, Pete?" Paul Gladston chimed in, as he turned and cast a smile at Burdette.

Clancy noticed Gladston's not-so-subtle attempt to gain Burdette's attention, and he wondered if the presentable young man with the brown hair and dark green eyes would get very far. *Ah, to be in my twenties again!*

"I'll tell you how," Burdette responded for Clancy.

Clancy remained standing, enjoying the interplay.

"They all belong to the union—or nearly all of them," Burdette said. "And from what Mayella Washington all but said—she's the union head there—it wouldn't matter who the Republicans put up this year, NTU is going to make a big donation to Williams. Period."

"So I guess, then, it's no surprise that they'd badger the Republicans," Gladston said, completing Burdette's thought.

"I'm going to stop this discussion," Dern intervened. "You two are speculating on hearsay, and while I'm not challenging what you say, Marlyn, that's the government's problem."

Clancy said, "NIS will endorse no one—officially or otherwise." He looked around at all eighty-some participants. "And while you're working for this company, we will not conduct ourselves in that fashion. Like I said, all it will take is one complaint."

The CNS crew positioned its first camera to the left of the stage with an up angle, a most flattering view of President Williams. Camera two, positioned for a straight-on shot, revealed worry lines and gray accents that might distract an audience. No microphone tricks were needed, however, to enhance what the president innately possessed: a beautiful and mellifluous speaking voice.

"Friends, I've come back to Ohio because I always enjoy coming here. And you know it's not just because of the campaign this year, because I've returned to the Buckeye State almost twenty-five times in the last few years. Some people are beginning to think this is my second home." He laughed into the mic, then waited for the applause and the Cleveland "Amens" to subside.

"Another reason I come here is that Ohioans represent the strength of our nation. They prove time and time again that recovery from the worst recession since the Great Depression is always possible, no matter how much the Republicans stand in their way."

The applause became louder. "You know that if the Republicans in Congress had their way, there would have been no stimulus plan to keep policemen, firemen, and teachers at their posts providing you and your children the services you're entitled to. Not only can't the Republicans decide how to help this nation, they can't even decide who from their party should lead them!" The audience roared.

Peter Marsden looked into the studio camera. "We'll listen a bit more to the crowds enjoying a visit from their president." Turning to the large video projected on the screen behind him, Marsden let the on-scene cameras continue coverage of the president's visit for a minute more of what was by now the standard Williams stump speech.

"Tony Duke will join us now with his observations. Tony?"

"You can see, Peter, that the crowd adores President Williams, a man who has no difficulty riveting an audience and getting them charged up."

"I can see that, and it appears that's no small group of people there. How many would you say, and is that pretty typical?"

"There are about twelve thousand people here, Peter, and yes, as you can imagine, the president has no trouble drawing crowds of this size wherever he goes."

"And the Hardy campaign? What do you see there?"

"Peter, the Hardy campaign plugs along with a steady barrage of standard Republican rhetoric, but it has yet to catch fire. Let's watch the presumptive nominee as he addresses a gathering of citizens at the Kenwood Towne Center, a tonier shopping venue not many miles north of downtown Cincinnati."

The studio played a video clip of Hardy campaigning. "As our national debt soars to a record sixteen trillion dollars, my fellow Americans, everyone needs to understand we will never climb out of the deep well of red ink unless someone who understands business takes charge in Washington, DC." The CNS camera panned the "Win with Hardy" signs and closed in on Hardy's tanned but aging face framed by polished graying hair. Then it showed a few faces in the crowd, some interested, some bored.

Tony Duke addressed the camera again. "I'd say that what you're seeing here in what should be a friendly venue for Hardy, the crowds have been well-managed by the campaign handlers, but they're only a fraction of the numbers that seem to gather for a presidential visit. I'd say the governor has a long way to go to be a true challenger for the November election."

"Thanks for that insight, Tony."

MAY

Politico/George Washington University Poll
April 29-May 3
Williams 47%
Hardy 48%

"Mare," Nelson Evers called to Marlyn Burdette across the office bullpen. "Got time for some Skyline?"

"For you, Nelson, anytime," said Burdette. It was an invitation not unexpected from the man who had trained her as a new investigator three years earlier. Though Evers possessed an entirely different generational outlook and background, he and Mare had hit it off immediately, and their three weeks together on the street went by quickly. For Evers, she held both admiration and affection.

"Well, then, little person, it's eleven thirty already, so let's get some Coneys before it gets crowded." At six foot three, he rose over a head taller than his companion.

Together, they headed to the Skyline Chili Parlor on Vine Street, near Fountain Square, and made small talk about the weather, unusually comfortable for the time of year. In a city that turned on its AC in April and kept it on until Halloween, this was a prized day, one on which it would be a pleasure to "do neighborhoods"—conduct interviews nearest a subject's residence as part of a background investigation.

Evers and Burdette agreed to get their Coneys—a smaller hot dog hugged by a large bun, leaving plenty of room for Skyline's chili, mustard, onions, and grated mild cheddar—and find an outside seat in the sun.

"How can someone so little eat two of those?" demanded Evers when the five-foot-four engine of energy retrieved her order. They walked back to the square and found a spot on the limestone benching.

"So what's on your mind, old man?" Burdette teased, though she knew Evers, in his sixties, was getting sensitive about age issues.

"Don't 'old man' me, little one. I can out-get you any day of the week," he laughed. "Although I have to admit you're the best of the eleven new investigators I've ever trained."

Burdette grinned. "Okay, I won't let that go to my head, and thanks, but quit stalling. I know there's something you want to talk about."

"What you said in Columbus at our meeting."

Burdette waited. It was a trick Evers himself had taught her. Be silent and wait. The other party will talk. She remembered reading in a popular bio of President Williams that he, too, used it. What Evers told her was that everyone understood the technique, but almost no one had the patience to use it. She ate her Coney and studied the fountain.

"That business about the IRS across the river really hit home with me," Evers said after a bit. "I've had more than a few friends and relatives working there. For years, those were low-end jobs, and they could easily hire a lot of black people to fill them, but when the IRS became more and more automated, a good number of the sharper ones were promoted into bigger and better jobs."

"Did I say something that offended you, then?"

"No, it wasn't that. It's just that my gut tells me you might be right. Of course, nearly all African Americans are Democrats, and almost to a body they voted for Williams and will again. Why wouldn't they?" He paused. "Do you know that next January first will be the hundred and fiftieth anniversary of Lincoln issuing his Emancipation Proclamation? And naturally, we're proud to have a man like us sit in Lincoln's chair, so to speak."

"But Nelson, those aren't all black people in the Covington office."

"Oh, I know that, but I also know that when civil rights finally began to be real under Lyndon Johnson, the best jobs were with the federal government, and I'm sad to say a lot of people who took those jobs weren't the least bit grateful. They thought they were owed. And when people who think they're owed have a union to protect them and their jobs, that feeling of entitlement becomes even stronger."

"But why would they want to bother Republicans?"

"I know you're not very political, but look, African Americans never seem to remember that Lincoln was a Republican or that Wilson and FDR were plain racists. Ever since JFK—who didn't help us much either—and LBJ, black votes have been in the *D* column. Period."

"Why do I think you don't feel the same way?"

"It's this way. I grew up here and went to Hughes High School in the sixties—a very tough place for a kid like me who didn't want to sit around or do the gang thing. Four years in the army after a degree in political science from the University of Cincinnati left me looking for any kind of decent job, and I remember my minister suggesting I take the Federal Service Entrance Exam.

"To me, it was just another job application, and was I surprised when someone from the US Civil Service Commission called me for an interview to become an Investigator, GS-7." He laughed. "I'm sure the two white guys conducting the interview hadn't realized I was black, but when they saw me, they had to go ahead with it. They asked every kind of question to see if they could find something to rate me out, and when they told me about the background investigation, they tried to scare the crap out of me. The one old guy with a white mustache said they'd find out about every window I broke, every candy bar I stole.

"I just smiled at them and said, 'Go ahead. Dig deep.' To my greater surprise—and theirs, I later learned—I was called to report for training at the US Post Office and Courthouse at the corner of Fifth and Main in March 1972, one of the first black men ever to be hired for this job. Think of that, Mare. Ever!"

"I get it. They didn't have women doing this when they hired you, did they?"

"You know, you're right. Got me there."

"But you're more steamed up about all this than most people. What's up with that?"

"Because Emancipation was a hundred and fifty years ago, over seven generations, and nobody owes me nothin'. I worked my ass off for everything I've ever had. That's why I've always felt good about working for the US Civil Service Commission and, then, OPM—since the seventies, anyway, politics and race have not been a part of the crap we deal with every day. And at NIS, well, it's been like arriving in a new country where everybody gets a shot."

"I'm actually honored that you're willing to talk to me about stuff like this, but where are we going?"

"Don't you get it? When you have all these conservatives wanting to abolish the tax code, to IRS people that means the end of their cushy jobs. Those folks have forgotten what they're supposed to be about. Every kid should know that without free speech, Lincoln himself couldn't have been elected, Clarence Darrow couldn't have fought for Scopes, women still couldn't vote, and Martin could never have told us about his dream. So what you said in Columbus makes me mad as hell—that federal workers would break the rules that give us all our freedom, and I'm even madder that some of my own friends might be part of the problem."

Burdette noticed the glisten in his eyes. "What do you want to do about it?" she asked gently.

"Next time you have a need to go there, let's see if Dern'll let the work be reassigned to me," he said, his voice nearly a whisper. "I haven't been there in a while. If you don't mind, I want to see what I can see for myself. Okay with you?"

"For you, old man? Anything."

"Dammit, Norty," said the president into the phone. "Why am I reading this crap from the Associated Press about the bomb plot in Yemen? Just what the hell is my attorney general doing about the leaks out of this administration?"

"Mr. President," Norton Sweeney answered, attempting to tame the tremble in his voice and the almost uncontrolled blink reflex. Never had he heard Averell Williams speak to him in that fashion in the two decades of their association. "We're doing all we can to find out what happened here, sir."

"Well, 'all we can,' Norty, isn't good enough by half, apparently. What was published by the AP was supposed to be classified information, which means, last I heard, that the attempted bombing of that airliner two weeks ago was never supposed to be in the public domain." Sarcasm dripped from his voice.

"You are absolutely correct, Mr. President."

"You're damn right I am, and what's more, this administration has made a point of assuring the American people over the past few weeks that there have been no credible threats to Americans or our security as the anniversary of bin Laden's death approached."

Sweeney remained silent.

"It makes us all out to be liars," Williams went on, "and it doesn't fit with the narrative we're playing this campaign year. Connect the dots, dammit. We can't keep assuring the people they're safe, when crap like this hits the press."

"Yes, sir. We're presently drafting warrants..."

Williams interrupted. "What about that News Global guy, Joshua Powell, and the North Korean business? Did you ever do anything about him?"

"The Justice Department usually doesn't go after reporters, sir. Just the leakers."

"Bullshit. It's time they get the message."

Sweeney hesitated and blinked rapidly, but he knew he couldn't keep silent long. He nodded. "We'll sweep him up as well. As to the Yemen airliner, we think we know who the guy is who leaked this stuff, and shortly, we'll prove it."

"Okay, okay, Norty, that sounds better."

"The warrants we get from FISA court will dampen more than a few of them as the campaign goes on."

"So you think the Foreign Intelligence Surveillance Act will cover us?"

"Yes, sir."

"Well, it and you better do something. Look, I can't have a bunch of leakers and reporters messing up our al-Qaeda success story this year."

"Got it, sir. Loud and clear." When he heard the click on the line, he put his own receiver in its place. "Ouch!" he said, so loud he was afraid his secretary might hear.

Before doing another thing, Sweeney leaned back in his chair and processed the phone call he'd just experienced. It was a far cry from the Averell Williams who encouraged leaks from the Bush Administration about its intended surge in Iraq. How times had changed. Power, like water, did indeed seek its own level.

He picked up the phone and summoned a lieutenant for a task on which he intended to leave few of his own fingerprints.

"I don't think this is going to work," Amber Bustamente said, dropping her words into the middle of a morning wake-up.

"What's not going to work, sweetie?" Nutsy Conaway responded sleepily, at the same time wondering why many of their conversations took place in or around a bed.

"Us, you fat ass. Us. I think you're cheating on me, so why would I want to stay with you?"

Suddenly wide awake and sitting up, Conaway nearly shouted, "What? Cheating? On you? What are you talkin' about, girl?"

"When I asked you about all those women you listed as references on your clearance papers, you gave me a dumb answer. It made me think."

"My answer on that was my answer. I've worked with and for a lot of women, and they can recommend me when the investigator comes around."

"So who is this Marilyn Burdette?"

"Who? Marilyn who?"

"I looked at your phone this morning before you got up, you jerk, and there are two calls from this Marilyn. And you said you barely had time for me. You lyin' sack." She pushed herself upright and faced him.

"Wait. Gimme that phone, Amby. I wanna see what the hell you're talkin' about."

She reached back, tossed him his iPhone, and began to step away while he fumbled with it and the bedcovers at the same time.

"Hon. Here, look at this. These calls are from somebody named Marlyn—not Marilyn—Burdette. Her voice message says she's an NIS investigator for OPM and she's doing my background check. Here—you can listen to the message yourself."

Haltingly, Bustamente turned and reached for the phone. She listened to the voice mail. "Mr. Conaway, this is Marlyn Burdette, an investigator with NIS working for OPM, and we're conducting your background investigation for the US Election Assistance Commission. As you might know, there's some urgency to this case, and we need to sit down and review your Standard Form 86. Please return my call as soon as possible so we can set up an appointment. My cell number is..."

Sheepishly, Bustamente handed the phone back to Conaway and sat next to him, nuzzling his shoulder and neck with penitent kisses. "I'm sorry, Nutsy, but you can imagine what I was thinking."

"What I'm thinking is that you should not be looking at my phone, because there's a lotta work stuff on it that you should not know about."

"Don't you trust me?"

"Of course I do," he whispered softly, and he kissed her forehead and then her cheek before finding her lips. "We have got to be together on this," he said, gently pushing her down on the bed. Her panties slid off easily and he began to touch her in the places she liked best.

"This is Lew Michaels on News Global's *Weekend*, and this morning, we're pleased to have Governor Winston Hardy of Colorado, the nominee presumptive of the Republican Party. Good morning, governor, and thank you for letting us have a few minutes with you on the campaign trail."

"Good morning and thank you for having me, Lew." Hardy's bright white smile lit up the camera lens.

"Well, so far, governor, May has been a good month for you. You picked up a slew of delegates in the first week, and when Oregon votes in two days, it is also expected to go your way."

"Let's hope so. We have two more before we get to Texas at the end of the month. If all goes well, our campaign will have won the eleven hundred and forty-four delegate votes needed for the nomination. That is," he added, "if the convention agrees."

"Well, I won't congratulate you now, but I'll ask a few questions, if I may. The race so far has been a damaging one for Republicans, many have said. There are commercials, video clips, campaign releases from the other candidates that they cannot now take back. How hard do you think it will be to bring them together under your banner—if that's the way it turns out?"

"First, Lew, the race is not over officially, and I don't want to be presumptuous. Yet, the candidates are honorable people, and when it's all over, I expect that we'll all unite behind one leader. At least, it's my own view that I would support the party nominee, whoever it is."

"A fair answer for now, sir, and a few more questions before we let you go. A week ago, there was a little noticed piece from the Associated Press about an abortive airliner bombing attempt by an al-Qaeda affiliate in Yemen. Would you care to comment on how this story matches up with the administration claims about the terrorist group?"

"Actually, I'd prefer not to comment on that issue," said Hardy, mindful of the briefing paper contents he'd read the week before. He'd made a decision early in the campaign not to undercut the president, especially when he'd been made privy to substantially the same Presidential Daily Briefing (PDB) provided to Williams. "I expect the president to be handling the matter in the way he sees fit."

"But, sir," said Michaels, "while I'm not expecting you to compromise national security information, do you not find it puzzling that the Associated Press is reporting this while the administration has stated on two separate occasions that there have been no known or credible threats by al-Qaeda?"

"For now, I'll have to stand by my answer."

Michaels took a deep breath and continued. "Sir, surely you've noticed all the polls that show the president's dropping approval numbers. Does it comfort you at all to know that not a single president since Truman has been reelected with an approval rating below fifty percent?

"What gives me comfort, Lew, is that the American people are beginning to understand that we need someone new in the Oval Office."

Michaels' smile held no emotion. "And lastly, governor—and I know you must be expecting this question—now that the president has come out in favor of same-sex marriage, how will his new position affect your own and that of the Republican Party?"

"While I haven't decided whether or not my own position needs to be reevaluated, Lew, this decision of the president's has more far-reaching implications than you might imagine. No matter how you feel about same-sex marriage, will people wonder how many more times this president will simply toss aside standing law, like the Defense of Marriage Act, just to name his most recent move. There have now been a string of capricious decisions on his part, not based on law or precedent, but based on his personal views on the matters involved."

"I can see that I struck a nerve there, governor."

"Not your fault. These decisions should strike a nerve with every American, Democrat or Republican, who understands we elected a president, not a king."

"Thank you, sir, and as I would say to any of our guests, good luck on the campaign trail."

In a setting that some might have described as regal, but one that Joe Morrison had thought totally appropriate, the hotel in the 900 block of San Francisco's Mason Street seemed to flutter its many flags in a saluted farewell to the vice president and his entourage of staffers and Secret Service personnel. Morrison shunned the campaign bus for an Escalade after he'd been alerted to take an important call at two forty-five. It was a call he did not want to miss.

Over his shoulder, he glanced back at the Fairmont and thought of the Gold Room, where he'd given what he considered a thumper of a speech to the leadership of several unions and specially selected members and their spouses. The machinists and mechanics had paid their dues, thought Morrison, and he had given them a good message—gaffe-free, thank God—to take back to their brethren. He was savoring the moment when his cell phone chimed.

To Averell Williams, LA and Hollywood were places of sustenance, just as oases quenched the thirst of the wayfarer. As Air Force One touched the ground, he checked with his staff to see if he could fit one more thing into the schedule, and grudgingly, Sheldon Ingber's on-the-ground shepherds agreed when their charge promised only a brief delay.

Williams secluded himself in the onboard office and waited for his call to be connected. Having put the conversation off for weeks, he consoled himself with the notion that a phone call might limit certain possibilities for discussion, thereby allowing him to achieve his goal without giving away that which he had little intention to concede.

When he heard the click, he began talking, without making sure it was Vice President Morrison to whom he was linked. "Joe, this is Av. I was hoping to catch you before your flight and my speech. How did your fundraiser go today?"

"Any time is a good time, Mr. President, and yes, the luncheon went well—made a half million or so."

"Joe, that's great, and for you, it's always Av," the president said in as affable a tone as he could manage with someone he hardly knew. "Listen, Joe, I'm really sorry about the timing and the venue, but we need to have a quick talk."

"Whatever you need, Av."

The president thought he'd detected a bit of anxiety in the man's voice. "What I need is for you to remain on the ticket with me this fall. I know these past four years haven't been the easiest for you, and I regret not having done better by you, but I have some ideas about that going forward. First, I need your reassurance that you wouldn't be leaving me for a better offer."

"Why, I'd be honored to serve in any way I can as your vice president, and I look forward to having a good conversation about our next term before the election."

Joe Morrison was sharper than some gave him credit for, Williams scribed to his memory. "We'll have that talk, but for now I wanted to thank you for taking a load off my mind."

"You're most welcome, Av," Morrison responded. "Good luck with your dinner tonight."

"And you, Joe, have a safe flight home."

Why that clever bastard! He finessed it with a phone call. Not even a West Wing lunch to ask me the big question! Though delighted that the conversation had finally taken place, Morrison knew his mental whining was both ridiculous and self-destructive, and after a few moments, he put it all aside to make his next phone call.

"Sharon, honey, how are you doing, and how are the kids?" he asked, with uncommon interest.

"All fine, Joe. And how did it go on the coast?"

"Terrific, hon. I thought I'd catch up with you before jumping on the plane to Detroit to tell you he finally asked me."

"Who finally asked you what?"

"The president asked me to be his running mate again."

"Oh, that's wonderful. That's a relief, isn't it! Did you talk to him about the second term?" she asked hopefully.

"I didn't have to. He brought it up and promised me a good conversation about it before the election."

"You must be walking on air. You've gotten what you wanted. Did you ask him what took so long?"

"Now, hon."

"You're too loyal. Well, now we have to win."

"Don't we, though? Gotta go. Call you in the morning. Love you."

Once again, Morrison figured the time change and called a Texas number he knew well. "Morisa, this is Joe. I wasn't sure if you had gone to dinner yet."

"For you, Joe, my stop for a taco at La Fruta Feliz can wait."

"You're making my mouth water, Morisa. Have one for me, and some days, I wish I was home."

"What can I do for you when you're not homesick, Mr. VP?"

"Quit raggin' me," he laughed. "All things considered, you as secretary of state for the great state of Texas have a more important job than I do."

"Don't make me laugh. You don't need to work for my vote, Joe."

"That's in part what I wanted to talk to you about. Have you ever heard of Enrique McCord—a another Texan like us?"

"I know of him, but not personally. Texas uses SoftSec stuff for our elections, but only in a few big cities. What about him?"

"When he comes to visit you, just work with him, okay?"

"Sure. Not a problem. Is that all you called me to ask? You're slackin'."

"Thanks, Morisa. Regards to all the Riveras. See ya."

Last, Morrison checked his contacts and found Ricky McCord's number, one he chose not to put on speed dial. He waited for the expected answer and could hear delight in the man's voice. "Ricky, we need to talk about strategy. Soon."

"Sure, Joe, anything you want."

The president's next order of business was to tape a Jay Leno segment before moving on to the W Hotel in Hollywood. There, film and Silicon Valley executives had clamored for the right to pay $25,000 a couple for the privilege of sharing an intimate dinner with eighty-four other pairs that, in California, would not likely be evenly divided between men and women. As the motorcade approached, Williams could see that the venue itself shaped the metaphor of his presidency in the way the reflective glass in the glitzy hotel veneer made the upcoming, uncluttered social structure he planned appear translucent, if not transparent.

In the ballroom, it was an anything goes crowd, President Williams noticed, and that was just the way he would want it to be in the egalitarian society he had hoped to advance in his second term. These moguls of electronic wizardry and cine-magic were exactly the right kind of people to make it happen because it would require mystic levels of their arts to make his vision palatable to the people.

In the warm applause that enveloped the room, he rose to his place of comfort and spoke, to the surprise of many, without a teleprompter. "My friends, you have come here tonight because you appreciate all that art and science may someday offer a hungering world. You appreciate that there are those who would stifle your creative impulses to satisfy a debt, keep food and education from the poor to satisfy a shareholder's demand, deny an American job to a deserving woman and ship it overseas to satisfy profit requirements. Yes, you are here because you know that paying a fair share of your income is the least you can do to take us to a land where every child has a healthy lunch, where everyone who wants a job has one, where medical care is a reality not just a dream." Each comma permitted the expected applause to become louder and louder, and the speaker was not disappointed.

The evening's only lament was that more donors couldn't be squeezed into the W's venue. Secret Service control requirements, plus the need for media attention by the attendees—an addiction exceeded only by his own, Williams had to admit—had held down the numbers of deep pockets. Even so, for twenty minutes of mic time with a friendly audience and two hours of photos he thoroughly enjoyed, the evening netted his campaign an easy four million dollars.

"Marlyn, this is Paul Gladston, and I needed to talk to you about a part of the case I have on Enrique McCord here in Columbus."

"Oh, hey, Paul, sorry we didn't get to talk much at Pete's meeting. What's on your mind?"

"I saw on the system where most of the McCord case is in Cincinnati, and you have it. Are you working on it now?"

"Just about to start on him and his senior techie, a guy named Conaway. With Memorial Day, neither subject seems to be available."

"Yeah. Conaway's name has come up more than once in my contacts with the Ohio secretary of state's office."

"Are you getting a lot of cooperation?" she asked.

"Sorta. They seem to be wondering why EAC would let this contract go to SoftSec when the company is also the largest provider of hardware and software in the state. To Kathlyn Hopkins—she's the secretary of state—it seemed like an odd set of circumstances, but she hastened to say that she had no objection to it."

"Don't you just hate it when these cases start to get political, and these witnesses don't seem to understand that we don't care about their politics."

"You're right," Gladston said, "but there are some politics here, and that's why I'm calling. What's clear here is that Hopkins is a strong Democrat, and apparently, this McCord guy is Vice President Morrison's old Texas buddy—or at least, that what she said the rumors have been—and that's why this is a rush-rush bunch of cases."

"You said she's a Democrat? Isn't our governor a Republican? Oh, that's right," she hurried to say, "they're all elected independently, unlike the federal setup."

"So what's beginning to stink a bit—and I know this is stuff we're not supposed to be interested in—"

"And can't go in our reports," Burdette inserted.

"Yeah, but we have a buddy of Morrison's who is in a position to access all the votes in our state—one that everybody says is key to this election."

"Don't get wound up about this, Paul. Maybe we should just get these cases done and not worry about crap like that."

"You're right, I suppose, and so far, there's no dirt on this guy, but I'm wondering if there aren't some big time ethics questions just under the surface here."

"You'd better be able to prove that, or your ass will be in a sling. You know darn well what Pete Clancy was saying. Cases like this one have the attention of Morrison himself, apparently."

"Sorta ties it all up with a bow, doesn't it?"

"There you go again, and you're going to get us all into trouble."

"Hey, look, Marlyn, I was just calling to give you a heads up about some possibly sticky stuff with this company."

"Got it, and I'll keep that in mind, but I'm not a political type, and frankly, I don't much care one way or the other."

"Maybe you will, one day. Hey, before you go, maybe I'm way out of line, but do you ever go out with guys from Columbus?"

Burdette laughed. "Paul, I'm truly flattered, but I'm in a relationship right now." She hoped her voice hadn't betrayed the bit of regret she felt, but she didn't want Gladston's attentions when she was trying to figure out if her present situation was worth it.

"Well, I thought I'd try. Thanks. And if anything comes up there on McCord, how about letting me know before I wrap up my part."

"Will do," she said, hoping there was. "By the way, my friends call me Mare."

"Good evening, ladies and gentlemen. This is *The World Journal* and I'm Peter Marsden. Tonight's lead story is how the president's fundraising juggernaut is upping the ante for this year's election to levels previously unheard of." Over Marsden's shoulder played extended clips of the president at the Hotel W in Hollywood. "Here we see President Williams hobnobbing with some of the country's most influential men and women, and obviously, they're enjoying each other's company. Reportedly, the president raised some four million dollars for his efforts there and provided photo ops for the Hollywood stars present.

"Meanwhile, Governor Hardy of Colorado has taken a hundred and five delegates of the hundred and thirty-five at stake in the Texas primary, and he is now the GOP's probable nominee. Despite his strong showings of late, it remains unclear whether and how the governor can unite bruised Republicans and shed the image of being the party of white wealth in this country. We shall see."

JUNE

Reuters/Ipsos Poll
June 7-11
Williams 45%
Hardy 44%

Investigator Burdette consulted the ream of case papers in front of her and decided that first on her list had better be the Enrique McCord and Nathan Conaway cases. The other seven assigned to her she would work in as she could. Nelson Evers, she knew, had two other SoftSec cases in hand. She believed Evers would be much better handling her assignment, but she appreciated the challenge, and made a mental note to connect with him in a few days.

Cell phone in hand, she dialed Conaway's number for the third time in the past week and was surprised when he failed to answer. She would give him one more opportunity before speaking with her supervisor about a failure-to-respond situation.

The McCord case papers seemed generally clean, but Gladston's information from the state capital bothered her. Conaway's papers, on the other hand, left much to the imagination, and she knew his might likely be the more difficult case.

Burdette then tried McCord's number, two previous voice messages to him having gone unacknowledged. Ordinarily, she would have wanted to get with McCord first; then, the rest of the SoftSec cases would go easier. When she heard the change in rings at the other end, she knew his calls were being forwarded.

Finally, she heard a voice: "This is SoftSec, the company supplying every election need," the female said without a hello, but with such a perky greeting that it wasn't missed. "Can I help you?" she asked at the end.

Burdette went through her standard introduction and asked for the woman's name before asking to speak with Enrique McCord directly.

"This is Heather Lake," she said, hesitating, but seemed pleased to add, "I'm afraid that will not be possible, Ms. Burdette, as he is in Columbus today and tomorrow."

"But he can talk by phone?" Burdette had been trained to be politely persistent. It was always amazing to her that even when completion of a background investigation meant actual employment or a clearance required for a specific contract or job, some subjects were awfully slow to get things going. For an investigator, subject delays were always a sign of trouble. "We need to set up an appointment to begin his background investigation."

"I'll see what I can do, Ms. Burdette."

"Please pass on to Mr. McCord that I'll expect his return call by COB today, and give him my thanks as well."

When she clicked off Miss Perky, her phone chimed, and she saw it was Nathan Conaway. He sounded nervous, even uncertain, but he shifted out of neutral when she stressed that she would have to turn the case back in if he couldn't find the time to talk with her. Finally, he agreed to block off at least one hour for her later that afternoon.

Having slogged in and out of the rain visiting employments and references on other cases, Burdette finally approached the address in an iffy neighborhood on Madison Road, not too far north of DeSales Corners. She was surprised that SoftSec headquartered itself in a small-ish, older three-story building, but the space seemed more like what she expected when she made her way to the second level.

Taken to Conaway's office by the not-so-welcoming Heather Lake, there began the patter of small talk investigators used to help them decide how to approach the interview. Conaway himself answered the question she hadn't asked by mentioning that SoftSec was a highly successful firm that didn't need an upmarket office because customers rarely came to them. Besides him and McCord, he explained, SoftSec had twelve salespeople in the field for the calls and installation Conaway did not make himself, along with other support staff in Cincinnati.

Curiosity getting the better of her, and keeping in mind the Gladston remarks, she asked Conaway a general question about the nature of the work SoftSec would be doing for USEAC, if that wasn't in some way classified, of course.

"Tell you the truth, Ms. Burdette, I don't know everything there is to know about this deal. What I know is what Mr. McCord shares with me, and that our job this November will be to place ourselves—electronically that is—in the middle, I mean between the local voting precinct and the state level to ensure that what each precinct is reporting as a total vote count agrees with what the county reports. Sort of a quality and integrity control measure, I guess."

"So you'll be doing this work 'in the middle' in all the states?"

"No, just in a dozen or less—where the vote could make actually make a difference in the outcome."

"Ah, I see. I suppose that's reason enough to be sure that the people doing this work are completely trustworthy, eh?"

"You got it."

"By the way, call me Marlyn, if you want, but I'll stick to Mister—I see your nickname is Nutsy, and somehow, I don't feel comfortable doing that." She laughed, as did Conaway.

After making him raise his hand and take an oath that the information he provided was correct, they spent seventy-five minutes going over every line and data point in Conaway's case papers, and along the way, cleaned up a few messes regarding employment dates, periods of unemployment, and places of residence. So far, so good, Burdette thought.

"Now let's go over Part B." The second part of the SF-86 had to do with a subject's use of drugs—prescription and illegal—and alcohol, and mental health, credit, and law enforcement histories, among other areas of interest.

"You say here that you've used marijuana, is that correct?" The yes answer triggered a half dozen other questions, the answers to which prompted a few more. The same was true for Conaway's law enforcement record—one DUI followed by a court-mandated alcohol seminar.

Burdette brought the interview to a close with further questions about his friends, means of contact, and lead information to verify some of his other activities.

"Gee," Conaway said. "That wasn't as bad as I thought. How long will the rest of the investigation take?"

"As long as what you told me was the truth, the end won't be bad either," she smiled, her gray-blue eyes piercing the brown slits just below the forehead opposite her. "As to how long, well, that'll depend on the availability of the people I need to see and what I find. Now, Mr. Conaway, we need to talk about Mr. McCord."

The return smile was there, but it was weak and forced.

Burdette proceeded to take his statement about his boss, though nothing of interest materialized. As someone who loved a job where she got to deal with people—all kinds—one that allowed her to be outside a confining office most of the time, and one that gave her people puzzles better than the *New York Times* could provide, Burdette wondered just how interesting the two cases in front of her might become.

Norton Sweeney's office faced the inner courtyard of the vast Department of Justice building situated on an angled plot of land between Pennsylvania and Constitution Avenues. There were times when Sweeney mused to others that the symbolism of the DOJ's placement between the avenue of political demands and that of constitutional ones was more than accidental. It required the attorney general to ride a constant roller coaster buffeted by ill and otherwise whimsical winds.

Not far down the hall, there existed a compact conference room for discrete meetings with a small number of people. Sweeney checked his watch upon entering the soundproof room and was pleased to see the only other two attendees already present. "So what do we have?" he asked in lieu of addressing the man and woman there, both very senior attorneys within the department, each steeped in a particular and unusual specialty. As the Harvard Law grads opened their folders, he wondered to what degree these seasoned staffers could be trusted. Both Merton Bruns and Sheila Sullivan were career appointees, and he knew little about their political sympathies.

"Sir, we have before us warrants for a fairly broad range," Bruns began, stumbling just a bit on the word *broad*, "of Associated Press phone numbers both in the White House press room and in their offices on the Hill."

"Sorry to interrupt you, Merton, but who's doing the minutes for this one?"

Bruns raised an index finger. "My turn."

"Then would you mind having the minutes reflect that you brought these warrants to me?"

"Of course, that is technically true, Norton, but you'll recall that it was you who directed us, in secret, to do the research and prep the warrants."

Sweeney blinked a few times, then nodded, as if to avoid saying it out loud, in case the room was plugged into audio. "But you are bringing these to me now, aren't you, Sheila?"

"Yes, sir," she said, and glanced at her colleague.

"Then, let's proceed."

For the next twenty minutes, Merton and Sullivan discussed the facts and time line regarding the abortive bomb attack by an al-Qaeda operative in Yemen some weeks earlier. Sweeney had no questions or challenges. Since it had been the AP that published the story without administration approval, naturally their communications were suspect.

"That's an easy one," Sweeney said as he reached over to sign the document.

"Before you do that, sir, you might want to consider the breadth of the searches we're contemplating; no administration has ever issued a search warrant so far reaching."

"Sheila, let me assure you the president is adamant about this issue, and those who work for this administration and leak classified information are going to be dealt with."

"I understand, sir," Sullivan said as Sweeney affixed his signature to the warrants. "Now, we turn to the matter of Joshua Powell, the News Global reporter whose activities you tasked us to review. Of course, this matter reaches back to 2009 and a news piece in which Powell purportedly used intelligence gathered on North Korea."

"Given that this matter has gone unattended to for three years, there will no doubt be some wondering as to why we waited so long," Bruns noted.

Sweeney looked up from the AP warrants, blinking. "There's no statute of limitations here, Merton, and it has not gone unnoticed that Powell and News Global have been particularly aggressive in reporting stories counterproductive to the president's goals." He looked across the table and, noticing their expressions, added, "Don't look so horrified. This will just be a shot across the bow for them, but it is probably appropriate that I don't authorize the warrant. Take it to some magistrate and get a signature on it."

Bruns and Sullivan rose, clearly uncomfortable with some facets of their work.

Acknowledging their body language, Sweeney expressed a final thought. "You might be surprised to know that as this meeting began, once again it occurred to me that unlike the Goddess of Justice, we cannot be blind as we try to step near but not on or over the fine, faint line between doing the right thing and the wrong thing. Like you, I'm not totally comfortable with the actions we've approved today, but that's why I'm a political appointee and you're not. Let the risk lie with me." Without another exchange, Sweeney made sure his bow tie was straight, rose, and left the room.

"You have your callback, Ms. Burdette," shot Enrique McCord, "but be sure this is not the end of it."

"Is this Mr. McCord?" she asked. "Is there some problem, sir? I've called your office more than once to obtain an appointment with you, and with all due respect, I haven't heard back from you until today."

"You bullied my secretary, and you're trying to bully me. What gives you the right?"

"I apologize if you think me doing my job is bullying you, sir," she said as pleasantly as possible. "But if I understand things correctly, you and your company sought this contract with USEAC, and it requires key personnel to undergo background investigations. This is not something the government is dragging you to do, is it? What time tomorrow or the next day can we meet?"

"There you go again, pushing me into an appointment time convenient for you. I don't like your snotty attitude, Ms. Burdette, and you should know I'm a personal friend of the vice president. Doesn't your outfit report to him?"

"Sir, I'm asking you what time is good for you tomorrow or the next day, and again, with all respect, most people would think what we're doing here at taxpayer expense is for your benefit, not mine. If you think I've been rude or unprofessional in any way while helping you and your company to complete a key part of the contracting process, please call my supervisor. I'll be happy to give you her number in Columbus."

"I'll decide that later, Ms. Burdette. And I'll see you at ten a.m. on the twelfth, at my office. Understood?"

"Of course, sir."

After hanging up, Burdette went to speed dial and called Janice Dern to report the entire incident.

Dern said she understood. She herself had run into people who were like that. "Is there anything stinky about his case?" she asked.

"No indication of any derog anywhere."

"When are you doing the subject interview?"

"This coming Tuesday."

"You know, Marlyn, if you think this is going to be a hot spot for us, why not take Nelson along? You can tell McCord it's a standard observation exercise. Your call."

"Thanks," she said, not sure if she'd been handed a life preserver or a problem. Working with Nelson Evers ordinarily would be a pleasure. On the other hand, she didn't want McCord to think she needed reinforcements. "Let me think about it."

The meeting began after a pleasant lunch provided for Governor Hardy's key campaign staff. Promptly at 1:00 p.m., the candidate came in and introduced his wife, Susan, to the few who had not met her. "Part of the reason we called you all together," Hardy began, "is to think about strategy for the general election, now that the nomination is all but assured. Today, we want to talk about the country's hot buttons and how to push them going forward."

Lisa Hoxworth spoke. "Win, I wouldn't let President Williams manage your campaign for you. By that, I mean his sudden turnabout on same-sex marriage should not change what you do. Having said that, you're going to have to address it, one way or the other, but we should find a way to have you spell out your position without making it seem like a response to Williams."

"You're right," Hardy said, "and perhaps we need to line up a few surrogates to support our position when I do address it."

"Next, of course, Win, is the economy," Hoxworth continued. "It's one thing to talk about unemployment numbers—they're important—but you have to make them personal to people. Talk about gas prices and what that means to the average Joe and Jane struggling to get to work and get their kids to soccer practice."

Hardy gave what he thought was a good smile, but it was the one most people saw, a thin and seemingly forced replica of the real thing. "I'm listenting." He nodded politely.

"Two other issues, governor," Hoxworth added, brushing the wave of rapidly graying hair from her face. "Gun control and abortion, and what some call 'women's rights.'"

"Hold on a minute," Hardy said. "Let me sum up so far: same-sex marriage, unemployment, gun control, abortion. Gee, gang, that's a plateful, and I've spoken out on many already."

"Your positions were articulated in mixed campaigns against a host of competitors. Now that you've won, we need to fashion position statements on all of these. They will be for much broader consumption in the general, and once made, can no longer be adjusted."

"What about priorities?" Hardy asked. "All of these can't be equal."

"Win, I'd suggest thinking about them this way: Unemployment and the economy matters to all sections of society, but it's a truism that it matters most to those who do not have a job and are having trouble getting one—African Americans, Hispanics, recent college grads. It does *not* matter as much to the ninety percent of the people who've managed to get through this recession.

"Next, while the women's rights thing might seem to matter most to the Democrats' base, that's not true. Catholic women who are white and Hispanic, for example, have very mixed views on this matter—while they themselves might not approve of abortion, they want respect. So again, you want to speak to Independent and Republican women voters and give them a reason to vote for you.

"Foreign affairs. Enough said there. The Democrats have no game and you have to exploit it by taking the air out of the Emerson Grantham and Averell Williams balloon. They've accomplished next to nothing, and you don't have to be a foreign affairs expert to point that out. Once again, Independents want you to present a position of firm reasonableness. No saber rattling.

"On the last two, care is important because gun control and same-sex marriage issues are important to your own base. We need to craft these statements so as not to alienate Independents who will constantly look for a reason to stick with Williams as they did in '08."

"Is there any chance for an erosion of African American and Hispanic votes to our side? And what about people under thirty?"

Hoxworth looked down, took a deep breath, and continued. "Now that you're the likely nominee, your negatives with these groups will likely diminish, but rest assured, the Williams crowd will constantly portray you as a rich white guy who cares little for them or their needs. It gets down to image, image, image, sir, and we need to reach out. When you're in Florida, for example, don't just visit The Villages—go to Miami and Naples. Speak some Spanish, and make sure Marco Rubio is at your side. As for the younger crowd, we might try to lessen their enthusiasm for Williams. But getting them to move to us in droves? I don't think so."

"I think I understand. My message is not enough. My principles will not get through."

Hoxworth said, "We have got to make your principles their principles. We've got to appeal to everyone's better nature."

The SoftSec receptionist announced the arrival of two NIS investigators to Enrique McCord, who remained seated and silent, eyebrows raised. Warning signs.

Marlyn Burdette and Nelson Evers approached his desk, each presenting the official credentials issued by their mother agency. McCord took both of them, turned toward the HP Officejet All-in-One behind him, and lifted the scanner cover.

Evers rumbled the air with his deep voice. "That's a no-no, Mr. McCord. Return our credentials, please."

"But I want a copy."

Evers said nothing, just looked McCord in the eye, and put out his hand to retrieve the pair of leather badge cases.

McCord hesitated for a second, as if he was in control, then returned them. "Give me your names again, then," he said with an authoritative air. "I want to write them down."

"It's Marlyn Burdette, and this is Nelson Evers, Mr. McCord. Can we start over, sir? We're not here to cause you a problem, and we're hoping you won't be one for us." She put out her hand to shake.

Lamely, McCord half rose and shook her hand, then lost his in Evers's catcher's mitt. "Okay, I guess we can do that, but I can tell you I'm not happy about all of this."

"Mr. McCord, NIS people have this kind of interaction at least four million times a year," Evers said, taking the lead. "And rarely do we have a problem with anyone. We don't have guns, and nobody's going to waterboard you. This procedure is just Uncle Sam's way of making sure that only the right people have access to the government's secrets."

"You know," McCord said, looking directly at Evers, "I wouldn't have expected to have a problem with you."

"Why would that be?" Evers asked in his diesel-engine voice.

"Why, I'm sure you're one of the team, aren't you, Evers?"

"What team? What are you talking about, Mr. McCord?"

"The president's team, of course. Every African American man and woman voted for him," McCord laughed nervously.

"Not every black man did, Mr. McCord. And politics is not a subject for our discussion. I hope we understand that, sir." Evers said nothing further, but gave him a hard look, then turned and nodded to his partner.

Burdette began the standard process of verifying and clarifying information, confirming witness contact information, and making small talk along the way. In an hour of sometimes tense give-and-take, they covered everything.

McCord said, "I understand you people have been talking to state employees in Columbus. I didn't give you their names. What right have you got to do that?"

Burdette responded. "It's not just our right but our obligation to obtain the statements from a good variety of people who know you, Mr. McCord. As you can imagine, if we talked only to people you identified for us, those interviews would be pretty much pointless."

"Okay. I get it," he said grudgingly. "But I don't like all these different people knowing my business. Know what I mean?"

"We don't share anything about your business or personal life, Mr. McCord. Our job is to get information, not give it."

"Please remember, sir," Evers added, "when you sought this contract, you asked us to do the work. Right?"

"Right. I just want you to know I intend to give plenty of feedback to the vice president, with whom I just played golf recently."

"Nice," Evers said, impassively. "You do that."

"I will. This is an important contract that will help the government, uh, er, manage the voting process as never before. That's why the vice president is interested."

"We'll make note of that," he said.

"And now, Mr. McCord, we need to talk with you about your employees being cleared," Burdette said.

McCord rolled his eyes and exhaled loudly in exasperation. Burdette and Evers remained silent, waiting.

After a few seconds, McCord surrendered, and said, "Oh, what the hell. Who do you want to talk about first?"

They agreed on Conaway, followed by the staffers. Evers had been assigned those cases, and for the next forty-five minutes, Burdette and Evers tag teamed their captive. By the time they finished, Burdette thought she could hear in McCord's voice a newfound respect for their thoroughness, while despising the use of his time.

She thanked the SoftSec CEO, and when they'd left the building and stood on the sidewalk riding the curb of Madison Road, Evers said, "Maybe you should come back for other statements on this guy when he's not around to intimidate anyone."

"Probably a good idea."

"Mare, why would the vice president be so damned interested in a little ol' contract with the EAC?"

"It might be because McCord is obviously on one team already. So it's not like he'd be a totally neutral guy administering a contract that counts votes, would he?"

Evers nodded. "You saw what you saw at the IRS—and I'm gonna check that myself—and now we have this. I wonder what else is out there. Hey, can I tag along on some interviews with you?"

"I already told you, Nelson. Anytime. Any reason in particular?"

"Way too many people—perhaps, African Americans in particular—have been through too much to make this a free country, and I don't like the stink that's around these guys. We'd better be careful out here."

In the same conference room in which he'd met his man many times earlier, Ron Shope waited. At precisely 2:00 p.m., the IRS head walked in, the look on his face scribing a sad story.

"Hello, Gordon. Is there a problem?"

"Yes. Yes, there is. I am becoming increasingly uncomfortable with what we're doing, and I want to talk to Sondra herself."

"No way, man. You know she's chief of staff to the president, and she just can't run up here every time you have a worry on."

"Get her, Shope, or I'll start thinking about alternatives."

After two more exchanges of the same sort, Shope said, "Wait here." He stepped into the hall, took a deep breath, and sent his boss a text expressing the urgency of a stop upstairs.

Within two minutes, Thompson appeared. "Something you can't handle, Ron?" she said.

"I can handle a lot, Sondra, but this one's above my pay grade. If you have a trump card in your pocket, now's the time to play it."

"Watch me," she said, and plowed through the door with Shope behind her.

"Look, Gordon, I don't have time for crap like this, so unbunch your panties. What's the problem?"

"I can see where this is going to go." His eyes darted. His forehead beaded with perspiration. "It's going to unravel, and you'll pretend you don't know me. The employees won't go to jail, I will."

"Nonsense, Gordon. No one's going to jail. Have you noticed who's president? Who's attorney general? We control all the strings."

"I don't like it," he insisted.

Thompson did not raise her voice above a tense whisper, but her words hit the air like a steady electrical storm, syllables arcing the air. "What you won't like, Gordon Hellman, is what happens when somebody calls your high-powered wife, a big player in New York left-wing politics and a big Williams supporter, and she wonders why you're not on our team. You can think about a no-risk situation with us or face Georgina and her friends and let them all toast you alive." Pausing for but one second, she added, "I'm stepping out of this room now, and I don't want to see you again until 2013. See Ron Shope—every damn week. And for the next six months, make sure you run every conservative through the IRS buzz saw. Understood?"

Swallowing hard with a dry throat, Hellman gasped. He only nodded as Thompson, Shope in tow, brushed past him and out of the room.

❖

Once in Hyde Park Square, Burdette surveyed Nathan Conaway's residence and what was around it. It would be unusual if anyone outside the building knew him, Evers observed, but they'd find out. Above Graeter's ice cream shop, the door to the apartment was solid oak with surrounding woodwork that put the building into a much earlier era. Burdette could hear heavy steps come to the door and stop to look through the eyepiece.

"Who's there?" a female voice yelled out.

"Marlyn Burdette, investigator working with OPM. Can we speak to you?"

The barrier opened soundlessly, a surprise for an eighty-year-old structure, and Amber Bustamente stood barefoot, hugging her chemise. "What is it that you want?"

"Amber Bustamente?" Burdette didn't wait for an answer. At the same moment, she and Evers displayed their credentials. "We're here about Nathan Conaway. This is his address, isn't it?" After a bit more word dancing, Bustamente swung the door wide and gestured Burdette and Evers to a couch.

"You can call me Amber. They only call me Ms. Bustamente at work."

"Oh, where is that?"

"I work in the IT department at Xavier University, not far from here."

"What's it like with all the basketball mania there?" Evers joined in. "Don't hold it against me that I went to UC."

"Love it. Xavier's a great school and they're all about being for others. That's actually where I met Nathan—at a party for nerdy people like us about two years ago." Without knowing it, she was answering a number of questions Burdette and Evers would have asked about the nature and extent of her relationship with Conaway.

"Before we go further, Amber, I should mention that according to the Privacy Act of 1974, Nathan can see a copy of his report when we're finished—if he asks for it—and that would include the names of people we talked to and what they said. That okay with you?"

"No problem at all. And I'm glad you're telling me what the deal is with the investigation, but I would never lie to you, and Nathan can see anything I have to say."

Having heard the never-lie-to-you line more times than there were years since the birth of Christ, Burdette simply continued, but she made a mental note of it. When people insist they would never lie, they'll usually lie. "I'm guessing Nathan told you we'd be coming around?"

"Oh, sure," she said. "He told me to tell you everything." She giggled.

"You live together here?"

"You get right to it, don't you. Is that a problem?"

"Not at all, Amber. I just need to get a pretty good idea just how well you know Nathan Conaway."

Another giggle was Bustamente's first response. "Sorry. I guess we know each other pretty well."

Next, Burdette covered her witness's knowledge of Conaway's past education, residence, and employment histories. Bustamente told her Conaway had worked for SoftSec since a least a year before they moved in together.

"As for his life before we met, I don't know that much. I only ask him about his other girlfriends." Giggling still again, she added, "You'll laugh, but when I saw your name on his cell phone, I thought he was cheating on me with you."

Burdette could feel her face turn as red as her hair. She smiled, thinly. She also noticed that Evers spent the time eyeing everything he could about the apartment.

"Nice place you two have here. Hyde Park's pretty expensive. How do you manage that, if I might ask?"

"Well," she said nervously, "we both work, and in IT, they pay us pretty well. But before you ask, I don't know how much Nutsy—I mean Nathan—makes. And I'm sorry I said 'Nutsy.'"

"That's okay, Amber—he put it on his SF-86. How'd he get that name?"

She did her best to suppress another giggle. "Sorry to laugh so much. I guess I'm just nervous, that's all," she said. "I think he got the name in school because he could go more than a full day at his PC without sleep or a break except to pee or have a sandwich. He's just crazy about his work, is all."

"Really?" Burdette suspected this was Amber's second untruth. She next covered the usual questions about character, honesty, and integrity. Receiving good answers to those and to questions about physical and mental health, she moved on to a few more questions about Conaway's financial responsibility and his history with law enforcement agencies. All the answers came easily.

"What about alcohol and illegal drugs, Amber? Does Nathan do any of that?"

"Well, like everybody, he'll have a glass of wine or a beer, but never to excess."

Burdette's eyes never left Bustamente's face. Though she had been taking notes during the entire interview, she let her pen point rest on the page. The slower, more hesitating pace of the witness's speech pattern told her to focus closely. She remained silent, watching.

"Naturally, we might stay longer at the Cock & Bull than we should at times, but we never drive," said Bustamente, as if to mitigate their visits across the street.

Her response prompted a few more questions about the extent of Conaway's alcohol use, and once Burdette was satisfied, she moved on. "You didn't say anything about drugs, Amber. Does Nathan smoke a little pot now and then?" She could see Bustamente let her eyes drop, and they darted to and fro, as if searching for the answer somewhere on the magazine-strewn coffee table.

"Well, you know," she began, "everybody in our generation does a little weed now and then, but never before work or anything." She sighed audibly when she thought the topic was closed.

Evers said, "If you haven't told us the truth, Amber, and we found out about his drug use from others, how would that look for you?" It wasn't a threat, and in actuality, it wouldn't make a bit of difference, but Burdette knew Evers wanted her to think it did.

"Now, let's move on to security matters," he said. "Do you think Nathan would abide by regulations dealing with sensitive or classified information? Has he ever talked about things like that?"

"He never talks about his work," she said flatly, her eyes going rapidly from Burdette to Evers.

"Do you know if he is in any way vulnerable to blackmail for anything he's ever said or done in the area of moral conduct or anything else?"

Bustamente remained silent for a moment. "That's a big question. Unless you might think sleeping with me makes him vulnerable," she tittered weakly, "no, there's nothing." She looked like she was thinking about something.

"Does he have any friends or associations that would make you wonder about his loyalty to the United States?"

"No. None at all."

"So you think he would uphold our Constitution at all costs?"

"Yes," she answered without hesitating, but looked toward the window, as if she was checking the weather.

"You're sure?" asked Evers, apparently noticing her sideways glance.

"Sure."

"Would you have any hesitation at all in recommending him for work that may be sensitive to the national security?"

"I recommend him." Knowing that the interview had concluded, Bustamente exhaled as if she'd held her air for the entire twenty-five minutes.

"May I call you again if I have another question?" Burdette asked, looking at her closely, knowing there was more to be had.

"Sure. Anytime."

Glad of Evers's presence, Burdette knocked on the doors of others in the building and found only one person home. They identified themselves and asked for a minute of her time, but the elderly woman knew little, except to verify some basic information of Conaway's residence and provide a few observations, none of them significant.

Downstairs at Graeter's, they sought the oldest person behind the counter and began to run through the same drill. The woman referred them to the store manager who had rental records that verified exactly what Conaway had claimed on his SF-86 about his residential and employment history. The manager saw Conaway sporadically, since he worked long hours, but she saw Amber, the girlfriend, more regularly, since she was a frequent customer after she moved in with him. The manager was glad to have a tenant like Nathan Conaway, but otherwise, knew little about him, good or bad.

On the sidewalk, under an awning, the two investigators compared their thoughts.

"This works out well," Evers said. "Next time you see McCord and Conaway, have a few more questions for each about the other. It'll bug them, especially McCord, and one of them may say something stupid, but you'll have a hell of a time getting corroboration. Finding people who know guys like Conaway well will take a little work, but I hope you put in the sweat. There's something hinky about this deal, isn't there?"

"You're probably right. Bustamente has more to tell us, so," she chuckled, "we'll be talking soon."

"Joe, we have to talk," McCord rattled into the phone. "Why did you send those FBI people here?"

"Ricky, calm down," the vice president said, swiveling his chair to look out at the sun-drenched day, "and what the hell are you talking about, anyway?"

"I thought you said the background investigation was just a formality, that some contractor was going to come around and go through a little checklist or something like that?"

"Listen, Ricky, and listen carefully. One, they were not FBI agents. The Office of Personnel Management uses a contractor for this job. And it's more than a checklist, but in your case, it is pretty much a formality, because I will see that everything is taken care of. The EAC contract is already yours, and that's that."

McCord's voice came in a burst. "But they were damn good and they asked a helluva lot of questions, Joe."

"So what. What is there to find, Ricky? You're clean, and why would they have anything to be suspicious about?"

"Nothing, I suppose. I'm just getting a little nervous about some things you and I talked about, if you know what I mean."

"Stop right there, Ricky, and don't say another word. I want you to call me when you have a problem, my friend, but never to discuss election matters. Understand? And relax, I'll make a call or two, and you won't have to worry about the OPM contractor. Got it?"

"Yes, sir. Got it. I feel better," he said, though his voice did not vouch for his words. "Thanks for listening, Joe."

"Glad you called." Morrison drummed his fingers while he thought about the bureaucratic path of least resistance. When he picked up his landline for a call to the OPM director, a political appointee who owed her job to him, he knew how things would go. She would immediately call Kristen Bartley, a career woman who wanted to keep her job, but someone who also valued federal power and employees she could actually control. *Nothing beats a work force that appreciates the bennies of government work with nary a risk.*

His next call was also one not to be initiated by an intermediary. The voice of a flustered assistant greeted him at the other end, and Morrison was obliged to wait a moment.

"Mr. Vice President," said Milton Jennings, one of the richest men in America. "It is a rare honor and privilege, indeed. How can I help you?"

"Milton, let's get right to first names. We haven't known each other long, and you've been making billions almost twice as long as I've been alive, but I consider you a powerful friend to have."

"You're too kind, Joe," Jennings said, adding nothing.

"I have an unusual request to make, so I hope you will be in a position to accommodate me."

"Whatever you or the president want, I'm your servant."

"My staff informs me that back in December, Appalachian Shires purchased control of the *Missouri Courier*. Is that correct?"

"Shires has hundreds of holdings, but I believe you're correct."

"Interestingly, one of the *Courier* holdings is a company called SoftSec, and as it turns out, the CEO is a fellow Texan who happens to be the winner of a contract let by the US Election Assistance Commission."

"And?"

Why does he sound impatient? "This contract is one that's important to the administration because it will assist in ensuring we eliminate vote fraud in the November election."

"Does this have something to do with Voter ID, Joe?"

"Indirectly, perhaps," Morrison said, knowing it was a Jennings hot button. He could almost see Jennings twisting his bushy eyebrows. "We're concerned about vote counting irregularities by local and state officials in red states, if you want me to be blunt about it."

"Ahh, I can see why that would be important to every American. So what's the problem?"

"Well, it seems that Enrique McCord, SoftSec's CEO, is getting balky about the contract because he fears it will interfere with so many other state and local voting hardware and software contracts he has, and if the pending antitrust suit moves along, it would definitely affect the profit picture so dear to the heart of Appalachian Shires."

"So what do you want me to do? I would have thought a call from you to a fellow Texan would have been most effective."

"That's just it. McCord is an honorable guy who doesn't like the appearance of a conflict of interest. I don't want to burden you with unnecessary details, so here's all I'm asking. Just give McCord a quick call and let him know the EAC thing is important to you as well, along with the American people, and that he has your full support. That's all you have to say. For that, the president and I would be grateful."

"That I can do, and by the way, Joe, I'm glad you'll be on the ticket again and that you and the president are working on election integrity without a gimmick like Voter ID."

"Thank you, Milton. You won't regret it."

As part of a western swing, Winston Hardy couldn't resist spending time in a part of Utah just beginning to feel the steady, warm breezes of summer, and he relished both the beauty of the state and at Provo, the relative proximity to the center of his Mormon faith: Temple Square in Salt Lake City. Of the former, he spoke with public gusto. Of the latter, he kept his feelings in his heart, lest he unnecessarily inflame the same classes of religious bigots who attempted to spear Jack Kennedy's Catholicism to the dome of Saint Peter's.

He stood in the shimmering sun exuding an earnestness that could not be studied. His audience knew that in him, it was genuine. Too, his visit served as a respite with the GOP contests in California, Montana, New Jersey, New Mexico, and South Dakota soon becoming pleasant afterthoughts. As the 22,000 people said to be there listened, he waded into his remarks. What he said, they seemed to know, had not been poll tested. As long as it met the Hardy test, that was all it took.

"Just what kind of country have we lived in the past few years, ladies and gentlemen, and just what kind of country do we want to have for the rest of our lives and, more importantly, for the lives of our children?

"Have you noticed how our president talks about people who look at freedom of speech differently than he does? Have you noticed what the other side does about people who disagree with them? It's very simple, you see. A man named Saul Alinsky wrote a book called *Rules for Radicals*, and in it, he describes how to eliminate your enemies. First, you demonize them, then you marginalize and mock them, and soon, they're irrelevant.

"So what does that have to do with our president? All across our country the past two years, people have begun associating with like-minded people who believe that we're too much in debt, that government is too big and too much in their lives. These folks aptly call themselves the Tea Party." Scattered cheers erupted from around the audience. Others seemed keen on what Hardy might say next.

"Yet, our president has gathered around him people like former Speaker Tesoro and Senate Majority Leader Riordan. And together, they've so enthusiastically endorsed the Occupy Wall Street movement—a group that is not just exercising its free speech rights, but actually breaking the law. So what has our president been saying?

"In August 2010, President Williams called out a group named Americans for Prosperity, funded by successful entrepreneurs. He said these groups with harmless sounding names that are running millions

of dollars worth of ads might well be foreign-controlled corporations."
Hardy looked at his audience, and asked, "Is there any evidence for that
charge, Mr. President?"

"No," the audience shouted, at first not sure if that was what they
were supposed to do.

"Two days later, the Democratic National Committee blasted the
so-called Gardner Stewart-inspired groups as if they were a Communist
front of some kind. Is there any evidence of wrongdoing here, Mr.
President?"

"No," the audience shouted, more together now.

"A few weeks later, in his radio address, the president once again
referred to 'attack ads run by shadowy groups with harmless-sounding
names. We don't know who's behind those groups,' our president said,
and 'you don't know if it's a foreign-controlled corporation.' Really, Mr.
President, is there any evidence for what you're saying?"

"No," the crowd roared.

"A few days later, an article in the *New Yorker* claimed these were
'slippery organizations with generic-sounding names.' Sounds like the
writer was following the president's script, eh? Then there was the
White House adviser who claimed the Prosperity group does 'not pay
corporate income taxes.' This one's important on two points, ladies and
gentlemen. How would a White House staffer know whether anyone
pays taxes? And, Mr. President, does your administration have any evidence for the charges it makes?"

"No," yelled the crowd again, and it pressed closer to the stage,
angry about the words it heard.

"There are more examples, but, well, you get the idea." After pausing for effect, Hardy went on. "My friends, the President of the United
States sets the tone for our country. His words and his actions should
lift us to a newer, higher notch on the yardstick of freedom. Given what
I have accurately reported to you here today," do you think our president is taking us to new heights of freedom in our land?"

"No," the crowd responded, but in this answer there was a somber
tone, one of concern, perhaps fear.

"My friends," Hardy said, cocking his head to the left, "the Tea Party is not a threat to democracy, and neither are conservatives who want Americans and our immigrant guests to abide by the law, who want us to live within our means. All we conservatives want is for all Americans to have every freedom our founders dreamed of. Over three hundred years ago, refugees from England and Europe risked everything to come to a place where they could speak their minds and worship as they pleased, and over the centuries we have become an inclusive people that welcomes diversity of background and opinion. Those are not just fine words spinning out of a speechwriter and a teleprompter, Mr. President, and I can assure you, no Hardy staffer or I will ever try to demonize and marginalize our American opponents or their motives. We Americans are a decent people—or should be. Take us to that high place we have earned with our blood and treasure, Mr. President—or the people will ask you to step aside."

The thousands roared, and the cameras clicked and whirred, but as he later learned from Lisa Hoxworth, only one or two news outlets played much of the speech. ABS News, Newshare, and CNS played two minutes of President Williams declaring that "the economy is fine," with no critique from the broadcasters.

"Amby, what's wrong?" Obviously concerned, Conaway's tone begged and demanded at the same time.

Amber Bustamente turned away. In the corners of her eyes, she could feel wetness forming, and she tried to suppress the emotion behind them. Desperately, she wanted to stay with Conaway, but she wondered if a long-term relationship could ever be possible with him.

All her life, she had struggled with weight issues. Both parents became what people generously described as "heavy," but the fact was that they were morbidly obese. Even their chocolate Lab came to resemble a very fat pony, and other people laughed at them, calling them "the Bustabuttons." It didn't make any difference that in 2012, over a third of the nation's population was headed in the same direction in terms of weight.

What she knew was that she and Nutsy Conaway had some key qualities in common: they were big people who shared the same profession, had no real religious beliefs, and probably, they each knew finding someone for themselves would nob be an easy task. Like herself, Nutsy was emotionally immature and insecure, and in any relationship, only one party can have that baggage. *Would he always be looking for someone else better looking and more stable?*

When she still didn't answer, Conaway pursued her. "Amby, we have to work this out. You're the best thing that's ever happened to me, and now I think I'm losing you."

"I only wish you truly believed that I'd be so good for you. The first girl you meet who's a runway model attracted to nerds, well, you'll be gone in a hot minute."

"Not true, Amby," he said, putting his hands on her shoulders when he walked up behind her. "You have no idea how badly I need you. Especially now."

"Why now?" She regretted asking the question as soon as the words left her mouth.

"Because this contract we're getting from the Election Commission is a big deal, that's why."

"What's so big deal about them? You told me all they do is watch the voting."

"Well, they don't know it yet, but this year we're gonna do more than that."

"What do you mean?" she asked, anxious for a reason—any reason—to stay.

"I'm not supposed to talk about it."

"That's not fair," she whined, turning to tap him on the chest, as if to push him away.

"Well, sweetie, you could talk me into it," he said teasingly, drawing out the words.

"Don't flirt with me, you big phony."

"Nuthin' phony about Nutsy," he murmured, pressing himself to her.

She inhaled, succumbing to the moment. She closed her eyes, waiting for him to slide his fingers along her special place. She found his sweet spot, hardened for the occasion. As she worked her hands, she moaned and whispered at the same time. "You've got me all excited, you hunk."

Less than twenty minutes later, when each had had the moment of satisfaction they'd craved, she spoke into his ear, mocking them both. "Well, did I talk you into it?" And she giggled into his neck.

"Um-hmmm," he sighed. "Give me a minute to get past ecstasy." They both laughed out loud. Then, speaking slowly, softly, he said, "It's this way, sweetie, and you're one of the few people I know outside of work who would get this. When we set up our interfaces with the states we're supposed to be monitoring, those states won't know we'll be able to do more than watch."

"What do you mean?"

"Just what I said. In some cases, that's all we'll do, according to Mr. McCord." A wicked smile lit up his eyes. "But in others, we'll actually be able to turn the votes from one candidate over to the other—in any race we choose."

"Why would Mr. McCord want to get himself involved with stuff like that? What does he care, anyway?"

"He didn't tell me this directly, but I think it's this way. Somehow, he and Morrison—"

"Who's Morrison?"

"Oh, God, you're like the people they interview in the street. Morrison. Morrison! The Vice President of the United States? That Morrison?"

Her insecurities rising, she said, "Well, I didn't know which Morrison you meant. So what about him?"

"Mr. McCord and the VP are ol' Texas boys, and somehow McCord got this contract through his new best friend. Now that he has it, the big guy is expecting us to do something with it."

"Like?"

"Like make the only race that matters come out the right way, silly."

Her eyes widened with fascination, amazement, and then, fear. "And you're the one who's gonna make sure that happens?"

"You're lookin' at him. Nutsy Conaway, the new kingmaker—behind the scenes, of course."

"Oh, this scares me." She backed away a bit, as if he now carried live voltage.

"Nuthin' to worry about with Nutsy!" he said. "And no one will ever be the wiser. Because in most cases anymore—except right here in Hyde Park—there's no paper ballot to check against the record, no one will ever know where it happens or how many votes I'll turn over from one guy to the next."

"But why would you do something like that?" she said. "It's just wrong."

Backing away himself and shocked at her reaction, he said, "Wrong? That has nuthin' to do with anything."

"But why would you do such a thing—to change what the people want." She could hear her voice rising.

"Because we can, sweetie. How cool would it be that one man—me—can control the whole damn thing." A different look appeared on his face. "This stays between us, right? Tell me it stays here, Amby."

She bit her lip, but said, "Okay, it stays here, whether I stay or not."

"C'mon, sweetie, don't start that again. This is gonna be a tough couple of months while I go around the country and set this stuff up. I'm gonna need you bad."

"Just give me some space, okay?" She rose from the bed and took a step away, grabbing a sheet as she did so. For some reason, she no longer felt good being naked in front of him, and she stepped quickly from the room.

One thing nagging at her was the fact that she lied for him to the federal investigators. The implications of too many questions they had asked left her very unsure of her roommate. Mental health? Drugs? Integrity? Keeping secrets? Amber now had reason to doubt Nutsy Conaway would ever keep faith with their relationship when he had just admitted to her he made much bigger promises he never intended to keep.

The whole business bothered her like nothing ever before. Nutsy—the guy she thought she loved—was ready to undo what their country stood for and why? *Because he could?*

At the halfway mark of the six o'clock news, Barnes Ward turned to the cameras at the News Global studios in Washington, DC, and the viewers could see the backdrop of the Washington Monument while they heard him say, "And now to the campaign trail. Well, panel, this was a big week for Governor Hardy. It was a clean sweep for him in the last five states, with no other GOP competitor receiving a single vote in any of them. As for the president, the Democratic primaries have been largely non-events." He introduced his guests, before turning to the man on his right. "Going forward, William, how do you see things shaping up?"

William Herzog took a labored breath, providing oxygen to a mind crisp and clear as a silver dollar pinging off steel on a cold day. "It's over, of course, as it's been for some time. The governor has had the past month to polish his positions and raise his poll numbers, and to some degree he has succeeded."

"Marta? Do you agree?" Ward asked, shifting his gaze to Marta Andresson.

"Yes, I do, in part. I have to say, though, that Governor Hardy has still not connected with women, the fifty percent of the voting population that does not know what to expect of him. He has only a short time left, and given that his words are so heavily filtered by the media at large, he'll have a hard time sending that message."

"And Steven Harrison. Steve, I know you've had some reservations about the governor. Now that he'll be the nominee, how do you feel?"

"I'm having a change of view on him, I have to admit. If you saw and listened to his whole speech on civil liberties in Utah the other day, any conservative in the country should have stood up and cheered. Can we play that clip now?"

Several call-and-response segments from the Utah stage filled the News Global screen. Then the cameras returned to the panel, and William Herzog spoke first.

"I agree with Steve," he said. "And if Governor Hardy spoke with such passion on topics like the economy, immigration, and health care, just to name three—and if the other news services would air his speeches—he could turn the thing in his direction."

The sultry weather outside the president's private dining room near the Oval Office bore no resemblance to the conversation inside, thought Sheldon Ingber. The president had invited him on the spur of the moment and gave him the strictest of instructions: listen and note what Tesoro, Riordan, and Sweeney were saying. At a dinner meeting like this, where time was limited, each would mention what was most important to them, and these were the points for which Ingber would need to forge a talking point during for the campaign ahead.

First, he appraised Angela Tesoro, Speaker of the House when the president had majorities in both House and Senate the first two years of his term. She had served the president well in passing a trillion-dollar stimulus package and a comprehensive immigration bill.

As for Harry Riordan, the old man smiled with satisfaction, the only person in the room considered a friend to both the Williams and Morrison camps. The fact that Morrison himself was not present spoke volumes, Ingber wrote to his mental journal.

Then, there sat Norton Sweeney, resting comfortably in a well-padded chair. Though his friendship with the president went back to Albany days, those ties could be broken in a moment if any DOJ issues became a political embarrassment to the president and a bus happened to be gliding by.

Ingber savored with anticipation a discussion he knew would be all about power. Such discussions always were.

As the evening traffic died away and the lights of Washington began to glitter the night, the president entered from his study and took the seat everyone knew he would choose. The dining table itself, eight feet around, was more than commodious for five, but it also meant no one felt uncomfortably intimate, like the political conspirators they all knew themselves to be.

President Williams opened the dinner with a toast to them and another four years.

"Here, here," was heard four separate times, if one listened carefully, and there began light conversation with a simple julienne salad. First names prevailed in the trusted, convivial, and totally private setting.

"Av, how do you see the general?" Sweeney prompted.

"If I had to bet right now, I'd say we were in," he responded. "Sure, the economy sucks, but the public still ties that bag of rocks around the necks of the Republicans, and I'm not about to remove it."

Everyone laughed, and Tesoro decided to weigh in. "You know, Av," she said in her semisweet voice, one that some would call bittersweet, "I wonder if you're going to have to strengthen the public's perception on your views regarding abortion."

Ingber noticed the president eyeing her carefully. Though no media reps were in the room, her question sounded like she'd had it written on her palm. Tesoro reminded him of a wrinkled Bette Davis attempting to smile without breaking the skin stretched over her cheeks. Sweeney and Riordan studied their plates.

"You're right, Angie, but you know, what folks in Maryland want to hear isn't exactly what housewives in Ohio want to hear."

"I agree, Mr....uh...Av, but you must speak out. There's confusion out there."

"The vice president makes it clear that this administration is for unfettered women's rights as far as that goes. That's a pretty powerful endorsement, Angie," Ingber said.

"It will take good words from you, Av," she said, ignoring Ingber's kibitzing. "What Morrison says and does is not always perceived as accurately representing your policies."

Her response raised a chuckle with Senator Riordan, and he joined in. "For a Baltimore Catholic, Angie, I'm always surprised by your views on abortion, and you don't hold back like a lot of Catholic Democrats. You put it right out there."

"For a hard-shell Missouri Baptist who shouldn't smoke," she teased, "you shouldn't talk. Look, gentlemen, we've worked too hard from *Roe v. Wade* in 1973 through *Stenberg v. Carhart* in 2000 to leave an impression—by omission—that our party is abandoning women's rights."

"I understand your view," Riordan said. "But I sometimes wonder if some people feel we're so over the top on women's rights that viable fetuses are left to die."

"Don't you start that nonsense, you old so-and-so," Tesoro said affably but with a sufficiently clear conviction that the men in the room could have no doubt that the issue had a high voltage warning all over it.

Sweeney looked at his boss. "Back to second-term expectations, Av. If national health care is your next objective, as well as effective control of school curricula, not to mention centralized fiscal policy, what constitutional hurdles do your foresee?"

"Ha. That should be a question for you, Norty. As far as the Constitution is concerned, I see it the way I always have: it's a lovely old document steeped in history, but one with little relevance today. Each legislative initiative we can pass will shape the view of that parchment in the minds of the people, and when we can't get the legislation we want, there's always my pen." He chuckled. "I know you'll chastise me, Norty, that as someone who studied constitutional law, I should respect and understand it more than most, but that's precisely why I've come to my own conclusion: it is a dead letter in the annals of progress. The Constitution and the Supreme Court are an obstacle to every progressive impulse this nation has ever had—from slavery to women's rights to a fair distribution of wealth. It's the latter challenge that we'll tackle in our second term and health care will be one of the hinges that swings the door."

"The Republicans and the Court will give us fits," Tesoro countered.

"Let them. We'll manage our obstacles, one at a time." The president's eyes went from Sweeney to Ingber. "Steps have already been taken to ensure that the media types in our pocket remain there, and for outfits like News Global, well, there are things we can do, too. The only thing Gardner Stewart and I have ever agreed on is when he referred to CNS and the old networks as 'State Media.' He's almost right."

The conspirators offered up a collective smile.

Sweeney said, as if for any recording device present: "It's the president's view of the Constitution that allows us to do what we think best for the greater good, and as long as he gives me the green light on certain initiatives, I intend to carry them through."

"Averell," said Riordan's old voice sandpapered by the cigarettes of his youth and the cigars of middle age, "there are some old dog Democrats and more than a few Independents who do not care much for an extra-constitutional view of governance, if you don't mind my saying so. There were more than a few nellies out there when you were howling about the Tea Party being foreign-controlled. Nobody believed that, and I think you hurt yourself there. How will you handle them?"

"One at a time. The key thing about adversarial relationships, Harry, is to know exactly who is against you." The president smiled and winked. "And we have ways to know that too."

As if on cue, Freddie Frederick appeared at the dining room door and quietly walked to the president's side. Leaning over, she spoke into his ear. "Secretary Grantham is on the line. He says the two of you need to talk about concerns Ambassador Stevens has raised. There's some urgency."

"One minute, Freddie," he said. And as he stood, he couldn't resist it. "Even as we talk about presidential politics, Emerson Grantham needs a word." A round of chuckles accompanied his exit.

In his private study, President Williams picked up the line. "Emerson! Freddie says something is up that needs my attention, and for you, I'm always ready to listen."

"Averell, we have been in this business too long for you to waste your time on flattery." He paused. "I'm not sure our approach in Libya is panning out for us, and we need to reconsider some of its parameters."

"Look, Emerson, you and I have been through this," he said as patiently as he could manage. "I laid out for you my vision for managing Middle Eastern affairs—a clear departure from the Bush years."

"Yes, sir, you did," he said, injecting some formality into the conversation, as if it were for the record.

"And as I recall, you disagreed but have been a good soldier—and I appreciate it very much. I just hope that Stevens and others haven't undercut it."

"That's not it at all, Averell. We supported Qaddafi's ouster and his fledging replacement, but it is a very fragile situation teetering between raw democracy and open chaos. We have to go slow here. Stevens is now reporting, as of two days ago, extremists are operating openly in Benghazi, and indeed, in Libya as a whole. It's likely he'll ask for beefed up security forces at our stations there."

"That would be exactly the wrong signal, in my opinion. It would show we have no faith in the new government."

"And there's good reason for that. They haven't proven they can be trusted to maintain order and protect our ambassador, not to mention our other operatives there. When you and I met with CIA Director Warner at the end of February, we mentioned that more serious unrest was highly likely."

"I know you did, and even then, I told you that installing barbed wire on the tops of compound walls in Benghazi and elsewhere would be seen as offending local officials."

"Offended or not, sir, we have to show signs we're willing to protect our soil."

"We are staying the course, Emerson."

JULY

CNN/Time/Opinion Research Poll
July 1
Williams 49%
Hardy 46%

"Janice, are Burdette and Evers ready to talk?"

"They'll be dialing in any second, Pete." The Verizon telecom operator confirmed her.

"We're here. Evers and Burdette," reported the older investigator.

"Thanks, you two," Clancy began. "Look, I'll get right to it. The big ball of you-know-what rolled downhill and landed on my desk via a call from Kristen Bartley this morning. As she informed me, the vice president himself called the director of OPM who called Bartley and so on, and it's all about the McCord case for USEAC. That means you, Marlyn," he said for effect, but without anger. "According to the thirdhand version of events, you intimated Mr. McCord and his secretary with officious demands for their time. So, let's have your side of the story."

"For cryin' out loud, Pete. You know me, probably the shortest, least intimidating investigator you have. I tried several times to set up an appointment with this guy for his subject interview, and he kept blowin' me off, and so, maybe I was a bit pushy when I told his secretary I needed a callback. And following Janice's advice, I took Nelson with me for the interview. This guy's a piece of work."

"More than a piece of work," Evers said. "He may have powerful friends, but something's bugging this guy—otherwise, why mention his buddy, Joe Morrison?"

Clancy heard Dern's chuckle at the forthrightness of her people, then asked a few more questions. Satisfied he had the whole picture, he said, "Okay, I get it. This isn't the first time a subject of investigation with political connections tried some indirect pressure on us, and—sorry Janice—given this administration, it won't be the last. All right, you two, just try to make nice as these EAC cases move through the mill. Are we close to done with them yet?"

Dern explained that the work was split between Evers, Burdette, and Gladston in her region, and most of the fieldwork was complete.

"Any derog anywhere?" Clancy wanted to know.

"Nothing on McCord so far," Burdette said, "and if you check the system, nobody else has anything. Conaway's another story. Besides his live-in girlfriend who might know too much about his work—that I can't prove—he's got some drug use, but nothing big."

Clancy knew that by "the system," Burdette was referring to OPM's electronic reporting system for background investigations. "I looked, but I just wanted to see if there's anything else you hadn't reported yet."

Evers chimed in. "Nothing except an old man's hunch that something is truly hinky here, Pete. Naturally, that won't be going into any report unless some witness tells us something."

"Okay, Nelson. You're the senior guy on these cases, so I'll trust you to keep us all in the loop. And Marlyn, don't worry about any pressure from the political types. Just do it right. Thanks, and be safe out there."

Nelson Evers knew that with the Fourth of July being in the middle of the week, devising an efficient work plan would not be easy. Finally, he thought it a good time to tackle his northern Kentucky work—at least that was what he'd mentioned to Janice Dern when she casually asked about his cases on hand.

Dripping from the humidity, he was grateful for the brief, air-conditioned ride across the Roebling Bridge to the IRS Center in Covington. Modern fabrics were great, but he still felt the unremitting dampness of his pressed white shirt against his chest, and there was no way he would loosen his tie or remove his jacket. He'd been a professional for too long, and it would take more than a hot day to make him change.

The identification and security formalities had been at a higher level for ten years, but they felt no less overdone. Today, the drill took longer to accomplish, and he wondered why that would be. Not that he expected any better treatment from the black officers there because he was black or a fellow fed, but because he'd been coming to the building for decades and these guys knew him by name. Maybe they just had a case of "the slows."

As he finished, he saw that Mayella Washington was headed his way, and he immediately regretted whatever karma he brought with him. When he took a last glance at the three men who had checked him in, all averting his gaze, he connected the dots—they had tipped her off and had taken their sweet time with the rigmarole.

"Hey, Nelson, what's up today?"

Evers always thought Washington's voice was the personification of shards of glass scratching each other in the wind. "Nothin' much, Mayella. What's goin' on witchu?"

"Just the usual. Protectin' the workers from evil management and the likes of you." Her forced chuckle matched the poor attempt at humor.

"Your folks got nothin' to fear from me, long as they tell me the truth about things."

"Ah, but the truth will not make them free, my man. It might get them fired, and most people here think these jobs belong to them."

"Oh, I didn't know they owned 'em. Anyway, I need to get on with it, and what I got today will not need a union rep, so keep your dogs in the kennel."

"Dogs, Nelson?" she whined in her high-pitched imitation of offended honor. "The employees need us, and don't you forget it."

"Look, Mayella Michelle, I didn't come to debate you on this stuff, but in my humble opinion, these folks need you no more'n a dog needs fleas."

"Watch yourself, Nelson Evers. You soundin' like a white man's boy."

"Don't start wit me. Remember, we grew up together in Mount Auburn and got in lotsa trouble together Over the Rhine, so I know what you're about. You're about the easiest gig there is, and in this building, it don't get any easier than this."

"Listen, you wanna get your work done here, you better be nice."

"I'll always be nice to the folks, but if you start any shit, I'm gonna finish it."

"What's in your craw, anyway? You don't usually come in here with a stone in your shoe. What's goin' on?"

"I don't know what news you watch, but when I saw Senator Marshall on TV the other night talkin' about IRS people targeting certain people for, shall I say, special treatment, I was wonderin', would that be your people here—the ones you say need protectin'?"

The President of Local 2450, National Treasury Union, glared at him and said not a word.

For a moment, he looked into her deep, black eyes, bottomless wells of memory and anger. "Look, Mayella, I remember when our people couldn't get good jobs, and then work came for so many—those without a big education. They did nothin' all day but move piles of paper from one desk to another before computers, and later, a lot of our people were lucky enough to get better jobs outta the deal. Management wanted them to succeed because they needed black faces to fill slots—not so hard since black people flocked to government jobs. So for the last fifty years here, it's been a big love-in between management and labor, and the only conflicts here are the ones you start so these folks think they need you. And they pay dues so NTU can bribe candidates with contributions. And that keeps your jobs cushy. So who's enslaving our people now? So let's cut out the crap. One day, somebody's gonna make some real noise, and I hope you're ready."

"You through makin' your speech, big boy? Well, don't you worry. We may be from the same 'hood, but don't ever think we won't run over you in a minute if you mess us up. Sure, we gotta good deal here, just like the white man had for hundreds of years before that. So what? And now, *Mister* Evers, we gotta black man in the White House. And this union, along with these people, intends to keep him there, no matter what. Are you gettin' that, *Mister* Evers?"

"Got it." He stopped himself cold. He'd want to come back—and be welcomed back—without any interference. Evers switched faces from one of confrontation to one of conciliation. "And you know what? I don't know why I'm makin' such a fuss witchu, sweet girl that you've always been. Just a bad day in the heat is all. Will you take an apology from an old man like me?"

She half smiled, victorious but wary. "Okay, Nelson. No harm. You just do whatchu came to do, and we won't get in your way—if you don't get in ours. I guess I just don't understand why a black man like you doesn't know where your bread is buttered." Her smile became broad, like the salesman just before the signature.

They hugged in mutual, faux forgiveness. Evers took a few steps in the direction of his first witnesses, but turned just in time to see Mayella Washington take herself, purposefully, into the office of the IRS Center's director.

Inside a small interview room, Evers popped his cell phone from his pocket and speed dialed the Columbus office. "Hello, Janice? I got somethin' to tell you." For the next few minutes he recalled for her some of the talk at their April meeting and what he'd just heard with his own ears. "I always knew it, but for the first time, Washington took her gloves off. What Burdette was sayin' was right on the money."

"And what do you want us to do about it?"

"Maybe nothin', but I just want it on the record. I ain't nobody's boy, and you're nobody's house girl, but black people in these agencies are sharecroppin' just like they used to. They're just workin' for another man. You can mark my word."

"I think, you're taking this way out of context. I'm glad the workers have their reps, and in my opinion, there's nothing wrong with their unions making political contributions."

"Would you be just as happy if they were making those contributions to Winston Hardy?"

"Never fear. That'll never happen if there's a Democrat in the race, and how could you make a choice other than Averell Williams?"

Mayella Washington asked to see the Center's director, and within minutes of her entering his office, he picked up his phone and dialed a number he knew well in Washington, DC. "This is Evan Hughes for Gordon Hellman, please."

"Mr. Hellman," he said, after a curious hello. "Maybe it's nothing, sir, but you know, Senator Marshall was on the news not that long ago alleging certain misconduct by our people, and—"

"What of it, Hughes?" Hellman asked, cutting him off. "Marshall's letter will wait here for a few months more before he gets an answer."

"Yes, sir, I understand, but there was an investigator here just now, an old friend of our union chief, and in a private conversation with him, he made some noise about it as well and—"

"So?" he said, impatiently. "What agency?"

"OPM."

"OPM? Is he there about Hatch Act violations? If so, no matter. OPM can be managed and feds usually don't mess with other feds on stuff like this."

"He's not a fed, sir. This guy works for their contractor, NIS."

"Even better. I'll take care of it. And Hughes?"

"Yes, sir?"

"Just keep doing what you're doing, and don't worry about it. Nobody is going to get in our way."

"Is this Marlyn Burdette?"

"Speaking," she said without inflection.

"This is Amber. You remember me? Nathan's girlfriend?"

"Oh, sure, Amber. It's been a little while. What can I do for you?"

"Well..."

"You must be breaking up, Amber. I can't hear you."

"I know," she whispered, forlorn. "I..."

"Amber, you're still cutting out. Is something wrong?"

"No...Yes. I shouldn't be calling you Ms. Burdette, but—"

"Marlyn is okay, Amber. What's on your mind?"

"Can I call you back in a minute? Maybe two minutes. I'm going to walk downstairs and across to the little park. Up here makes me nervous. I'll call when get to a good spot." She hung up.

Bustamente eased herself into a presentable chemise, slipped on a pair of flip-flops, and carefully negotiated the stairs. At the entrance to Graeter's, she promised herself a raspberry chocolate chip right after the call. When she found a vacant bench in the park—not hard, since it was so hot—she punched in Burdette's number. In the few minutes it had taken her to free herself of the apartment, his things, his smell, she felt better about what she needed to do.

"Hello, again, Marlyn. Sorry about all that. It's just that I didn't want to talk up there."

"Something is bothering you, Amber. You can tell me what it is."

"I didn't tell you the entire truth about things."

Silence.

"Nathan smokes more pot than I told you about."

Silence.

"And there's the other stuff."

"You mean other drugs, Amber?"

"No. Remember when you—or maybe it was Mr. Evers—asked me some stuff at the end about Nathan following the rules and being loyal and stuff like that?"

Silence.

"Well, I'm not political if you know what I mean, but where I work, people always talk about doing the right thing," she said. Sweat beads formed on her forehead despite the shade. "Unless Nathan was lyin' to me, I think he's going to do somethin' with the votes."

"I'm not sure what you mean."

"He didn't say much, because I told him I was gonna leave him, so he wanted me to know how important he was and that he would really need me for the election."

"You mean this November, for the presidential election?"

"Yeah. He said he could fix it so Williams wins, and that's why they got this contract from the vice president."

"Amber, the contract is with the US Election Assistance Commission, not the vice president. Is there some confusion there?"

"No. Somehow this guy Morrison is involved with Nathan's boss, and they're gonna fix it."

"Amber, do you know what you're saying?"

"I don't know, really. I'm just trying to repeat what he told me."

"What else did he say?"

"Nothing that I can remember right now."

"Please think about it for a minute, Amber. Anything would be important."

"Nothing, and I'm sure. Oh, crap," she said, and she began to cry.

"Amber, let me come to where you are and I'll listen to whatever you have to say."

"No," she sniffled. "I'm glad I called you, but I hate myself for it. Don't call me. I gotta go."

"Paul, you're never gonna believe this," Burdette said when she connected with Gladston in Columbus a minute later.

"What, that you want to go out with me again?" he asked playfully. "Put that aside, Paul," she said, wondering where another date with him would lead. They'd been out twice her breakup with Randy, and she couldn't take her mind from his deep olive eyes and his way of look-ing so directly at her. It was almost a stare, but a most flattering one, softened by the slight smile his lips easily offered.

"Okay," he responded, and stopped there.

"Hey! This is serious, and no comebacks, Paul. I need you to think about the McCord case for a minute."

"I'm about to turn that one in, Mare. It's all clear here, and I have four solid witnesses testifying to his good character."

"Fine. Now zero in on his number two—Nathan Conaway."

"What about him?"

"His girlfriend just called me and said he told her he and McCord were going to fix the election."

"What? Oh, bullshit!"

"Paul, this chick was serious. Conaway was bragging to her, trying to impress her so she wouldn't give him the heave-ho."

"Holy crap. What else have you gotten on this?"

"Absolutely nothing. I was about to turn my stuff in as well. You know, when Evers and I talked to him about some of his employees, you could see him do the double-think when it occurred to him the questions I was asking were the same ones I'd ask his people about him. It was funny to watch. I think the guy lost a pound or two when I brought up security regs, the Constitution, and loyalty."

"But he didn't tumble?"

"No, and neither did anybody else I talked to."

"What about the employment sources at SoftSec—nothing?

"Not a whisper. If there's anything going on, it's with McCord and Conaway and nobody else."

"And Conaway said nothing?"

"Same. According to Conaway, McCord is the best boss, SoftSec is the best company, and God's in His heaven."

"Somethin's gotta give. Have you talked to Evers?"

"Not yet."

"I wouldn't wait. Maybe he has an idea or two."

"Why don't I see if he and I can drive up to Columbus and we'll have a sit-down with Janice."

"Good idea. She can decide about getting Clancy involved."

"I hate stuff like this, and I hate all the political crap. That Bustamente chick could be crazier than a bedbug, and she's the only one who's said anything."

"You know, Mare, it used to be that politics was something people talked about a few months before every election. Now it seems to be a part of our everyday lives."

"Except for the totally ignorant, Paul, and maybe for people like me, who are afraid to care about it."

"This is Peter Marsden's *World Journal*, and this is the news. Today's appearance by Governor Hardy at the NAACP convention did nothing to raise the GOP narrative above a low roar. Tony Duke, what do you have for us?"

"Low roar, indeed, Peter but not of approval. He was booed today by the thousand-member NAACP convention here in Houston."

"He was not received well there, you're saying?"

"That would be putting it mildly. While the governor did receive polite applause when he reached the podium and at the conclusion of his speech, there was clear disapproval when he talked about entitlement reform—Social Security, welfare, Medicaid—and this organization, since 1909, has been the voice of African American voters all across the country."

"Thank you, Tony. Otherwise, on the campaign trail, the governor now has fourteen hundred and sixty-two delegates sown up for the Republican convention. This number is significant, ladies and gentlemen, but now largely irrelevant. Barring some unforeseen calamity befalling Governor Hardy's campaign, he will be the Republican nominee for President of the United States."

Marsden turned to face the large screen dominating the studio backdrop, and on it appeared the president, smiling and shaking hands with eager, approving fans. "President Averell Williams not only enjoys a comfortable lead in the polls, he has a substantial fundraising lead all across the country. Easily a hundred million dollars ahead of his opponent, Averell Harriman Williams will be a hard man to beat."

"Why are they always doing construction around Lebanon?" Nelson Evers wondered, as he and Burdette streaked up I-71 for their face-to-face with Janice Dern.

"I don't know," she said, "but we both know ten ways around it if we get stopped. And don't get me wrong. I don't mind going to Columbus, but what will we accomplish in person that we can't by phone?"

"It's this way," he said, hands firmly on the wheel. "I'm not sure where Janice stands on stuff like this, and I want her lookin' me in the eye if she tells us to write a memo and move on."

"Just a minute. Even if what Amber says is true, it's not our job to investigate it. And think about it. From what we've learned on these cases, there's no smokin' gun, and there won't be one even after the election, and not even the EAC will know what happened."

"So you're telling me that even if Amber Bustamente takes and passes a polygraph test, there's not a damn thing that can be done?"

"The EAC needs to know about what this woman is alleging, and that's where the memo comes in," Burdette said. "I'll bet that's what it all comes down to. We put her allegations in the report and write a memo to Bartley through Janice and Pete, and she decides whether to send it to the EAC or bring in the FBI."

"And I'm supposed to be the mature, old investigator. You're probably right, and I'm a damn fool."

"Just what kind of difference did you think we could make, Nelson? This isn't a movie," she said teasingly.

He chuckled. "You mean I'm not Morgan Freeman and you're not Amy Adams?" They both laughed. "Seriously, all I want to do is throw a wrench into their plans, assuming they're real."

"Just to put it on the table, Nelson, I could care less about this or any election—I just want to do my job the right way and not be bothered with all the bull crap."

"Nice work if you can get it, young lady. Not caring about what goes on in Washington is no longer the luxury it used to be. Now they can reach right into your living room, and for that matter, your bedroom, and there's nothin' you can say about it. What's more, this president thinks he can kill American citizens with drones if he thinks they're bad guys."

"I'm not sure about the drone thing," Burdette said, clutching her seatbelt.

"Exactly," Evers said, "and I now I'd better second-guess what I say to people."

"You got that right."

Fifty miles later, Burdette and Evers parked their sedan just off of North High Street, downtown, and made their way to the NIS offices. Janice Dern greeted them warmly, if curiously, and asked to speak with Evers alone.

"Marlyn, Paul is just down the hall. Maybe you want to say, hi."

"This must indeed be important, Nelson, for you to insist that you and Burdette come up here on the clock," she said after she'd closed the door.

"It's that important, Janice."

"Not more about the IRS business, is it?"

"No, ma'am. Well, not exactly. Whether any of it's connected, you can decide. Gladston should be part of this too."

"Yes, and that's another investigator here on the clock. Not many cases getting done with you guys not out there ringing doorbells."

"I know you're dubious, Janice, but this could be big-time stuff. Now, if you really want us to get back out on the street, maybe we could get Pete Clancy on the phone so we ain't tellin' this story more than once."

"You know, Nelson, you have a lot of nerve making my decisions for me."

"You should be no stranger to that. You've been lettin' some other people do your thinkin' for you on other matters, wouldn't you say?"

"You're way out of line. If you weren't the senior investigator in Cincinnati, you'd be movin' to Butte."

"You know, you are soundin' just like Mayella Washington."

"Mayella?"

"The union head at the IRS. She tried to threaten me, too."

"Be careful, Nelson," she said, seemingly relieved. "You're way out there."

"I'm tryin', but just so's you know, I ain't nobody's slave anymore, and I'm off the plantation." As Dern rose to conclude their encounter, Evers's eyes were drawn to the wall of fame behind her desk.

Gladston and Burdette were summoned, and once all were convened at her small conference table, she began their meeting. "Nelson knows I'm not comfortable with all of you taking so much time to relay this tale." There was the slightest emphasis on the last word. "But here you are. To save time, let me see if Pete Clancy can join us on the phone." Clancy answered the phone on the second ring.

"Yes, Janice, what's on fire today?"

Everyone in the room laughed.

"Sorry, Pete, I should have warned you we have three investigators with us you may remember. Paul Gladston, Nelson Evers, and Marlyn Burdette."

"I do remember them—names even the vice president might remember." The chuckles at his little joke were nervous and short. Clancy cleared his throat. "So what's up?"

"Pete, I'm going to turn this over to the Three Unlikely Musketeers here. Nelson?"

"Not me, Janice. Mare should talk. It's her case."

Burdette wrinkled her jaw. "Well, Pete and Janice," she began, cogently laying out the story. She emphasized how odd it was that McCord was so difficult when it was a probably lucrative contract for his company from the EAC, how heavy-handed he was about his relationship to Vice President Morrison, how the same impression of self-importance came through during the subject interview with Nathan Conaway, how they reacted to questions about national security, loyalty, etc., and lastly, how Conaway's girlfriend relayed his braggadocio about fixing the election when he thought Bustamente was going to dump him. She recited what she knew in less than theee minutes. When she finished, there was total silence in the room, and at the other end of the line.

Clancy cleared his throat again. "That's quite a story, and except for the last little bit, every new investigator could explain the other behaviors you described."

"I know, Pete," she responded. "Taken one by one, what we observed means little, but together, it suggests there could be a problem."

"You said, 'we'?"

Nelson Evers spoke up. "Hi, Pete, it's Nelson. Maybe you remember that I was there when we did the subject interview with McCord and the original contact with Bustamente. Of course, I did not take her phone call about the election fix."

"So if I have this straight," Clancy said, "we have all sorts of funny aroma, but only one piece that's a bit more solid, and you alone heard it by phone?"

"Ye...yes," Burdette stammered. It was all on her.

"You know how this would look to anyone outside this call, don't you?"

"Sure I do, Pete, and maybe somebody could stitch something together if politics was my passion, but everybody who knows me knows that I could care less about either Williams or Hardy. Truly, Pete, I do not have a dog in this fight."

"All of us can vouch for her, Pete," Gladston said.

"Ditto on that," Evers said.

"So what to do," Clancy ruminated aloud. "One, it's not ours to investigate. This will be an FBI matter, I'm sure, but I hate to send this forward with so little." There was silence for a long moment. "Marlyn, I want you to see this Amber Bustamente in person and get her to repeat what she said to you face-to-face. Take Evers with you, since she thinks you two work together. Then go back to see Conaway on the pretext that you needed a bit more information on something and get him talking about the contract. Let's just see if he says anything. Janice, do you agree?"

"I'm not sure it's worth it, Pete, but if you think so."

"Well, it's this way. I can't *not* report this to Bartley, but I'd rather have something more substantial before I do. I want our credibility to be as high as it can be on this, but for God's sake, everybody, don't do any more than what I've directed. And by the way, let's get this done before I get another call. These were hot cases to begin with. Good luck." The line went dead.

"Okay, boys and girls, that's it. Let's get this done and get back to getting our cases out. The customer is waiting."

While Evers headed for the restroom, Burdette and Gladston rounded the corner for more private conversation. "I'm worried about you," said Gladston. "Be careful. This is beginning to sound real, and it's out of our league."

Burdette smiled at him, pleased at his concern, but she sang a different tune. "Listen, Paul, I can take care of myself, and besides, this is no big deal—just some chick who's insecure as hell and immature to boot. We'll be all done with it by early next week." She touched his arm and gave him a peck on the cheek. "Thanks, though," she said, and she hurried off, not wanting him to see her face blushed to match her hair.

The friendly crowd broiled in Roanoke's noonday sun, and the shirt-sleeved Averell Williams let his speech flow like melting butter on a fresh-roasted cob of corn. After the usually perfect litany of thanks and shout-outs to local officials and political wannabes, he reminded his audience that man does not live by his own sweat alone. "You know," he said, "there are folks on the other side of this debate who think that every man is an island unto himself, somebody who can live without rules or regard for his fellow man."

"You got it, man," someone shouted.

"But you know and I know that every man, woman, and child in our land exists and thrives only if there are others they can depend on—whether it be friends, family, neighbors, the local food bank, or what have you."

"Say it again," shouted someone as the crowd applauded.

"And when times are hard, when the problems are big—like the ones the Republicans left us in '08—there simply aren't enough friends and neighbors, and the food bank just won't do it. That's when you need a government big enough, strong enough, and ready enough."

The applause was louder now.

"Ready enough to take care of those who need help. My father used to say that Republicans will stand by a creek and give the drowning man a lot of encouragement to hang on, to swim harder, but they won't throw him a life saver."

"That's right," somebody yelled.

"Or if they throw the man a rope, they throw him the whole thing and won't hold on to the other end."

Derisive laughter rippled through the crowd.

"And when they talk about the power of hard work, starting a business, and being a success, well, somebody needs to tell them, 'You didn't build that!' It was the government that built the roads to get to your business. It provided the streetlights to show the way and the police and fire departments to protect it. It's the government that does all the hard work and makes it all possible."

There was more applause, but it was light and uncertain.

"That's what a Williams Administration is all about. We're about providing the infrastructure so that all the dreams of the individual become possible, because without a government strong enough and big enough to do what it takes, nothing is possible. And all of our dreams can happen when the rich pay their fair share."

Shouts of approval rang out along with strong applause.

"My friends, it's taken a long time to fix what the Republicans broke, and we're not finished yet. We need more time to give you the country you deserve! If you vote for the other side, they'll just give you more of what got us into the mess in the first place. Think about us going forward together, about what's good for you, and when you do, I'm confident of your vote for our team."

The crowd roared its endorsement.

"This is Chad Kent with News Global, and with me is Jackson Armitage, deputy campaign manager for what will officially become the Democratic ticket in September." Kent turned to his guest. "What did the president mean by 'You didn't build that,' Jackson?"

"He meant what he said. For many people, and certainly for African Americans, given their history in this country, government is the only answer. And even the rich need the helping hand of a central government to foster their success."

"How do you think the president's speech will go over with moderates and independents?"

"It'll go over well, Chad, when those groups consider what the future will be all about and that President Williams is the only way to achieve that vision."

"Thanks for letting us stop by," Burdette said. "You remember Nelson Evers, don't you?"

"Ye...yes, I do. Hello, Mr. Evers," said Amber Bustamente.

"Are you okay, Amber?" Evers asked immediately. "You seem a little jumpy."

"I'm okay," she said, looking at Burdette.

Burdette took the cue. "Amber, we were hoping to catch up with Nathan. Is he around?"

"N...no, he's not. Nathan's in Texas for a few days, then Colorado and Iowa."

"Working on election stuff, is he?"

"Yeah, I guess so. He's supposed to check on a bunch of equipment that's already out there, but he's checkin' in at the state capitals as well. Gotta make contact with the higher-ups, he said."

"Something is bothering you. What's goin' on?" Burdette asked, managing to sound both casual and concerned.

"I guess I'm all messed up."

Rather than respond, Burdette reached out and let her hand rest on Amber's forearm.

"I want to leave that son of a bitch," she said, squeezing back tears. "But I just can't. I guess I need him more'n he needs me." She broke down.

"It's okay, Amber. We're here to listen." Burdette waited. "I'm wondering what changed your mind. When you called me, you were pretty upset."

"Oh, I know."

"Is the same thing bothering you? All that stuff he said about fixing the election?"

"I suppose so. I know I was really pissed at him when I called you."

"But he did say all those things, didn't he?"

"Oh, yeah. I didn't make any of that up."

Burdette breathed a sigh of relief and glanced at Evers, now another witness to the admission. "I just want to make sure I heard what you said, because that's pretty big stuff."

"What I said, I said. He thinks he's pretty cool because they're gonna fix the election—him and McCord."

"Who will do all the work?"

"I think most of it will be Nathan—right from the office on Madison Road."

"But Nathan isn't that political, is he? How will he know what to do exactly?"

"From what he said, they would have to have somebody else to guide him."

"Oh, so there will be someone who's not a SoftSec employee?" Evers asked, ever so easily.

"All night long or whatever it takes, he told me the other day." She brushed away tears as she spoke, and didn't look at either of them. "Nathan didn't know the details, but just said it could be an all-nighter for him, McCord, and whoever else."

Elated that Bustamente was actually filling in some gaps, she proceeded. "You know, Amber, we're awfully glad you felt you could talk to us, but you know, this is too big for us to keep just between us."

Bustamente suddenly looked up, first at Evers, and then she let her gaze land on Burdette. She looked at the person across from her, a third her size, and asked, incredulously, "You mean you'll have to make it an official report?"

Burdette had seen such behavior before and knew that Evers had seen it a thousand times. The boyfriend or girlfriend spills the beans and thinks the investigator is really a priest, bound by the seal of confession. "Well, naturally," she began, her tone as sympathetic as she could make it. "If this is true, someone will have to deal with it."

Immediately, she regretted the phrase "deal with it" and all its connotations.

"You mean he might be arrested?"

"That we don't know," Evers said firmly, "but what happens next is above our pay grade, if you know what I mean."

"Oh, I don't know," she mumbled, the words conveying an image of a building about to crumble. "I can't be responsible for something like that."

"Who else might know about this?" Evers knew it was a long shot.

"Nobody. He wouldn't tell nobody but me."

"Do you know if he's had any second thoughts? His conscience beginning to bother him?" Burdette said.

"Nutsy?" she said, her voice weepy. "I mean, Nathan? Hell no!" He thinks it's cool as hell to be the big kingmaker."

"And you still think that's a no-no for our country, don't you?"

"Of course, I do, but I can't rat him out, can I? I love the stupid shit. He's all I got."

"But Amber, we can't forget what you told us."

"Yes, you can. You can forget we ever talked."

With a voice that was both gentle and firm, Evers said, "Doesn't work that way. Now we have to make a report, one way or the other."

"Can't I be a secret witness, or somethin'?"

"Down the road, that'll be somebody else's call," Burdette said. "But we have to put your name in the report 'cause they're gonna want to know where we heard something like this. See what I mean?"

Bustamente leaned back into the couch, attempting to disappear into what cushion was left. "If I can't be secret, I'll deny I ever talked to you."

"Of course, there is such a thing as a confidential witness," Burdette said. "The security officer and whoever needs to know will see your name, but Nathan won't be able to see your identity if he asks for his report under the Privacy Act. Remember me mentioning that?"

"Yeah. Well, okay. I guess we could do it that way, but I'm kinda scared about all this. Make sure your report says so. Okay?"

"Don't' worry." Burdette then tried a slightly different tack. "Amber, you talked a lot about leaving Nathan, but now you sound like you love him more than your country." She could see Evers rolling his eyes.

Bustamente hesitated. "I do love my country." She hesitated again. "But why is it my responsibility to save it?"

On the curb outside the lighted windows of the ice cream shop, Burdette exhaled, as if to squeeze out every molecule of carbon dioxide humanly possible. "Whew! Thank you, God! She confirmed it, added to it, and at least agreed to own up to it."

"You're lucky as hell, Mare. She coulda told us to get the hell out, and we'd have had nothin' but our notebooks."

"Of course, if Nathan won't be back until the end of July, we can't talk to him until then."

"I don't think they'll want us to wait that long. I'll bet we go with what you've got and wait for it to hit the fan."

Nearby, the desk phone sat, like a mute manservant waiting for its signal. The vice president knew he had a choice to make. He had to be certain of the outcome before any other risks could be considered. Now that he was secure in his position on the ticket, he needed to ensure victory. Otherwise, his one real shot at history—a likely buzzer-beater—would be another thwang on the rim, just another missed shot in the career of Joseph P. Morrison.

His hand shaking about the irrevocable move he was about to make, Morrison picked up the receiver and punched in the direct number to Langley. Managing McCord and his flunky was one thing. CIA Director Warner was quite another.

"Mr. Vice President. To what do I owe the honor, sir?" said Andrew Warner.

"Oh, stop the false courtesy, Drew," Morrison said with a laugh. Then he stopped and said nothing.

"So this is really a serious call. What can I do for you, Joe?"

"I hesitate to ask, because I usually conduct my business quietly. I like it that way—especially around spooks like you guys." He laughed again. "But I need a favor, something only you guys do well."

"We're not killing anybody for you, Joe, not even Angie Tesoro."

"Ha-ha. You're talkin' to a Democrat, not John Whitaker. Maybe he might make such a request."

It was Warner's turn to enjoy the comeback. "So what's up,?"

"I need to meet some people here in DC, or in the outskirts. Leesburg would be okay, I suppose. But it has to be a safe house that my visitors do not remember. And, Drew, it can't be bugged."

"God Almighty, Joe. You know everything we own is bugged."

"Then you'll have to pull the plug for one evening. Can I trust you to do that?"

"Sure. I'll see that it's done, and call you with details, but Leesburg wouldn't be my choice. Let me figure something out."

"Thanks. I need this done ASAP."

"Hi, Kristen. I was just about to call you," said Pete Clancy into his office phone, but he could get no further.

"No friendly greetings today, Pete," Kristen Bartley said flatly. "I got a bone to pick—a big one."

"Is somebody higher up calling about cases?" Clancy could picture her at the desk that used to be his, pelting the blotter with her left index finger while she hammered him with words.

"No. It's me, and I'm high enough. Don't make light of anything I say, Pete, and no small talk. I'm hearing things out in the field, and I don't like them."

"Jesus, Kristen. What are you talking about?"

"Is it true that you've been out in the field bad-mouthing OPM and implying you might not be doing thorough case review?"

"That's not correct, Kristen. Somebody's been turning your crank. What I thought I've been conveying to the field staff is that if they want review off their backs, they're going to have to do a helluva lot better job with their casework before they press the send button."

"That's not good enough, Pete. I'm hearing that you won't be doing review on cases before turning them in."

"Not so, and if I were you, I'd check your sources. If we adopted any reduced review practices or triaged the work in any way, you'd be the first to know. And by the way, if we did that, it would only be a practice that we used at OPM in the good old days."

"Still not good enough. That was then. A contract is a contract, now you're going to tell me that because we give you a few extra cases, you can't handle it? The whole purpose of the privatization exercise was that the private sector could handle anything we threw at it."

"And we can—with the same considerations that customers and businesses do in the private sector. We both know that your customer agencies are supposed to review the casework in full before granting a clearance, and if there's a problem, we're always happy to fix it. The real scandal is the agency isn't reading the case. They're just glancing at your system codes, and if no issue pops up, they give out Top Secrets like candy."

"We're the government, Pete, and we can do any damn thing we want, and if you can't handle what we give you, we'll do it ourselves or find somebody who can. I just hope short-term profit isn't what drives your shareholders."

"No one ever thought OPM would be both our customer and competitor. Right now, there's no one else but NIS, and the only way you can do the work is if you steal our people from us."

"And that'll be easy. Government pay and benefits have crept up over the past ten years to the point where we pay as well as you do—and it's a lifetime job."

Clancy knew she held the best cards. "You're making it impossible for NIS to perform under this contract."

Silence, then line buzz, filled his ear.

Clancy waited five minutes until the steam began to leave his already broiling office. The agenda Bartley had outlined months before had become a palpable presence in his everyday work life, and their just-ended conversation made the wound fresh. Were the rumors true that people representing the new owners were already undercutting him? Was it true the board planned to replace him with someone more profit minded?

What the new bottom-line guys didn't understand was that profits could be reasonable and forever if NIS kept its focus on quality and thoroughness. Running the business any other way only played into the hands of Kristen Bartley. He didn't know if she could execute her plan, but there were few ways to stop a clever woman, he'd learned long ago.

Ah, well, he'd had a good run, and he couldn't stay forever. He took a deep breath and called his customer back. The chill he felt on the line was what she must have intended.

"What is it, Pete? I'm very busy and don't wish to debate this matter further. I'll just tell you that if I hear any more garbage like that, we'll go for your throat."

"Understood. That's not why I called, however. You'll remember at the beginning of our last conversation I had been about to call you."

"Well?"

"You'll also remember the USEAC cases you called me about some time ago. There's a development with them, and you'll have a memo from me on it no later than tomorrow morning."

"You mean the cases that are already late?"

"Please don't exaggerate, Kristen. It doesn't serve you well. All the cases but two were submitted and complete well before the deadline. We were about to complete both McCord and Conaway when the latter's live-in girlfriend called our investigator—the same one you called and complained about, by the way—and told her over the phone that McCord and Conaway were going to tamper with the presidential election via the EAC contract."

"That's crazy. I'll make sure the vice president knows about it pronto."

"That's the problem. According to our source, what SoftSec will do this November may be at the behest of Vice President Morrison."

"That's even crazier, Pete. So how many witnesses do you have on this, and why would we trust this investigator—Burdette was it?"

Clancy could hear the tension frizz the electronic air between them. "Nelson Evers, one our senior guys and an old OPM-er, was with Burdette at the first in-person interview with the girlfriend. Obviously, he wasn't privy to the phone call, but as they should, they called me, and we decided to give her a day or two, then visit her in person. Evers and Burdette did so together, and the girlfriend gave them even more damning information. We were going to see Conaway again, but he was out west visiting various states, setting up the interface between SoftSec and the state capitals."

"Pete, this is unbelievable. What makes anybody think they can steal a whole election?"

"Apparently, it's simpler than either of us would ever have thought. This won't happen in all the states, by the way, just a few of the so-called battleground states, plus a few others where things might be undecided. My memo will give you all we've got, but it's from only one witness who now insists on confidentiality."

"One witness?"

"But isn't that what we're here for? To capture information like this and give it to our customer?"

"But the vice president? They'll laugh us out of town."

"Not us, Kristen. You. And isn't this what the public sector is here for? Before it's too late?"

After they hung up, Bartley began to perspire as she thought through the ramifications of accusing the Vice President of the United States of a high crime. What did the Constitution say about vice presidents? What would a charge like this do to her agenda for refederalizing the program?

She remembered vividly what Jefferson Harper's vice president did to OPM when the FBI developed derogatory information on too many Harper appointees. What would happen to OPM and its vaunted personnel security investigations program?

With her chest still pounding, she placed both hands on her desk blotter and pushed herself up to full height, as if she could rise above the unsavory aroma beginning to saturate her air. The vice president wasn't some contractor she could dump. He was the number-two federal employee and, perhaps, her next rabbi. She would make no phone calls until after she'd received Clancy's memo. Perhaps not even then.

Off a country road in McLean, Virginia, at a house on Holyrood buried behind leafy birches and ancient rhododendron, the solitary black Escalade, lights off, crept up the drive and paused while Secret Service Agent Marty Cox quietly exited the vehicle and walked on the grass bordering the asphalt. In a minute, he returned and nodded to his charge.

Clad in dark summer slacks, a golf shirt, and a straw plantation hat pulled low, the vice president walked to the front door, the existence of which was marked only by the illuminated doorbell. Otherwise, the house rested in complete darkness.

At the threshold, a man in a black jersey and slacks waited quietly.

Without touching anything, Morrison entered and directed the doorman to wait outside. Following the only light into a dining room with blacked-out windows, he saw seated there the only other parties to the meeting. So quiet were Morrison's steps that Ricky McCord jumped—two feet in the air, it seemed.

"Jesus Christ, Joe. I mean—"

"It's Joe, Ricky. Let's keep it at that. And this is?"

"Joe, this is Nathan Conaway, who is going to work the election-day magic for you."

"Not for me, Ricky, for the American people. Nice to meet you, Nathan. Pardon me if we don't shake hands and if I keep my hat on. It's more comfortable for me that way."

"Sure, Joe, but what's with all the hocus-pocus," McCord said. "We've been seen in public before, right?"

"That was then, Ricky, and this is now—much closer to show time—and this meeting couldn't have been held at a restaurant or a golf course, don't you see?"

"Yeah, I guess so."

"Nathan? We haven't met before, but Ricky will tell you I'm serious about everything I do. Are we clear?"

Conaway nodded, beads of perspiration forming on his forehead.

"So let's skip all the other pleasantries," Morrison began. When we're finished, you'll be escorted back to Dulles and dropped there in time for your flight to Cincinnati. And this meeting never happened. Are we clear on that?"

There was hurried acquiescence. Conaway began, as if he were a software salesman at a techie convention. "The best way to demo this, sir, is by example. These three laptops represent a mock-up of the 2000 presidential election setup in Florida. I don't need to tell you how that turned out. On this computer," he said, pointing to the leftmost one, "are the results for all the counties as they were originally reported to Tallahassee. So here you see Volusia County with 45 percent of the vote for Bush and 55 percent for Grayson. Here's Palm Beach County with 36 to 63 for Grayson, and Gadsden with 32 to 66 for Grayson. On the other side, here's Santa Rosa County with 73 percent for Bush and 26 percent for Grayson; Walton County with 67 to 31, Bush; and Okaloosa, 74 to 24 for Bush.

"So, on election night, sir, Bush apparently had a lead of 1784 votes, and, technically, he won. But that small margin triggered a recount, with Bush eventually winning by less than 600 votes."

"We know all this, Nathan. Where are you going with it?"

"Let's say this second computer, the one in the middle, was me sitting in my office in Cincinnati—but electronically, it was in between each county and the state capital. If we wanted Grayson to win the election—and avoid a recount—here's what we would have done, and we have two choices. We either inflate Grayson's win in the counties where he did win, or we shave votes from Bush where he won strongly but wouldn't miss a few thousand here or there, or we could do both."

"Do both," Morrison suggested.

"OK. Remembering that we need to avoid a recount, Grayson has to win the state by about sixty thousand votes. I recommend we do not change the state's totals, only who gets which votes."

"Agreed."

"There are sixty-seven counties total in the state," Conaway said. "So let's say that in Volusia County, already strong for Grayson, we give him two thousand more votes, and we do something similar in Jefferson, Leon, Dade, Saint Lucie, and Palm Beach Counties. With a few clicks here and there, we come up with twenty-four thousand votes. Now let's go to the strong Bush counties I mentioned, along with others, and we come up with another eighteen thousand. "

Conaway's voice rasped with excitement. "You might remember that Republicans won fifteen of the twenty-three congressional districts in the state. By turning over more votes, one way or the other, from the other forty-some counties, Grayson would win our mock election by about sixty-seven thousand votes, give or take a few. And the Democrats would win twelve of the twenty-three congressional races. And that all appears on laptop number three, here on the right, representing the Tallahassee official counts."

Morrison pulled up a chair behind Conaway and sat down, mouth hanging wide open. "It would have been that easy?"

"Well, in 2000 the right software wasn't in place in many of the states we would have needed."

"According to what you just showed me, Grayson needed help in only one."

They continued on like this for several minutes.

"This is incredible—better than I thought," Morrison said. "It's good you're ready to go in all those states, Nathan, but when we get right down to it, perhaps we'll target a smaller number someplace where we want it to count the most." The vice-president became ebullient. "After all, we don't want to be greedy, do we?" With that, he stood up and slapped the backs of both men, as if they'd enjoyed a good joke after a round of golf.

"All that'll be necessary, Joe," McCord said, "is for someone with the right political savvy to give us guidance on where to turn the votes over to the Williams–Morrison ticket and how many to turn to make it appear reasonable."

"And you're sure there can be no trail?"

"If you think about it, sir," Conaway said, "with electronic voting, and no paper, how could there be?"

Morrison nodded. "I'll see that you get the expert you need. You'll be doing all of this from your Cincinnati offices, Ricky?"

"Yes, sir."

"That'll make everything easy," Morrison said, upbeat and smiling.

"This is Nelson Evers, Janice," said Cincinnati's senior investigator when he reached the voice-mail box of his regional manager in Columbus late on the last Sunday of July. He doubted she would check it over the weekend.

"Since our last telecon about the Amber Bustamente accusation against SoftSec and the vice president, I've been thinking a lot about my experience at the IRS in Covington and what that woman said about the election. I know you're gonna think I'm off my toot, but I think those two events are connected, and if more information comes out that this administration is manipulating the news, I'm gonna more than think it.

"I'm gonna know it like I know you're Mayella Washington's sister. How do I know that? When Marlyn and I came to Columbus a few weeks ago—when we first talked to Pete Clancy about this whole thing—you remember we were in your office? I noticed your college diploma from the University of Dayton and there it was—Janice Michelle Washington. I didn't have to work hard to check that out. Only people I ever knew who would give both their daughters the same middle name? The Washingtons—but I never remembered you as a kid in Mount Auburn.

"You know, Janice, you should have mentioned that when the whole IRS thing first came up at our meeting a few months ago, and when I called you about Mayella just recently. The fact that you didn't makes me wonder just what you're all about.

"So for now, I'll keep this to myself. But I gotta tell you, I'm this close to writin' one big memo—not to you or Pete or the attorney general, but to the media, people who won't drop it down the toilet.

"I'll be waitin' for your call Monday morning. Good night. But I don't know how you sleep, sister."

AUGUST

Rasmussen Tracking Poll
August 3-6
Williams 47%
Hardy 45%

"I sleep very well, Mr. Evers," Janice Dern spat into the phone when she reached her subordinate. "How dare you talk to me that way? I'm saving that voice message and will use it to fire your ass when the time comes."

"Perfect. I want you to save that message because it lays out your credibility problem for anyone to hear. Just remember, Mrs. Dern, I'm retirement age, divorced, and my kids can feed themselves, so I've got nothing to lose."

"I don't know what it is that you don't get. Every other black man and woman in this country gets it. Why can't you?"

"Oh, I get it, but I'm tired of being the bought-and-paid-for, down-in-the ghetto black man that white Democrats still think they own, but I guess you're happy being in the bag for any Democrat that comes along. And when it's a black politician, he thinks he's entitled to our vote. What's the matter with you, Janice? You've succeeded in ways that your sister hasn't—and you were that scrawny little kid no one ever noticed. Shame on me for takin' so long to figure it out. So, when're you gonna break free of the old chains?"

"There're no chains on me, brother, but you better know this, Nelson Evers: you are swimmin' against the tsunami, and when it washes over you, you'll be gone, and nobody will care."

"Nice. You and Mayella like to talk about how I should kowtow to the black tide, but look how you treat me. You didn't even trust me enough to tell me she's your sister, and you know what they're doin' down there is just plain wrong, now, isn't it?"

"Whether it's wrong or right is not my problem. I just hope you don't become my problem."

After hanging up with Nelson Evers, Dern pulled the iPhone from her purse and called Mayella's cell. "Remember when you called me and whined about the uppity black who works for me?" she said after her sister answered. "The one who was so high and mighty with you about what you all are doin' to Republicans at the Center?"

"Yeah. Nelson Evers. I knew he was gonna be a big pain in the ass when we used to walk to school together over fifty years ago."

"Well, you were right, sis. I had never told him we were sisters, and now he's got a buzz on about that, what you're doin' on the job, and somethin' else that's come up. He says he's gonna go to the media about it one of these days. So just watch your p's and q's down there, y'hear?"

"Got it, Jannie, and don't you worry, Nelson Evers ain't no big deal."

Mayella Washington trod the well-worn path into the Center director's office and made Evan Hughes's already busy day busier when she relayed the latest development on Nelson Evers. In turn, as the union chief expected, he hit his speed dial for a number in Washington, DC, at which moment she turned and headed out of his office, the smile on her face hidden from his view. Not my problem anymore, she thought, and she returned to her comfortable office not very far down the hall.

"I know what our marching orders are, Mr. Hellman," Evan Hughes said into the phone. "But no one here will want to carry them out if this NIS guy is bird-doggin' us."

Hellman didn't answer right away. "I'll have to make a call I'd rather not, Hughes, and both of us should assume OPM's contractor will get the message."

Everything in Kristen Bartley's career was built upon her matchless understanding of computing capabilities and the boundless opportunities in data mining. Yet, her reliance on the digital universe did not preclude an old-fashioned, physical Rolodex, painstakingly kept current. She thumbed through it for the second time.

Then she saw the name. Remy Carlson. 2010. The Executive Development Retreat at Johns Hopkins University, sponsored by OPM. When the name flipped to her gaze, she saw it as the manna she craved. She exhaled completely. *Be careful what you wish for!*

Pete Clancy's memo three days earlier made her wrestle with the responsibilities. Ordinarily, she would speak to OPM's director, who reported directly to Vice President Morrison. But then the circle of people with knowledge of the memo would widen rapidly, and that would anger a man with a deserved reputation for being a bit off plumb. More people knowing about it would also limit the options.

Why bring a possible scandal upon the administration when the allegation was likely the figment of a lively imagination? Why expose ourselves to scrutiny and ridicule?

Sipping a cup of hot orange tea, she let her mind do its work. *And if the allegation is true, why take a chance on a Winston Hardy administration, one likely to cut government to size rather than grow the federal employee base? Why not reelect a man whose big government polices so nicely coincides with my own agenda?*

Bartley reached for her phone and punched in the number Carlson had given her in the week they'd become pals a few years earlier. Mulitple rings meant she'd have to leave a message. *What will I say?* Finally, the younger woman's voice came on the line, and in a moment, she remembered their friendship in Baltimore.

"Why, Kristen, how nice of you to call." After exchanging a few pleasantries, Carlson said, "What I remember most about you from the program was that you're a person who does everything with a reason, and while I'm flattered that you called, I suspect there's something you want to say to me."

"Remy," Bartley said, laughing out loud, "am I that easy to read? I must be. And you're right. I have a very ticklish situation, something that's come up in a very ordinary background investigation, but something the vice president would not want to deal with officially, if you know what I mean. If I sent you a memo from me to him in a sealed envelope, would you be good enough to walk it in and see that he opens it immediately?"

"Oooh—cloak and dagger! For you, Kristen, I would do it because you're assuring me such a favor to you would not be a waste of my time or Joe Morrison's?"

"Most definitely, Remy. You won't regret doing this, and you can relay every word of this conversation to your boss."

"If you say it's legit, consider it done."

"Mr. Vice President, I have a sealed envelope from a friend, Kristen Bartley, who heads OPM's Federal Investigations Service," Remy Carlson said.

"What's it all about, Remy?" Morrison looked up from his desk, interested.

"I don't know, sir. She called me and said you'd be grateful if I delivered this envelope to you—unopened. She said you'd want to open it right away."

Morrison raised his eyebrows. "Okay, let's have it." When Carlson left the office, he slit the envelope and was stunned by its contents. *How could a little pissant outfit like OPM find out about something like this?* Aloud, he said, "Jesus, they don't even carry guns."

The memo was a page and a half and laid out in fair detail the names of the people under investigation, the names of the witnesses, one in particular, and the names of the NIS investigators. "Damn those people!" He read on. *Thank God there's only one witness, the girlfriend. Two, if you count the idiot who spilled the beans. And McCord!* "What a dumb ass!" For the next few minutes, he thought about the way forward.

It didn't take long to conclude that options, plural, were a luxury for others. His only choice was to plunge on with the original plan. He had worked too hard not to have his chance. And he was not about to be forced into a resignation "for health reasons" so that an appointed vice president could duplicate Gerald Ford's ascendancy.

One thing is for sure: we're going to be reelected, and if Williams loses his battle with cancer, well then, political nature will take its course. And nothing—nobody—will get in the way!

Clipped to the second page was Bartley's business card, a gift for which he was grateful, because he wouldn't have to involve Carlson in any communications link. *This can wait a bit.* Carlson would be expecting a reaction to the envelope, and he would provide it.

In the outer office, he paused by her desk and said, as casually as he could manage, "Thanks. That was interesting stuff, and I'm glad you brought it in."

"Is everything all right, sir?"

"Sure is, Remy. Sure is. Anything else cookin' down the hall?"

"That I don't know, sir," she said, and she laughed as if to indicate there was always something cooking in the political kitchen that was the Oval Office. "But there is one thing that's odd. Actually, it's been odd for a long time and I meant to mention it before, but I saw something recently that makes it even more curious."

"Oh, what's that?" he asked, knowing she wouldn't mention it unless it was worth mentioning.

"I think you've met Gordon Hellman, Director of the IRS. I've noticed him here in the West Wing quite a few times, and that's pretty unusual for a guy in his position. So I asked. It turns out he's visited this building well over a hundred times over the last three-plus years."

Morrison raised his eyebrows in interest.

"Can you imagine that?" she asked, rhetorically. "And then, a few weeks ago, I think, I saw Sondra Thompson walking out of that little second-floor conference room. She was mad as hell. In another minute, out walked Gordon Hellman. I don't know what that was all about, sir, but it was weird, even for this place."

Morrison chuckled. "I'm glad you love your job so much, and I won't ask what you were doing hanging around the second-floor hall, but I'm always glad when you do. Thanks again."

His own curiosity piqued, Vice President Morrison had only to step out of his office, turn right, walk down the hall, and enter what everyone called "the Beehive." Sondra Thompson's office was, indeed, a busy place, but serendipitously, she was in and available.

"Joe, what brings you down to the slums?"

"Slums? You mean where the Williams Administration power center really exists?" The two enjoyed their banter, and he knew Thompson would always give him deference, but not her loyalty.

"Actually, I'm happy you dropped in. We have a little problem with one of your agencies, and perhaps, you can sic your dogs on this one."

"Anything to help. What's up?"

Thompson inhaled deeply and said, "Sit down, Joe. I need to bring you up to speed." For the several minutes, she described in the broadest of terms the administration's ongoing meetings with IRS management. "These sessions involve highly sensitive tax matters and certain organizations applying for non-profit status." She paused. "For your protection, however, I should not give you any further information, unless you want to forfeit your deniability."

Morrison nodded. "I'll accept that, for now. So what's the problem?"

"The problem is with OPM's contractor, NIS. It seems there's an investigator stationed in Cincinnati—some guy named Nelson Evers—who has begun to make loud noises about the so-called political atmosphere around the IRS Center in Covington, and in particular, about possible union involvement. Oh, by the way, Evers is African American, if you can believe it."

"Interesting." At the same time he couldn't believe that lightning was striking twice. *What dumb bastards! Al Grayson might have solved a problem one way, but I'll solve it another.* "So, I take it you're dumping this one in my lap, then?"

"Joe, the president would be grateful if you made sure this did not become an election-year problem."

"Your saying this request is coming from Averell?"

"I didn't say that, Joe," she said with a laugh. "I said he'd be grateful.'"

"I understand perfectly." He started to leave, and then, a bit theatrically, turned back to Thompson, winked, and said, "For you, Sondra, consider it done."

The vice president passed several people in the hallway but said not a word to them as he strode back to his office with a purpose. In one sense, he resented being Williams's fix-it guy when the man barely gave him the time of day, but loyalty and persistence had their own rewards.

First, he called Ricky McCord, and though tempted to read him the riot act, he kept the conversation lighthearted and purposeful. "How are things going, Ricky?"

"Very well, sir. Our team has nearly all of the fifteen states connected to our network, and we plan to have everything hooked up before the end of September."

"Things have gone according to plan?"

"Definitely. And by the way, Morisa Rivera sends her regards."

"Any issues out there, Ricky?"

"Not a thing. The background investigations are finished and the EAC security officer called to tell me he expects clearances to come through in a few days."

"That's excellent. Keep up the good work. We'll be talking soon."

Next, Morrison retrieved the business card he'd seen earlier and called the number. An unusual step to be sure, but a necessary one.

"Is this Ms. Kristen Bartley?" he inquired easily when she answered.

"Yes, and how can I help you, sir?"

"This is Vice President Morrison calling to thank you for trusting Remy Carlson to pass me a message." On the other end, he heard the expected gasp of disbelief.

"Yes, Mr. Vice President. I might have thought you were one of my prankster friends, but no one knew of my call to Remy. I hope you found my memo useful, sir."

"To be sure, Kristen. To be sure. First, let me thank you for avoiding an unnecessary embarrassment for this administration, all because an apparent braggart came to a terrible misunderstanding about the purpose of the EAC contract. I can assure you, there's nothing untoward here, and nothing inappropriate will occur because of this contract in the upcoming presidential election. Far from it. Mr. McCord's company will ensure the votes are counted accurately the first time around and that no one will be disenfranchised. What's more, I apologize that you have had to deal with this nonsense. I'll take care of it from this end."

"Thank you, sir, for your good words, but you needn't have explained anything to me. What the woman alleged was simply not believable, and certainly not corroborated."

"Totally correct. You appear to be a quick study, and I'll remember it."

"Thank you, sir. Is there anything else?"

"Actually, there is, I'm afraid. It's about NIS, your principal contractor?"

"Yes, sir. You'll remember that NIS was created by the Harper Administration in 1996."

"Yes, I'm well aware that privatizing your program was a Democratic initiative, but times—and attitudes—have changed. This administration is more about having a federal work force that will be more manageable and responsive in carrying out policy than a contractor. This NIS has proven to be too..." He was about to say, 'good.' "Too... independent, shall we say."

"I couldn't agree more, sir."

"Ahh, a kindred spirit. I'm aware of your career at Treasury before coming to OPM. You'll no doubt have a brilliant future."

"Thank you, sir."

"Well, Kristen, there's no time to think about refederalizing your program like the present. I take it you would not object if the director of OPM received guidance from this office requiring you to make that happen?"

"Not at all, Mr. Vice President. It would be a pleasure."

Elation energized Kristen Bartley as she contemplated the future of her program, a totally federal entity, once again. For two hours, she made preliminary notes outlining her plans. All at once, she stopped.

The Vice President of the United States didn't need to call me. Or did he? Why hadn't he had Remy make the call? She sat staring at the wall, desperately wishing the next logical thought would not take shape in her thoroughly quick mind. *He called me because he told no one about the accusation.* If it were laughably untrue, he wouldn't have wanted to bother with it, and Carlson would have called with instructions on how to proceed. *Why would he need to control NIS?*

In her mind's eye, Bartley saw the next questions and answers attacking her thoughts out of the mist. Desperately, she wanted them to evaporate: *Did he take the trouble to call because it was true? Yessss,* her conscience hissed. You've just been bribed, the inner voice shouted over the rumble in her chest. And you loved it.

Thwang! The Spalding Never-Flat slapped the rim and fell easily into the waiting hands of Marty Cox. "Nice shot, Joe. Just a little off," he said to Vice President Morrison, as they breathed in the sauna-like August air clinging to the District.

"Yeah, just a little. Story of my life, Marty."

"Couldn't be. You're the vice president of the United States. A heartbeat away and all that."

"Well, you've got a point there. And in the second term, I won't have much time for basketball."

"Why is that?"

"I don't want to be indelicate, Marty, but the president will be over seventy when he finishes his term." Morrison made sure his eyes met those of the agent. He knew that his listener would be in tune with the same rule of courtesy around the White House. No one ever used the word *if* when referring to a president's longevity and the possibility of an unfinished term. Unspoken though it was, the word's presence was as palpable as the 93 percent humidity drenching them. "And that means that I will likely have more duties and responsibilities than at present. In fact, I can virtually assure you of that."

"You mean like some cabinet positions reporting to you?"

"Perhaps, Marty. Perhaps. Homeland Security could be one," he suggested, knowing that such an assignment would carry great weight with his listener, given that the Secret Service was an agency under the broad DHS umbrella. "But of course, that hasn't been settled yet, so our little conversation has to remain here. Right?"

"You got it, sir," the agent responded.

The change in courtesy wasn't lost on Morrison, who said, "You know, Marty, there's a federal contractor causing some inconvenience, shall we say. It'd be nice if they got a message."

"Say more."

"Have you heard of NIS, OPM's contractor that does backgrounds for about a hundred federal agencies?"

"Sure. In fact, OPM does some work for us. Most of them are former feds—Secret Service even—pretty good guys, most of them."

"But they're not feds now, Marty. They're not part of us, if you know what I mean. Now they're private and independent, and they don't seem to have much sense about what they hear in the field. Unlike you guys, who know when the golden rule should apply."

"I know what you mean, sir."

"I'd ask some others to do this for us, but we—the president and I—were hoping you might make a few phone calls. You know, keep this all in the family."

"That's no big deal. We can do that."

"You're right, Marty. It's not a big deal. All we want you to do is scare the crap out of one or two people—maybe it'll help them get the idea. If I give you the information you need, do you think your guys can take care of this for us—quietly?"

"Anything you say, sir."

"It's Joe, Marty. Always Joe."

"If you elect me and Joe Morrison," President Averell Williams told the carefully chosen crowd in Piqua, Ohio, "I can promise you one thing." With his tie off, he stood white-shirted and jacketless in the ninety-degree heat, delivering what had become a polished stump speech, punctuated occasionally by an airborne hand purposed with a pointing index finger. "No matter who the Republicans nominate for president and vice president, no matter what they propose, and no matter what they claim about me, the best bet for the American people is to give us the levers of power for a second term."

The applause allowed him to take a breath while he panned the audience and saw what he wanted: unwavering, unquestioning support. "Why? Because I won't ever have to run for reelection again, and that means you can count on me to do what I said I would when I ran in 2008. Then, I promised to fundamentally transform America, and regrettably, I am only part way done. So here's my pledge to you: if you reelect me, I will appoint the right people, I will make the right policies, and if Congress will not enact them, I will break that gridlock and issue the right executive orders to make the right policies real."

Cheers broke out among the faithful. "And what kind of policies will they be? You know what they'll be. They'll be the kind that allows everyone in this country to have an equal shot at a bright future, the kind that'll make everyone pay their fair share to spread a social justice that gives the least of us the same rights as the richest of us."

He talked over the crowd's loving noise. "And that's why another four years will give us the chance to fix this economy, to finish what we started, and will allow us to transform America for you!" The noise grew louder and broader as it filled the air with the sweet music of voting levers pulled for the Williams-Morrison ticket.

As the president exited the stage, Jackson Armitage walked up and spoke in his ear. "Sir, I've been asked to pass a message that Secretary Grantham wishes a moment. Staff has a secure connection for you this way," he said, leading his candidate off to a side hallway blocked at both ends by Secret Service agents.

Having just enjoyed the applause and adulation he appreciated most about his job, President Williams resented the Secretary's intrusion on the campaign. He snatched up the phone. "This is not the best time, Emerson. What's up?"

"Sorry, Mr. President," he said, as if reading his mind. "Ambassador Stevens has sent an urgent cable to my office requesting a protective detail bodyguard. I had not mentioned to you that last month he requested at least thirteen additional security personnel, citing what is becoming an unpredictable situation in Libya. I should also point out that our Regional Security Officer has concluded that the risk to US officials there is high."

Williams let silence reign while he gathered his patience. "I understand, but I do not see how this requires us to abort our current policy there. Insulting the local populace with squads of heavily armed escorts will only inflame tensions."

"They will also protect our people there, sir."

"I see no reason to alter our course, Mr. Secretary."

Winston Hardy held up both hands, as if their combined waves would hold back the volume of applause greeting him in Norfolk, Virginia. "It's always good to be back in a state where the likes of Patrick Henry, George Washington, and yes, even Thomas Jefferson once regaled their neighbors with their reasoned burning for liberty."

Warm applause, if not rocking excitement, greeted his remarks. "Here in a bastion of freedom is where I come to share with you my choice for Vice President of the United States. Fortunately for me and for all of you, there are many fine candidates from whom I could have chosen.

"I am deeply honored to introduce you to one of our country's outstanding US senators, a two-term incumbent who knows the halls of Congress as I know the Rocky Mountains, a person whose legislative skills are unparalleled, and not least, a wife and mother of four. I give you Olivia Johnson Smith of Indiana."

Cheers, applause, and pandemonium charged the nearly full basketball arena at Old Dominion University when Senator Smith, a prim forty-two-year-old, entered the spotlight with a wave and a smile and stepped to the microphone.

"I am a Hoosier and proud of it," she began. "But I am prouder still to represent my fellow Americans as Governor Hardy's choice for vice president. When we take the stage in Tampa two weeks from now, the American people will know they have a choice for their future. Not four more years of dithering ineptitude! Not four more years of hardworking people unable to find a decent job! Not four more years in a world where we may be likable, but not respected!"

Unorchestrated noise, loud and long, filled the air.

"Yes, my friends, what Governor Hardy and I hope to bring is simple leadership. Leadership that creates twelve million new jobs in the next four years. Leadership that breaks congressional gridlock with sound legislative proposals that a majority can live by. Leadership so that, more than E. F. Hutton, the world listens when an American president speaks!"

The crowd jumped to its feet and roared its approval as Winston Hardy stood by with a smile as broad as the foothills of the Rockies. "And the candidate to restore American greatness for a sound economy, a responsible congress, and an unstable planet, is no one but Governor Winston Hardy!"

Still standing, the crowd crazed themselves with a withering noise of endorsement. Hardy and Smith walked back and forth across the stage smiling and waving, nearly blinded by the constant blinking of flashed photos being recorded for family histories. Off to the side, the media mavens spun silky webs of news snippets they knew would be played over and over for several hours.

"Well, are you willing to compromise?" Marlyn Burdette's voice purred into her cell phone.

"Compromise how?" asked Paul Gladston. "We've been dating for less than two months and we're talking about compromise? What happened to individual rights run rampant and personal selfishness?"

"Are you mocking me?" She laughed, half hoping her all-too-serious boyfriend was doing just that.

"I would never mock one of the little people," he responded, whimsically referring to the less-than-intimidating distance between the ground and the top of her head.

"Watch it, smart guy. This could be one of your shorter romances."

"Haha. Nice play on words. So romance, is it? Well, now you're talkin', but just what compromise do I have to make?"

"Well, I know it's your birthday, and in the era of female rights and responsibilities, I should drive to Columbus, but if you're interested, why not come down here and take me to one of my favorite restaurants?"

Gladston laughed out loud for what seemed a full minute, and he heard her laughing, too, but in embarrassment. "Now there's a let's-meet-halfway proposal if I ever heard one. We compromise by me driving a hundred miles to take you to dinner. Such a deal you have for me."

"So we have a deal?" she asked, the limitless gall lost in her laughter.

"Deal. I'm just hoping your favorite restaurant isn't some three-star wallet whopper. Remember, I'm a low-paid NIS sleuth just like you."

"Don't worry. I was going to take you to Via Vite on Fountain Square, but they're completely booked."

"Wait. You already checked? Why you so-and so."

"That's what you get for making fun of the little people," she tittered. "But Teller's in Hyde Park Square has room for us at seven. Can you make it?"

"Pick you up at six thirty."

After a quiet, but delicious dinner on Teller's less-noisy second floor, they agreed to a walk around the square. "I didn't know you liked this area so much," Paul said, agreeing to a stroll only because it was with Mare.

"Actually, I don't. I lied. Do you know where we are?" she asked as they stepped into the flow of foot traffic outside Teller's front door.

"Not my territory," he said slowly, cautiously. "Why would you lie to me?"

"Trust me. C'mon, let's get across this traffic lane and sit in the park for a few minutes."

"Mare, just what the hell is going on?" he demanded, becoming warier by the second.

"Wait." She led him to a bench in the island park that centered the square. They found a bench in the deepening evening shade.

"In this heat, I'm going to be patient and trustful only a few seconds longer."

"Sit. Check out the apartment just above Graeter's. It's where Nathan and Amber live."

"Jesus H. Christ, Mare. Just what the hell do you hope to accomplish?"

"I don't know. It just feels good to do more than listen to the bull crap people like Conaway and McCord pour on us. Anyway, I was curious."

"And you wanted an accomplice. Lucky me."

"Don't be sarcastic. You're right, though, I had no idea what we might see. Maybe it was a dumb idea after all."

"Thanks. Do you believe Amber?"

"Yeah, I do. She'd have no reason to lie to us about any of it. She's a mixed-up technocrat who doesn't realize what she's gotten herself into."

"You're probably right about that. So are you telling me we came here just so you could look up into their windows?"

She turned to look him in his deep, inviting eyes. "That was one reason. The other was that I wanted you here, in Cincinnati, with me."

"If that's baloney, I'd like my sandwich with mustard and mayo, please."

Mare said nothing but looked right into his eyes with a message that was unmistakable.

"Well, then, why didn't you say so?" He grasped her hand and led her to his car.

Two hours later, as the very last sliver of Saturday's sun crept through the front windows of Mare's Ellison Avenue apartment in Mount Lookout, the two lay next to each other, a glistening sheen of lovemaking bathing each of them. She lay on her stomach, the beautiful curves of her naked backside completing a perfectly proportioned body. Paul lay face up, and as he studied the ceiling, he wondered if there was a single square inch of her body that he had not kissed at least once. He leaned over and kissed the nape of her neck again, just where reddish-brown hair began to cover the flush of her skin. She smelled of a body lotion that took him into another state of pleasant reverie.

"I think you like to use your lips," she whimpered.

"But you know that's not all I can use. Want me to show you?"

Mare turned over and clung to him, nosing his cheeks and lips. "I dare you."

For another hour they caressed like two people who had been deprived of sensory pleasure their entire lives. Their love was greedy, grateful, grand.

Finally, she said, "You know, Paul, I'm a little scared."

"You're scared! I'm the one who should be scared. Hell, I know hardly anything about the woman I just slept with," he said, a mischievous smile accompanying his words.

"Okay, wise guy, here's the one-sentence bio. I grew up on a farm in southeastern Indiana—not more than fifty miles from here, in fact—and I loved every minute of it."

"That's it? That's all you're going to tell me?"

"Well, I went to Xavier University here in town—BS in education. I never mentioned that little bit to Amber Bustamente. And I'm glad I didn't."

"More. I want more. What was it like growing up in Indiana?"

Mare didn't hesitate. "What I remember most were the fabulous chicken dinners our church used to throw at the end of the summer. People came from miles around to feast on the homegrown everything and the best fried chicken you could eat."

"For a little person, you sure are a foodie."

Mare smacked his bare backside. "Hey, let's get serious. This whole thing is really bothering me."

"Now there's a non sequitur," he said with a smile. "Just what are you scared of?"

"You know. This whole election thing. The IRS crap. Usually, I could care less about politics and stuff like that, but I'm beginning to wonder if I need to get interested just to survive."

"It's all about greed for power. I suppose that's where we're different, Mare. I do care about this stuff. What you and Evers experienced at the IRS Center is positively crazy, and people thinking it's perfectly okay to fix an entire presidential election. That's the real scary part. We're becoming like the two-bit banana republics we used to hear about and laugh."

"You're scaring me even more," she said clinging tightly.

"I don't mean to. This is still America, and on a totally personal level, you shouldn't be scared of anything. I mean, what're they going to do to you?"

"I don't know. I wonder what this country got itself into with Williams."

"You don't mean because he's black."

"Hell, no. Dammit, he seems like a decent guy. I voted for him because I felt the same way so many did. We wanted change. It was time for an African American, and he's as well qualified as any white guy we've ever had."

"Nobody would argue there, Mare. He's not Joe Morrison, a one-term senator who's never even held a job or done much with his abilities. All that guy does is get on stage, look good, and blabber platitudes."

"You're right. At least we didn't put somebody like him in the top spot. But Williams is different. He was a governor of a big state. Did he allow crazy stuff like that in New York?"

"It's not the same thing. Some of these guys, black and white, get off on power politics. It's all about control and manipulation of the people. And from what Amber Bustamente says, Williams and company are set to take four more years from us."

"Do you think there's anything they can do to us?"

Silence claimed four or five seconds. "Nah. Like I said, this is still America."

"Are you sure, Paul?"

The storm changed everyone's schedule, especially Winston Hardy's. As Tampa battened itself down, the 2012 GOP convention had to be delayed given concerns for the safety of travelers and all the others flocking to the site.

"That's the best decision, Governor," Lisa Hoxworth said, her face grim and damp from the summer heat and rain. "Somehow we'll have to make up for the loss of airtime before the country, because you can bet the Democrats won't be cutting their convention short."

"What's done is done," Hardy said affably. "Let's concentrate on making the most of the time we have left. Any platform battles we have to head off?"

"No, sir. The conservative wing seems relatively happy with your stand on abortion, the debt, the budget, and, of course, the growing bureaucracy the president is foisting off on the American people."

"Sounds like lines from a speech," he said with a chuckle.

"Actually, that's my subliminal suggestion for topics you have to hit in every one of the sidebar group talks and conversations you have while you're here. It'll be important for you and Senator Smith to remember that. Whatever you say to people individually will be carried back to their states and repeated ten times over."

"Delegates and fellow Americans. Tonight I thank you for your nomination just as I thank you for nominating Olivia Johnson Smith to be at my side during this campaign—and for the next four years.

"I am honored to be your standard bearer and privileged to represent conservative values that every American can agree with. Let's test that statement. Do you think that Americans are happy with the highest gas prices since the president took office four years ago?"

"No!" came the low growl of the crowd.

"Are Americans happy with an unemployment rate of eight point one percent—higher than when the president was inaugurated?"

"No!" they said again.

"Is the president doing anything about an unemployment rate for Hispanic Americans at just under ten percent and an unemployment rate for African Americans of over thirteen percent?"

"No!"

"Will our children be happy," he said, pointing to the tabulating clock above their heads, "with a national debt that will be over eighteen trillion dollars in a few years?"

"No!" they shouted.

"And what does the president do with his time? Speechmaking? Photo ops? Playing golf? Fundraising?"

The crowd applauded each question, the noise getting louder as Hardy went on.

"Speaking of fundraising, do you know what their latest gimmick is? If you want to write a check to the president's campaign for something over thirty thousand dollars, why you'll get to sit down and have lunch with him—you and a bunch of others—and you'll get at least two minutes to make your pitch directly to him. Oh, and by the way, if that price is just a bit too high for you, a little check for ten thousand dollars will get you in the same ballroom with the president, and for a mere six thousand more, you can have your picture taken with him. Now let me ask you. Is that something many of our fellow Americans can afford to do these days?"

"No!" the crowd yelled in a mass of unbroken noise.

"The problem with President Williams is his political philosophy. You'd think a two-term governor of New York would have been well qualified to be president, but if you're a governor of a state with high taxes, a strong welfare mentality, and that's hard on business, then your philosophy might fit in New York, but not fit for the entire United States. Don't you agree?"

"Yes!"

"In a place like New York, some also think the state should be all things to all people, whereas most people in our country think we should take care of ourselves and only ask the state for help as a last resort. Don't you agree?"

"Yes!"

Hardy paused and edged his voice toward a more somber pitch. "One big difference between our philosophy and theirs has to do with the right to privacy. We hear more and more hints that our government, using national security as its excuse, is intruding into our daily lives, and we won't have it!"

Cheers filled the arena.

"We think privacy means the government should stay out of our business. They think the right to privacy has only to do with what they say is a woman's right to take the life of an unborn infant. Some have advised me not to discuss this here tonight, and I suppose the liberal media will have a field day with me, but personally, I don't believe a woman has the right to end the viable life of her child on demand."

The crowd roared, the noise rattling the seams of the entire building.

"Let me be more specific. There are many views about abortion early in a pregnancy, before the heart begins to beat, and I'm not here to debate those views. We should agree, I think, that a woman should be able to terminate a pregnancy—early on—in cases of rape, incest, or serious threat to her physical well-being. Here's where we must differ with our radical friends on the other side, however. Most women, I venture to say, would agree that an abortion in the third trimester should be permitted only in the rarest of circumstances. Don't you agree?"

"Yes!" they shouted and thundered.

"That's because, my friends, when a fetus is viable outside the womb, we should be talking not about women's rights, but human rights!"

The din became a life of its own.

"That's right. Human rights, because when that heart begins to beat, when that brain begins to sense, when that little being feels hungry or is in pain, we're not talking about some 'thing.' We're talking about a human with all the inalienable rights God has bestowed upon all of us."

The crowd surged, a heavy rumble of approval vibrating even the speaker's podium.

"So you see? That's what this race is really all about. Respect for life. Respect for each other. Respect for our many cultures within one large one. Respect for differing views, religions, and ways of life. In a Hardy-Smith administration, we will work with all people, not just those of our own party, to forge the steel we'll need to tame our government, not just grow it. To lower our debt, not just pass it on. To reduce our taxes, not just raise everyone's bill. To educate our children, not just train them. And we'll do it together. May God bless you and all of America."

The bands struck up, the balloons dropped, and the conventioneers went wild.

In the spin room just off the convention floor, CNS's TonyDuke leaned toward the camera, as if conspiring with his audience. "And there it is," he began, "Governor Hardy's continuing attempt to overcome the apparent voting gap with Averell Williams, the popular sitting president. Let me see what Sheldon Ingber, the president's campaign manager, has to say about the Hardy speech. Shel?"

"Much of it, Tony, was what you might expect of a campaign desperately trying to catch up with a president who's worked harder than anyone in the country to overcome a Republican mess. Governor Hardy spent most of the time running down a good and decent man and presented no concrete, new proposals of his own. And that shabby attempt to deny women their constitutional rights? I don't have to say much on that score. By tomorrow, a good part of the country will have something to say, and it won't be favorable to the Republican position."

"This is Meredith Ramirez here with William Herzog. What did you think, my friend?"

"I think it was a call to arms for the Republican base and it was an appeal to that mass of Independent voters out there who will make the difference in this race. More important than what I think, Meredith, is how Lisa Hoxworth feels about her candidate's performance."

"Lisa," Ramirez said. "Tell us. Do you think the governor hit a homer here tonight?"

"I sure do," Hoxworth responded. "I think he nailed it. He concisely identified what's been wrong with this administration's approach to our economy and our whole national being, and then he promised what a Hardy administration would look like."

"What about his position on abortion? I'm sure many were surprised to hear a candidate put it right out there."

Hoxworth smiled broadly. "Speaking as a woman, I'm glad someone finally spoke for most of us, I believe, who do not think a woman has unilateral control over the life of an unborn. For fifty years now, the Democrats have been pandering to women—maybe in guilt for their past views—telling them they have total control over their own bodies. And we do, but we shouldn't have total control over another body that's inside us, especially in the third trimester of pregnancy."

"So, William," Ramirez said, "do you think that most women will take his words to heart?"

"Yes—although you won't be able to tell that from the liberal media and the party puppets we'll hear tomorrow," Herzog said. "As for women, I think they've been waiting for someone with the courage to take that view, and Olivia Johnson Smith appears totally behind Governor Hardy on this."

"Pete, Janice here. I hate to drop this on you, but I've received two calls I'd just as soon never received."

"What's wrong? Tell me."

"The first one came a few days ago, and frankly, I decided to ignore it. The other one came just now, and I'm still shaking."

"For cryin' out loud, will you tell me?"

"Pete, they were threats. The caller, a man's voice, very deep, maybe disguised, said as plainly as I'm now talking to you that I'd better control my people, or there'd be a reckoning."

"Okay, so it's a nasty call, but what of it? You and I have heard a lot worse."

"That was the first call, and you're right. All by itself, it's no big deal."

"And?"

"Sorry," she said, her eyes dampening rapidly. "But then the second call came in—same voice. This time, he said, 'I hope I got your attention the first time, bitch. Blacks should stay bought, and you got one who doesn't get it. Make him understand, or there'll be a problem.'"

"Sorry I barked at you. I can hear the fear in your voice. Is that exactly what he said?"

Dern took a deep breath. "No. He used the n-word. The way this guy said it was something out of the fifties, when I was in the sixth grade in Cincinnati."

"Damn. Sorry you had to listen to that. Look, I know you have friends in the Bureau there. I want you to call them this afternoon, right after you carefully write everything down, quoting both calls as closely as you can, and send a copy to me. If the local guys aren't interested, let me know, and I will personally call the Hoover Building."

"Okay, I'll do just that."

"And by the way, I also think you should have one-on-one conversations with Evers, Burdette, and Gladston, and tell them to keep it quiet. It's just for them to be extra careful."

"Why them alone?"

"You and I don't believe in coincidences. These calls coming on the tail of the allegation against the vice president, and less than a week after I called Bartley? Gotta be some connection there."

"Oh, Pete—coming from the feds? Are you serious?"

"Just concerned—and those are the only dots that connect."

As soon as she hung up, Dern put her head in her hands and cried like no other time since she lost her child to leukemia. As she thought about the threats and the conversation with Clancy, she shook. What he didn't know and she did was that there was another possible cause for the threats. Some people at the IRS had a lot to lose if Nelson Evers made too much noise, but she refused to think that her sister...She refused to complete the thought. All she could say for sure was that her conversation with Mayella was something she would never mention to anyone.

Then, it occurred to her that the only person in the eye of both storms—the IRS and the election issue—was Nelson Evers.

SEPTEMBER

CNN/Opinion Research Poll
August 31-September 3
Williams 48%
Hardy 48%

Pete Clancy walked toward the door of the Little River Turnpike office knowing the summer's warmth would soon be blown away along with the coloring leaves. Carefully, he held on to his McDonald's coffee and briefcase as he managed the front door. With the Labor Day weekend over and the Democratic convention just beginning in Charlotte, he expected a quiet day.

At his desk, a refuge from the morning noise of I-495 a hundred yards away, he perused the morning mail while his Dell went through its wake-up phase. Sipping his coffeee, Clancy's gaze fastened on an official-looking envelope with the OPM logo on the return address. Its thickness suggested it wasn't to him personally as an OPM retiree, but to him as CEO of NIS.

Immediately curious, he sliced the envelope as if it might be an explosive of sorts, and he chuckled at his own paranoia. When he let the half-inch sheaf of paper escape its manila binding, he zeroed in on the one-page cover letter, the signature on which he recognized immediately: Kristen Bartley, Director, Federal Investigations Service. He felt his heart beat faster, and the missive's first few words told him his instincts were correct. The package contained lit dynamite.

As the words went by, he realized Kristen had somehow achieved her aim. The three-year contract with OPM was being terminated "for the convenience of the government," effective December 31, 2012.

Wow. That's quick. Especially for the government. One week, she's reading me the riot act, and next, we're getting the ax. He glanced through the boiler plate material with the obligatory language about appeal rights, but he knew it was over. Rereading the letter, nevertheless, he hoped for a syllable of relief.

The fact that OPM levied no charges of misconduct or contract violations was a bit of solace. Yet, it was a brutal, bullet-to-the-head affair, and in some respects, he was grateful for that. He knew from experience that two things would likely happen. The first was that the termination could be delayed for a negotiated period while OPM made arrangements to continue its investigative mission. The second was that all or nearly all of the NIS investigators would be taken by the NIS replacement or OPM itself. *Dammit to hell!*

As for the rest of NIS's contracts with other agencies and its private customers, he suspected the NIS board would blame him for the loss of the OPM contract, whether it made sense or not, and that would be that.

After a few minutes thinking it all through, he realized his first priority was for NIS to complete its responsibilities under the contract with as much class and grace as possible, and right next to that in importance was the care of all the people under the company's wing. It would be futile, he knew, to call Bartley and fall on his sword or beg for a reprieve.

For her to have acted so quickly, with all other options apparently blocked, she had to have had backing—from on high. "Just what the hell is going on?" he demanded of the room's warming air a few stories above the snarling street traffic. Then, he picked up the phone and dialed the number of the NIS board chairman.

"Here in Charlotte," announced Peter Marsden, "we have a bird's-eye view of the quadrennial Democratic Convention as they spend their time with—I hesitate to say it—not much of substance this year. Of course, that is always true when a sitting president of either party runs for reelection, and it is unfortunate that in recent years, the American people know the names of both nominees before the first convention gavel comes down. That may explain why viewership of these spectacles has continued to decline.

"In Charlotte, however, the president continues to excite the throngs like very few other politicians in the last twenty years, and I think most people will agree that although the GOP's Governor Hardy is gaining in popularity, he may be no match for President Williams when it comes to the heartbeat of a crowd.

"Having said all that, Tony Duke, it's hard to explain why the CNN/ Opinion Research poll showing the race all tied up. What do you make of that?" He put his hand to his earpiece. "Tony Duke is down on the floor. Do you hear me, Tony?"

"With all the noise down here, Peter, I'll do the best I can," he said, holding the earpiece tight to his head. "So what do I make of the apparent tie? The easiest answer is that Governor Hardy is reaping a bit of a bounce from the GOP convention, and that should be expected. One might suggest, then, that after all the hoopla here in Charlotte, and with the benefit of a convention a full day longer than the Republicans, the president ought to surge ahead when the polls come out early next week."

"And that's a good answer. Thank you, Tony."

"I want to speak to Vice President Morrison," the voice insisted.

"There's no way, sir. The vice president is in Charlotte at the convention and completely unavailable."

"I want you to find him and tell him that it's Enrique McCord. We're well acquainted and have played golf together, young lady. I need his attention, urgently."

"Sir, I will telephone his chief of staff and ask her to give him a message, but that may take a few minutes. Will you hold?"

"Yes, I'm holding." While he sat in his second-floor office in Cincinnati, he watched the traffic on Madison Road, not too far above

Saint Francis de Sales church, where he had attended seven-thirty Mass that morning. He had forsaken Mass for many years, but at the rite's opening, when the priest reminded the congregants to seek comfort in God's forgiveness of all sins, McCord wondered what it would take to chuck it all and go back to Texas where he knew he and Bridget could be happiest together.

Such was the vision occupying his mind when the line clicked, and the young operator came back on. "The vice president will be with you in a few minutes, Mr. McCord. Please hold on."

"Thank you," he said, returning to an image of life uncomplicated by what he'd come to think of as the evil an unbridled ego allowed him to embrace. In his soul, he knew what the vice president was asking him to do was wrong. It was why his grandfathers left Mexico and came to a country where a person's vote spoke for them and that right was inviolate. The importance of that right was what inspired him to excel in the election software and hardware business. Then the line clicked again.

"This is Joe Morrison."

"Joe, it's me, Ricky."

"Oh." Morrison sounded surprised. "They didn't tell me who it was, just that it was important. What is it?"

"I don't want to go through with it, Joe. I want out of the whole project."

"Ricky. Do you realize that I'm here at the convention with the President of the United States? The president, Ricky. We're in a tight race—haven't you seen the polls? If ever we needed a little help this November, it's now, and I've already promised the president that he would be in the White House for four more years to transform this country so that all the folks who've had the bad end of the deal would get a fair shake. That means all the people with names like yours, Enrique. Don't you see?"

"I do see, Joe, but the people should speak. And if President Williams is who the voters want, they will speak with their votes."

"God dammit, Ricky, don't give me any of that pious bullshit. You were the eager beaver who suggested to me that you could help in a big way this fall. Yes, you gave us a big check, but we both know you talked about something else."

"But, Joe, it's—"

"Now, we're both Texas boys, Ricky, and Texans never break their word to each other, and when you said you'd do this thing, you were giving me your word."

"I know I said that, but—"

"Are you still worried about those investigators? Forget them. That problem will go away."

"Joe, I know you spoke to Milton Jennings, and the word came down that he's personally interested in our project."

"And?"

"Why did you have to do that, Joe?"

"You gave me no choice, Ricky, and I wanted you to know that it wasn't just the president who wanted you to do what's good for the country. It's everybody who knows anything. Don't you trust Milton Jennings?"

"Does he really know what this is all about?"

"Of course he does. You don't think he'd call you without knowing what was at stake, do you?"

"Milton Jennings is a good man, and you're saying he's onboard with everything?"

"Yes, he is, but Ricky, I gotta say, this is the second time you've called me with a hair up your ass about this. If there's a third, I'm not gonna know you, and you'll be done in the election business."

"O-okay, Joe. I guess I just needed some reassurance about this whole thing."

"Don't get squeamish on me. After it's all over, you and I will have a nice long talk about the future, and I can promise you it will be very rewarding."

"Well, okay. I wish I was as certain as you are about stuff like this."

"You need to trust me, Ricky. Remember, we're Texans!" he hooted, as if they were at a fraternity party. "And now if you'll excuse me, President Williams is delivering his acceptance speech, and he'll be wanting me on stage with him right after."

When they hung up, Morrison's heart raced. His head pounded. How long could he play the game of the double lie? Harry Riordan had taught it to him his first year in the Senate. "It's this way, son," he had explained. "For the sake of discussion, let's say you're Smith and you're dealing with Jones and Brown. First, you tell Jones that Brown is for it, or against it, and then you tell Brown the same thing about Jones. You can play that game until the cows come home, but the trick is to do it when Jones is highly unlikely to ever to talk to Brown."

Even so, the pressure was becoming more intense than a presidential campaign. Massaging his temples eased the thumping but not the feeling of being squeezed in a vise. He'd used this little trick for a lotta years, but he'd never had so many double lies going at the same time.

Remy Carlson walked up and gave him the two-minute warning. Morrison couldn't help but smile to himself as he heard the president talking about his foreign policy successes.

"We can sum up our war against terrorists, my friends, by recalling what Joe Morrison likes to say at this point: GM is alive, Osama bin Laden is dead, and al-Qaeda is on the run."

As the makeup people finished tamping the perspiration growing on his upper lip and forehead, Morrison stood and walked toward the opening where he could see as well as hear the president's peroration. He knew the face the American people were about to see would belie the concerns darkening his thoughts, and worse, the resolutions beginning to shape themselves.

"And so, my fellow Americans," the president continued with pieces of a speech he'd given a hundred times, "if you want a return to the policies and practices that got us into the mess we're working so hard to fix, you can take a backward step and vote for the other side. If you want an America where the distance between the haves and have-nots continues to widen, and if you want an America where the middle class disappears under the crush, well, then, you know who to vote for.

"But if you want an America where every man, woman, and child, no matter what their color or where they came from, can dare to aspire, and dare to succeed, will you vote for Williams and Morrison?"

"Yes!" The crowd's energy had been pent up and was ready to explode.

"And if you want an America where the rich pay their fair share so that our children can face a brighter future, will you vote for the party that'll make it happen?"

"Yes," they shouted, and the electricity took form as it crackled through the thousands.

"And if you want an America where every American can have affordable health care—as their inalienable right—will you vote for Joe Morrison and me?"

The expected yes was drowned by the applause and cheers bursting from the loudspeakers.

"I am, indeed, proud to have at my side for another four years your vice president and mine, Joe Morrison. C'mon out here, Joe!"

In the News Global booth, Forbes Flannery had his captive duo seated and ready to pronounce their verdicts. "What say you, Jack Rispoli?"

"I'd say the president did exactly what he was expected to do: rally and excite the throng with a speech like no one else can give."

"And you, Gardner?"

Stewart held up his chalkboard for the camera and the millions. "As you can see what's on my board, it's a big fat zero. So what do I mean by that? First, he gave a heart-thumping speech for the adoring masses on the floor and his liberal base at home. That I'll give him, and I agree with you, Jack, nobody does it better."

"So what's the zero for?" Rispoli asked impatiently.

"The zero is for anybody else who was listening. All throughout his speech, I kept my grease pencil poised above the whiteboard in my lap so that I could tick off all the points the president might make to convince Independents and a few Republicans to vote for him. At the point the speech was finished, my grease pencil never touched the board. So, I wrote down a zero."

"And there you have it, ladies and gentlemen," Flannery said as the camera cut to him. "The Democratic National Convention is now over, and the race is on."

"Mare, did you watch those guys?"

"Paul, I just can't get excited about this stuff. To me, it still doesn't matter who wins in November. It'll be the same old, same old."

"But Morrison strutted on that stage like he owned it. Doesn't that bother you?"

"Not yet."

"I don't want to have our first fight over politics, Mare, but you're wrong about not caring. Maybe there was a time when we could coast along, but not when some guy is planning to steal the entire election."

"But what if they don't need to steal the election? Maybe this guy Hardy doesn't measure up."

"Right now, though, it's all tied up."

"You wait," she said. "Williams will be on top within a few days."

"I thought you said you weren't interested, crafty pants."

Mare began laughing. "Of course, I'm interested, you idiot. I just wanted to see what you get all fired up about. But I can guarantee you I'm not nearly as obsessed by this election as you are."

"I'm not obsessed, just worried."

"Did Dern talk to you about the threats she received?"

"Yeah," said Paul. "She called me in—didn't think it was a huge, big deal."

"Who? You or Dern?"

"Me. I know I'm only a few years older than you, but I've been doing this job longer, and we had some moron make a threat a few years ago— turned out to be nothing. I'm just gonna ignore it."

"Is this the person who was so concerned about me not that long ago?"

"Same, and still am. What did Dern say to you?"

"Probably the same as you, but she mentioned the focus of the phone message seemed to be Nelson."

"Did she say how she knew that?"

"She said the caller used the n-word and said, in effect, people like Evers 'should stay bought.'"

"Hmmm. Not nice. How does Evers feel about the whole thing?"

"He's pissed. You know him, six three and all hard. I've never seen him back down from anything. He won't stand back and let the IRS union goons bully him, and he won't roll over just because some jerk like Morrison wants to mess with our votes. He'll make some noise. You just watch."

"This is *America Now*, with Meredith Ramirez this Tuesday, September eleventh, and our lead story centers on the memorial services taking place in three special locations across our country: the heart of New York, the Pentagon in Washington, and an eerie field in Shanksville, Pennsylvania." Ramirez and the News Global staff spent the next hour fully focused on the tragic anniversary.

"Next, we have some interesting poll numbers to share with you. According to a CNN/Opinion Research poll, the president made the most of the Democratic Convention. He now leads his challenger by a margin of six, fifty-two to forty-six percent. Now, you would think that's convincing, wouldn't you? But this morning I have with me Gardner Stewart with a totally different set of numbers.

"Gardner," she said as she addressed the cherubic face of her guest, electronically present from Texas, "so what do you have that's so interesting it waters down the CNN poll?"

"Two things. One is that we might have expected a bounce after the DNC extravaganza, and giving the president his due, they did a pretty fair job grabbing public attention. However, and this is point two, there's a *Washington Post*/ABC News poll out today showing the president's disapproval rating at fifty percent, with an approval rating of only forty-eight percent, and indications are that it's dropping."

"So how do you explain those two disparate sets of numbers—an anomaly we've seen before?"

"I have no scientific explanation for your viewers, but I do have this fact. No president has been reelected in the last fifty years without a fifty percent or better approval rating as of Labor Day."

At three forty-five, as downtown Washington, DC, traffic began to bake the asphalt with a half a million tires and hot exhausts, Joe Morrison and his erstwhile opponent met on the White House court for a quick dance of a male rite. Away from the afternoon babble of staffers, visitors, and media on the paths not far from their hoop hideaway, the two men limbered up briefly before taking a few practice shots.

"How are you feeling after Charlotte, sir?"

"As well as you could expect, Marty, and naturally, it'll be a while before we can enjoy our little luxury out here on gorgeous days like this. The campaign staff has the usual murderous schedule ahead of us, and..." He laughed. "Why am I telling you? You'll be with us most of the time."

Smiling back, Cox nodded with the grim understanding of what a campaign tour meant to Secret Service agents and their families.

"Which means," Morrison continued, "we won't have many opportunities for a totally private conversation."

"I understand, sir. And, by the way, I made the phone calls you suggested."

"I wish I could say they were enough."

"What do you mean?"

"What I mean is that the calls may have put the fear of God into some, but the others involved didn't get the message. That's a tougher bunch than I thought they were." The silence on the court was so complete that the sounds of Pennsylvania Avenue traffic on the south side of the White House complex evaporated.

"What is it you want me to do, sir?"

"Right now, nothing. Just wait for it. What happens then can't be, shall we say, a short-term fix."

Cox eased the air from his lungs as slowly as possible. He did not want the vice president to see how tense he'd become imagining what he might be asked to do. "All right, sir. I'll wait to hear from you."

Saying the words made his gut tighten again, and he wasn't sure he should have been so eager to agree. *What choice do I have? It's my job, my pension, college for my kids.* He looked directly at Morrison, as if he was seeing someone for the first time. Making his best effort, he cranked up a smile. As the sun peeking through the trees prickled his skin, he wondered how much hotter it might become.

Not long after four o'clock, September the eleventh, Remy Carlson appeared at the court, out of breath. "Mr. Vice President," she called, just as Morrison's layup did its expected ricochet into the basket. "You need to return to your office."

"What's going on, Remy? I don't have another appointment until five."

"That's all been canceled, sir. You're to meet with Secretary of Defense Roberts and the president in the Oval Office at five, and I thought you'd want time to shower and change." Urgency and tension marked her voice.

"Remy, do you have any idea about what's going on?"

Carlson glanced quickly at Marty Cox, a clear signal to Morrison that it was not for other ears. "Sondra said it's something about Libya. Let's go, sir."

Morrison knew a firm request when he heard one. Forty-five minutes later, he walked into the Oval Office where Jensen Roberts was already waiting. They shook hands and waited for the president to join them.

Roberts said, "Our Libyan policy is in flames. The ambassador is missing and it doesn't look good."

"Where is Secretary Grantham?" Morrison asked.

Roberts answered the question with only a look.

"Oh, are you telling me there'd be blood on the floor if he were here?"

An ever so faint smile crossed the defense secretary's lips. "You might say that. The fact is, Emerson is unaccountably unavailable, and if I were you, I wouldn't bring it up when the old man comes in. Also unfortunate is that CIA Director Warner is out of town."

At 5:00 p.m. precisely, Averell Williams strode in and offered a grim face to the other two. "Sondra will join us in a moment, and if you don't mind, I'll have Jack Sennett in as well. He will be facing most of the flack, and should be read in."

"Av, let's bring Jack in after we've talked about some of the truly sensitive stuff," said Roberts.

"Agreed. Go ahead, Jensen."

As Roberts began, Thompson entered the room. "I'm going over the highlights of our recent Libyan moves so that everyone is on the same page. And, Sondra, you can decide—with the president's approval, of course—what Jack should be allowed to dispense.

"You may remember that in late March, on the twenty-eighth to be exact, Ambassador Stevens requested additional security assets in both Tripoli and Benghazi in particular; this was after terrorists threw an IED over the consulate wall in Benghazi. In Secretary Grantham's name, the request was refused. In late May, terrorists attacked the Red Cross and blew a hole through our consulate gate. Then, in June, the British ambassador barely survived an assassination attempt. Some or all of the above prompted another request for a security team from Ambassador Stevens on June twenty-second. Stevens made further requests along the same lines in early July and on August second.

"For reasons unknown to me," Roberts continued, "the ambassador's security team was ordered removed from Libya, and a week later, the Regional Security Officer e-mailed Secretary Grantham about a worsening situation there. Al-Qaeda operatives were openly rallying in Benghazi by this time.

"On September sixth and tenth, Benghazi security officials issued further warnings of attacks against US interests there. Then this afternoon, at seven thirty Benghazi time—remember, they are six hours ahead of us—Stevens began a meeting with a Turkish diplomat and ended it an hour later. Just ten minutes afterward, the first shots were fired. Stevens called Gregory Hicks in Tripoli and told him they were under attack. Just a little more than an hour ago, at four oh five exactly our time, the State Department notified the White House of the situation. To whit: the consulate was in flames and Ambassador Stevens was missing.

"Just before our meeting, a few minutes before five, we learned that the firing had stopped and that the consulate was abandoned. And right now, that's all we know. I might point out that the last time we lost a US Ambassador was, they tell me, in the late 1970s."

All during Roberts's recitation, the president sat with his elbows resting on the arms of his leather chair, his fingers splayed and touching their counterparts. Morrison noticed that the isometric exercise Williams was performing caused the tops of his fingertips to turn a bloodless white.

At the recitation's completion, all waited for Williams to speak. After a half a minute or so, he said, "I will make some public comments in my Rose Garden talk tomorrow morning, but I do not intend to portray this as a terrorist attack, and I do not want this administration's spokespeople to use the word, either. Sondra, make sure that Jack understands that."

Thompson nodded and took a note.

"For now, we will say nothing at all until some news outlet—God forbid it's News Global—tumbles to what's transpired. Jensen, how much time do we have, do you think?"

"A few hours at most, Av. Even if our people don't have it soon, Al Jazeera will hit the wires with it, and if we're not careful, we'll take a lot of flack for not getting something out there before the others do."

"Nice point. Thanks, Jensen. Then, we say nothing, at least not until I've had a chance to talk to Emerson Grantham, or unless our hand is forced."

Thompson said, "We've lined him up for a ten o'clock telecon with you this evening, sir." She clicked her pen several times, but stopped when Williams looked in her direction.

"Perfect. I have a dinner date with Andrea and may be unavailable for a bit, but before dinner, you should craft something plausible to put out there." Williams seemed a man without emotion.

Roberts said, "Do you have any suggestions, Av?" He seemed pained, unbelieving.

"How about something as innocuous as there was a demonstration that got out of hand, and we will expect the Libyan government to investigate it and take the proper steps to see that it doesn't happen again." He paused. "Need I mention," he said, looking at each one in the room, "that we're in the midst of an election campaign in which a hallmark of our foreign policy success has been that al-Qaeda is on the run? I know I'm repeating myself, but I stress that as far as this administration is concerned, this was a demonstration run amok, or some such thing." He looked at Thompson. "Just let me know how you plan to play it."

Morrison spoke for the first time. "Av, Ambassador Stevens? Other staffers? Perhaps, we should have some idea about their safety before issuing anything that puts us in a box."

"Good one, Joe. Thanks. Jensen, between you and Grantham, let's make sure we know about those folks before we say anything to the media. Who? How many? Their situation? You know the drill. And by the way, if I'm not directly available, Sondra, keep Joe in the loop when you work something up. And in the meantime, I want you, Jack Sennett, and one of Jensen's people, and perhaps Joe here, to craft something I can look at before we call it a day. Okay, gang. That's it for now."

The president completed his deskwork and stood for the photo ops fat cat donors needed in trade for their checks. With a worn out smile, he made his way upstairs. It was just before seven in the evening. Waiting for him in the dining room was Andrea Williams, a ravishingly beautiful woman and a brilliant intellect in her own right. The cold glare greeting him was not an intellectual one.

He wondered what mistake he'd made, and told himself to tread carefully.

"Hon," he ventured, and he leaned forward to kiss her on the cheek.

"Don't 'hon' me, Averell Williams! I am so mad at you, I don't know if I'll even speak to you until after November sixth."

The president never thought about a black woman getting red in the face, but if there was a way to manage it, Andrea had done it. "Andie," he tried again, using a more intimate term. "What in the world is going on?"

"Today, Mr. President, I had my annual physical in Commander Bolling's office."

"Yes?" he asked interestedly, but looking away.

"Don't you dare evade me. You know exactly what I'm talking about."

"For cryin' out loud, Andie, would you mind not keeping me in suspense?"

"Jeremy Bolling is a good and decent doctor, and when he finished with me and gave me the Good Housekeeping seal of approval, I looked him right in the eye and asked him straight out, 'I assume you gave the same to my husband.' And like you, Averell, he did the man thing and looked someplace else."

If it weren't so serious a situation, he would have enjoyed her reversion to her Arkansas beginnings, both in voice and mannerisms. Wisely deciding not to smile, he stumbled a bit. "He...he didn't violate doctor-patient privilege, did he?"

"I reminded him I'm your emergency contact, and that I damn well had a right to know what was up with you."

"So let's get to it, Andie. What did he tell you?"

"Why, you damn fool, he told me about the cancer and that you decided to put things off until after the election. Are you serious, Averell? Is this crazy job so damned important to you?"

"You know it is. And you know what kind of feeding frenzy the media would have if the *C* word even formed on Commander Bolling's lips. It would be all over for me, and the first African American president would wind up a failed one termer. Would we have been happy with that in our later years? Huh?"

A syllable of some sort started to leave her throat. She stopped and began again. "Oh, sweetheart, you know what hurts the most?" She didn't wait for an answer. "You didn't trust me enough to tell me so that we could work through this, together."

Just at that moment, they heard a knock, and Freddie Frederick entered to say that there'd been a development in the Libya situation.

"Not now, Freddie. Have Sondra get with the others. Please don't interrupt unless you have to."

Williams lowered his eyes and his head. Then he said, "You're right, Andie, and I'm ashamed that you, my best friend, lover, and partner, weren't the second person to know it. I'm sorry."

She threw her arms around him and said, "I'm sorry, too. I just don't want to lose the only man I've ever loved." She teared up, as did he. "C'mon, my wonderful fool. Let's have a drink before dinner."

Morrison's head swirled as he left the Oval Office. When Sondra Thompson told him they would rendezvous in an hour to see what Jack Sennett and Jensen Roberts worked up, he merely nodded, dazed as he was by the naked manipulation of the truth he had just witnessed. *Jesus!* After a moment, he thought, *Who am I to judge?*

He made his way down the long hallway, past Thompson's office and to his own, not far off the West Wing's north entrance. He let himself fall into the $12,000 executive leather chair that housed his agile frame on most business days and swung around to face his empty blotter.

"Jesus," he said aloud, but from that point on he contained himself, lest he invite interruption. Leaning back, he lifted his shiny black Allen Edmonds-clad feet onto his favorite corner of the desk and began to assess what he'd heard.

Until the five o'clock meeting, he hadn't worried about the election outcome because often enough, the incumbents received the benefit of all doubters, and Ricky McCord and his gang was there to eliminate any question. But if a sudden, full-blown scandal were to brew, manipulating the vote could be harder to carry off. And yet, by taking their right to vote for granted, by showing so little interest in safeguarding that right, the American people were making his choice easy. *The voters were committing the biggest turnover of all, weren't they?*

The way he saw it, there were two threats to his plan for a Williams reelection and a possible Morrison succession. First were the usual presidential campaign challenges: a powerful candidate or resurgent opposing party on the one hand, and on the other, a big administration scandal or failure, or an impaired incumbent.

What they had going for them was the most competitive president in two decades, a man not seen as impaired because the public didn't know the truth about his health. Against them was the perception of a stagnant economy, but very little else. Until now, foreign policy had been iffy in some places, but nothing they couldn't deal with. On the other side, Hardy was a formidable candidate with a stroke-of-genius choice for vice president, and while Republicans could play the economy card, the administration was getting high marks for trying. Now Benghazi. "Dammit!" That, along with an IRS scandal, could blow Morrison's play off the court.

As to Benghazi, that would have to be a Williams problem, and it appeared he had a plan to manage it away, or at least, get past the election before it all came apart. The IRS problem had become Morrison's. That, and his plan for the election were connected, and in a moment, he knew exactly what to do. "And I get a two-fer!"

Carlson poked her head in and asked, "Did you call for me, sir?"

"You bet, Remy. Get Cox on the phone." *In for a penny...* He laughed out loud.

A few minutes before ten Washington time, long after the president and first lady had begun to relax for the evening, Freddie Frederick knocked on the door and reminded the president of his call with Secretary Grantham.

"I'm coming down to my office for this, Freddie. Have him wait if he's on before I get there." Williams leaned over and kissed his wife before rising to duty.

He never liked entering the Oval Office at night. Even with all the lights on, he felt he was in a well-lit tomb. But like it or not, there were some bits of presidential business that should be done in one and only one place. It was silly of him to allow such a caveat to rule his day, but it was his caveat, come what may. When he sat down, he saw the line blinking and knew his most difficult charge was waiting at the other end.

"Emerson," he said, gripping the phone. Without pleasantries, he launched right in. "You're aware, I'm sure, of my earlier meeting with Roberts, Morrison, and Sondra Thompson. I'm up to speed as of about three hours ago."

"Then, Mr. President, I regret to inform you about that time—three hours ago—the mangled and burned body of Chris Stevens was found by Benghazi locals. Five or six others were taken to the hospital. At this moment, my information is that three others were killed as well."

"Three hours ago? Why wasn't I informed?"

"I sent Freddie in to tell you, but she said you couldn't be disturbed."

"Yes." He closed his eyes, damning the physical law that he couldn't be in two places at once. "Well, I am truly sorry for you and your department," he began again, knowing Grantham was mad as hell. "I know your staff will provide Sondra with names and phone numbers so I can make those calls when we know what we know for certain."

"Thank you, sir."

"And there's no doubt who's responsible?"

"None. Gregory Hicks, Deputy Chief of Mission in Libya—I don't think you know him—called me at eight in the evening our time to tell me in no uncertain terms it was a terrorist attack, possibly an al-Qaeda affiliate."

"From where we sit, it was a demonstration gone wild. A very unfortunate incident stemming from God knows what."

Grantham did not answer immediately. "A demonstration? Provoked by what?"

"We're not sure yet. Sondra and a few others are checking that out right now and will let you know shortly."

"So that's our narrative, Averell? That it was a demonstration? You know, way too many people know that's simply not the case."

"And I suspect all of them work for you. And if there's a way for you to make sure they don't say the wrong things, I'm sure you'll find it."

"Is this the way we paste over your ill-fated policy in Libya?"

"Watch it, Emerson. All the policy papers have your signature on them, not mine."

"That may be, but you and I know that in all of this, I've been your good soldier. Nearly all of this administration's foreign policy has your fingerprints all over it."

"You're about the only person who knows that. The whole world thinks you're a terrific secretary of state, logging more miles and working longer hours than any of your predecessors, even the fabled Condi Rice. That's how both of us wanted the world to see it, and there's no way you can change that view now."

"You've got this all figured out, don't you?"

"You bet I do, and because you want to run for president in 2016, it'll be in your best interest to make sure what happens about Benghazi is all according to script. My script." He delivered his words unemotionally, to leave no doubt anger was not involved, only commitment.

"I understand fully," Grantham said. "But I can't be held responsible if someone talks out of school."

"One or two truants can be managed in the usual way. That's what we have most of the media for."

"On that score, I agree. And the understanding is that we have each other's back on this? Is that what you're saying?"

"That's one way of putting it.."

"Then when can I submit my resignation?"

"Do you really want to do that? You don't want to serve for three more years or so, so that the public has you firmly in their eye for 2016?"

"No. And why I don't want to do that, Averell, is that your foreign policy approach—leading from behind, as your critics say—is going to come off the wheels. In my opinion, whatever good image you think we have now will disintegrate early in your next term—if you get one—and I don't want to be part of it. The Russians and the Chinese in particular know we don't have the balls to play on their stage, and al-Qaeda knows it too."

The president's voice grew cold. "That's your opinion. All right, Mr. Secretary, you can submit your resignation sometime in December. That work for you?"

"Deal," he said. "I'll do my best with my people. You take care of the rest."

"Agreed. By the way, for appearance's sake, you and I will meet at State tomorrow morning, where we'll catch up on the miscellaneous details of the attack. Sondra will give you a time. I'll be leaving for a Las Vegas fundraiser right afterward, so I'll be depending on you and only a few others to mind the store here."

"I'll tell you one thing. I'm not going in front of the media to peddle a pound of bullshit."

"Then send somebody else if you're not available. Just make sure it's someone with enough rank to make it credible—we'll manage the talking points from here."

"Fine. I have someone in mind."

Williams clicked off the line.

Nelson Evers had always hated the weekends, and that was just one reason why Althea divorced him. Whenever he thought about his marriage of twenty-six years and the three beautiful daughters he and his wife produced, he wondered if he could have changed enough to make a difference. Maybe he married too late to change. Maybe work was his life, his proof to himself that he could be better than what many whites thought he could be. Althea hated him for that, too, and his need to succeed was a source of many long nights, many nasty weekends.

Finally, it happened. One day, Althea came home and said she'd found someone else, someone who would give her a good time, someone willing to spend money for a good party. It hadn't been bitter, and he was glad for that. When they split, two of the girls had been raised, one of them married with a child he never saw, the other unmarried with two children he saw more than he wanted to. Jackie, his third, remained uncertain about her feelings for him, and he was content to give her time.

With the way things were going, maybe he'd retire earlier than he'd planned, and then there'd be plenty of time to make things up to all three. He'd made up his mind in Columbus when he heard things about people at the IRS, some them friends and relatives. He felt the water was too high and the current too strong for him to swim with the likes of Mayella Washington and Janice Dern. He had one shot.

After the divorce, Evers had purchased a little house on Germania Avenue, just off of Wooster Pike, in eastern Cincinnati. Actually it was the Village of Fairfax. The location appealed to him for a number of reasons. When he first became an investigator in 1973, no blacks lived in the neighborhood where he now collected his mail. He was proud of the fact that he was just one of several African Americans who had purchased property there and kept it in tip-top shape. Never would he give anyone a reason to say he didn't belong there.

Second, he told all of his friends and fellow investigators, was the fact he was one block away from a Skyline Chili and two blocks away from the Frisch's Mainliner, where he had worked bussing tables all through high school and college. Now he was closest to his two favorite food sources. "What more could a guy want in his old age?" he'd said more than once.

The third reason was one he shared with no one except Mare Burdette. Wooster Pike was US 50, and, unlike many people, he knew that if he got on that road heading east, it would take him to the foot of the Lincoln Memorial. Pretty soon, he'd promised himself, he was going to do just that: see face-to-face the man who set his people free.

It used to be that he hated weekends because there'd be a lot of hours spent listening to Althea complain about their drab little life.

Now weekends passed without another ear or voice nearby, and the interminable hours gave him plenty of time to think about things.

One of the things he thought about most the past few months was what he called "the IRS disgrace." By itself, he could chalk it up to one agency gone crazy that would be fixed in due course. What Amber Bustamente alleged was something else altogether. How could someone who thrived in the shadow of Lincoln even think of stealing from every American what had been denied to so many: to vote and to have that vote count.

The more ingredients that fell into his stew, especially given the 24-7 election coverage, the more he felt compelled to take a next step. As of that morning, the Williams Administration script about Benghazi filled the hours. Evers watched as an ambassador tried to push a story even friendly networks found hard to believe. *Why would such a smart black woman allow herself to be used by the likes of Emerson Grantham?* He dawdled.

By Sunday evening, Germania Avenue was quiet, a beautiful September day having just left the horizon. From somewhere on Grace Avenue less than a block away, he heard loud music, probably a teenager who hadn't yet adjusted to a school schedule. Stepping out onto his little front porch, he noticed all the vehicles lining both sides of the street as they always did when people were through with weekend playtime, but otherwise, nobody was out. In a minute, as if some kid's parents had read his mind, the music stopped.

At the kitchen table, with the debris of several meals pushed aside, he fired up his Hewlett Packard laptop, and after its usual Windows startup loads and hard-drive rattles, the home screen, with an old photo of his three daughters as his wallpaper, seemed to beckon him to the Microsoft Word icon. With a new document on the screen, he began to type quickly the words he had formed in his head many times over the last weeks. Paragraph after paragraph filled the pages, and after an hour of typing, reading, editing, and rereading, he finally printed four sets of his three-page opus. One set, he put where he thought it would be safe. For the other three, he found envelopes, and addressed and stamped them.

Evers placed the envelopes on the counter, intending to mail them in the morning when he went downtown. One was addressed to the *Cincinnati Enquirer*, one to News Global, and the third to OPM's Inspector General. He couldn't take his eyes from them because he wanted them on their way.

Heck, this is a good night for a walk to the mailbox. And he smiled broadly as he thought about the fact that Frisch's was open late. A piece of peach pie and coffee sounded good. Grabbing the objects of his compulsion, he walked outside, smelled the cooling night air, and turned south, walking briskly toward Wooster Pike. Once there, he turned right and continued toward the Big Boy sign flashing its neon lure.

Only a few steps into the long parking lot on the east side of the diner, he heard the heavy engine roaring up over the curb. Evers just had time to turn his head toward the oncoming headlights before feeling the the SUV's high hood smash him full in the back, slapping him to the pavement.

"Jeff, how are you doing? We haven't seen each other for a few months now," President Williams purred into the phone. He was alone in the Oval Office and expected no interruptions.

The raspy voice answered quickly. "Why, Averell, how nice of you to take a call from an old has-been like me!" The smile in his voice was infectious, and it hummed through the phone as if by magic.

"Has-been, my ass, Jeff Harper! Your name carries more cachet than mine in many circles, so I'll always take your calls," said Williams, continuing the charade.

"Well, this is a quiet Sunday night for me, Averell, but I suspect it isn't for you. This Benghazi thing must be driving you nuts."

"It's not too bad, Jeff, but you know how this kind of thing goes."

"Indeed, I do, and that's why I thought I'd call before it gets out of hand."

"What's on your mind?"

"I hear tell you might be thinking of throwing my Connecticut cousin under the bus over this Benghazi stink."

"Jeff, I have no such plans for Secretary Grantham, but why would that bother you?" Williams was taking a chance, but everyone in politics knew about Former President Jefferson Harper and his cousin.

"Emerson and I are hardly close. That's no secret. But he is family, and if he is to have a successful run in 2016, Benghazi can't be pullin' him down."

"So you were calling to offer your thoughts?"

"It's lookin' more and more like you need some help as this race closes, and you sure as hell wouldn't want me to take a long nap between now and November, would you?"

It was clear that Emerson Grantham had not told his cousin of his planned resignation. "Good thing they're not close!" was what he had said some months earlier. "No, I wouldn't. If I understand you, then, you'd be willing to do some campaigning for me if...?"

"If you treat Emerson right, Mr. President."

Williams let the silence hang. "You know, when something like this happens, Jeff, it's not the president who takes the fall..."

"I know that, Av." Harper paused. "I'm willing to make it worth it to you between now and November sixth if that's means something to you."

Aha! He'll get off the couch. "We have eight weeks left. How about a half dozen appearances?"

"Jeeesus! That's pretty steep. We may both be Democrats, but we're not the same, Av, and honestly, my heart wasn't in it. Now, I have a reason. Sorry. I'm just being straight with you."

"I understand perfectly," Williams said slowly, "and I respect you for it. In fact, I would have been disappointed had you said anything else. Now, however, you have the best of all reasons to put our differences aside. Hell, I'm betting you want Emerson in the White House in 2016 more than he does." Williams chuckled.

"Well..." Harper responded in kind.

"God forbid the Republicans get in and get access to people and paper—that would really mess him up, wouldn't it?"

"I think you just played your trump card. You can count me in—for six appearances only. Just have Shel Ingber get with my people with some proposed dates and talking points, and we'll go from there."

"Glad you're on board, Jeff. Really glad."

Gladys, the NIS secretary for the Cincinnati duty station, poked her head into the squad bay and said, "Mare, two policemen are here."

In the reception area, Burdette saw two officers waiting, but she didn't recognize their uniforms. "Yes?" she called out.

"Could we see your identification, please?" one of them said when they stepped forward.

"From me? What's up?" she asked, lifting her credentials from her jacket pocket.

"Let's go where we can sit," one of the uniforms said.

They followed her into the back room, and the taller one began. "Does a Nelson Evers work here? African American, in his sixties, about six three or six four?"

"Yeah, he does," she said, confused. "He's our senior investigator. Don't tell me he's done anything wrong, 'cause that's just not possible."

The two men said nothing.

"Hey! What the hell is going on?"

"I'm sorry to have to tell you this, Ms. Burdette, but he was run down and killed last night."

"What?" she said, fighting to keep the tears from filling her eyes. "How can that be? A hit and run?"

"Apparently," said the officer. "An odd one, though. It wasn't on the street. It was in the Frisch's parking lot. You know, the one on Wooster Pike? That's not how this usually goes. The, uh, evidence suggests it might not have been an accident."

"What...what department are you guys from?"

"Village of Fairfax, Ms. Burdette. You don't often see us downtown, but we knew Mr. Evers lived within our jurisdiction and what he did for a living. We're here as a courtesy to him."

"I can't believe it," she said, her comment a non sequitur. "Nobody would want to hurt Nelson." Then she nodded her head. "I know the Frisch's you mean. It's near his house. He was divorced and lived alone. He ate at Frisch's and Skyline a lot. I still can't believe it."

"You know, we got lucky here. He had a couple of bucks in his pocket, but no ID. The manager came out. She said everybody there knew him because he worked there when he was a kid. Anyway, she knew where he lived, and we found his credentials in the house."

"Oh, God. But wait a minute. So this might have been delierate? What else do we know about it? My bosses will want to know. This doesn't happen to our people."

"Whoa! We're not sure of anything yet. There was an older couple in Frisch's dining area and almost nobody else at that hour—about ten thirty last night. They saw a big black SUV, but only noticed it when it stopped and backed up. They didn't see the impact, but they saw someone laying on the asphalt."

"Nothing else?"

"Just that the driver was Caucasian with short, light colored hair, dark clothes. He got out, looked right at the couple in the window, but the light wasn't good for them to make out a face. He stooped to pick something up—like he had dropped it, then jumped back in the vehicle and sped past the window. All the old man could say was the vehicle did not have an Ohio plate. The driver made a loud U-turn and headed east on US 50. That's it. No other witnesses. Actually, I shouldn't have told you any of that. The investigation's in progress. You know how it goes."

"Yeah, I get it, but we're practically his only real family." Burdette swore. "He was the neatest guy. Trained me. Who'd want to hurt him?" She paused, staring at the floor. "Look, you two, I've never been through this before—one of ours getting killed. Let me call my boss in Columbus. There's some government stuff we'll have to get." She remembered the phone threats and didn't know what she should say.

"Do it quickly, if you don't mind me suggesting it," the talker of the two cops said. "If this is a murder investigation, everything might be held as evidence. Otherwise, once we find next of kin, that stuff may just get swept up, if you know what I mean."

"Gimme a card. I'll call you in an hour or so." By this time, Gladys was standing at the door, crying.

Picking up the phone as soon as the cops left, Burdette dialed Janice Dern's number, but it went to voice mail. Burdette said only to call her back ASAP. She knew it couldn't wait, so she called Pete Clancy directly and was glad for his answer on the second ring.

Passed mutual greetings, Clancy expressed his surprise by the call.

"Pete, Nelson Evers was the victim of a hit and run last night. He's dead." She could hardly get the word out. She'd experienced very few deaths in her life, and the simple idea that she and Nelson Evers would never be hitting the Skyline again had not yet settled in. "The police say it might have been deliberate. It happened in a parking lot." Her voice was flat.

"Dammit. Janice talked to you about the threats we received, correct?"

"Yeah, and I know she talked to Paul. I don't know about Nelson."

"Doesn't matter now, but she and I will talk. For now, call the cop back and give him my number, nothing else. Either I or Janice will give him what info we have."

"Got it. Pete?"

"Yeah?"

"This just wasn't supposed to be like this. We don't carry guns. We have no way to protect ourselves from people who would harm us. Just exactly who would do a thing like this, anyway?"

"No guess. Maybe Janice has an idea. She's closer to it than I am."

"Yeah. Maybe."

Two hours later, Janice Dern returned Pete Clancy's call, and he gave her the news about Nelson Evers. "I am so sorry about this, Janice. I wish we could have protected him." He could hear her choking up.

"Janice, are you okay?"

"Yes," she said, her voice unsure.

"Do you have any idea what this could be about?"

"No," she said, uncertain of what she knew.

"You should be the one to talk to the police. Tell them everything. The threats are connected, and we don't believe in coincidences, do we? I want to know if we need to do anything to protect anybody else."

"Will do."

Oh, and by the way, make sure to get his laptop and case papers back ASAP. Otherwise, we'll have another problem with Bartley."

"I'm sending Gladston down there to help with all the details, and he can help Burdette finish the cases Evers was working on."

"I'll let Bartley know."

"Mayella? Hey, did you hear about Nelson? He was run down last night—maybe not an accident."

"No way. Why would anybody want to do that?"

"That's one reason why I'm calling you. You're the only person I've talked to about him. Nobody's ever had a beef with him except you. Nobody in the union went crazy there, did they?"

"You just shut up, Janice Washington! We would never do anything like that. It's too bad, but maybe Nelson brought it on himself with his big mouth an' all."

"Nice, Mayella. Nice. He was a good man who just wound up on the wrong side of the political fence. No reason to kill him."

"There had to be some reason, didn't there? It wasn't his ex or his kids, that's for damn sure."

"That's right," Janice said, shakily. "It had to be somebody who really needed him dead."

After their phone call, Dern sat alone in her office, her eye catching the diploma that caught her in a lie. She thought about Nelson Evers, one of the most honorable men she had ever known. Why did he have to be so stubborn? So obstinate! The more she thought about it, the more she thought—and hoped—her sister's IRS people were not involved. *Then who?*

After a few more minutes, she sat straight up in her chair. *The election thing? The vice president? No. Couldn't be. Now I'm thinking like those crazy Tea Party people!* Then she remembered: *Nelson Evers was the only one to speak out.* She saw where the road went, but she refused to follow it home.

When she hung up with Clancy, Bartley snagged Nelson Evers's profile and picture from her database. She sent out an e-mail to all OPM staff, many of whom would have known and worked with him. The secret memo to Morrison crossed her mind. The more she busied herself at her desk, the more she felt an unwelcome presence around her. She looked around, but she was alone. She reached for a cigarette, but it wasn't there. Then, she knew. What was beginning to crowd her desk, the seat of power she was close to having, was her conscience, and it screamed out a truth.

A sickening feeling crept its way across her midsection like icy tingles signaling something unpleasant about to happen. She grabbed for her wastebasket as her stomach expelled her lunch.

The vice president was slipping on his Nikes, getting ready for another game, when Carlson came in and reported that Cox was delayed getting in from his out-of-state assignment.

"What a loss. What else do I have today, Remy?"

"You're to meet with Secretary Grantham, Sondra Thompson, and Andrew Warner on the Benghazi thing."

"I think I'd rather play ball. Did you see how our UN ambassador did with it yesterday?"

"Too bad Secretary Grantham couldn't have done those shows himself."

"Yeah. Good point. It was like he wanted no part of it. Funny, eh?"

"Funny isn't the word," Carlson said.

Two days later, Paul Gladston sped the familiar ninety miles from downtown Columbus and went directly to Marlyn Burdette's Mount Lookout apartment on Ellison Avenue. "Dern is detailing me to Cincinnati to finish Evers's cases and help you with some of the administrative crap," he had told her.

All she said was, "Okay." There was no reaction, no interest.

All the way down I-71, Gladston thought about their conversation, and he began to worry about the young woman for whom he was beginning to care. This was not something casual, he admitted. Mare was somebody real, someone to spend time with, somebody to...It seemed too soon to complete the thought.

He pounded up the stairs to the second-floor two-bedroom. The door opened when he tried the knob. He saw her sitting by the window overlooking Ellison. She must have seen him come up. She didn't move, but he heard her breathing hard. Was she crying?

"I never asked him," Mare said when she turned her face toward him, her cheeks wet with tears. "I thought about it, but never asked. I always thought I'd get the chance sometime."

"What, Mare? What didn't you ask who?"

"Nelson. I always wondered if he was related to Medgar Evers. Whenever I thought of Nelson, words like *brave, heroic,* and *character* jumped into my mind. If ever there were heroes for all of us..."

Paul sat down opposite her and let her talk. The more she did, he noticed, the firmer her voice became. She moved from sentiment and pity and grief to another emotion altogether.

"And do you know what the Fairfax Police said to me today when I called?" She didn't wait for an answer. "They said their official report will say that it was an accidental hit and run."

"Accidental?" Paul all but bellowed in surprise. "What the hell is going on here?"

"Yeah," she said, her eyes hard and cold. "Accidental. What the hell is that all about? Just any old black man run down in a Frisch's parking lot. Bullshit. It happens every day doesn't it?" She stopped to look at him. "Well, doesn't it?"

"Mare, you're talking to me, remember? We both know damn well this is all connected to the stuff Nelson saw at the IRS and to this SoftSec thing. What else could it be? And don't you wonder why he was out so late on a Sunday night?"

"Somebody put an analog drone on him, didn't they?" Burdette shot back. "And you know, I wondered about him being out, but heck, half his diet was Frisch's and Skyline. Maybe he just had a taste for a Big Boy or something." Both became silent. "Hey, that reminds me. When are we going to reclaim his laptop and case papers? OPM will be getting antsy if we don't get their stuff soon."

Paul nodded.

"Try this out," Mare said, not through. "First, the police said they had to keep the stuff because it was a vehicular homicide. Now, they're washing their hands of it, and they say the stuff has to be inventoried and processed, whatever the hell that means."

They both let out all their air, as if their venting was also a necessary process.

"I was worried about you, Mare."

"Don't be," she answered dismissively. "Look, I didn't mean it that way." She smiled at him. "You know what I remember most about Nelson's funeral service? It was what his minister said. Something about walking a different path, one of righteousness.'"

"Something's changed with you. I can hear it."

"You're damn right something's changed. You know, Paul, when you and Nelson used to talk about political stuff and what you call the grand scheme of things, I always thought you guys were smart and all that, but that you took yourselves a little too seriously, that none of the Washington bull crap meant anything to ordinary people. People like me." She looked at him, her lips pressed together. "Don't you see, Paul? None of it used to matter. Now I am pissed."

He looked at her, appraising someone he'd never seen before, someone he admired even more than the other Mare Burdette.

"Now I know it does matter," she went on. "If they can knock down a giant of a man like Nelson Evers just like that, then this country has a problem. Character and integrity should mean something—it should give you some armor. You know, Paul, when he trained me, I thought he'd come from another age, and at first, I rolled my eyes every time I saw him in action."

"But?"

"But then, I saw that he was a man whose conscience didn't have a lien against it. He never had to borrow honesty, because it was always in stock with him. The guy was amazing. And now, some creepy bastard has taken him away from us. For what? I want to know who that bastard is, and somehow we're going to get some points on the board for Nelson."

"Look, Mare, I'm with you, but you know, we are not going to die to make that happen. Nelson wasn't careful, and I'm not being funny, but he didn't watch his back, and he didn't have anyone around to do that for him. You and I aren't going to make that mistake, because that's what it was."

"What's this you-and-I stuff, Mr. Gladston?"

He smiled into her shimmering eyes. "Just what I said, Ms. Burdette. We are going to get through this together. If, uh, when it's all over, you're, um, not interested, then we'll part company—but not until I know you're safe. Understand?"

"Yes, I understand," she said in a low whisper. Her tone wasn't at all romantic. Just committed. "But just you understand that goes both ways, Paul, and don't ever underestimate the little people."

They laughed together, small, sad sounds though they were. "And now, get out of here, because if anybody's watching us, we're not giving them any ammunition. Where are you staying?"

"There's no place close—some hotel in Norwood. You sure you want me to go?"

At the podium, Winston Hardy could be seen working the private gathering's political emotions in the grainy video playing on the

News Global screen. "I need your support," Hardy was saying in May, "because nearly forty-seven percent of Americans are already on the government payroll and I don't expect them to vote for me. If all of us here—right in this room—want to achieve a conservative agenda, our victory has to begin right here."

"And there you have it, ladies and gentlemen," Forbes Flannery said into the camera. "Governor Hardy's lament about the forty-seven percent is on every news channel tonight, some four months after it was secretly videoed. Let's have William Herzog give us his take. William, what say you?"

"This video was shot in May of this year, even before Hardy had secured the nomination, and so he was peddling his conservative credentials—carefully. Back then, he needed to convince the base he was one of them, and that's what he was doing.

"Often we hear the lame excuse that someone's words were taken out of context, but that is exactly what has happened here, cleverly purloined by an obvious plant from the Williams campaign. Way to go, Sheldon Ingber."

"And what about that forty-seven percent? Do you think that's accurate?"

"Whether it's forty-seven percent or some other number close to it is irrelevant, in my opinion. The fact is that over the past three years in particular, the number and percentage of Americans comprising such a number has grown substantially—witness the USDA's Food Stamp program, to name just one."

"Former President Jefferson Harper has already started naming at least one other. Let's take a look at this clip from, of all places, The Villages, in Florida, usually considered a Republican stronghold. Here he is making the pitch for President Williams. Roll it."

"And what is Governor Hardy saying now, my friends?" Harper's drawl was as unmistakable as the Dixie bartender asking if you'd like a shot and a beer. "He's saying that forty-seven percent of all Americans are on the dole, on the government payroll, on the couch collecting checks paid for by their fellow citizens. Well, you of all people know he's wrong about that, now don't you? Looking around at this crowd, you all look like you're of age to collect Social Security. Of course, none of the women look that old, just the men."

Polite laughter broke the calm.

"We laugh, but everyone here, I suspect, receives a government check every single month. You earned it, and you depend on it. The governor is saying all of you are part of the president's base, and you know what, folks, I hope he's right."

Flannery chuckled out loud at the former president's delivery. "Well, William, what do you think about what President Harper is saying these days?"

"That he's saying anything on Averell Williams's behalf at all is what is amazing," Herzog said. "In 2008, his cousin called the then-candidate Williams inept, inexperienced, and, legislatively speaking, inert. Until today, one would have thought Jefferson Harper had taken a trip to the moon for all of 2012, but now, he wheels out the charm. Does he have an issue? Of course, he does. Will he play the card well? Of course, he will. That he is doing so at all, I repeat, is most mysterious."

"I agree. William, I was wondering if you would agree with me on another point. Over the past ten days or so, the most important story out there has been the Benghazi attack, and one has to believe the Administration needed something else grabbing the public's attention. So a video made in May suddenly surfaces in late September. It almost seems as if the Democrats kept this on the shelf for just the right moment, and this forty-seven percent story sure takes some of the oxygen away from Libya, doesn't it?"

Herzog turned toward the camera with a sly smile usually reserved for a magician and his rabbit. "Of course. Just in the past few days, Secretaries Roberts and Grantham admitted the obvious, that Benghazi was a terrorist attack, almost *sotto voce* insofar as the mainstream media is concerned. Rolling out the Hardy gaffe couldn't have been more timely."

"Thank you, William. I'd just like to point out that early voting has already begun in some states, and perhaps as the campaign rolls along, we'll find out just what it was that lifted President Harper off of his couch to gather up some of those votes."

"Nathan, how're we coming?" Enrique McCord needed to ask the question but didn't want to know the answer. He kept hoping there'd be some electronic obstacle to the Turnover Project, as the vice president had come to call it, but what he'd conceived, and Nathan Conaway was building, was totally foolproof. As he asked the question, his voice was unsteady and overcaffeinated. *No sleep and a clouded conscience would do that.* Bridget did not know the risks he'd taken to build his business, and if he could help it, she'd never know of this one.

"Excuse me, sir. Did you say something else?"

"No. Just wanted to know if you're satisfied with all the arrangements."

"I'm satisfied, but in the end, it's you and you-know-who," he said, jerking his thumb up above his head, "who has to be happy." He clacked on his keyboard, completing another instruction for the ether. "As for me, this is the coolest thing I think I'll ever do. I can't imagine anything bigger or more important. The only other question will be, 'What's next?'" He laughed with the satisfaction of a man from another era smoking a Cuban cigar and sipping a rare brandy.

"Nathan," McCord said, hesitatingly. "Have you had any doubts about what we're doing?"

"You mean what our business is all about?"

"No. Providing election hardware and software is a good thing. It serves the interests of the American people, don't you see?"

"Of course. So, what are you talking about then?"

"The Turnover Project, Nathan. Does what we're doing bother you in any way?"

"No way, boss. If this is what the big guy wants, why not give it to him? Besides, like I said, it's totally cool."

"Have you considered that this little dirty trick actually makes our core business irrelevant?"

"No." Conaway laughed out loud. "I hadn't thought of that, but it's damn funny, isn't it? SoftSec makes a lot of money on the one end, and cashes in, so to speak, on the other. It makes this whole thing even cooler, now that you put it that way." He turned to his keyboard. "Hey boss, no offense, but you better let me get to this. I have just a few more instructional interfaces to prepare, and then we're done."

McCord nodded, his face expressionless. He went to the restroom and, without thinking about it, washed his hands and looked into the mirror. What he saw was a man trapped in his own success. Again, thoughts of Bridget and their boys came to his mind's eye.

"Paul," Mare said, on her cell. "I just received a call from Janice, who finally heard back from somebody at the Fairfax Police Department. They're releasing Nelson Evers's effects, including all of his NIS stuff. Can you meet me at the Fairfax PD?"

"I'll find it," he spoke into his cellphone.

Thirty minutes later, at the dispatcher's window, they asked to see the officers who had called on Burdette earlier, but were told the men were not available. They presented their credentials, filled out several forms, and were handed the large equivalent of a Ziploc bag.

Gladston checked the laptop as carefully as he could, and riffled through the case material. Whether anything had been copied or tampered with, he couldn't tell. Last, he picked up Evers's standard-issue notebook, a small flip-top affair, with about fifty pages in it, all in Evers' personal shorthand. The clerk looked bored as she asked several questions for the record before the NIS pair left the station.

"Tomorrow, when we have a minute," Mare said, "we can look at all this stuff more closely. Nelson had his act together, so I don't think we'll find any surprises."

"That's a plan. Since we're here, want to go to the Frisch's Evers was heading for? I could use a Big Boy."

"Sure," she agreed, but disinterestedly.

Once inside the diner, Mare approached the two officers eating at the counter. "Hey, do you remember me?"

The talker of the two turned, clearly surprised. "Sure I do. It's Burdette, isn't it? What can I do for you?"

"We learned your department is now classifying our investigator's death as a hit and run, not the vehicular homicide you thought it was. What's up with that?"

"That was the chief's decision after he reviewed our reports," he said, looking at his shoes.

"Sorry, that's not a good answer. That driver ran down one of the best investigators in this country, and that was no accident. You said so yourself."

"Look, Burdette, I can't talk about it. You'll have to see the chief."

Gladston spoke up. "You look like decent guys, and we have good relationships with PDs all over the United States, but when one of ours gets run down in your jurisdiction, you're not going to talk about it? What if he had been your partner?"

Red-faced with either anger or embarrassment, the policeman began to speak, but the silent partner cut in. "Look, you two," he said, looking around carefully. "You never heard this from us, but the chief got a call from somebody in DC, and all of a sudden, it's no longer a possible homicide." He lowered his eyes. "I'm really sorry about Evers. There's nothing we can do."

Burdette and Gladston looked at the two officers, nodded in silent thanks, and left. Outside, Gladston said, "I guess I'm not so hungry now."

"Well, we've both got work to do. We'd better get at it."

"Hey, workaholic. Why so down?"

"Why? For God's sake, Paul, we're handling a dead man's stuff and it's not just any man. It's somebody who could have been my uncle, my father. It's a guy who was run down and killed, no matter what the village idiots have been paid to say."

"Take it easy."

"I won't take it easy. I told you. I'm mad as hell, and seeing his stuff just makes me madder."

"Sorry. I need to remember how close you two became."

Squinting in the sunlight, she looked up at him and slowly let a smile come to her lips. "You might be a keeper, Paul. Thanks." She stretched up and kissed him, then looked around to make sure they were not seen.

"Gee, what are you afraid of?" he kidded her.

"One of the bags I carry, Paul—fatefully fearful. And now, scared as hell."

OCTOBER

Politico/George Washington University Poll
October 1-4
Williams 49%
Hardy 48%

Pew Research Center Poll
October 4-7
Williams 45%
Hardy 49%

Milton Jennings wondered if New York City's weather could have been more welcoming to President Williams as he hosted the last campaign fundraiser of the quadrennial cycle. At the Palace, the Secret Service had its own nightmare screening and protecting both the courtyard, which faced the back of St. Patrick's Cathedral across Madison Avenue, and the gathering space up the stairs and inside the hotel. The parties finally agreed there were too many windows looking down on the courtyard for the president to be safe. POTUS would remain indoors, the Secret Service ordered, while most of the guests—those who had not pledged sufficiently large contributions—could drink and mingle in the perfect autumn air.

Wherever they found themselves, Jennings noted, the guests were all well heeled. He knew most Wall Streeters were not as enthusiastic this time around, simply because the president had not been all that friendly toward business in his first term. Most of tonight's attendees were old money or East Coast entertainment moguls, who, like maple trees in season, were waiting to be tapped.

At the top of the steps, he eyed the courtyard until he found the target. Sheldon Ingber was schmoozing both a name-brand hotelier and a jewelry magnate at the same time. Jennings chuckled to himself as he ambled over to the threesome.

A drink in hand, the slightly rotund, the bushy-headed Ingber never stopped to sip his beverage, his clever patter in full spill. The group welcomed Jennings the billionaire, and the political urgency revved up a notch. Financial commitments having been pledged, the two marks excused themselves, and Jennings took advantage of the opportunity.

"Shel, you and I have to talk. Let's step over here for an uninterrupted moment."

"Milt, you have a very serious look on your face."

"Damn right, I do. Look, I do a lot of things for people who move a progressive agenda, but there are limits."

"What in the heck are you talking about?" he asked in a most respectful tone.

"You're his campaign manager, for heaven's sake. You should know what's bothering me. That call you had Morrison ask me to make." Jennings saw the look of total bewilderment on Ingber's face, his fabled moustache totally immobile. "Are you telling me Morrison's call did not come at your request—or Averell's?"

"Jesus, Milt, please tell me what you're talking about. I honestly don't know a thing about it."

"As you may know, one of our holdings in turn owns something called SoftSec, one of the largest election hardware and software firms in the country. In fact, they recently became even larger through the purchase of a large competitor. Anyway, SoftSec's CEO, a guy named McCord—who happens to hail from Texas—was apparently getting balky about executing a contract with the EAC."

"The EAC? Who or what is that?"

"A little known federal agency—the Election Assistance Commission. They assist in and oversee certain election procedures."

"So what does that have to do with anything?"

"According to Joe Morrison, the president and he have been concerned about voter irregularity, possible fraud, and SoftSec's contract requires it to perform a monitoring service this time around. So Morrison wanted me to lean on him."

"So why is that a problem?"

"Don't you see, Shel? McCord views it as a conflict of interest, and he's nervous because their recent purchase is being looked at by the antitrust people. But that isn't the real problem."

"I'm still not following."

"What I just explained to you was Morrison's pitch, but I think there's something ethically tacky about that contract and the relationship between McCord and Morrison. When I talked to McCord, he wasn't balky so much as scared to death. Does that make sense to you?"

"No, it still doesn't, Milt." Ingber looked like a freight train was coming at him. "I'm sure it was legit, but because of your concern, I will personally check this out. You can rest easy, old friend."

As he walked away, Jennings turned back in time to see Ingber texting someone on his iPhone as if his life depended on it.

"Shel, I can give you fifteen minutes," the vice president said coolly as his visitor pushed through the door of his West Wing office. "What's so important that I have to delay my campaign flight—one that you set up for me?"

He watched as Ingber slammed the door, walked directly to where he stood, and put his face within a half-dozen inches of his own.

Before Ingber could speak, Morrison said, "Do I need Secret Service protection here?" and he was serious.

"I wouldn't want to tell you what protection you'll need if what I heard is true, Joe. Tell me you haven't finagled some contract with the EAC to have one of your Texas pals manipulate votes this November. Tell me it's not true you've enlisted Milton Jennings in this same hare-brained scheme to taint the election. Tell me why I shouldn't walk down that hall and give Averell Williams every reason to make you resign from this ticket." His face and scalp scarlet with rage, Ingber took a breath and waited.

JOHN P WARREN

Vice President Morrison looked his prosecutor in the eye, took a deliberate step backward, and placed himself behind his desk. He let several seconds elapse before he spoke. "We will win this November more because of me than because of you. And you will not whisper a word to him about it."

"What's to stop me?"

"The president has cancer." He said it without drama because the words carried a punch all their own.

Instantly, all of the blood that had rushed to the peaks of Mount Ingber drained away, leaving a colorless face staring back. He took a step and sank into one of the chairs facing Morrison's desk. "Ca...cancer? How do you know? How could you know?"

"Never mind how I know, but I believe it's aggressive."

"Oh, God. What kind of cancer? Why hasn't he told anyone?"

"You'll have to ask him, Shel, but I wouldn't do that if I were you. It's not to be revealed until after the election, when he'll undergo treatment."

"He's told you this?"

"No, we've never discussed it, and you have just confirmed that he's not discussed it with anyone, except perhaps, the First Lady."

"This could kill us if it got out."

"That's why I took out an insurance policy, Sheldon, my friend. You've watched the polls. The race is even. Averell's disapproval rating is growing. And now there's Benghazi, the truth about which is being barely contained. Leaks about cancer would indeed end our one best chance at transforming our society. I simply could not depend upon your mythic campaign skills to see us through."

"And you think he's going to die in office?" Ingber's voice had flattened to a whimper.

"I don't know, Shel, but if he does, I was not about to let Emerson Grantham—or anyone else—succeed him." He let the last few words hang in the air.

Ingber appeared both speechless and frightened at the same time. All the steam had left him. After a few seconds, a wan smile found a place beneath the moustache. "You need to read me into the circle of knowledge, Joe."

"I'm not sure about that, and besides, what you don't know you won't have to lie about. Right?" He didn't wait for Ingber's assent. "Take my word for it that the election is all but over, and from you I need only one thing."

"What's that?"

"On Election Day, I need one of your geniuses—just one—who has at his mental fingertips the voting patterns of every fucking county in every fucking swing state. All the rest don't matter. If I have this one guy, somebody you trust like your mother, we can pull this off and no one will ever—that's ever, Shel—be able to prove a thing."

"Sounds like you've thought things through, Joe," Ingber said slowly and carefully. "Just one thing."

"What's that?"

"Don't leave any breadcrumbs."

"I'm way ahead of you. Way ahead."

With obvious effort, Ingber stood, walked over to the vice president, and extended his hand.

Morrison shook it and flashed the smile of one who has jumped the last hurdle.

"Give 'em hell in Madison, Joe."

After a three-hour flight to the Central Time Zone, Morrison's plane touched down and was met by an enthusiastic crowd of union members, always his strongest allies. Within an hour, the Vice President of the United States was introduced to the annual luncheon meeting of Planned Parenthood executives and staff from Iowa, Illinois, and Wisconsin, and his welcome could have been no finer. On their feet, the attendees applauded with their hands at head level as the vice president walked to the podium amid the bright lights and flashing cameras. Once there, he held his arms up in a double wave and broadcast his wide smile. When the applause subsided, he placed his hands on the podium, as if holding on for support, and wore a sober expression on his face. Taking their cue, the audience sat, stone quiet.

"My friends, we live in dangerous times. Ever since *Roe v. Wade*, so many of us have fought for the unfettered right of a woman to control her own body. Because of your unwavering support, with your safety often threatened, we have managed to establish against great odds the reproductive rights of women in every state, and let me say with no embarrassment whatsoever, I am proud of what we've done." The crowd rose and cheered.

"Despite all of our accomplishments, my friends, I also stand by my opening statement. We live in dangerous times. Why do I say that? Because women in this country face the greatest threat to their personal rights since the day before *Roe v. Wade* became law. And what is that threat? Winston Hardy and Olivia Johnson Smith! The Republicans have never been so bold as in this election. In the past, there has never been a woman nominated to a presidential ticket by the Republican Party. But now, Winston Hardy has had the audacity to insult us all by attempting to bury women's rights in a noble speech about human rights. And we all know what he'll do as president.

"He'll attempt to impose his worn-out ideas on every woman in this country, and he thinks it'll go down easier because he's found an unwitting partner in Olivia Smith. How hard they must have searched to find a woman who would go along with policies that would return women to the back alleys? Yes, Hardy and Smith want to take us back to a darker time in our nation's history where women were second class and had no control over their lives.

"Yes, my friends, a vote for Hardy-Smith would be a return to the past. As for President Williams and myself, well you know where I stand, because I haven't changed my views with every new breeze that blows. And I can assure you the president feels the same. I put it that plainly, my friends. We have to put everything we've got into defeating our opponents, and with your help, we will stop at nothing."

❖

"Jeremy, I know you've been trying to get a minute with me for over a week now, so consider this the return phone call," the president said cautiously. He was alone in the master suite of the suburban Denver estate a local billionaire loaned to the campaign for the first presidential debate.

"Sir, are you sure you want to have this conversation today? You know, I initiated the call last week so that it wouldn't get in the way of the debate and matters of state."

"Thanks for your consideration, but I suppose you're telling me the news isn't that good if you're now wanting to postpone a conversation you wanted to have some days ago."

Commander Bolling cleared his throat. "Well, yes, sir, but you know, this could wait for tomorrow. One day won't matter."

"Let's skip the dance, Jeremy. We've known each other long enough, and we both know what's at stake. Let's have it."

"Well, sir, you'll recall that our earlier diagnosis was based both on a physical examination and biopsy as well as the series of PSA tests leading up to it."

"Hold on, Jeremy. What does PSA stand for again?"

"Prostate-specific antigen. It's a blood test that measures the protein level in your blood as secreted by your prostate gland. Generally, a level of four point or less is viewed to be in the safe zone, while levels above that number may be an indicator of cancer."

"And?"

"You'll also recall, sir, that when we'd performed the physical tests, your PSA was at eight point six, more than double the so-called good number. Of course, it's possible to have very high PSA numbers and not have cancer, and vice-versa. In your case, the biopsy showed conclusively that cancer had already developed."

"Don't keep me in suspense," the president said affably.

"We did the next PSA test in early May, and it came out less than nine point oh—about the same as in February. The blood draw we did ten days ago is another matter, sir. It is showing twelve point four."

"But you said a higher number may not be relevant." The president felt his confidence beginning to teeter, as if he could write the next part of the interchange himself.

"What some of us have come to suspect, sir, is that it isn't necessarily the number by itself. It's the rate and speed of its rise that's most relevant."

"In English, Jeremy, what does that mean for me?"

"It means, sir, that in my opinion there's little time to waste now—you have to agree to some action as soon as you are able."

"What exactly is involved?"

"I can give you some general information now, sir, but I am not a urologist and not a surgeon. Basically, these are your options: there's a cryogenic procedure that attempts to freeze things in place, there's a treatment with radioactive beads inserted in the prostate, and there are two varieties of surgery. There's the old-fashioned kind where they open you up, remove the gland, and eyeball and biopsy related structures. And there's the robotic version, which is less invasive, but accomplishes the same objectives."

"Where?"

"You're fortunate, sir, in that the best place in the world at the moment—in my opinion—is at Johns Hopkins in Baltimore, where the latest techniques were invented. The doctor who pioneered the best approach is now in Pittsburgh, but you needn't go there to have this done."

"When?"

"In the best possible scenario, Mr. President, it would be tomorrow, before the cancer invades your bladder and lymph system, or worse, metastasizes to your bones."

"My God, you're putting me into an impossible situation."

"I don't mean to, sir, but I must speak to you from a medical standpoint only. If not tomorrow, then within a few days of the election, for certain. Every week you delay, well...In the meantime, with your permission, I would like one or two people at Johns Hopkins to take another look at what we've got—without identifying the patient—so that I have more information to give you. You may even decide to listen to what they have to say yourself, sir."

"We'll see, Jeremy. And now," he said with a darkening cloud hovering in his psyche, "first things first."

In Cincinnati's NIS office, not long after business hours, Paul Gladston used his first opportunity to carefully inventory Nelson Evers's professional belongings. Without the password, he couldn't access the dead man's government laptop, but he reaffirmed that no one had breached its physical integrity. The other material, casepapers and witness notes, he catalogued and put aside. In addition, there was a white business envelope with "Insurance" printed in large letters across the front. He put it aside as well.

As dusk began to creep across Fountain Square, Gladston heard the old oak and pebbled glass door open in the outer office. Perhaps, he thought for a moment, his paranoia level was rising, and for once, he wished he was armed. Stepping through the doorway, he was relieved to see Mare standing there like she was happy to have a bad workday in her rearview mirror. "Ready for a nice dinner?" he said.

She walked up to him, let her head rest on his chest as his hands caressed her shoulders. "This is another reason to like you: sometimes I like being held, but not enclosed." She whispered into his suitjacket. "What is it about you, Paulie boy? How could I have gone from *A* to *Z* so quickly? Two months earlier, we were fellow investigators, barely friends, and now?" Finally, she looked up. "Dinner, you said? Where to?"

Paul smiled at her. "Did you want to repeat all that after dinner at The Wine Guy? A flight of whatever, some good food, and then...you never know."

She poked him in the ribs. "I do know, buddy. I'm tired." She cast a glance toward the back room. "Finished back there?"

"Yeah, for tonight—Nelson's stuff. Tomorrow or Thursday, I'll put it all together and write the memo to Clancy and OPM. There's no urgency since I'm about to complete his cases and have all of his notes. Let's go."

They drove in silence to the restaurant where a twenty-minute wait got them a table for two in a quiet corner. "Now don't yell at me, little one," he said. "But in about an hour, the first presidential debate begins. Do you mind if I watch it at your place?"

"An hour ago you had your mind on something else."

"And you told me to get another plan. Right?"

"Don't you ever multitask?"

Since Pete Clancy had scheduled a national telecom for midmorning, and they had plenty to do downtown, Paul and Mare decided to share a ride to the office.

"I wonder what the polls will show after Hardy said he'd kill Big Bird," said Paul.

Mare laughed. "Oh, I know. He seems like a decent guy, but someone not used to public speaking without a script. He just doesn't have the experience Williams has."

"But it was as if President Williams wasn't even there last night. I mean, the guy was practically speechless. I'll be surprised if Hardy doesn't come out on top when the polls are published."

"You might be right. Williams picked one hell of a time for an off night. Wonder what he had on his mind?"

"Benghazi," Paul guessed. "They've really been busy figuring out how they're going to lie about it."

"All right. Enough. I'm not spending my day with you listening to the truly live version of News Global."

"Okay, okay. Truce."

"Hey, Paul, what do you suppose Clancy wants to talk to all of us about?"

"Maybe more about the contract termination. I suppose that's why it's at ten thirty our time. He's not getting the west coasters up too early."

They parked, picked up some coffee, and lugged their heavy briefcases to the NIS offices diagonally across from the federal courthouse where Nelson had once said they used to camp. They both chatted with Gladys, checked their mail, and made a few phone calls.

In the back office, Burdette spotted the envelope marked "Insurance."

"Paul, what's this?"

"Oh, that. I found it in Nelson's stuff—it was buried in his case papers, and I didn't notice it when I gave it a once over at the Fairfax PD. I just assumed it was some personal stuff, and I didn't want to open it."

"Got it. Maybe you should send Pete a quick e-mail about it."

"Why not just ask Dern?" she said. "Clancy is getting ready for the phone call."

"I don't know, but the last few times I talked with Nelson, he didn't seem all that keen on Dern. I don't know why, but I think you should just send Pete something."

"Okay. Janice can yell at me later if she doesn't like it." Immediately, he cranked up his desktop and sent the message, not expecting a quick answer. He was surprised when within a few minutes his computer beeped. "Jeez," he said aloud. "He's quick. He's saying just open it and take care of it if it's something we need to get to the family."

"We've still got time before the telecon, so go ahead. I'm curious."

Once slit open, the envelope revealed several typewritten pages. Paul began to read. Halfway down the first page, he whispered, "Holy shit, Mare!"

"What, for cryin' out loud?"

"Wait, let me finish it." It took a full minute before he spoke again. "This is something Nelson typed up the night he died." He turned the document toward her. "See? The date is right here. And his penciled note indicates he was going to send this to the *Enquirer*, News Global, and the OPM inspector general. Read it if you want to, but I can tell you what it says." He handed her the sheets, but she waited for him to speak.

"Nelson laid out what he thought was happening at the IRS in Covington—suppressing conservative views—and the crooked contract with SoftSec to fix the election. At the end he says Benghazi was the last straw for him, that it was plain to him Williams and Morrison were deceiving the American people, and he needed to bring it all to somebody's attention."

"But Paul, there were no unmailed envelopes found by PD."

"Maybe he had already mailed them," he said.

"Couldn't have. I don't think he had the chance to mail them." Mare stared out the large square window, her brow wrinkled in concentration.

"What are you thinking about?"

"Somewhere along the line—I think it was those two Fairfax cops right here in this office—somebody told me the only witnesses were an old couple inside who saw the SUV stop and back up. Yes! The guy got out and picked something up. These letters, maybe?"

"But where the hit happened is at least a hundred feet from that window in a not-so-well lighted parking lot."

"Exactly," she said. "But it proves to me, anyway, that he didn't mail them. If he had, Paul—that was over three weeks ago—somebody would have made some noise about it. If not the *Enquirer*, then News Global— one of them would have been around to ask a question or two—especially since he was killed. But nothing."

"Son of a bitch."

Just then, Gladys entered the back room and told them to click on the speakerphone so they could all tune in to Pete Clancy's call.

"Good morning." Clancy began. "In my mid-September telecon, I gave you the news about our contract with OPM, and since then, you've received several communications from me and others with more information. Today, I want to give you further assurance that one way or another, all of you who wish to work as investigators will have good opportunities to do so, a few with NIS on other contracts, but most with other contractors or OPM itself."

Clancy went over other workload and personnel details. "Between now and December thirty-first, I expect all of us to comport ourselves like the true professionals we have been in conducting the government's business to the best of our ability, confident in the knowledge that virtually no one will be out of a job over this. Lastly," he said, concluding the twenty-minute call, "and once again, I extend my deepest thanks to the best background investigators this country has ever produced."

When it was over, Gladys began to cry softly, the second time in a month. Though ready for retirement, she had spent forty years in honorable duty to the US Civil Service Commission, then OPM, and now, NIS, and she said, "I refuse to let any mud be thrown at my reputation." Then she rose and left the room.

"Oh, crap." Mare said. "What should we do now?"

"First, I'm going to call Pete directly and tell him what this is before I fax it to him," said Paul. "No one else needs to see it for now."

"Good luck with that," she said. "I'm sure Pete will be bombarded with calls."

"Then I'll tell his secretary to pass him my name with a note about Nelson Evers's 'Insurance papers.'"

"And what about us, Paul? What the heck do we do? If I was scared outside the Fairfax PD the other day, I'm out of my freakin' mind right this second."

Glancing at the communicating door to Gladys's space, Paul put a hand on each of Mare's shoulders, looked her in the eye, and said, "Whatever happens, we will not be going it alone, Mare. Never forget that."

She looked back at him and said nothing, as tears of her own began to flow.

"The 2012 presidential election season is nearly at an end, ladies and gentlemen," Forbes Flannery noted after his opening monologue. "And what interesting twists and turns it has taken. Here with their latest pithy observations on the electorate's recorded opinions is the Dubious Duo, Jack Rispoli and Gardner Stewart."

"Forbes, you sound positively giddy that this feast for political junkies is about to end," said Rispoli.

"You're right on that score, Jack. I've enjoyed having you two on the show once or twice a week for months on end now." Flannery looked at the camera and rolled his eyes in mock agony.

"There's nothing humble about you, Forbes," said Stewart, enjoying the opportunity for a playful dig. "This country has no more important decision to make in the next three weeks than to elect either the man who will increase the national debt or the man who has the skills to help us all move on to a better deal."

"Point taken, Mr. Stewart," Flannery said in a serious tone. "What I'm fascinated about is that not that long ago guys like you, Gardner, wouldn't have given Winston Hardy a snowball's chance at the presidency, and now look where we are."

"What a nice segue. Thank you." Stewart raised his chalkboard with two figures scribbled in red. "As of today," he said, fetching another board from below the desk, "Gallup shows Hardy ahead by a point in a poll of twenty-seven hundred likely voters."

"And what does that mean, Jack?" said Flannery to the Democratic strategist.

"That means the president could be in trouble," answered Rispoli, his face in funereal repose. "But it is still too soon to count out a sitting president, in my opinion. And a professional betting man would still put money on Averell Harriman Williams."

Flannery said, "Will tomorrow night's debate between Joe Morrison and Olivia Johnson Smith make any difference?"

"Not much, in my opinion," Rispoli said. "Yet, if Smith carries the water against a skilled rhetorical aggressor like Joe Morrison, her performance will only add to the growing momentum for Hardy."

Stewart smiled as broadly as his face allowed him. "I'm so pleased to be in agreement with Joe on that one, but it's not the debates that Hardy has to worry about at the moment."

"C'mon, Gardner, don't tease us."

"Hardy's biggest problem is the media. Even though most of America clearly judged Hardy the big winner of the first debate, you couldn't tell that from the *New York Times*, CNS, Newshare, or CBN News."

"So you agree that the media's been in the tank for Williams?"

"No doubt about it. Just give those guys half a chance and they'll put their thumb on the scale."

"Jack, you say?"

Rispoli half smiled with the guilt of having eaten too many cookies before dinner. "I'd have to agree that the president has had a pretty easy time of it with the media."

"Anything else, guys?"

"In elections past, campaigns always worried about the October surprise," Stewart said.

Cheshire grin in place, Rispoli added, "You bet. There's always a wild card out there."

Mare began to feel like someone was watching her. When she turned around, checked her rearview mirror, or looked out her apartment window, she expected the boogieman, but no one was ever there. Nonetheless, she found herself changing her personal routine, something Paul advised her to do.

On a chilly mid-October night, she would have preferred walking down Ellison Avenue's slope and ducking into Zip's at the edge of Mount Lookout Square for a darn good cheeseburger and a beer. They knew her there, and with Paul stuck over the river doing neighborhood investigations, she wanted to get out. On the other hand, the short walk would be on a dimly lit street, usually a very safe neighborhood, but in the past few days, she shunned dark spaces.

She drove over to Hyde Park, and after navigating the square twice, found a well-lighted parking space close to her intended destination, the Cock & Bull, just across Edwards Road but within sight of her car. At the bar, she planted herself in front of one of the high-definition TV screens, the only company she hoped for. When someone touched her forearm, she half jumped and turned to defend herself.

"Oh, Ms. Burdette, I'm so sorry, I didn't mean to startle you. Do you remember me?"

A woman Burdette could never forget—someone who'd given her the most extraordinary witness statement she'd ever heard—occupied much of the space around her. "Sure, Amber," she said, steadying her hand on a cold glass of beer, "I remember you. How are things going?"

"Are you alone. I mean, I don't want to bother you."

"I am alone, and tonight you're welcome company. This stool is free—want to sit?"

Relief filled the woman's ample cheeks with color. "Oh, thank you, but I have a confession to make."

"Oh?" In the flash of a moment, Burdette envisioned her recanting the allegation about the election, the ripple effect of which would be hard to measure.

"Yes. You know, since not long after you and that nice Mr. Evers came to see me that day, I've hardly seen Nathan."

At that moment, Burdette felt Evers's presence as if he were somehow in the space between her and Bustamente, and she worked hard to hold the tears she knew would come if she let them. She guessed Amber didn't know what had happened.

Bustamente continued. "After work—and I've been putting in longer hours at Xavier—I come home and sit by the bay window of our apartment."

"Amber, is that your confession?" she said with a laugh.

She inhaled deeply and lowered her eyes. "Well, Marlyn, my confession is that I saw you park your car and walk over here. I don't have many friends in town, and well, I've been alone so much and..."

"Say no more. C'mon, have something to eat. I'm having the turkey wrap and fries. And here it's a good choice."

She laughed. "Oh, thanks. Nathan and I used to come here, but...I haven't been in lately." She sighed. "You know he's been on the road so much...I miss him."

When the bartender came, she ordered the French dip with fries and a Diet Coke. They ate in silence as Martha Raddatz came on the screen and introduced the only vice-presidential debate to occur. "Tonight, we are honored to have with us two Americans who have distinguished themselves in different ways. On the one hand, we have a sitting vice president who, along with the head of their ticket, seeks a reaffirmation by the American people. On the other hand, we have a US senator from Indiana, the first female nominee for either spot on a Republican ticket."

Speaking directly to the combatants, Raddatz continued. "Mr. Vice President, Senator, you know the rules. There will be three areas for discussion, two questions in each for each of you, and time for rebuttal.

The first question goes to Senator Olivia Smith. Senator," she said, allowing the cameras to pivot correctly. "The American people want to know what is it that makes you qualified to be a heartbeat away from the presidency."

"Thank you Martha. I am, indeed, honored to be here tonight in Danville, Kentucky, a sister state to four others in America's heartland, including my own, Indiana. Before I answer your question, I'd like to address a comment to Vice President Morrison." Senator Smith turned to look her opponent in the eye. "Not long ago, Mr. Vice President, you made public remarks showing a great deal of disrespect to me as the Republican nominee for your office, as a senator from Indiana, and as a woman. In fact, you insinuated that my party chose me to somehow hide behind when Governor Hardy articulated his views about human rights. You should know, sir, that along with millions of other women and mothers in this country, I wholeheartedly believe there should be clear restrictions on third trimester abortions, and on behalf of those millions of women just like me, I insist you show us respect for our views, even if they differ from yours!"

Despite rules to the contrary, the applause was more than polite, and Morrison was starting from behind.

"I'm glad someone has finally said what so many of us believe," Bustamente whispered. Both women turned with a smile when there was applause behind them as well.

"I wonder if some of these women are clapping because a woman like Smith stood up to a bully like Morrison," Burdette said.

"You may be right about that. But we know who's going to be elected, don't we?" She lowered her voice even more. "And this is one time I'd like to know how the people really feel."

"Yeah, me too."

Their food came. After a few bites, Bustamente broke the silence. "Marlyn, did your people pass on what I said?"

"We sure did, Amber, but guess who's in the chain of command." She inclined her head toward the screen on which Morrison's face now appeared. "It's not that easy."

"Isn't there somebody else you can tell?"

"The same people you can. There's nothing stopping you from calling the newspapers or a TV station, you know."

"But they'll just think I'm some crazy woman."

"What do you think they'd think of me, then? You see what I mean?"

"Then, there's something I need to tell you. You know when I'm sitting at my window watching the square, I see lots of things."

Burdette laughed softly. "Yeah, like me walking into a bar."

"That too. But last weekend, there was a car, a big black Tahoe SUV with Virginia plates, parked just below our apartment. It had the moonroof pulled back, and when I looked down at it, I saw a face looking back at my window."

"For God's sake, Amber, are you sure?" Chills ran up her arm to the back of her neck. "You weren't seeing things?"

"I'm sure what I saw—a man, very tan, with blond hair that you could hardly see. He had a crew cut." She paused. "Because of the curtains, I don't think he saw me, but it scared the crap out of me. There's a two-hour limit there, so he moved a few times when a spot close to that one was open, but it was the same guy, both Saturday and Sunday. Just watching."

"Did you call the police?"

"No. I don't know who to trust. Do you?"

"And now he's gone?"

"Yeah, and after the election, maybe I'll be gone too."

"If you're thinking about leaving Nathan, why not leave now?"

"Oh, I don't know, Marlyn," she answered, almost in a whine. "I really care for him. I guess I'll see what happens."

In Danville, polite, sustained applause ended the debate, and both candidates shook hands, each carrying the biggest smile of victory they could muster. They waved, gathered their families around, and made the kind of small talk that made every viewer in the land long to eavesdrop. When the scene played itself out, Morrison exited stage left with Sharon and their children, and the famous grin exited as well. "Look, honey," he whispered to his wife, "I need to make one phone call and attend to the usual postgame bullshit, so let the guys take you and the kids back to the airport and get comfortable on the plane. I'll be along shortly."

Sharon Morrison said, "Good job, dear."

Morrison went directly to one of his two Secret Service minders. "Marty," the vice president said with a biting tone, "I take it you haven't completed your all of your extra assignments as yet. I want you to get that done—and soon."

"One's already taken care of, sir, but you know I just can't disappear. I was in Cincinnati over the weekend checking some things out, and I'll head back again when there's a hole in your schedule."

"Hole or not, everything must be taken care of by close of business November sixth."

"Yes, sir. I think I understand."

"Just so you do, Marty. Remember what you said about missed shots—they'll get you every time. No loose ends."

The knock on the door was firm and insistent. Inside, Paul approached as quietly as he could and looked through the peephole. Smiling, he opened to the young delivery guy from LaRosa's bringing their sausage pizza. After grabbing a few Diet Pepsis from the fridge, Paul and Mare planted the pizza, plates, and sodas on the coffee table in front the TV and began switching back and forth between CNS, News Global, and ABS for their reportage of the second presidential debate, this one at Hofstra University.

While waiting for it to begin, Mare said she had a couple of things to tell him. "First, you'll never guess who I ran into the other night when you couldn't see your way clear to have dinner with me."

Inhaling two bites of one of his favorite Cincinnati treats, Paul said, "I was bustin' my butt in Kentucky while you were hangin' out at some bar, I suppose."

"Not just any bar—the Cock & Bull in Hyde Park—catty-corner across the street from where Nathan Conaway and Amber Bustamente park their pillows."

"Yeah, and I suppose Nathan Conaway, the human hairball, came in hittin' on you. Hope you had fun."

She laughed, almost choking on her Pepsi. "No, idiot. It was Amber—a sweet girl but a little dumb about stuff—who followed me in and told me some scary story about a black Tahoe—Virginia plates—and a guy checkin' out their apartment."

"Jesus, Mare. That was what ran Evers down? Would Bustamente have known about that?"

"Wait. The cops never said it was a Tahoe. The old folks just said it was a big, black SUV with out-of-state plates, and that's what was in the papers and the news. Evers's death got a lot of air noise for a few days around here."

"It could be the same vehicle. Could she have been makin' that up about the SUV and the guy?"

Jim Lehrer's voice filled the room. "In just a moment, we will have the second of three debates, this one hosted by Candy Crowley of CNN. Candy?"

The reporter began her introductions and laid out the rules, then began with the first question.

Mare looked at Paul. "I don't think so. Why would she? She's scared. And then, you'd think she made up all the other stuff, but for that we have too many other bits to back it up, when you think of what McCord and Conaway said."

"And then there's the secretary of state—a Democrat—up in Columbus. Even she thought the whole thing was shaky."

"Then the Tahoe thing might be real," she said slowly. "But so far, they've only come after Evers."

"I don't know, Mare. There's a lot at stake. If killing a retired federal investigator is no big deal to somebody, then..." They went on for many minutes dicing the known facts as finely as they were able.

Then the debate on the TV caught their attention. "Governor, I have to step in here and say that President Williams is correct," said

Candy Crowley. "He did, in fact, label the Benghazi incident as a terrorist attack in his Rose Garden comments the next day."

Mare and Paul watched as the inexplicable occurred. A news media person from a cable news network intervened on behalf of one of the political gladiators she was there to referee. "Holy Hell," Burdette said. "I guess I'm starting to see why you're so into this stuff. It's unbelievable that she could tilt the debate like that. Now this is something nobody could make up."

"Why should anyone be all that surprised? Hardy's momentum is growing and with only a few weeks left, he stands a good chance, but now the libs are desperate, and I guess interfering with a debate is okay if your guy needs help."

"My question is, why does a news reporter think the President of the United States needs her help? Can't Williams defend himself?"

"Nice point."

"Hey, back to Nelson Evers for a minute," Mare said. "Do you remember when we were up there in Dern's office for the telecon with Clancy? Well, on the way back down I-71, Nelson said something really strange to me I've never figured out."

"Which is?"

"He said something like, 'You know, Mare, sometimes a college diploma can tell the real story about a person.' And he was kinda sad when he said it."

"Strange thing to say," Paul said, and then stuffed the last bit of pizza into his mouth. "Can we switch back to News Global?"

"I'm starting to love these two guys," Mare said, pointing to Jack Rispoli and Gardner Stewart sitting in the spin room with Meredith Ramirez.

"So guys," said Ramirez on the screen. "What do you think? Aside from the Benghazi interchange, did Hardy hold his own?"

Stewart addressed the camera on cue. "What we know, Meredith, is that Winston Hardy is more than holding his own with a president that thus far in this campaign, has raised over seven hundred million dollars against Hardy's four hundred fifty million. With such a huge advantage, this race shouldn't be this close, but it is."

"And you, Jack, what do you think?"

"What I think, Meredith, is that this race is about over. The president certainly gave the lie to all that had been said about his performance in the first debate, and there's no doubt he's mastered his talking points."

Gladston turned to Mare. "You're gonna hate this, but I have to go to Columbus tomorrow. Dern is pissed about somethin' and wants to see me. I don't want to leave, especially with all that's goin' on. I want you to plan your day so you're with a lot of people as much of the time as possible."

"Hey, Paulie boy, don't think twice about me. I'll watch out, but you'd better be back soon."

"Let's see what Dern says. Maybe I can come back the next day unless she has some hot case there."

"For cryin' out loud, Paul. It's not as if we're the only two NIS investigators in Ohio. Don't take this wrong, but I want you with me."

"I am taking it wrong," he said, leaning over and kissing her hard, and holding on tight.

Up at five, Paul kept the lights off as he worked his way around Mare's apartment. She had windows looking onto Ellison Avenue and onto the side driveway leading back to the four single garages under her building. Approaching each window from the side, he scanned what he could see. Much relieved, he donned his running shorts, shoes, and a light sweatshirt before quietly going down the back stairs. In the small rear parking lot, he glanced in every direction, and because of the hilly topography, he didn't think anybody would approach from the rear.

He climbed the small fence of the adjoining building and exited to the street from that building's driveway. Once again, he scanned the entire street looking for a black Tahoe or any vehicle that looked occupied. Nothing. He ran several blocks in every direction an approach could be made to Mare's building. Nothing.

Returning in thirty minutes, he shaved, showered, and dressed without waking the woman he knew he loved. Leaning over the bed, he pecked her forehead and whispered, "Love you, lazybones," then left, feeling that Mare, *his* Mare, was safe, at least for the moment.

Gladston nosed his car onto I-71 at the Redbank Road entrance and headed north while the seven o'clock traffic was mostly headed south into the city. Adjusting his lanky frame to the car's snug interior, he settled in for the ninety-minute ride to downtown Columbus. His plan was to see what was bugging Janice Dern and take care of some case-work before checking out his apartment somewhat northeast of Ohio State's sprawling campus.

The office was quiet. Either everyone was out working, or after Pete Clancy's telecon, they were job hunting in a city full of federal, state, and private sector opportunities for personable self-starters who could write a sentence without breaking into a sweat. He skittered by Dern's office, but not more than ten feet down the hall, he heard her voice.

"Ready whenever you are, Mr. Gladston."

"I'm here, and at your service."

"Have a seat," she said, and began ticking off concerns she had about him. "You're spending too much time in Cincinnati with Marlyn Burdette, and yes, I know there's a lot of work there and I sent you there, but you need to finish up. Second—"

Her cell phone buzzed and she picked it up. "Excuse me, I need to take this. Hold on a second, Paul."

"Hi," she said into the phone. "I'm in the middle of something, so I have only a minute." She became silent when her caller took over the conversation.

Gladston tried not to listen, but could hear a loud, strident, apparently female voice on the other end. While she talked, he let his eyes roam around Dern's office, and soon his gaze caught a clutch of diplomas and certificates on the wall immediately behind her. At first, he couldn't read the archaic printing on most, but he began to focus on them as best he could, remembering Nelson Evers's insight about what someone could learn from a college diploma.

"Look, Sis—" Dern said, but again her caller cut her off.

When his eyes met Dern's, she looked embarrassed but maintained her focus on the space directly in front of her.

Gladston saw the federal certificates for superior service, the performance awards, and in the center, the Bachelor of Science degree from the University of Dayton. It took him a further few seconds to notice the name.

"Bye, Mayella," said Dern, and she hung up the phone.

Then Paul realized the name on the diploma was "Janice Michele Washington." He smiled at her, hoping the carpet ride would end soon.

"Where was I?" she said. "Oh, yes. Paul, second is that you sent your request about Nelson Evers's envelope directly to Pete Clancy. You should have sent that to me and sought my guidance. In fact, you never sent me a copy of it. That is just plain disrespect, in my opinion."

"I'm sorry, Janice. I didn't think it through," he responded. Looking up, his eyes landed on the diploma once more, and with what he knew was a trick of the mind, names floated in his consciousness, combining and recombining. Nelson Evers. Janice Dern. Janice Washington. Mayella Washington? In a flash, he realized how glad he was to be there so that he could see what Nelson Evers saw.

"All right, Paul, I'll accept that, but I am your direct supervisor, and you can trust me with anything."

Once out of Dern's earshot, he called Burdette on his cell. No answer. She was probably in an interview, and she was fine. He settled for an innocuous message saying he'd call later. In the afternoon, there was a text message saying she would wait for his call around seven. After a stop at a Wendy's, Gladston headed home and waited a long twenty minutes, like a teenager impatient to call a girl for a date. At the earliest moment, he hit her number on speed dial and listened to the electronic rings.

"Hey," she said, a Burdette version of hello. "Tell me again what you said when you left this morning."

"Didn't I say, 'Bye, lazybones'?"

"No, you didn't, Paul Gladston. I do object to the lazybones part, but not to the other words I heard."

"In that case, I love you, and I hope there's a big smile at the other end of this call."

"Yes, there is, and I feel the same way, and I can't believe it."

"Can't believe what?"

"It's only been maybe three months since we went beyond case talk."

"I'm okay with that, and I hope you are."

"I'm getting used to the idea," she said, her voice still dizzy with disbelief. "Is this what you called to get settled? That we're a real pair, you and I?"

"I wish that were the only reason. For me, now, it's the most important, but there is another reason, and I don't know where it goes."

"Well, let's try it out."

"Okay, but be patient with me on this. You knew I was going to get my butt kicked when I went to see Dern today, and I was okay with that. I have no regrets—or apologies—about anything we've done—together or work related, especially in connection with Nelson Evers."

"Paul, skip the prologue."

"I guess we're a pair. You're already giving me directions. All of it's important, Mare, so just listen. Well, anyway, while I'm in Dern's office, a minute or so after she started in, she gets a call on her cell, and from what little was said on Dern's end, it was clear that she was talking to somebody named Mayella and that she is her sister." He heard Burdette start to speak. "Wait. Remember what you said just the other day about Nelson Evers telling you about what a diploma says about a person?"

"Yeah?"

"While Dern was on the phone, I checked out her wall of fame, and of course, smack behind her head with a bunch of other stuff is her college diploma. Did you know her maiden name was Washington?"

"No shit! So you think the Mayella Washington who likes to give me a hard time whenever I show up in Covington is Dern's sister? Like I'm there to beat on 'her people,' as she likes to say? Are you kiddin' me? She's Dern's fuckin' sister?"

"You eat with that mouth, lazybones?"

"Don't piss me off, Paulie boy."

"Yeah, her sister, but what the hell does that all mean?"

"Well, let's see, Sherlock. If Dern is Washington's sister, then both knew Nelson was really torqued about the crap at the IRS with conservatives. And since Dern knew about the SoftSec allegation, she's the only one who knew what Evers knew about the IRS and the election—and them being sisters."

"Yeah, but Jesus, Mare, Janice Dern wouldn't have had Nelson killed. He may have been something of a pain in the ass to Janice and her sister, but he was no threat to them. And when you think about it, as nasty as some union people can be, I can't believe NTU types would run somebody down somebody like that. What happened was cold. It was done by people who saw it as their job."

"Let's assume that what Amber Bustamente said, and what the old folks at Frisch's said, connects the dots—a black Tahoe with Virginia plates."

"Think about it," said Paul. "A black SUV was here to kill Evers and a black Tahoe was here a few nights ago checking out Amber's apartment. Virginia plates. This is coming from somebody in Washington."

"From the IRS? I just can't believe they'd kill somebody to keep secret what apparently is an open secret in the department. It doesn't make sense. Something else triggered this."

"Suppose the same people in DC have something to do with the IRS and SoftSec?"

"I don't see any link."

"The only connection is us, Mare—NIS or OPM. And, okay, Kristen Bartley isn't out to kill anyone, but this is an election year, and a scandal at the IRS along with the SoftSec thing goes a lot higher than OPM. And NIS just lost its contract."

"And OPM reports to the vice president. What Amber told me ties it all together. Oh, my God, Paul. You think Morrison would go this far?"

"Crazy, isn't it. We almost said it out loud the other night. And now we did."

"Yeah, crazy," said Mare. "All this to get reelected?"

"They're not tellin' us about Benghazi. Why would they tell us about the IRS, which somebody up top had to initiate? No union flunky thought that one up. And they sure as hell wouldn't fess up to a plot to steal the election!"

"This isn't a freakin' movie, Paul. This is real life."

"Right. Now it's real life."

Alone in his apartment, Gladston couldn't stop thinking about Nelson Evers and replaying the tapes, as it were. Despite what he and Mare had concluded, this was the United States, dammit, and people didn't pull that crap here. Yet, it couldn't have been Dern, and it wouldn't have been her sister. He wouldn't buy that no matter how angry he could get about the IRS and what they were doing to conservatives. *Even if the IRS thing went all the way up, would Evers be killed to keep it a secret? No way!*

It was all about the election, and nothing else. People who craved power would not kill just to hide dirty tricks regarding the Tea Party, but they would kill to hide the fact they were going to pervert the one right that's at the heart of our democracy—the right to vote. That would be something even the liberals would get upset about, because they knew if they could do it to the Republicans, the Republicans could do it to them. Stealing Illinois in 1960 was one thing, but stealing a bunch of states in 2012—that was another.

In fact, until Evers's death, most people would have dismissed Amber Bustamente's nasty secret as the imaginings of a depressed woman jilted by an electronics junkie. Evers's death actually confirmed that the plot to steal the election was real and that people at the top were prepared to do whatever it took.

If he thought about that fact first, everything else fell into place. The IRS activities were designed to suppress the conservative vote by limiting their fundraising. The Benghazi talking points were designed to deceive the public into thinking they're safer than they are. But stealing the election? That must have been somebody's backup plan in case all the other tricks failed. *Why only Evers? Because his name showed up on two screens at the same time?*

It was getting late, and the *Daily Show* came on. Jon Stewart's patter blurred in the background as Evers's murder—and what he had come to think of it—lurked in the shadows of his mind. Suddenly, he was drawn to the other screen in front of him when President Williams appeared. In an instant, he switched off his mental ramblings, and tuned in.

Williams was letting Stewart interview him about Benghazi. *Really?* The president wouldn't let objective journalists ask him real questions about the attack, but he would let a comedian tackle the subject? *Must be a another softball game.* Then he heard Stewart gently point out that the administration's performance in managing the communications with the American people was "not optimal."

"An understatement, to say the least," Paul whispered with derision.

The president responded, "Here's what I'll say. If four Americans get killed, it's not optimal. We're going to fix it. All of it."

The words made him wonder if the president hadn't made the biggest slip of all. "Not optimal." *Is life so trivial to him?* "We're going to fix it." *Fix what?*

Evers's murder wouldn't leave the front of his consciousness. *Evers. Why just him?* Why would they—whomever they worked for—be watching Amber Bustamente, and only part time, apparently? That says there are only a few people involved—a very small circle. The vice president, McCord, Conaway, and by extension, Bustamente. *Why bother her? Because she spoke out? That, and because she's a loose end. And to quote the president, that is "not optimal."*

What about anybody else in the knowledge chain? Clancy? No, he's jaded—he won't be a hero. Dern? Not her. With her, it's about race, and it's their turn on top. Me? Mare? Maybe they killed Evers to warn everybody else. Maybe they'll leave us alone. As they say in Cincinnati: maybe when pigs fly.

Lives are nothing to people who think drones are a great answer for one's enemies. Somebody ordered a drone to hit Nelson Evers. A drone is watching Bustamente. It would be back—before the sixth of November. *For us?*

"Pete, this is Paul Gladston. I'm here in Cincinnati with Mare Burdette, and we'd like to talk to you."

"Sure, Paul. Is this without Janice or around Janice?"

He hesitated. "Around."

"I think you'd better explain yourself. Janice and I have worked together for a lot of years and she's next in your chain."

"I know that, sir, but we're hoping you'll listen to us. It's about Nelson Evers and what happened to him."

"What does that have to do with Janice Dern?"

"Maybe nothing. Maybe everything."

"All right. Get on with it."

Mare spoke up, "Do you remember when you were on your swing through Columbus a few months ago and I stood up and talked about what I'd seen at the IRS in Covington? And I mentioned the political atmosphere there?"

"And?"

"Well, afterward, Nelson and I spoke about it more than once, and he asked if he could take a few of my cases and see it all for himself. I guess he hadn't been there in a while."

"Get to it, please."

"He had a run-in with a woman he'd known as a kid in Cincinnati—Mayella Washington—the union chief. From what Nelson told me later, it got pretty hot."

"Where's this going?" "She warned him not to get too talky about what goes on at the IRS, and you know Nelson—he told her in no uncertain terms that he planned to make some noise about it."

"I'm still waiting."

"Pete, you have to be patient—follow the bouncing ball, please. Well, the day Nelson and I drove up here to have a telecon with you, Nelson met with Janice privately. He never told us what was said, but it wasn't all that pleasant. On the way home, he said something odd—about a college diploma telling the whole story about somebody."

"C'mon, Marlyn. Our contract's been canceled and I have a lot to do."

"Then he gets run down. First, the police say it's deliberate. Then they say it's accidental. We collect his stuff and find the letter we sent you. What we may not have mentioned is that the only witnesses, an old couple in Frisch's, said they saw the driver back up and stop. We think he picked up the letters Nelson was going to mail but didn't get the chance to."

"I'm listening."

"Then Janice gave Paul a hard time about spending so much time in Cincinnati."

Paul jumped in. "And in the interest of full disclosure as they say, I've been spending time here—cleaning up Nelson's cases, working others here, and, not that it matters, dating Mare." He cleared his throat in embarrassment. "Anyway, when Janice had me on the carpet in her office, she got a phone call from somebody named Mayella. I didn't remember who that was, but Dern called her 'sis' during the conversation. While they were talking, I noticed Janice's college diploma. I took a good look, remembering what Nelson had said to Mare, and son of a gun, her maiden name is Washington."

"So how are you going to connect this?"

"Janice and Mayella are sisters," Paul said. "It's not a stretch to think that when Nelson and Mayella had their run-in, she and Janice talked about it. And if Nelson confronted Janice when he realized they were sisters, it's not a stretch to think that Janice talked to Mayella about that."

"Big deal."

"Janice is the only person of all of us who knew Nelson was planning to say something out loud about the IRS and that he knew about the allegation concerning the vice president."

"For God's sake, Paul. Are you saying Janice killed Nelson?"

"Hold on, Pete. At Frisch's, the old folks said it was a big black SUV with out-of-state plates. Since then, Amber Bustamente found Mare and told her that a black SUV with Virginia plates has been watching their apartment. So, you're right, it's not Janice, but somehow there's a link between what Janice knew and Washington, DC."

"You have a hell of an imagination, Paul. Some people would say you've been smokin' somethin'."

"Have I? The fact that Evers never got to mail his letters—"

"How do you know that for sure?"

"Well," Paul said, "according to his pencil notes—you saw them—he planned to send three letters. Have you heard or seen anything on this from any source yet?"

"No, but someone might have thought it was just a crank letter."

"Not someone with knowledge of certain background investigations involving the EAC and the Vice President of the United States. Somebody would be saying something if any one of the letters had reached their destinations. Especially if Evers wound up dead. Right? And you, Pete."

"Me?"

"We're assuming you passed Nelson's letter on to somebody?"

"I certainly did—to Bartley—right away."

"You hear anything? Besides our contract being canceled?"

"No."

"Awfully quiet everywhere, ain't it?" Mare said.

His voice barely above a whisper, Clancy answered, "Yeah, it is."

"So Pete," Paul asked, "what the hell do we do?"

"What do you mean?"

"I'm starting to think Mare and I are loose ends—like Evers."

"Couldn't be," Clancy said, but his voice was uncertain.

"And Bustamente and her boyfriend, not to mention McCord. Pete, somebody is playing for keeps. This election means a lot to somebody."

"I just don't think Williams would go that far."

"Because it wouldn't be 'optimal'?" Paul said sarcastically.

"If this is real. Bear in mind, Evers's death could have been a more ordinary crime, and what Bustamente thought she saw could have been mostly in her imagination."

"That's what we'd like to think, but for Mare and me, I don't want to take any chances."

"It's not Williams," Clancy said. "It has to be Morrison, but why he would want to risk everything for this election, I don't know, and unless there's a good reason, it makes no sense. What I am pretty sure of is that it was him who nailed us on the contract."

"How do you know?" Mare asked.

"Because neither Bartley nor the director of OPM could do this on their own. It looks like all roads lead to Morrison."

"Then who can we tell? How can we stop this?" Paul asked.

"I honestly don't know. When one of the two top guys can pull any string he wants to, it's hard to say. You may think that some bad guy from DC killed Evers, but who would believe you? And who's going to believe this whole election thing? It's just too fantastic."

"Couldn't we go to somebody like News Global?" Mare said.

Clancy said, "They're the only ones who would listen to you—politely—but they could never go public with anything so farfetched. Not in time for the election. There's only two weeks left."

"What about the FBI?" Paul asked.

"I honestly don't know who to trust these days. With these people, saying anything puts a target on your back."

"Pete, could we be in danger?" Mare asked.

"Maybe. Why don't the two of you take some leave and disappear for a while?"

"What about Bustamente and the others?"

"At the very least, call them. Warn them to be careful. Mention Nelson Evers. If anybody sees anything—you two or the rest of them—don't hesitate to call the police. At this point, that's all you can do."

"Jesus, Pete, what kind of country do we live in?"

"Anymore, I'm sure I don't know."

"Milt, what a pleasant surprise," Ingber said into his cell phone. He tried to keep his voice at the level of a low steroidal high but found it hard to do so. The third presidential debate would be the next day and he was wound, not in the least by the fact he felt certain of the election's outcome. *What timing. Uncle Miltie could wreck my mood with a dose of scruples.* "How can I help you this afternoon?"

"I suppose you're prepping the president for the last bout, eh?"

"You got that right, Milt, so I do not have much time to chat. What's up?"

"I know you'll remember our conversation at the Palace three weeks ago—about Joe Morrison and the EAC contract?"

"I do."

"I want you to know, Shel, that conversation has never left my mind. It hangs over this election like a giant raven hovering over its kill."

"You've never been quite so poetic, Milt, but I want to assure you that I spoke to the vice president the very next day before he left for Wisconsin, and I am embarrassed to confess something to you."

Jennings remained silent.

"It's not what you think, though," he said, attempting a chuckle. "Joe reminded me in no uncertain terms that what he had said to you was entirely accurate. Apparently, he and the president had had a conversation about voter fraud, and EAC is one of those agencies in Joe's kit bag of responsibilities." Ingber could hear the older man exhale in relief. *So far, so good.*

"But what about the relationship between Morrison and McCord? And what about McCord, in effect, overseeing a process for which he also has a contract?"

"You are a very astute man, Milton, but why should I be surprised? I'm talking to one of the most successful businessmen in the United States."

"And the answer is?"

"An easy one. Joe assures me his relationship with McCord is at the proper arm's length, given the SoftSec contracts. He also assures me there is no conflict, because the EAC thing has nothing to do with his state and county level contracts. The way he explains it to me," Ingber ventured, with only the vaguest idea of the sensibility of it, "is that although SoftSec provides hardware and software for voting purposes, the contract with EAC is to ensure that each vote cast in the precinct is exactly what is eventually reported to each state capital." He hoped his blast of hot air would sit well with a man apparently desperate not to have his bubble burst.

"Well, I'll accept that, Shel, but why didn't Morrison have the courtesy to explain that to me originally?"

"You should ask him." He chuckled. "Actually, no, don't. You and I are sophisticated people, Milt, but there are many in the media and the citizenry who would not appreciate the subtleties here."

"God, you're glib, Shel. Now I know why you've been so successful at what you do."

"Thank you, sir, and I intend to add another win to that string on November sixth."

After the old man severed the call, Ingber stood with his cell in his hand, as if he was studying the latest stock reports. At the bottom of it all, he liked winning, and to have another four years in which to embed the social agenda of Averell Williams deeper into the fibers of the American fabric meant that winning was absolutely everything.

"You'd think we don't know of any other place to have a drink and a sandwich in Cincinnati," Paul pondered aloud. "In a city famous for its top-end dining and culture, we wind up at the Cock & Bull, for heaven's sake." He meant his tone as a tease and was glad to see the smile on Mare's face.

"Not my choice, Paul. When I called Amber about a little get-together, it was clear she was scared out of her mind and didn't want to venture far from her nest."

"Want to sit at the bar so we can watch the last debate?"

"For God's sake, you know there must be medicine for an addiction like that." She leaned into him so only he would hear her in the din. "And you know how it's all going to come out, for the love of God. That would be like watching the 1919 World Series after paying off Chicago."

"That was different. That was a team paid to lose. Now we have a team that owns the scoreboard. Fascinating as hell to watch. C'mon, we're early. Let's get a beer and stand by the bar for the pregame."

"Just this once, Paul Gladston, will I give in to your disease."

They both laughed and ordered their beers as Peter Marsden's voice could be heard—barely—over the patrons' other interest, baseball talk shows. "At least these guys didn't plan the debate on the same night as the World Series opener," Mare shouted over the din. "I'm not sure which channel this crowd would want to watch."

"Oh, I'd bet on baseball," he said. He ordered a Blue Moon and a Guinness. Then he turned toward the HDTV just above his head.

Peter Marsden was speaking. "Tony, you're there at Lynn University for the last debate before this November's contest. What can you tell us?"

"The crowd here is polite but excited, Peter, and Bob Schieffer will have his job cut out for him to keep it from taking over the evening. I understand President Williams and Governor Hardy have worked hard in preparing for this joust. Both men have been cordial and respectful, and I'm sure the audience must wonder how they can say the things they do about each other and at the end, act like two brothers at a family reunion."

"That's an interesting insight, Tony, especially when we take a look at the most recent polling. As of yesterday, according to the NBC/ *Wall Street Journal* poll, along with Public Policy Polling of two thousand voters altogether, the race is essentially tied, with little or no air between them."

"That's right, Peter. There's a lot riding on this one."

"Hi," Amber Bustamente said weakly, looking everywhere around the bar as she spoke the one syllable.

"Amber," Burdette said, touching the other's arm, "Paul has a booth over here for us."

"Paul?"

"Oh, that's right. You've never met him, have you?" She made the introductions. "Paul is one of our investigators from Columbus, and he's here to help with our workload for a while."

Bustamente eyed Gladston warily. "Okay," she said, still nervous. "But I'm not sure why you wanted to see me again."

"Because we think you have reason to be scared," Mare's tone was empathetic. "We're here to warn you."

Bustamente's face wrinkled in horror. "Is it that bad?"

"We can't be a certain," Paul said, "but if you're sure about a black Tahoe in front of your apartment, you should know it was a black SUV that killed our Nelson Evers."

"Well, I'm pretty sure it was a Tahoe, but at this point, I could imagine it to be anything if the whole thing would just go away," she whimpered. "I just don't know what to do."

"Amber," Mare said forcefully. "You have to think logically here. You know there's something very wrong about what Nathan is doing, otherwise you wouldn't have told us about it."

"Maybe he lied to me just to impress me, just to keep me around for him. Oh, I don't know what to think."

"You might think about getting away for a few weeks," Paul suggested.

"Oh, I could. I work for pretty good people and I haven't taken much vacation, but I have to admit, I haven't seen that Tahoe or...or him—the crew-cut guy—since that weekend. Maybe he was one of your people, checking on Nathan."

"We have nobody like that," Mare said flatly. "You have to trust your instincts about what you saw and felt."

"Maybe I'm just upset because of how things are going between Nathan and me."

"You seem to want to give yourself reasons not to worry," said Paul. "But we think there is something going on, and we all need to be on our guard."

"But I can't live like that, Mr. Gladston," she said, tears beginning to dampen her cheeks.

"Please. It's Paul. Is there a good way to reach Conaway or McCord right now?" he asked.

"I doubt it—I haven't seen Nathan for a week now, but he calls every few days. And McCord? I wouldn't have any idea. Just their cellphones."

"Have you encouraged Nathan to get out of whatever he's doing?"

"A hundred times. He won't listen to me. He says he wants to do it. He keeps saying it will be the coolest thing on earth."

Burdette said, "I want you to know that we'll give him and McCord each a call suggesting they abandon the contract."

"Good luck with that," Bustamente said, letting her sarcasm flow.

On Saturday the twenty-ninth, Paul and Mare watched the news in horror as a deadly hurricane struck land at Brigantine, New Jersey, with such force that it soon became clear all other news would be blown off screen. They lay in bed, and Mare held Paul tight as they soon saw an indescribable swath of destruction. Amongst other things, it was announced that Hardy would suspend his campaign as the wags suggested that President Williams had been dealt the best trump card in the deck by his new friend, Hurricane Sandy.

"He's working this like he really needs it," Paul observed. "Makes you wonder, Mare."

"You don't think he's just there because he should be?" Mare challenged.

"That's part of it, and I'll give him that. He's doing his job, and getting a public French kiss from a Republican governor certainly doesn't hurt him, does it?"

"I suppose so. Maybe it was a mistake for Hardy to put his campaign on hold."

"Maybe, but it doesn't matter," Paul said. "You said you called both McCord and Conaway today and they think what they're doing is no big deal. To them, it's just an election."

"But Williams is out there as if McCord doesn't exist. We keep coming back to the same question. If he's not involved, what's in it for Morrison?"

They watched in silence as the storm's rage knocked buildings end over end, and in a surreal view, they saw an amusement park roller coaster sitting in the ocean as if an angry god had tossed it there.

"Oh, Christ," Paul exclaimed. "I can't believe I let you do that."

"You're scarin' the hell out of me, Paul. Do what?"

"Clancy was only thinking of doing the right thing. He didn't think of the risk."

"What? Calling those two guys?"

"Yes," Paul said. You think those guys would keep your calls a secret? McCord is in it too deep. Oh, Jesus!" He looked at her, and for the first time he could not hide his own fear. "He's probably called Morrison already. That means we have no choice."

NOVEMBER

Washington Post/ABC News Poll
October 27-30
Williams 49%
Hardy 49%

T he set for News Global's *Weekend* was primed and ready. Making
the rounds were principals from both campaigns, and Lew
Michaels paced the back hallway, calming himself before interviews
he knew would be filled with overconfidence, bluster, and braggadocio.

First up was Lisa Hoxworth, who, with her high-wire personality, took no prisoners in word battles. At the two minute warning, he
looked across at Hoxworth and gave her a genuine smile.

"Live in 10, 9, 8..."

Michaels made last-second adjustments in his seat and waited for
the pointed finger. "Good morning, ladies and gentlemen. Today, we
are fortunate to have both Lisa Hoxworth and Sheldon Ingber, gurus of
the Hardy and Williams campaigns." Turning to his right, he said, "Lisa
Hoxworth is an old hand in the Winston Hardy organization and most
qualified to let us peek behind the GOP curtain, as it were. Lisa, how are
things going?"

"Thanks for having me, Lew. We think the Hardy campaign is on fire
and that's demonstrated by the tight race we have. Everywhere we've
been in Ohio, Virginia, and Florida these past few days, the crowds have
been unbelievable. Both the governor and his running mate have done a
marvelous job, we believe, in bringing the issues to the people."

"Lisa, I have several polls in front of me, and I'd like your comment.
As of a week ago, Gallup had Hardy over Williams by three. Rasmussen's

result was similar, showing a spread of four, and even the *Washington Post*/ABC News poll had Hardy up by one. As of October thirty-first, Rasmussen's poll of three thousand voters has Hardy up by two, and the *Washington Post*/ABC News poll has the race a tie. So what to you think?"

"You know what I'd think, Lew. The fact that the governor is ahead of or tied with a sitting popular president does not bode well for the incumbent, and in a few days, we should be celebrating."

After a few minutes of continued banter, Michaels gave her another smile and said, "You know, Lisa, there's somebody else on the set who will not likely agree with you. So, let me say thank you for coming on this morning, and now we'll give Sheldon Ingber his opportunity to provide a rebuttal." Michaels pivoted to his left.

"Mr. Ingber," he said, the fabled impish grin in full view.

"Why, Lew, one might think you suppose this is the very last time you'll see me."

"Not at all, Sheldon. I don't want you or the viewers to think that. You heard, no doubt, the poll results I mentioned to Lisa Hoxworth. What's your take on those numbers?"

"Oh, that's an easy one. Surely, the numbers are the numbers, but you've no doubt noticed that the governor's momentum may have crested last week—"

"Just before Hurricane Sandy jumped into the race," Michaels said.

"Whether Sandy had anything to do with anything, I couldn't say," Ingber continued, a half smile of his own in view. "As to the polls, they seem to suggest that Governor Hardy's presumed lead—all the numbers were within the margin of error, I should note—his presumed lead has evaporated. And we all know what that has meant historically: the benefit of the doubt goes to the incumbent."

"Sheldon, I understand you have a bet going with someone over at another network about that famous head of hair of yours—that you'll be shaving it off if you lose. And so I ask you, do you have your razor and shaving cream at the ready?"

Ingber chuckled. "I won't give Peter Marsden the satisfaction. Lew, my wife knows only what you see, and I have no plans to change that now, so in answer to your question, absolutely not!"

Pete Clancy paced back and forth on the flagstone patio tucked in behind the townhouse on South Fairfax Street. At Mass that morning, he had been so lost in his own thoughts that someone had to poke him at Communion just to bring him to the gathering at hand. He didn't remember the short walk from South Royal Street back to his own house and the Sunday *Washington Post* waiting for him there. Two cups of coffee and a sweet roll disappeared without so much as a taste he could savor.

In seven weeks, he knew without checking a calendar, he'd be making his last daily commute on I-495 to the Little River Turnpike office where he'd spent more than a decade building what had turned out to be his castle of sand. As he'd learned to expect, his board notified him of his termination not long after he updated them on OPM's decision to end their long contractual relationship with NIS. All the reasons cited were, in the end, irrelevant to him, the employees, and the company. The failure was his, however it occurred, and there was no longer a place for the entrepreneurial miracle man who had produced NIS in the first place. Peace with all of it had come with difficulty, and his biggest concern, the employees themselves, had solved itself.

His reverie of contentment for the people who served NIS salved his ego for weeks, but it could never quite smooth over the witness statement of one young woman in Cincinnati, Ohio. And no matter how detached politically he had allowed himself to become in a capital city where even the taps spewed partisan waters, he could not stow away his frustration at the murder of Nelson Evers.

The afternoon drifted on, and he couldn't get past it. A good soldier his whole life, Clancy did what he was asked and rarely upset the applecart, but Nelson Evers wasn't an applecart. If there was a hero anywhere, he was the number one choice. What churned his bile was not the cancellation of the contract, and not the end of his career. After the September Surprise—what he called Bartley's letter of cancellation—and after he learned the Fairfax PD had been neutralized, he tried to call Bartley several times about Evers, but could never get through, and his voice messages went ignored.

His e-mails to her disappeared into the ether, he supposed, because he heard nothing in response to them either. Once, he talked to her deputy, but the man said the agency had no jurisdiction in the matter and had no reason to challenge the police report. Mr. Evers was not a federal employee, in any event, the bureaucrat seemed relieved to say, and therefore, no federal law could cover what had happened to him, if indeed, it was more than a simple hit and run.

Simple hit and run! The killing of a heroic black man was the proof of all that had become rotten in an administration pledged to transparency. The man's death was the first harvest of a ruthless power grab, and he wondered what decisions people like Marlyn, Paul, and Janice were yet to make. What about Amber Bustamente herself? Who would protect her?

By four o'clock, when the chill winds off the harbor whipped their way down the alleys and byways to his little courtyard, he'd decided. Next to his Dell Latitude laptop, which he had courtesy of NIS, sat his Jameson manhattan with two cherries swimming in the swirl of whiskey, vermouth, and bitters. He took a long sip before beginning his letters to old friends in the Offices of the Inspector General at the IRS and OPM, as well as a midlevel field office manager at the FBI.

All three letters focused on the dubious EAC contract, the fix, the IRS mess, and the death of a good man to his last breath. To each, he attached a copy of the letter he'd sent to Bartley in the summer, along with the Fairfax incident report, and the observations of Gladston and Burdette. He carefully laid out his reasons for not having put up a flare sooner and gave no indication that his e-mail and surface mailings were going to others. Were he to do so, his friends, decent and honest men and women though they were, would each hope the others would act, thus relieving their consciences of a troublesome burden. A letter to News Global was next.

Human nature was generally predictable, he reminded himself, but with his little precaution, perhaps one of them would be moved to do his or her duty to the American people, and to a dead hero. Such duty he no longer hoped to expect from an administration that considered the Constitution no more relevant than several of the Commandments.

Tuning to the six o'clock news, he heard the latest so-called experts make their calls on the election result but felt no satisfaction in knowing the race was already over.

Amber Bustamente had become bored with the self-assigned guard duty in the bay window above Graeter's. Through the newly bared trees, she could see the firehouse diagonally across the way, at the opposite end of the square from the Cock & Bull, but otherwise, the streets were mostly empty of people and cars in the chilly weather. There were but a few lights on in the storefronts below. Abandoning her observation post, she retreated to a warmer part of the apartment to try her call one more time.

"Hey, Becca," she said when her best friend, Rebecca Garrity, finally answered her cell. "I thought I'd never get you."

"It's been a few days since we talked, and I was beginning to worry about you."

"I've had a lot to think about, and if you weren't up in Cleveland, we'd be having dinner and you'd be totally caught up with my crazy life." She attempted a laugh at the end, but her heart wasn't in it.

"Just what's bugging you? Is it Nathan? Is he still on the same project you mentioned?" Garrity asked, peppering her friend.

"Yes to everything. Only I never told you exactly what he was working on. I was too scared. But I don't care anymore, so I hope you're ready to listen, because you're not going to believe what's going on."

"Jeez, you sure know how to give it a buildup."

"Remember I told you how Nathan was going around the country setting up computer links with certain states?"

"Yeah, he's been on the road all summer, right?"

"Right, but it's been more than that. Hey, wait a minute. There's someone at the door."

Amber held the phone in her left hand and put her right hand on the knob, preparing to open the door. "Who is it?" she called through the oaken barrier.

"Little Joe's delivery."

"Really? I didn't order out." *Maybe Nathan called in a pizza for us!* She opened the door. Two men stood there, one with a face she'd seen before—a face with a yellow crew cut on top of it. It was in an SUV looking up at her apartment.

The men pushed in and grabbed her. She tried to scream through the heavy cloth placed over her mouth, but managed nothing more than a muffled groan. *Why?*

A frantic voice came through the phone, but the tall one with the crew cut ripped it from Bustamente's clenched hand. Then he pressed the icon ending the call.

The vice president's Bethesda mansion was unusually quiet. No gala dinner with Washington heavy hitters. No campaign aides running everywhere with changing details for the next day's hustle. No Secret Service people at every doorway.

Sharon Morrison sat in the small second-floor sitting room because she liked to be there. It was the only place in the residence that could be described as cozy, and it was a pleasant change from the hotel ballrooms, arenas, and stadiums she been in all over the country. She'd insisted that after the kids were in bed, she and Joe should spend one evening together pretending they were everyday people, and she'd gotten her wish.

With a smile, he agreed, but not without protest. "Hon, we'll never be ordinary people again."

"You're right, and that's why tonight is important," she had said earlier in the day. When her husband brought her a glass of Santa Margherita pinot grigio and sat down next to her with a Sprite, she continued in that same vein. "I can't tell you why, but I feel content tonight, and I hope you do too. I want you to put your feet up. And you know, I'm glad your key Secret Service people got some time off as well."

"Don't worry about them, hon. People like Marty Cox always have something to do."

"That's just who I was thinking of. He's one of your favorites, isn't he?"

"You might say that. Anything tricky that comes along, why, Marty will always take care of it."

"Let's focus on *my* favorite," she said coyly. "You have to be awfully proud of yourself, Joe. Despite all the noise from the eastern establishment, you remained on the ticket and you're cutting a deal with the president on second-term responsibilities." She laughed. "It would be perfect, if we'd win."

"You don't have to worry about that, hon."

"Oh, I am, Joe. It's not that I doubt you or Averell Williams. You guys have put on a hell of a campaign. Still, I'm worried. All the polls show Hardy ahead or tied up. Tell me we'll pull it out, Joe."

"Like I said, Share, don't even waste a second on it. In my mind," he said, winking at her, "it's in the bag."

"Well, I'm sure your relationship with the president will become just what you want it to be."

"In some ways, Share, it won't matter."

She could see he was peering into the distance, somehow present with her and at the same time, in some other year. "That's an odd thing to say. What do you mean by that?"

"I'm sorry, hon. I was just thinking that if he does what I expect him to do, it can't help but get better for me."

The driveway bracketing one side of Marlyn Burdette's fourplex descended from the street to the back of the building where four garage doors banked the basement level. Paul parked his car there, a used Volvo sedan, and crept up the drive until his head was just above grade. He couldn't see much in the dark, but he could hear clearly the small animal noises mingling with the crisp November gusts coming up Ellison Avenue.

He returned to her second-floor flat. "Are you ready?"

"Yes," she said, her voice loaded with tension. "Paul, are you sure we have to do this?"

"As sure as Nelson Evers is dead, Mare. Sorry to put it that way, but you have to understand. If they're going to do something, it'll be before Election Day, not afterward. If they waited, they'd be taking the chance that one of us would speak out."

"I hear you, but I can't believe this is happening."

"No tears now, Mare. You can cry in the car. Did you turn off your phone?"

"Yes. I've got all my cash, credit cards, passport—everything. And I have just one suitcase with enough clothes for a week, like you said."

"Good. I don't want to be a jerk about the phone, but is it off? Not just in silent mode?

"Off."

"Okay. Take a peek out the front window."

The streetlight in front of the building next door cast its shadowy glow into the room. Mare slowly moved her face to the small crack in the gauzy white curtains. "Paul, there's a vehicle coming up the street."

"Somebody coming home?" Seeing the glow from his watch, he noted the time. Just after eight.

"Yeah, I guess. It's going on by. It's a CRV that belongs up the street. Oh, here's another one, coming up slow. Oh, crap! It's a black SUV!"

"C'mon, let's go!"

They slid into the hall, closed the door, and hustled down the back stairs and out the man door. Once in Paul's car, he said, "Get down. They know you live here. They might not be expecting me."

Lights off, Gladston propelled his Volvo up the drive. The SUV's taillights went slowly up the hill toward the crossing of Nash Avenue. He bumped out of the drive, turning right, and headed down the hill. Almost to the corner, he turned on his lights. Because Ellison curved away from his line of sight, he couldn't see the SUV. Hopefully, its driver couldn't see him.

At the bottom of the hill, where stood the cold stone edifice that was Christ the King church, Paul stopped briefly at the traffic light and waited for the one car leaving the square to drive by before turning.

Headlights were coming up behind him. "Stay down! Somebody's coming."

Down Linwood he coasted to the Herschel light, which was green, and cruised through. Hard as it was to do, Paul drove as if he was in no hurry. He didn't want them to make his plate. The guy he and Mare began to call Crew Cut had never seen him or his car. He hoped their focus would be Mare's bronze Ford Taurus.

When Linwood Avenue bottomed out at Columbia Parkway, Paul noticed the SUV was gone. His strategy had worked. He turned right again and drove west until he could see the city center's lights and the signs for I-71 north. "You can sit up now. They're gone."

"I don't believe it, but I want to believe it. Paul, I'm afraid. And you never said where we're going."

"We're going to stop in Columbus and pick up some stuff I was in too big a hurry to pack when I came down to get you. I've got only a day's change of clothes and my briefcase. Then, away we go. We're going to disappear for a while."

"Disappear? How can people do that these days? Somehow, we're always connected to the grid."

"When we get to Columbus, I'll stop at an ATM and get a load of cash before we head out. Where we're going, we won't need much, anyway." Out of the corner of his eye, he could see her watching him, then smiling.

"You're one lucky, guy, Paul Gladston."

"Why is that, Mare Burdette?"

"Because if I weren't so scared out of my wits, I'm not sure I'd get in a car and head off to God knows where."

Paul reached for her hand as she reclined her seat a bit. Somewhere near Lebanon, she drifted off to sleep.

Paul's headlights sliced the dark of the interstate, uninterrupted only by stalled traffic, construction, or the left laners he had come to despise. Originally, he'd intended to gas up just north of the city, but a glance at the gas gauge suggested a change in plan—he'd forgotten that on the drive to Mare's the Volvo had had its drink.

Washington Court House was a good stop for gas, a cup of coffee, and a clean restroom. Stirring in the passenger seat, Mare blinked her eyes at the station's bright lights and said she needed a pit stop herself. Less than ten minutes later, they were on the road, and he told her they were only forty minutes away. The remainder of their flight up I-71 was uneventful, and remained so as he maneuvered his Volvo onto the Dublin-Granville Road exit.

He turned north into the labyrinth of streets that took him to his modest apartment near Ambleside and Barnes, but he could feel his muscles tense as he turned into the long parking lot jammed with cars, their windows painted opaque by the settling frost. The one or two with clear windows belonged to people who'd just arrived home and had no doubt hastened to be inside their warm dwellings.

One vehicle caught his attention. It was backed in its spot, and tell-tale plumes of exhaust signaled the running engine. The small red glow from the dashboard's security light reflected off the faces of the two men inside a black SUV.

"Damn! Mare, slide down. We've got company."

"What are you going to do? Do you have a gun?"

"No, nothing. We're going to bluff it and keep going like we're look-ing for an address. If we're lucky, they won't connect us with Ellison Avenue."

"Jesus, Paul, I'm going to pray."

"Now would be a good time," he said, coasting by the SUV but look-ing the other way. "I'm past them now. I'm going to try something. There's an open spot coming up and if it goes through, I'm going to pull in, just like we belong here."

"Then what?" she whispered.

"You don't have to whisper. I'll kill my lights, glide through, and pull out the other side."

"You're nuts. When they see that, they'll know who you are."

"We'll see." About a dozen parked cars farther down, he did just as he said, steering his car into a slot on the far side of a van between them and the SUV. "Open your door, then close it in a few seconds. If they hear it, they'll think I got out of the car."

She did so.

"Okay. Here goes." Lights off, he eased the car forward and made a left out of the spot and kept going, but slowly. In a hundred feet or so, he saw the exit.

The plan went well until he reached Ambleside and turned on his lights. Looking backward over his right shoulder, over two rows of cars in between them, he saw the SUV's headlights come on and begin to move.

Paul turned left and raced up Ambleside, killed his lights at a dark spot on the boulevard, and veered right into another part of the maze. He couldn't tell if the SUV saw him. He kept going until he saw a drive-way with several cars. The house to which they belonged was dark. He pulled in next to a Ford Explorer and killed his engine. In a few seconds the SUV motored past and disappeared around a bend.

Paul backed out of the drive and retraced his route, turning north on Ambleside once again. Melding with the light traffic, he turned right on Schrock, a broad, well-lighted, always busy road. He drove in an easterly direction and felt safe until he saw the SUV pull into traffic four or five cars behind him. It must have been waiting for him.

In another minute, they were passing over the Outer Belt. He moved to the left lane and saw the SUV follow suit. Now it was only two cars behind him. In the bright lights of the roadway, when the cars shifted left or right a foot or so, he could see the SUV's driver—a tall man with light-colored hair cut short. It was Crew Cut! "Keep down, Mare, it's him, and we have only one chance ahead."

Traffic on the main roads thickened the closer they came to Cleveland Avenue. When he saw his opportunity, he sped up and elbowed his way into the lane to the right and over one more into the turn lane. Horns blared. He saw the SUV attempt the same maneuver, but its size, and the slowing traffic near the light at the intersection, penned it in.

The Volvo swerved into a right turn and answered its driver's foot on the gas pedal. Soon, Paul was propelling his gem of a car onto the entrance ramp of the beltway. Cars filed on behind him, but no black SUV.

One exit away, Paul angled right and, again, plowed north on I-71, pushing the Volvo to a bit over seventy miles per hour, as fast as the traffic, but no faster. He wanted to attract no further attention. Within a mile, the expressway guide lights disappeared and their company was the blinking wave of taillights in front of them.

Driving at night could be friend or foe, Paul knew. Just as it was harder to spot state troopers at night, it would be hard to spot a black SUV sneaking up behind.

"You can sit up again. We may have lost them."

"So do we have a plan? I don't know how much longer I can be a sack of potatoes sliding on and off this seat."

"Good thing you're one of the little people."

"Don't start that crap, Paulie boy," she countered, half seriously. "There's only so much of you I can take."

"Where we're going, you're going to have to put up with a lot more than me."

"I don't know what that means, but you'll tell me what happens next, right?"

"Yes, dear," he responded, like an old married man. "We're getting off at US 36. If Crew Cut figures we're heading north, he'd guess we stayed on I-71 and go like hell until he caught us. We're not going to make it easy."

"Okay, so we get off the interstate. Then what?"

"Then," he cocked his head sideways and gave her a sly smile, "we go see the spot where Humphrey Bogart and Lauren Bacall got married."

"Paul, all this crazy stuff has popped a few of your rivets."

"Just so long as you're with me, that's all that matters now."

"You know, you're a guy out of another era—and I think I like it."

He laughed, and laughed again. "You just wait."

MONDAY, NOVEMBER 5

I t had not been hard for the fugitives to snag a room at the Comfort Inn near Lexington, Ohio. By the time they had rolled in close to midnight, the adrenalin had worn off and both were exhausted.

A brilliant, but chilly morning greeted them as they dressed as warmly as their limited wardrobes allowed. "Didn't I tell you?" Paul teased as they inhaled the hotel-provided hot breakfast.

"Tell me what?" Mare said, "besides the fact you're a morning person, and I'm not."

"About Malabar Farm. That's where we're going today," he said, excitement sugaring his voice.

"For God's sake, Paul," she said, disbelievingly. "Are you telling me we're gonna be fuckin' tourists today? When we're running from a killer? Are you nuts?"

"Gee, I guess you can eat with that mouth," he said, amused. "Yes, dear, we're going to do exactly that because no one would ever expect it. Besides, Louis Bromfield's farm is in the middle of nowhere, where crazed killers tend not to be. This is the heart of America, for cryin' out loud."

"What's so special about this place?" she asked as the pair cradled cups of coffee in the lobby.

"I'll be happy to be your tour guide. Bromfield was to American fiction in the thirties and forties what Jodi Piccoult and John Grisham are to us today. Except that he won a Pulitzer Prize and, after a while, escaped Hollywood for the purity of rural life when few people did so. He built this experimental farm and humored his conservational instincts until he died."

"Was that baloney about Bogart and Bacall?"

"All true. Bromfield was a friend to many Hollywood types, and when Bogie and Bacall wanted to get married without a lot of hoopla, they came to Malabar and did it in Bromfield's foyer. You'll see. We'll be there before lunch."

"How do you know about stuff like this?"

"The same way you do. It's the best thing about being a street investigator. You meet the most interesting people and learn the most random stuff."

"Right. Then what?"

"Then, like Bromfield, we're going to escape for a while, only not in Ohio. It's to Pennsylvania we go, not far from where I grew up. My plan is to get there this evening."

"Won't Crew Cut think to look there for you?"

"Not unless he's read my background investigation, but it won't matter. He'll never find us, because we're going to our own Malabar."

"Are you going to keep secrets from me for the rest of our lives?"

In the parking lot next to his Volvo, he stopped in his tracks in. The wind gusts almost took his words. "Who said anything about the rest of our lives?"

"I did," she said plainly.

"There's sure nothing old-fashioned about you," he said, his voice becoming hoarse. "I guess opposites do attract." He paused, looking into her unwavering, expectant eyes. "And if you're proposing, it's one hell of a yes." They kissed.

"We have to go to the post office before we leave here," Paul said, as they settled in the cold front seat of the Volvo.

"Why on earth would we do that?"

"We're mailing three letters—in honor of Nelson Evers."

Tears welled up in Mare's eyes and for a full minute she couldn't speak, but she grabbed his hand and gave it a good squeeze.

Then she found her voice. "You still haven't said exactly where we're going."

"Just you wait."

"Oh, God. That's the second time you've said that."

"This is *America Now,* I'm Meredith Ramirez, and have we got a news day for you! It doesn't get any closer than this, ladies and gentlemen. All the latest polls show it's pretty much dead even. And here's Lew Michaels to give us his thoughts. Just to get right to the point, Lew, will Sheldon Ingber have to shave his head?" she asked, her broad smile seeming to have its own broad smile.

Michaels chuckled demurely. "Oh, just put me on the spot, won't you," he said. "Well, I'll say this. Winston Hardy has worked hard during this race, and he gets an A for effort despite the fact that campaigning isn't his most comfortable state of being. The president, on the other hand, is uncomfortable when he's not campaigning. I'd also remind our viewers that President Williams has raised nearly double the campaign contributions as has Governor Hardy, and contrary to some media spin, his seven hundred million dollars hasn't come from poor people."

"You're saying what, exactly?"

"That President Williams has attracted very wealthy donors. That his campaign has had the funding to saturate the states that continue to matter with TV ads. And that it will get down to who conducted a better campaign. In those three key areas, the president has the edge, in my opinion, but having said that, the momentum for Governor Hardy, especially in the last week or ten days, has been nothing short of astounding."

With her voice set to tease, Ramirez said, "Lew, you sure took a lot of words to tell our viewers it's a tossup." She laughed, as did her guest.

"Well, whatever I might think, there are millions of people who haven't made up their minds yet, and last I looked, I'm not employed by either campaign."

"Wouldn't it be nice if all the news people shared the same view?"

Jerry James jumped out of the taxi directly in front of the Madison Road address given him by Mr. Ingber himself. He stood looking at the less-than-impressive office building and wondered if he was in the right place, even the right neighborhood. In the dimming light, however, the SoftSec logo on institutional red brick told him no mistake had been made.

Certainly, he viewed himself as the right man for the job. Originally from Oklahoma, he had grafted himself onto the Morrison bandwagon when the man was running for US senator in Texas. Single and unattached, he had always stayed very much to himself, so much so that other campaign workers hardly knew him. That was the way Jerry liked it, and he noticed that those way above his pay grade liked it, too. That way, he could be assigned the most delicate task and it would be carried out discreetly. Moreover, he was not the least bit unwilling to execute every dirty trick on GOP opponents his betters could imagine for him. Along the way, he'd been pirated by the Williams people, and he was happy to be making the president a winner again.

But this? No scruples invaded his conscience as he stood wondering why he should direct the outcome of the election in so shabby a venue. Somehow, he had imagined a NASA control room, a la Houston. He laughed at his own Mittyesque daydream and propelled himself up the few steps and through the aluminum-framed glass vestibule.

Upstairs, he met Nathan Conaway, a hairy, overweight specimen, and again, he wondered if he was on a fool's errand. He and Conaway went through a wary handshake exercise, and he let the latter show him their workspace.

"Let's have a cup of coffee, Jerry, and we can talk about how this whole thing'll work." Conaway laughed nervously.

"A Mountain Dew for me, uh, Nathan, is it?"

"Friends call me Nutsy." He laughed again. "Don't ask me why."

"No, I won't," Jerry responded, and for the third time wondered why he was chosen for this. When the campaign manager himself, Mr. Ingber, had approached him—the two had never before spoken—he told him his special skills marked him for a project dear to the vice president's heart. That Morrison was involved was enough to seal the deal.

Nathan shambled over to a small fridge and pulled out a cold Dew. "I want you to know, Jerry, I understand you'll be in charge of this gig. The electronics and how it all goes together, that's my thing. If you give me timely direction, nobody will know or see a thing—nowhere, no how."

Jerry nodded. "Good. Glad we won't have to fight over a keyboard, my man," he said, and began to relax. "Don't undersell yourself, Nutsy. You must be held in high regard by a certain customer," he said, attempting to make up for having forgotten that Conaway and the venue in which he operated were two vastly different animals. "And that tells me you have it all together." He raised his can of Dew in salute.

"Thanks, but I don't take my abilities too seriously. I mean, giving a demo on how it could have been done in 2000 is one thing. Making properly calculated adjustments real time is another."

"Well, we won't need to fool around with the voting in all fifty states. Not even fifteen of them. We'll have to watch carefully how everything starts to play out, but I'm expecting to be paying attention to Florida, Virginia, and Ohio, of course. Possibly we'll do Wisconsin, Iowa, New Hampshire, and," he chuckled, "Colorado. Maybe New Mexico. Maybe not even all of them. We'll see how the real voting goes. We may tip Colorado just to let Hardy know who's in charge." Both men laughed, like a pair of muggers about to pistol-whip a victim for the hell of it.

For over an hour, they exchanged gritty tidbits about the process and bragged about their respective episodes of electronic mayhem and election trickery. Finally, Nathan asked if he was doing anything for dinner.

"You don't have a place to be?"

"Yeah, thanks, but I'm batchin' it tonight. I got a text this morning saying she was at her girlfriend's until after this is all over."

"Okay. Got it. In that case, I'm open for something good. Tomorrow and through the evening, I don't expect we'll get much."

"As for tomorrow, we'll get some Coneys brought in."

"Coneys? No such thing in Oklahoma. Chili dogs, maybe."

Nathan explained the local delicacy, but more important, he stressed that shortly after noon on Tuesday was when localities around the nation would begin populating their databases with the results from absentee balloting, military voting where it had not been suppressed, and early voting numbers. "I've always wondered why they permit people to vote a month ahead of time when stuff like Benghazi might change their minds before Election Day."

"Jeez, Nutsy, you sound like the League of Women Voters. What do you care? And this year especially. Why would you care at all?"

"Hon," Joe Morrison said into his cell. "The president and First Lady want us to join them for a little pregame warm-up tonight in the residence—just a small group with family and key campaign types."

"Oh, Joe, that's so nice—and only a few years late."

"Don't be that way, Share. Let's take it as a sign of a new relationship with them."

"Whatever you say," she said, not disagreeably. "My lunch today with the American Veterans group went well. Yours?"

"I'm all over the place here in Columbus, but I'll jet back in time to pick you up. Be ready at seven thirty."

His call-waiting notice chimed and he looked at the caller ID. "Oh, sorry, honey, gotta go."

He picked up the incoming call. "Just a quick update, Marty, without any details."

"Yes, sir. Good news and not so good news. Another one of the players has retired, but two others are still free agents. We'll get 'em later."

"Shit."

"Kept us busy. We're looking."

"A game plan for the others?"

"Yes, sir. Not to worry."

"It's too soon. Don't put a hex on it," Winston Hardy said with a chuckle as he and his wife walked to the elevator from the presidential suite at one of Denver's largest hotels.

"You're right, Win, but in twenty-four hours, I hope there will be millions of people thinking of you as Mr. President-Elect."

In the small suite reserved for their gathering of a few dozen senior people, pols, and staff, Lisa Hoxworth, waited, beaming. "Given the forward energy of the past week, sir, no one here knows how we can lose tomorrow."

"Well, my friends," Hardy said, addressing the crowd around him. "As I've said earlier today, let's not count the votes yet." Realizing that was too sober a thought for his closest allies, he added, with the broadest grin he possessed, "But tomorrow night—well, then, we'll have something to talk about."

"Well, we made it," Paul said with a deep expulsion of air along with his words. He turned his head toward Mare and gave her a smile of satisfaction and calm. Malabar Farm had been all pleasure and the ride up I-71, uneventful.

She touched his hand. "I'm all in, partner, but when you say, 'we made it,' just where the hell are we?" She laughed in amazement at his comfort level.

"You know, potty mouth, you're gonna have to clean that up for a while. Our hosts will not take kindly to it."

"Okay, Paulie boy. Enough. Just what are we doing?"

"Well, surely you noticed we crossed into Pennsylvania about twenty minutes ago. We came south on what everyone used to call 'Sixty,' and just passed through the little borough of New Wilmington. We'll go a few more miles along the Lawrence and Mercer County line and we'll be there."

"Sounds interplanetary to me."

Paul chuckled at her sarcasm. "You know, we never talked much about my growing-up years, but it was only about ten miles from where we're going, in a little town called Grove City."

"Where you went to college, right?"

"Yes and a darn good one, if you're a bit conservative like me."

"But I saw a sign for a school in New Wilmington as well."

"Yes, that's Westminster, another good liberal arts college."

"And?"

"And when I was growing up, my dad did something no other father ever did, to my knowledge. Just so I never forgot what most of us take for granted, he talked an Amish farmer into letting me work for his family over a few summers."

"You're kidding!"

"No, and it took some doing because with the Amish, it's usually the reverse. They have their children work for us—the English—to learn a trade or, mostly, earn money for the family. It's unheard of for them to take in an English kid."

"English? Is that your ancestry?"

Paul laughed. "It is, in fact, but to the Amish, if you're not one of them, you're 'English'."

"You know, Paulie boy, I'm afraid to connect the dots here."

"Look, Mare, we need to hide out for a while. Neither of us has a million in cash so we can stay off the grid. This is the only way to do it on a budget. The Schenks are the people I stayed with. I think of them as family and they think the same of me. I didn't try to corrupt them with English ways, and they told me I'd always be welcome."

"So you think we're going to be Amish farmers? Are you kidding me? Mare Burdette?"

"Yes, you, dear, because it's the only way I know to keep you safe. If we just took off and used our plastic, they could find us within a day or two. We'd be history." His tone changed. "Wait a darn minute. You told me you grew up on a farm. Indiana, right? You said you loved every minute of it, as I recall," he teased.

Mare chuckled. "I said I loved growing up on a farm. I never said I loved farming, but, Paulie boy, can I milk a cow!"

He laughed. "You'll get your chance."

"But what about our own families? What do we tell them?"

"I have a throwaway cell we'll use to make one call, and that'll be that. If they don't know where we are, nobody will bother them."

"Paul, don't you feel guilty running away like this? Is that supposed to happen in real life?"

"Look, sweetheart, this is real life, and neither of us are heroes. We're just ordinary people who did our jobs too well, and now we're in the crosshairs. Now they've got all the power, all the cards."

"Maybe," she said, thinking over what he said. Then she sighed and stared straight ahead. "I don't want to sound like a ninny, but do I have to wear the same getups I saw in the buggy we just passed?"

"Yes, and me, too—wool hat and canvas pants." He waited. "And it gets worse."

"I can't imagine how."

"We might not be able to stay together while we're with them."

"Jesus, there are limits, you know."

"There you go again. Of course, if we get married..."

Both smiled but looked straight ahead.

At the Schenks, not far from where the Indian Ridge and Sunken Bridge Roads converged, they pulled into the dirt and gravel two-track drive just at dusk. "I sent Andy a letter a few days ago, and I hope he got it in time."

They drove into a picturesque setting where the barn, house, and other outbuildings gleamed an immaculate white in the fading light. Everything was trimmed and neat, and in the fields, the last of the haystacks stood in long skirmish lines. The whole scene seemed like photoshopped calendar art, but indeed, it was real life—only a century earlier.

A gray-bearded man and his wife came out of the house, lanterns in hand. Both bore broad smiles. "Paul!" they shouted together. "Oh, Paul, it's so good to see you," Sadie Schenk said. "And the children will be delighted."

Andy Schenk hugged him and shook him. "English—you're back!" Their excitement and welcome were genuine. "Before it gets dark, drive that machine into the barn. No one will notice it there."

"Wait. You have to meet my fiancée," he said, not believing he actually said the words out loud to others. "This is Mare Burdette."

"Of course, she is a mare, Paul. We can see that. What is her real name?" Schenk bellowed in his mild German accent. Everyone laughed at the patriarch's corny joke, and at once Mare felt at home.

Paul and Mare were invited in to dinner, and for an hour or more, they spent time with the seven Schenk children before they were shooed off to bed.

"As for you two," Schenk said sternly, as if warning them that they'd better be telling the truth, "if you are, indeed, betrothed, you can stay in the smaller house behind ours."

Sadie nodded her approval.

Schenk lowered his eyes. "The old folks passed last year, and it stands empty now. There's some simple furniture and wood for a fire."

"If you are to stay with us, then you should dress like us." Sadie said, appraising them for size. "Then you will not be noticed. I will bring you some proper clothes now that I know how big they should be." She laughed. "And you, Mare, you can wear one of my daughter's dresses." She laughed again.

"Thank you so much, Sadie," Mare said, inhaling deeply. "We are so glad to be here."

Later that evening, under a sheet and two heavy woolen blankets, Paul and Mare lay staring into the utter darkness of a moonless night with no electricity circuiting their lives.

"I've never slept on a straw mattress in a rope bed before," Mare said in mock distress. "I don't know how to thank you for such a treat."

He squeezed her tight and said, "I might have a suggestion for you."

"Never mind that, Paulie boy. Do the Schenks know why we're running? Are they going to vote tomorrow? And you never answered my earlier question—about running away."

"Wow. Catch your breath. No. Yes. And yes, I did, but you were more interested in fashion issues than my answer, as I recall." He reached over and held her close.

❖

The White House gleamed in the frosty night air, with little left undone to make the key symbol of world power look grand, but not garish. As the vice president's limousine pulled up to the white stone pillars bracketing the reinforced steel gates, Sharon remarked, "One day, Joe, it would be nice not to be a visitor." Her tone was wistful, not demanding.

Morrison placed his hand on hers, his thin attempt at tenderness. "Patience, Share, patience." Immediately, he regretted his tone and manner; he had been thinking of the prize he believed would be his.

Upstairs, the gathering was small. In addition to Averell and Andrea Williams, there were Sheldon Ingber and his wife, Audra; Sondra Thompson and her mate, Katherine; and the Norton Sweeneys. Morrison thought he'd find Harry Riordan, Angela Tesoro, and Jensen Roberts there, but he realized this was the real inner circle, the one from which he'd been excluded for nearly four years. Mentally, he swept the self-pity aside and fixed his broadest smile.

The first to approach them was Andrea Williams, a tall, stately woman with fine features and a figure much younger than her years. "Sharon and Joe, how lovely it is you could join us. Av and I thought tomorrow night's vigil would be a bigger, louder, less intimate group, so tonight we wanted to relax and celebrate the end of the campaign." She couldn't have been more gracious, as if the Morrisons had been with them in private social settings dozens of times.

Joe Morrison went directly to his host, who was with Sweeney and Ingber. The president turned as if instinct told him someone was coming up behind him.

"Joe. So glad you and Sharon weren't tied up. I never know what Shelley here has you doing for us until the very last second. In fact, I'm surprised he didn't have both of us out there scouring the landscape for the very last undecided Independent voter." The men laughed.

Except for Sweeney, the men traded campaign anecdotes that allowed them to laugh even more. "At least this time around, Joe Six-Pack seems to be solidly in our corner," one of them said.

The mood became noticeably tense when Ingber brought up the latest private polling data. "Av," he said, his voice more serious than his news. "I think it's going to be ours. Maybe not a landslide, but a clear victory for you and your policies." Ingber looked directly at Morrison as he finished.

"Gee, Shel, is that all seven hundred million gets us?" said the president. He was teasing his campaign manager, but everyone listening knew he was disappointed in that prediction. "I hope we can do better, guys, 'cause I'm not doing this again."

He turned to Sweeney. "Since we're turning to more serious matters, Norty, let's you and I catch up on all the leakers my administration seems to have spawned."

Morrison and Ingber moved to the far side of the room, away from where the other men were in conclave and where the women had commandeered the couches. "Is your polling pretty good?" Morrison asked his companion.

"Not that good. Sorry. What I mean to say is that our polling is excellent, but the results were not quite as good as I just quoted them to be."

"What? Why the hell would you do that?"

Ingber studied him for a moment. "Because, Joe, I'm counting on you to deploy your secret weapon." He paused, sipping his bourbon. "So you see, there would be no point in being the bearer of bad news when you're going to make it good news in the end."

"Got it. Speaking of deployment, I understand our guy is in position and everything's set. That Jerry James is unbelievable."

"That's all I want to know."

"Then you haven't told the president, I take it."

Ingber looked at him over the top of his glass, took another sip, and moved his head in answer when he saw Williams approach.

The president said, "Shelly, you're going to have to excuse us. Joe and I have some business to talk over. This way, Joe, over to my study—the real oval office."

They exited the long salon at one end and Morrison found himself in a relatively small room, perhaps twelve by fifteen, but exquisitely paneled. There was no desk, just a couple of easy chairs, a place for the president's personal laptop and printer, and a pair of high-definition televisions. He also spotted a compact bank of electronics he assumed was for the president's use in case of a national emergency. There was room for only one visitor.

The president noticed Morrison's appreciation for his man cave in the White House. He chuckled. "This is where I hang out when I can, and sometimes Andrea joins me here and we watch a little *Boardwalk Empire*." He looked directly at Morrison and saw the expression on his face. "Surprised? Well, don't be. You already know that high-stakes politics can be a little like Atlantic City in the twenties at times."

"I suppose you're right," Morrison said, and he took the seat offered him. The two men sat and caressed their tumblers.

"I've always admired you, Joe, for staying away from alcohol. You've been a good example for me, you know. And it has always reminded me to take one drink and nurse it for an evening."

Nodding in appreciation of the compliment, Morrison decided not to say much. The president had not called him into his den to talk about the evils of liquor.

"Joe, we have two pieces of unfinished business between us. As for the one, I'm deeply sorry I haven't more wisely used your engaging talents to help me accomplish our agenda in Congress. I promised you a few months ago that would change, and assuming Shelly is right about the polls, that change will begin on Wednesday. It would be bad luck to talk about it now, but I wanted you to know I had not forgotten."

"You won't regret it, sir."

"But there's another thing, and when I tell it to you, you'll be only the third person to know it." He paused to ensure his listener's keenest attention. "Jeremy Bolling," he said, and he sighed.

Morrison tensed at the mere mention of the White House medical officer's name but remained stone-faced as he prepared himself for the correct reaction.

"Jeremy Bolling has informed me that I have a moderately aggressive form of prostate cancer. It's not something that most men talk about with each other, but should. I am guilty of shunning what I've always called the fickle finger of fate test, and that may or may not be why I'm in my present circumstance. My PSA tests have been abnormal and rising, and Jeremy makes two points with me—very insistently, I might add—and one is that I do not have the luxury of waiting it out. I will have to act, and I should tell you now, Sondra and Jack Sennett will have to work their magic with the media when the time comes."

Morrison waited.

"Jeremy tells me one of the best places in world for this kind of surgery is practically next door at Johns Hopkins. Which means I'll be under anesthetic for several hours and not fully able to carry out my constitutional duties for the better part of a day."

"Av, I don't know what to say. I'm so sorry you'll have to endure this. What do you want me to do?" Morrison did all he could not to crush the glass in his hand, his body tension tightening with each word. It was impossible to listen to the president's words and process what they meant for him.

"Joe, let's be candid. I know you're an ambitious guy, and so far, I haven't done much to help you if you intend a bid four years from now."

"Sir," he responded, not totally comfortable calling him by his given name. "That shouldn't be on your to-do list at the moment."

"But it is, and for good and practical reasons. Just before the surgery, I'll be executing documents as required by Section Three of the Twenty-Fifth Amendment, passing temporary power to you to act for me. We'll play that up a bit to let the world know I think you're a capable vice president."

"Thank you, sir."

"Needless to say, I expect you to exercise such powers in the most limited way possible, save a national emergency, and Sondra will be at your side the entire time to guide you through any difficulties. Having said that, there remain two potential problems."

"Sir?"

"One is that in surgery, as they say, shit happens. I don't expect it—these are the best guys in the business, I hear—but they're dealing with a sixty-seven-year-old machine with the warranty near its expiration, if I may put it that way." He chuckled. "Of course, if the worst does happen, then Section One of the amendment applies."

"Section One?" the vice president asked, and he felt like a total idiot as soon as the words left his lips. "Sorry, sir, I understand."

"That's right. You get to move in here, and now having served in this office for some time, I pray you're not so cursed. I have to say that only those who have occupied this office fully understand its miseries."

Morrison nodded once more, not quite believing the president's disclaimer and hoping he would have the benefit of that understanding himself.

"Oh, there's the other thing. The prognosis."

Morrison inhaled, his chest wall rattling to the point he thought the president could see his rising excitement.

"It's not bad—not bad at all. With the surgery, I have every expectation of living out my second term—if I have one—and then some."

Morrison forced his lips into a smile, but he knew it wasn't the thousand-watt smile for which he'd become famous. The words were not as hard. "Oh, that's wonderful, Av. Losing you would be devastating for the country."

"So nice of you to say, but as Charles de Gaulle liked to say, 'The cemeteries of Paris are full of indispensable people.'"

"How right you are," Morrison said, his heart pounding as on the last thrill of a roller coaster.

"So there you have it. We have our work to do, and we'll make an even better team this next time around."

"Glad to be on it, sir. I wouldn't have it any other way."

They left the den and returned to light sandwiches and snacks while they watched CNS and Newshare tell them their chances were better than even.

Just before everyone began to leave, the president held his hand up and asked for everyone's attention. "We've all heard so much about Ingber's bet. So I put it to you, Shel. Will you be shaving off the mop after tomorrow?"

Ingber milked the look of expectancy in everyone's face. "I've already given my prognostication—absolutely not!" All cheered and made their good-byes.

Riding home to Bethesda, Morrison remained deep in thought, a frown dragging his facial muscles downward. His world had just turned upside down. He had been so sure the president's luck in life was about to come up short, every single task of every single day of the campaign built on the premise he was preparing for the top spot. He had risked everything conjuring a bogus contract, chumming up to fools, conspiring in the...what? He couldn't say the word to himself.

Of course, he could call everything off and let the chips fall where they may. If the president lost the election, he'd be out, and he himself could run four years hence. And if they won, well, then the voters would have decided, and he himself would serve in the best way possible, biding his time.

By the time the limo reached the armed gates at the Naval Observatory, he realized he had no option whatsoever. If they lost, he would also lose the loyalties that power commands, and with a Hardy administration, all would come out. Disgrace? Dishonor? Jail? *It was all for nothing! Fucking nothing!*

Sickening him further was the gag that had been running in his mind the past nine months: game-changing turnovers in basketball, and with rue aplenty, a sudden turnover in his political fortunes.

With hesitation, he put his hand out, and Sharon took it in hers, clenching it tight. He gave her a weak smile, but hoped she didn't see his eyes glistening in the welcoming lights of the mansion. How could he tell her? *At the White House, we'll always be visitors.*

ELECTION DAY 2012

T O Enrique McCord, the SoftSec building, once one man's monument to the right to vote, had become a mere façade for deception.
He drove into one of its private garages and sat there in his silver 2010
E-Class Mercedes Benz, its engine running, as the door darkened the
concrete cavity in its descent. For a full minute, he contemplated letting
the car's exhaust take him to oblivion.

He knew the operation he was about to supervise was both illegal
and immoral, and he could find no way to justify what he himself had
put in motion. His thoughts turned to Bridget and their children and
the disgrace of a suicide, something Latino Catholics did not do. Such
a dishonor would be immediate, and worse, his beautiful wife and children would think he did not love them.

Finally, he turned off the ignition, but sat a moment longer. Having
met Jerry James and Nathan Conaway for drinks the night before, he
departed early to spend some time with his family, as if Election Day
would somehow be separate him from them. He couldn't wait to leave
the two gurus, in fact, because of their bragging to each other about
what they would do to decimate the Republicans—they wouldn't even
know what hit them, they said.

Not that he felt sympathy for the GOP. It was one of the greater iro-
nies of the election that at heart, most Latinos would have been natural Republicans, given their love for traditional family structure, their
respect for the sanctity of life, and their work ethic. Yet, the Republicans
had shunned his people, and in '08, Latinos had paid them back for the
slight. Now, they would do it again with the help of SoftSec, and that
was the only justification he would allow himself for what he was about
to do.

In the office, Nathan and Jerry were already busy watching the various states begin to populate their databases. Amid the overwhelming aroma of Skyline chili dogs with onion, mustard, and cheese, he walked up and said, "Hey, guys, how's it goin'?"

"Great, Mr. McCord. Jerry is already giving me a guided tour of the four states we need to turn over to the Democrats and make it convincing."

"Only four states? We're not working in all the battleground states?"

"We are, sir," Nathan responded. "But that's for the EAC contract, and we'll make good on that, delivering a fat report at the end of it. But Jerry here says that the powers have decided to go after Ohio, Virginia, Florida, and Colorado, and to let the others go their way because we can make sure Texas stays in the D column."

McCord looked at the third conspirator. "You're sure, Jerry?"

James turned and looked at McCord. "Right from Mr. Ingber himself, Ricky." His tone and his words announced who was really in charge.

"Look, guys," Nathan said. "We've got a long afternoon with nuthin' much to do until later. For the EAC contract, I'll direct the work, and here's how I think we should do it. The analysts in the other room have no idea what we'll be doing in here, and we can keep it that way by telling them they're not cleared at the same level under the contract. So they stay out, but I can feed them the raw data as it comes in from every state except the four key ones, and they can do their stuff. Once we massage the data from the four, we'll kick it over to them as if it was raw, and they'll do what needs to be done with it, just like it was real."

McCord and James nodded in appreciation. James offered that he had his own data prepopulated based on what happened in which counties four years earlier. If the voting patterns and totals remained roughly the same, he had constructed algorithms to match proportions to the 2012 totals and at the same time ensure the four states wound up called for the Democrats, yet with the correct total votes from each county.

McCord was impressed and saw that Conaway was, too, by the genius of political mathematics electronically formulated by the tall, skinny, otherwise unimpressive man in their midst.

Around dinnertime, all three men convened for a collection of Jimmy John's rounded up by Heather, the well-appointed, self-appointed guardian of the firm.

As Nathan pounded down his meat-lover's delight, he sputtered between bites that he couldn't wait for the electronic frenzy to begin at seven, when most polls in the East began to close. Given the varying types of software and hardware out there, a substantial bit of it belonging to SoftSec and VoteCount, all three expected glitches and incompatibilities. For the routine, McCord suggested that the analysts in the outer room could also handle them, especially if they were coming from heavily red or blue states. James and Conaway agreed.

The ostensible battleground states were another matter. Any issues connected with the nine to twelve that theoretically could go either way would be managed within the sanctum, with no discussion outside that space. Jerry James suggested that McCord himself deal with problems coming from Michigan, Wisconsin, Iowa, Nevada, and New Mexico, and the owner agreed. James and Conaway would team up to ensure Ohio, Florida, Virginia, and Colorado went the right way.

In front of the trio was a large-screen, HDTV tuned to CNS, and as the clock passed the seventh hour, the men watched intently. States in the Northeast and Southeast began to perform, domino-like, for their respective candidates. Maine and all of New England remained true blue for Williams, while Georgia, Mississippi, and all but two states of the Deep South stayed with Hardy. At 7:45 p.m., Williams had 59 electoral votes to Hardy's 45.

A few minutes before eight o'clock, in northwest Pennsylvania, when Paul Gladston knew that Andy and Sadie Schenk would be heading to bed, he approached the family's head and asked for a special permission. "Andy, I know you have no way of listening to the election news, but there is a way for Mare and I to do so."

"How so, my young man?"

"If you will allow me to back my car out of the barn, I will leave the lights off, and we can listen to the results as they come in on satellite radio."

"What is this kind of radio?"

"It's in my car, and you need not worry. We will not connect any of your buildings to the world. It would just be the two of us listening quietly. We will not disturb anyone."

Stroking his beard for a moment, he nodded and said, "It will be the three of us. It will be all right if I am in the backseat?" His smile was broad, even partially hidden though it was by all his whiskers. "You know, Paul, all of us, we voted today." He patted his chest proudly. "And this is important to us too."

The three of them trooped out to the barn, Schenk with a lantern in hand, allowing them to see their breath in the crisp, dark night. Paul slowly backed his beloved Volvo out of the barn and killed the lights. They tuned in to News Global and heard Meredith Ramirez announce, at 8:17 p.m., that New York went for Williams, but a number of central states, including Michigan, went for Hardy. "The Michigan surprise puts the governor ahead, with 88 for the president and a 106 for the governor," Ramirez said, as a small cheer when up from the car. "Don't go away, ladies and gentlemen. This looks to be a very close race, as all the polls had indicated."

Florida teetered on CNS's big board as Conaway called the numbers coming in from Broward, Volusia, and all the other counties of 2000 fame and James frantically worked his calculator, giving Conaway new numbers to insert before the data flowed to the secretary of state's office in Tallahassee. They had to perform their service several times throughout the evening for each county to make the shifts appear natural and real. Then, at 8:21 p.m., the results of their work became official for the first time, as the Sunshine State became the first key state to fall under SoftSec's electronic spell, and its 29 votes went in the president's column, making his total 117.

By 8:42 p.m., Governor Scott Walker's leadership dyed Wisconsin red, CNS reported, an event turning Jerry James's head with surprise. He asked McCord if someone needed to shepherd his states, but the SoftSec founder waved them off. When the central states' races were nearly accounted for, however, Peter Marsden declared Williams had 167, and Hardy, 146. To get there, Minnesota, Illinois, and Pennsylvania fell for the president, but Hardy had also taken Iowa, Missouri, Arkansas, and Louisiana. Once again, James peered at McCord and wondered aloud why three states intended for Williams—Michigan, Wisconsin, and Iowa—went the other way. That should not have happened, but McCord did not possess the sophistication to turn those states for Williams.

Exhaust billows displaced the November air behind the Volvo, while inside the steamed windows, Paul said to the other two, "We may be in trouble."

"Jee...for cryin' out loud," Mare exclaimed, careful not to take the Lord's name in vain in front of her Amish host. She wanted to be careful, too, not to say more about the election, since Paul had reminded her the Schenks didn't know what was certain to happen.

At SoftSec, the three conspirators looked at the CNS screen to see Virginia's 13 electoral votes called for the president, all because of votes shaved from Hardy's south and western county vote totals.

"We've been watching this state closely all day because the exit polls seemed to belie expectations," Peter Marsden noted on the big screen. "This, however, is a big win for the president, giving him a new total of 180 to the governor's 146. Given what our experts foresee with the remaining states, it's becoming difficult to see a path to victory for Governor Hardy."

James and Conaway cheered out loud to see their version of the voting results for the Old Dominion being accepted as valid. "Two down, two to go," James said. "And the last one doesn't even matter. Icing on the cake."

Texas went for the Williams-Morrison ticket with only a little assistance from the SoftSec cabal, and 38 more votes slid to the Democratic column. Hardy forces claimed both Dakotas, Kansas, Nebraska, and Oklahoma for 24 of their own, but the totals began to spread apart with 218 for Williams and 170 for Hardy. It was 9:22 p.m.

Exactly forty minutes later, CNS reported that New Mexico's 5 votes went to Williams while Montana, Wyoming, Idaho, Utah, and Arizona and their 27 votes remained firmly in the red zone. It was 223 to 197 when Conaway and James delivered their insult to the Republican challenger. They sliced Hardy votes from all Colorado's outlying counties, along with Fort Collins and the vast military bloc in Colorado Springs, and added them to Denver's liberal base, thus delivering Colorado's 9 votes to the president, a boost to 232 at 10:12 p.m.

While everyone was waiting for the remaining western states to declare themselves, Conaway and James had finished slicing, shaving, and dicing Ohio's southeastern counties, along with Cincinnati's own Hamilton County, and together with Cuyahoga for Cleveland and Franklin for Columbus. Ohio was finally called for President Williams by all major news organizations at 10:56 p.m.

Mare reached over and closed Paul's hand in hers as Meredith Ramirez summed it up for them.

"With Ohio's 18 votes, ladies and gentlemen, most observers would declare that, barring a successful challenge in one or two key states, or a miracle in a combination of the still-to-be called western states, the race is all but over. The president now has 250 votes, and despite the

Nevada surprise win for the governor with its 6 votes, the Hardy camp has a total of 203. It shouldn't be long now before this race's results are clear. Please stay with us."

McCord held his head in his hands. He had done what he'd agreed to do, and hated himself for it. He sat up straight and said to the other two, "Look, guys, there's nothing more for me to do here. We accomplished our goal, and the president will have four more years to accomplish his." Even as he said them, he knew his words fell flat, empty of emotion. "I'm going to head home. It's over. Call me if anything comes up."

"Sure, boss. Jerry and I can take it from here. The two of us are just going to enjoy the endgame."

Just then, CNS's man said, "And here we have it. As predicted, Washington, Oregon, and California with their 78 votes are going for President Williams, and that puts him over the magic 270 electoral votes needed for election. The president now has a total of 328, and with Alaska declaring its 3 for Hardy, he will likely finish at 206. Oh, wait a second. Here come Hawaii's 4 votes for Williams, and let the record show, the time is 11:51 p.m., and we have a certain winner, Averell Harriman Williams continues as the forty-fourth President of the United States."

As James watched McCord stand up, he reflected further on what had just happened. He did the mental math. If, indeed, Wisconsin, Iowa, Michigan, and Nevada truly went for Hardy on their own, and if SoftSec had not perverted the vote in Ohio, Florida, Virginia, and Colorado, Hardy would have won the election with 275 electoral votes to the president's 263. Realizing for the first time the enormity of what he and Conaway had perpetrated, James sealed those numbers in his memory—the true result of the 2012 election.

Leaving the sanctum of the sealed room, McCord thanked the others for their hard work throughout the evening and found his way out. After a day of junk food, soda, and coffee, he felt wired, but struck by the damp cold as he walked into the unheated garage. He fired up the Benz, and taking no pleasure in it, backed his way out until he could make the turn and exit the drive. Except for the occasional streetlamp, the street was devoid of warmth or life.

It was a route he'd used many times to his home in Anderson Township. He turned right onto Madison and went the short distance to make a left down Moorman. When he did so, he noticed the headlights behind him, but paid no attention until they came closer. He made a left on William Howard Taft and proceeded east as the road dipped down toward Columbia Parkway just above the Ohio River. The headlights stayed with him, but he thought nothing of it even when they remained with him when he continued onto the parkway.

He could see from the height of the lights that they belonged to an SUV, and they had come close enough for him to see the Chevy badge in his rear view mirror. It was a dark color, he told himself. Black, maybe. He'd make a report in the morning. "Asshole!" he said to his car's interior. CNS election experts were jabbering on his Sirius Radio, but he heard little of it. He was tired, a bit strung out, and had no patience for aggressive drivers on a completely empty road at midnight. It's as if they were waiting for him, he thought.

Then, he felt the first tap of the SUV's bumper against the low rear deck lid of the E-Class. McCord tried to speed up, but the black monster kept right with him. He reached up to press the emergency button near his visor. The SUV struck his car so hard that his finger missed the button he sought and jammed into the windshield. He swore as he heard metal crumple.

What McCord saw outside his window was a blur of lights across the Ohio on the Kentucky side. There were no side roads for him. No place to go. Once again, he floored the gas pedal, and the Benz seemed to respond.

Over his left shoulder, he saw the SUV shift to the left lane and begin to come alongside. Swerving to his left, he tried to break the SUV's attack, but did so only momentarily. He wanted to see who in hell was crazy enough to do this to him and turned his head as far as he could. Two men. The one nearest him he couldn't see because the front post blocked his view. The other man's face was light and clear with a prominent nose, and for a second, he caught a glimpse of short blond hair.

With a sudden rush, McCord saw the SUV attempt to turn full into him. Its right front caught the Benz's doorpost and shoved it rightward. When his wheels hit the curb a few feet before the guardrail, it had the effect of lifting and flipping the car over the rail and down the heavily wooded sheer drop below them. Rolling and turning through brush, bushes, and trees, the car struck a large oak, one branch of which pierced the driver's window and McCord's neck in the same instant.

As the SUV sped away, Crew Cut saw the fireball rise in the passenger-side mirror. Looking at his partner, he said, "Back we go. There are two more waiting up there. Those we'll have to do a bit cleaner and drop them off on the way."

"Jesus, Marty, good thing this baby has a reinforced front end!"

"Not to worry. With any luck, we'll be back home by breakfast. And then we celebrate victory at the ballot box."

Andy Schenk opened the rear door of the car, and said, "Thank you." His voice was quiet, steady, resigned. "Sadie said I should have waited. Right she was. I would have slept better this night." He left a lit lantern for them next to the barn door and stepped off toward the house.

Without a word, Paul slipped the car in gear and slowly pulled it into its former place of rest. On the way out, he reached for the lantern, which had gone out. A metaphor, he thought. Finding Mare's hand, they walked slowly to their abode, such as it was.

Once under the covers, Mare said, "Well, we knew. We knew it all day long as we did our chores here and ate our dinner and supper with the Schenks. We knew it when we played with their kids and listened to the oldest read the Bible after supper."

"I know, but I've been just another American fool, somebody from another age, I suppose. I'm one of those idiots who thinks this kind of crap can't happen here, that somebody always steps in."

"No Superman here, Paulie boy," she whispered gently. "Is there anything we could have done?"

"I don't think I told you, but I copied Nelson's original, and to each of those three letters we mailed on Monday, I added my own note."

"About?"

"The murder of Nelson Evers. The powers in Washington can lean on itty-bitty Fairfax, but that doesn't erase what happened. It was murder, and people need to know. He was the best of us, and what happened to him won't go away." He turned on his side and looked her way, though in the total darkness he could see nothing. Yet, he felt her presence as an extension of himself.

"Isn't there anything else we can do?"

"Now? Nothing."

"Then, when?"

"Right now, we lie low because they—the 'they' who are supposed to be working for us—have all the high cards." He didn't try to hide his disgust. "They stole our votes and maybe they think they'll impose a government most of us don't want—and won't have."

"But there are a lot of them. People who want the government to take care of them in every aspect of their lives. Hanging around you, I've come to see that and understand it. When will people see the truth—and do something!?"

"We can bide our time, Mare, but we don't have much of it. There are millions of us, people with self-respect, who want what our grandfathers wanted—a place where everyone, without exception—can live and learn and keep the freedoms so many have died for. Elections matter, and when the time comes, people will know what to do."

"When, then?"

Words that had become Paul's anthem sliced the lightless night, but this time they carried a different meaning. "Just wait."

ACKNOWLEDGMENTS

M uch of *Turnover* takes place in Cincinnati, Ohio, a city for which my wife and I have much love, and we always enjoy the times we spend there. Other locales in Colorado, Ohio, Pennsylvania, Washington, DC, and elsewhere are also places where I have lived or worked, yet about which a bit of imagination has been applied. Where literary imprecision has been used regarding a few geographical facts, this has been done largely to protect the privacy of others. Many thanks go to all of these locations and the people who make them the great places they are.

In my public and private sector careers, I have been privileged to have served under and with good men and women too numerous to mention here, but their collective examples of leadership, integrity, and followership have served as an inspiration to me for nearly forty years. To all of them I am forever indebted.

Other sources of support are worth mentioning. The past two summers, I was privileged to attend the Yale Writers Conference where much was taught and, I can only hope, some was absorbed. In western Pennsylvania, I am delighted to acknowledge the support and friendship of Dale Perelman (an imaginative writer himself) and his wife, Michele, for their abiding affirmation—and willingness to read—throughout the creative process.

Naturally, if one has a family, one does not research and write without their quiet support, and for that I'm always grateful.

Made in the USA
Middletown, DE
05 July 2015